OFFICIAL SECRETS

A NOVAK AND MITCHELL THRILLER

ANDREW RAYMOND

D1344786

ALSO BY ANDREW RAYMOND

"In a time of deceit telling the truth is a revolutionary act."

— *George Orwell*

1

Twenty-year-old Artur Korecki bounded through the waist-high grass in driving rain, holding onto his camera with an iron grip as the two American agents gave chase. They hadn't identified themselves as CIA, but Artur knew, given what he had just seen, that they were professionals of some sort. A minute earlier, they had escorted a shackled man in an orange jumpsuit down the jet's stairs. Something Artur had caught on video.

Both agents had a slimline flashlight in one hand, and a Glock 34 handgun in the other.

The senior agent in front shouted, 'Drop the camera!'

They're gaining on me, Artur thought, too terrified to turn around. His head start had already been halved, and now had barely one hundred yards on them. *Just keep running*, he told himself.

Dropping the camera wasn't an option. There were too many videos on the memory card that could be used to identify him. Even if he stopped and gave himself up there was no guarantee they wouldn't just shoot him.

The terrain underfoot shifted unevenly, unclear in the darkness. As he hurdled through the soaking wet grass, his foot landed in a small depression. His knee buckled and he fell to the ground. He couldn't get any purchase on the mud, his feet running a treadmill as he looked back: a pair of increasingly bright flashlight beams jerking in motion with the agents' swinging arms.

In that brief moment that made two seconds feel like ten, all Artur could think about was how much he didn't want to die. Not yet. Not before he'd made it out of tiny Szymany. Before he'd made anything of his life. He was going to show all those small-minded idiots back in town he had bigger dreams than taking a job in the dog food factory twenty miles away, then drinking the rest of his life away.

He at least had his YouTube channel, TruthArmy. And he was going to get his message out to the world no matter what it took.

First, he had to survive the next five minutes.

He scrambled to his feet, struggling to get his legs moving quickly again.

At the chain-link perimeter fence topped with razor wire, he squeezed through the small hole he had cut an hour ago to gain access to the military airport grounds.

For a few seconds the agents were close enough to see Artur's terrified mud-speckled face through the fence in their flashlights, and the patch on Artur's denim jacket. It carried the logo of his conspiracy theory vlog: an Illuminati pyramid with the words "Trust No One" inside. Below the pyramid, "TruthArmy on YouTube".

The agents lost time cutting a bigger hole in the fence so they could fit through. Sensing they were losing him, the senior agent called into his radio, 'I have a clear shot.' His voice was unmistakably American.

The response came into his radio earpiece. 'We need that video. Take it.'

He held his Spytac X-6 military-grade flashlight against the barrel of his Glock – the flashlight trained on Artur's back.

The pounding rain was no issue for the flashlight. It could hold up in the most extreme weather, and was so bright, if someone flashed it at you in broad daylight, you would be seeing spots for minutes.

The agent had a clear shot, his trigger finger about to squeeze.

Then Artur was gone.

The agent flicked his light from side to side, but Artur was nowhere to be seen.

They didn't know that Artur had fallen, and was now crawling to one side under cover of the tall grass.

As Artur caught his breath, he thought about the terrain ahead. It was even deeper and thicker grass, and it lasted for miles. He knew he didn't have that in him. If he couldn't outrun their bullets, he'd have to outsmart the agents instead.

He ran dead left, safely away from their flashlight beams, then crouched under the thickest weeds he could find.

The senior agent raised a hand. 'Keep your light low. If he's hiding you should be able to see his breath.'

The agents could no longer see the path Artur had taken, the grass so high it had just flopped back into place behind him.

The senior agent made a helicopter blade gesture with his hand, meaning a three-sixty search of the area.

During the agents' confusion, Artur pulled out the camera's SD card and inserted it into his phone, moving his most recent video clip there.

With his 4G connection he opened a new email. He didn't have time to write an explanation, only a subject line saying '*Get this out there. TRUST NO ONE*' and formatted the email for encryption. He attached the video clip, then searched through recipients. It didn't take long. He only had three in his whole address book: his mum, his friend Wally, and a man named Tom Novak.

His mum couldn't even work the toaster, let alone a laptop

with an encrypted video file. Wally had been his only friend since they were little boys, and the last thing Artur wanted was to bring a whole lot of heat down on him.

Then there was Tom Novak.

Tom Novak had never met Artur, never spoken to him, and lived nearly five thousand miles away in New York City. Yet he was the only person Artur could trust now.

He sent the email to Novak, then wiped his entire camera library and SD card. If they caught him, he would at least have a measure of deniability, except for trespassing. The phone was encrypted, so no one would be able to read the contents of the message or view the clip. But he wasn't ready to give in. Not yet.

Although it was two against one, Artur knew that if he could just get another head start, and the agents couldn't tell what direction he'd gone off in, he might still make it home. What he needed was a diversion. And quickly. There were several more flashlights approaching in the distance from the airport runway: more agents were coming for backup.

He woke up his phone screen, then tapped out an encrypted text message to Wally. 'Call me in thirty seconds. Life or death.'

They only ever communicated using encryption, knowing that the NSA was capable of tracking any unencrypted text or phone call in the world. Even with astronomical luck and years of computer processing, it would take centuries for a computer to unlock an encrypted message. All Artur needed was thirty seconds.

He hit send.

It was going to be the longest thirty seconds of his life.

He waited until both agents faced away from him. If he made the slightest sound while tossing the phone, the consequences could be fatal. Since 9/11 the American government and CIA hadn't exactly been sticklers for due process. Artur had read enough from Tom Novak's columns in *The Republic* to know that if they got him now they might put him away for years before even the prospect of a trial reared its head. That was the risk he had accepted.

After setting the volume to loudest, Artur lobbed his phone like a grenade as far as he could. It looped straight over the two agents, landing to their right. The gentle rustle of its landing was enough to make the closest agent jerk the torch towards the noise, his senses on highest alert.

'Over here...' he told his partner.

Artur tried to keep a count down from thirty in his head but lost count somewhere around ten. His heart shivered like it had been packed with ice.

He held his breath. If it was going to work, he couldn't get away with even a second's hesitation.

Artur prayed silently. *Come on, Wally. Don't let me down. Not now.*

Buried down in the grass somewhere the ringtone – *The X Files* theme tune – came out muffled and quiet, but it was like a foghorn to the agents. They both whipped around, assuming, as Artur had hoped, that the phone was still in their target's possession.

They took several strides towards the noise.

That was all Artur needed. He leapt out of his hiding spot, and took off towards his hometown of Szymany.

When the agent saw the lit-up screen down in the grass, he realised what Artur had done. He started a curse, 'Motherf...' then got on his radio. 'He got away. Get me Dennis Muller at NSA.' He turned to his partner. 'Did you see that badge on his jacket?'

They'd both clocked it. Even during the heightened tension of a foot chase through unfamiliar territory, it was impossible to switch that part of their brains off.

The agent got back on his radio. 'I need everything they've got on a YouTube channel called TruthArmy. I want names and addresses. And I want local assets up to kick in doors tonight.'

CIA black site, Camp Zero, outskirts of Szymany – Monday, 1:03am

Specialized Skills Officer Walter Sharp stared out the window of the CIA block of the Stare Kiejkuty military complex set deep in the forest, seeing only blackness. The Polish secret service, *Biuro Ochrony Rządu*, had operated from there since the Cold War, and had now turned over a large chunk of its incarceration units to CIA. What had started out as a temporary base during the early days of the War on Terror had turned into a seemingly permanent prison. A 'terror hotel' as Sharp called it.

Camp Zero's location in the heart of Europe was ideal for the Americans, who could rendition the most valuable terror suspects from the Middle East or Africa and have them on site within a few hours. Then the bureaucratic nightmare of figuring out where to send the suspects afterwards could begin. The White House had given spec ops permission to basically go anywhere it wanted, and take whomever they wanted. All with total immunity and secrecy.

The closest anyone had come to unearthing the location of such black sites was the U.S. Senate Intelligence Committee's so-called 'Torture Report', following the Abu Ghraib prison scandal. But the report was so heavily redacted it gave CIA complete deniability on national security grounds of the most egregious human rights abuses. It wouldn't even officially acknowledge the sites existed, let alone allow lawyers in to inspect conditions or prisoners.

In Camp Zero, the rule of law didn't exist.

From the outside it looked like a fairly anonymous warehouse, with a low corrugated metal roof, a barbed wire-gated entrance, and double rows of razor wire along a perimeter fence.

Guantanamo Bay might have had all the notoriety, but that was only because its existence had been made so public. Hidden away in the dark, endless woods of remotest Poland, Camp Zero housed the worst of the worst: jihadis who strapped suicide bombs to children then sent them into public markets for detonation; human traffickers and paedophiles; war-criminal fugitives from Congo, Sudan and Bosnia to name only a few; and the executors from ISIS beheading videos.

Put simply, it housed the scum of the earth.

The interrogation block was made up of three different types of cells. The Soft Room was a large cell with prayer mats and a rug, for cooperative, high-ranking detainees. The Blue Room had plywood walls painted sky blue and was smaller, six feet by ten, for medium-intensity interrogation, using the sort of techniques approved in the U.S. Army Field Manual.

Then there was the Black Room.

In there, all bets were off.

It was twelve feet by twelve, painted black from floor to ceiling. There were speakers in each corner, which played deafening music – most commonly extreme heavy metal, as detainees were less likely to be familiar with it, and caused a greater degree of confusion. A spotlight shone down from the middle of the room, and an air conditioner gusted on high, bringing the cell to a steady minus two.

Depending on cooperation levels, detainees would be shuttled from one room to the other, all day long. An endless schedule of terror and not knowing what would come next.

If detainees cooperated, they would get to sit, while shackled, on a soft carpet and pray. If they didn't, they would get the Black Room, where they would have to listen to Slayer's *Reign in Blood* on repeat for five hours.

· · ·

Sharp closed his eyes and leaned his forehead against the window. The coldness felt soothing, easing the headache that had been circling him the past hour. He listened to the throb of Metallica's *Black* album coming from the cell behind him, knowing with each bludgeoning guitar riff the detainee's resolve was withering.

Sharp's U.S. Army compatriot, Captain Luke Hampton, wanted to get straight to it, but Sharp had insisted that the suspect needed at least an hour for the confusion and disorientation to rise sufficiently. Sharp knew the drill by now: *Where am I? What's about to happen to me? How long will they keep me here?* Those were all good questions when you'd been snatched on the edge of an ISIS stronghold in Nimruz province two days ago, and hadn't seen daylight since. After about an hour, more immediate questions of discomfort came to the fore: *How long am I going to have to kneel like this? What on earth is this deafening music?*

Sharp, dressed down in casual long-sleeve khaki shirt and dark combats, ran his hand down his long, thick beard as he read through the detainee's file – slim as it was. What few details he had were sketchy to say the least.

The Polish *Biuro* were so used to collecting CIA-renditioned prisoners from Szymany Military Airport, they dropped them off at Camp Zero like they were delivering pizza. No records were kept on the Polish side. As far as the *Biuro* and Polish government were concerned, CIA did not exist there.

Sharp had been living at Camp Zero for six months. No casual strolls off site. No holiday time. Just one day off a week. Which put him in a similar position as the prisoners: he had no idea how long he would be there for. The only advice he'd been given on the matter was from a colleague back in Virginia: *'Make some valuable intel or break a case, Walt. It's the only way out of a place like Zero.'*

Promotion in CIA had become so laughably rare in recent

years, it had bred resentment among mid-level officers like Sharp. The only way to get ahead was playing your politics smartly. And Walter Sharp had never shown much aptitude for that.

Sharp turned the file towards Hampton. 'Known accomplices are vague, any intel linking him to any known groups is either anonymous or obtuse, and no one we've spoken to has ever mentioned the name Abdul al-Malik.'

'The lead is solid, sir,' Hampton said resolutely.

'How solid?'

'Army Ranger unit says a man fitting his description was spotted near an IED blast at another checkpoint the day before. It took out about a dozen friendlies.'

Sharp exhaled, troubled by something. 'I've got a British ISIS executioner in cell three who every newspaper in the world thinks was killed nine months ago. And cell eight is a guy who was arrested in his car in Brussels with fifty Ks of C4, boxes of nails and razor blades, and a map directing him to the nearest Jewish kids' school. I'm looking at *this* guy... He's a parking violator compared to these other sons of bitches.'

Hampton said, 'He had a bag on him with multiple passports and some maps of the Pakistan border. Who knows where he was going after that.'

Sharp shook his head. 'Something's not right.' He closed the file and went to the cell door, checking through the spy hole. 'Did you see his hands when he came in?'

'His hands?'

'They're soft. No calluses. You can't live out in the shit in Nimruz with soft hands like that. They're all farmers out there.' Sharp kept staring at Malik's face. 'He's hard to place isn't he? Nationality-wise. He'd make a good grey man.'

Hampton nodded.

A grey man was what every intelligence recruiter hunted for: someone who blended in; who, after meeting them, you instantly forgot. They left no mark on the world.

Malik looked in his mid-thirties. He was wearing only

blackout goggles and a pair of white shorts. His feet were shackled close together, and he stood directly under the spotlight in the centre of the room in a crucifixion pose. His arms trembled from exertion, the cold, and sleep deprivation. There were fresh bruises all up one side of his body where he'd been taking sustained kidney punches, and he had the same on the backs of his legs from a wooden cane.

'The NDS must have had a few turns on him,' Sharp said.

Afghanistan's recently assembled National Directorate of Security – a kind of FBI meets CIA – would have had officers at the IED blast checkpoint. Any suspect was bound to take a beating from them.

'Any notes from the agents on escort?' asked Sharp.

Hampton replied, 'They caught a guy filming from the bushes nearby. They got his phone, but it's encrypted so they're not going to get anything off it.'

'That's the *Biuro*'s problem not ours,' Sharp said. He took a long look at Malik. 'You turn up the AC in there?'

'Yeah. It's barely thirty,' Hampton confirmed.

Testing him, Sharp asked, 'Does his current physical state surprise you, Captain?'

'Most civilians or innocents would have deteriorated more by now. They're also more likely to strike out, voice their innocence in some way. He's shown no signs of defiance or anger. Enemy combatants are usually more serene. It suggests Malik's had military training. Maybe in Pakistan. That would fit, given the location of the IED attack.'

Sharp often posed such questions to Hampton, helping him on his way towards becoming an SSO like him. It could sometimes take weeks before Hampton could work out if he'd given the correct answer.

Hoping to prompt him a little, Hampton asked, 'What do you think?'

'He's had training, alright.' Sharp passed him the file, then made for the cell door. 'Whoever he is, he's not just some guy.'

A thin Afghan interpreter, Fahran, stood against the opposite wall, dressed in U.S. Army uniform, a black scarf around his neck, wraparound sunglasses perched on top of his head, casually smoking a roll-up cigarette. He was one of the nine thousand Afghan civilians put on the Army payroll as interpreters since the American invasion in 2003, and was one of the few to stay on after the American pull-out. He wasn't in any great hurry to return. Everyone he knew or loved had been killed. Now he had decided to just walk the earth, going wherever Sharp went, for as long as he needed him.

Sharp put out a fist to Fahran, then said, '*Takbir.*'

Fahran pulled the scarf up over his mouth and nose, and the sunglasses down over his eyes. He bumped fists with Sharp, then replied, '*Allahu Akbar.*'

A lifelong atheist, Sharp only did it to put Fahran at ease, and to remind him he was no apostate for assisting white Western 'infidels': those men in the cells who claimed to be messengers of Allah were the real enemy, and Fahran had nothing to fear in this life or the next.

Sharp opened the cell door just as Metallica's "Through the Never" was starting, a rush of cold air hitting him. Malik jerked his head from side to side, hearing Sharp's footsteps nearby.

Sharp nodded to Fahran, who said to Malik in Arabic, 'Lower your arms.' Hampton then guided Malik towards a table, and a wooden chair with no underside, only the wooden border. He linked Malik's shackles through two metal loops attached to the table top.

Sharp switched off the AC, wanting to make Malik wonder if things were about to get easier or harder.

When Hampton removed Malik's goggles, Malik blinked hard several times, trying to adjust to the light. His eyes darted around the room to get his bearings.

Sharp prowled around in front of him, his long beard

making him look like a feral animal. His thick neck and shoulders bulged under the wide, baggy neck of his t-shirt.

'I love reading about history,' Sharp said, pausing for Fahran to interpret. 'There's a lot you can learn. For example, the monks of Castillo la Coroño. They were some real sickos back in the Inquisition. But damn it if they didn't get results.'

Malik squirmed on the front edge of the seat, having to fight to not sink through it.

Hampton stepped back towards the cell door beside Fahran.

'They'd take a piece of cloth.' Sharp pulled out a small white piece of linen and put it on the table, then moved behind Malik, out of sight. He dipped the linen into a bucket of water, soaking it. 'They'd put it down the guy's throat, then they'd fill his mouth with water and hold his nose. The only way for the guy to breathe was to swallow the water. Problem is, the water soaked the cloth which stuck it to the guy's throat and made him choke.'

Fahran translated the information dispassionately, in a neutral tone.

Sharp grabbed hold of Malik's head from behind, then shoved the dripping cloth deep into Malik's mouth. 'The genius of it,' said Sharp, now holding Malik's nose, 'was that it choked you just enough for it to be agony, but not quite enough to kill you. A man in reasonable shape like yourself could handle it for, oh, I don't know, a couple hours. A guy could say he believed in anything after that.'

Malik closed his eyes, and kicked his feet up and down, heels slamming into the ground. His eyes bulged as he tried to invent some breath for himself.

Hampton looked at his feet, as if this somehow absolved him of complicity in what was going on.

Sharp spoke slowly. And clearly. 'The only thing. I want you to believe in. Is me. And that I'll do *anything*. To find out what I need to know.' He pulled the cloth back out and let go of Malik's nose.

As Malik spluttered and caught his breath, it seemed like he was trying to say something. Sharp leaned close, his ear up at Malik's mouth.

He heard him whisper in a soft English accent, 'Get rid of the others.'

The cloth trick seemed to have had little effect on his faculties. His eyes were clear and still held their focus.

After a few paces back to his chair, Sharp said to Hampton, 'Give me a few minutes alone.'

'I'll be right outside,' Hampton said, then motioned to Fahran. Interpreters names were never to be used in front of detainees. Not even aliases.

Sharp waited until they were alone. 'I've got three Brits down the hall, so right now you're only mildly interesting to me. What else you got, al-Britani?'

Malik craned his neck, trying to stretch it out. He whispered, keeping his head low. 'You've got to get me out.'

Sharp laughed. 'Of course, why didn't you say so.'

'I'm in danger here.'

'You don't know where you are, Abdul. What makes you think you're in danger?'

'Judging by the flight time from Bagram, I'd say we were either in Camp Zero, Poland, or Camp Romeo, Romania.'

The names of the camps, let alone their locations, were classified. Code word clearance only. Sharp stared hard at Malik. *Okay*, he thought. *You have my attention.*

Malik's speech was quickening. Sensing time was running out. 'I know what you're thinking,' he said. 'How does he know the names of CIA black sites? How could a detainee have code word clearance?'

The inconsistencies in Malik's file, and his uncommon physical and mental fortitude compared to almost every other detainee, were no longer such a mystery to Sharp.

Giving nothing away, he asked, 'What am I thinking right now?'

Malik answered, 'You're thinking, why has this guy not cracked yet? Normally, I would sit here and wait for your phone to ring. But that's not going to happen tonight. Not for the kind of trouble I'm in.' Malik smiled ever so faintly, knowing that Sharp had already worked it out.

Sharp held Malik's gaze. 'You know I need to hear you say it.'

Malik said, 'I'm MI6.'

2

Twenty-five-year-old Rebecca Fox sat alone in the living room of her small flat, a pair of PC monitors in front of her filled with hours' worth of LINUX code. Consumed with her task, her face was blank as she typed, fingers flying around the keyboard – she had been able to touch type since she was twelve. She showed no sense of irritation at the sound of her neighbours through the wall, laughing drunkenly, singing karaoke to eighties power ballads. She was used to it by now.

She didn't feel envy at her neighbours' happiness, or that she was missing out on life. She didn't feel anything. This was the life she had chosen.

She put in the earplugs she always kept on her desk, and continued her work.

Nothing about what made other people happy made sense to her. The drinks with co-workers, standing in crammed bars, their faces lit up by their phone screens. The only time they really shared anything was on social media. Which made Rebecca's job much easier.

The hack she'd been working on that night had started several weeks earlier. Thousands of lines of code and many all-nighters, her program was finally complete. Now it was time for its first real-world test run.

Earlier in the day, the unsuspecting Dr Annette Hopkins had opened an email seemingly from the Inland Revenue, but was in fact a phishing email loaded with malware from Rebecca. The email had a subject line that would intrigue most people ('An update in your tax status'), replete with an official logo, and warnings at the bottom to beware of fake emails.

Dr Hopkins had clicked a link which claimed to take her to "www.inland-revenue.gov", a page that didn't exist but looked and sounded like it did. A quick Google check would have revealed that the Inland Revenue didn't use a dash in their web addresses, but all people ever saw was the 'inland revenue' and '.gov' part. Trust in authority, and fear of not complying with instructions filled in the rest. Most major websites owned close derivations of their web addresses (typing theguardian.-co.uk took you to its actual address of theguardian.-com/uk), but the U.K. government hadn't bothered to invest in such things.

Using what she called a web masker, Rebecca could create a webpage full of malware, but call the address something that sounded trustworthy. The web address couldn't be exactly the same as the genuine one, but by simply adding a dash, it created a much more believable address than most of the spam that flooded the public's inboxes.

Dr Hopkins thought little of it when the link took her to a blank white page. She closed the window and, thinking herself diligent, ran a scan of her anti-virus software to be on the safe side. But against Rebecca's malware, that was like trying to push a breeze back out your open front door. The damage had already been done. Silent and untraceable.

Rebecca now had remote access to Hopkins' computer.

She clicked and scrolled past bank details, financial

records, and credit card information, coming to rest at a folder marked 'Bennington Patient Records'.

It was password protected, but no match for her new program, OPEN WINDOW.

The idea for it had come from Rebecca's first ever hack: logging keyboard strokes via a USB stick attached to the back of a laptop. The tech equivalent of sliding tracing paper under the keyboard while someone types in their password. Rebecca had just found a way to do it without physically accessing the target's computer.

OPEN WINDOW scanned for the most commonly typed words on Dr Hopkins' computer. There, wedged in the middle of common words like 'for' 'it' and 'if' was 'Banana54'.

Rebecca tapped the password in, then the files opened up.

Each record had a header – 'Dr Annette Hopkins. Chief psychiatrist, Bennington Hospital' – with records running from 1989 to 2001.

Rebecca pressed Control+F and typed in: 'Stanley Fox'.

When the patient records appeared on screen, Rebecca said, 'I knew I'd find you.' She started printing the documents: hundreds of pages of conversations between Stanley and Dr Hopkins, as well as her personal follow-up notes.

When the printing finished Rebecca took the first page and pinned it to her living room wall.

What had started as just a picture of her and her dad taken when she was eight years old – Rebecca sitting on his knee, her smile showing a gap in her front teeth – now ran the entire length and height of the wall.

A cursory glance at the wall suggested a randomly assorted mess of photos, newspaper cuttings, questions written by Rebecca on sticky notes, and Facebook profile printouts. A closer look, however, revealed intricate links.

The top half meticulously reconstructed her dad's movements and employment history in chronological order: from Cambridge University, where he had been Visiting Professor of Applied Mathematics at the age of just twenty-three, to his work as a cryptographer for Government Communications Headquarters (GCHQ), the British intelligence agency, three years later. The timeline stopped suddenly with a question mark against the year 2001.

The bottom half of the wall was filled with pictures and schematics of Bennington Hospital, and maps of the surrounding area. To the right were a series of overlapping newspaper clippings from 2001 (*'Fire crews battle deadly blaze at hospital'; 'Hospital fire kills seven'; 'Celebrated mathematician among dead in hospital fire'; 'Enquiry rules hospital fire accidental'*).

On the left of the wall were various printouts of Bennington employee personnel files, surrounding the newest addition: Dr Annette Hopkins.

Ten years of research, combing the internet, and library records; hundreds of hours of phone calls; tracking down people who didn't want to be found...

At the centre of all the chaos was the thing she always came back to: the time when she was happiest, sitting on her dad's knee, smiling, her tiny arms around his neck. The last known photo of Stanley Fox.

Across the room, Rebecca heard the muffled sound of her phone ringing. She took out her earplugs.

The phone screen said '***Work calling***'.

'Rebecca Fox,' she answered, expecting it to be the switchboard.

It was her boss.

'Rebecca,' he said. 'This is Alexander. We've got an orange alert. You need to come in.'

Korecki residence, Szymany – Monday, 1.13am

Artur wiped the mix of rain and sweat from his face before carefully opening the front door – his hand trembling with the afterburn of adrenaline.

His mother was passed out drunk, as usual, on the living room couch.

On his way past the living room, Artur noticed a cigarette still burning between his mother's fingers. He stubbed it out in the ashtray.

He whispered, 'Goodnight, mum.' Then he kissed her forehead.

He made his way to his bedroom in the basement, and stood at his desk. A copy of *The Republic* magazine sat on top of his laptop keyboard, lying open at a journalist profile for Tom Novak, the magazine's national security correspondent.

He put the magazine aside, then woke up his laptop screen. His webcam had been covered with black tape after reading a Tom Novak story about the NSA's ability to patch into any laptop connected to the internet, anywhere in the world, and watch you in real-time.

Given his current situation he needed to remove as much of himself from the internet as possible. Starting with YouTube.

He didn't have time to discriminate against the occasional video where he didn't actually appear on camera. For now, they would all have to go. He doubted they would be missed: after three years he only had three hundred and sixteen subscribers.

After attempting to log in, a message at the centre of the screen popped up:

"This account has been terminated for repeated or serious violations of our Terms of Service."

Artur's stomach churned. 'No, no, no...'

He clicked to the YouTube homepage and searched manually for his most recent video, '*How To Encrypt Your Emails (NSA CAN'T HACK THIS!)*' But it was gone.

It was surely too much of a coincidence that, tonight of all nights, his account had been deleted for no clear reason. Artur figured that it was the Americans' first attempt to start reeling back in any and all copies of the clip. Because once it went online, getting it back would be like trying to stop a virus spreading. The issue for Artur was that if the authorities had tracked him down online, then it wouldn't be long before they found him in person.

Before he could start packing his things up, his spare phone and laptop both beeped with the same email.

It was from Wally:

'*Get out. RUN. RIGHT NOW!*'

Artur slammed his laptop shut and bundled it into a backpack, along with a spare phone, a flash drive, an MP3 player with earphones, and his passport. Wherever he was going – and he had no idea beyond "as far away as possible" – he needed to pack light so he could move quickly, but also blend in and not look like a tourist.

About to go upstairs for a hurried goodbye to his mother, Artur paused halfway up the stairs.

Someone knocked heavily, rapidly, on the front door, followed by shouts of '*Policja!*'

Instead of waiting for the *Biuro* like they were ordered to, the local police had wanted to collar Artur themselves. But there were only two of them, and neither had wanted to be the man at the back in case they missed out on the arrest.

Artur gently opened the letterbox window leading out into the back garden. He had just managed to slide his feet clear of the window when the front door was broken down. The last thing he heard from his mum was her shouting, '*My Artur's a good boy. What do you want?*'

Artur fled through the maze of back gardens and washing lines, and disappeared into the night without looking back. He couldn't afford to listen to how exhausted his body was. He knew he had to keep moving forward. And that the next twenty-four hours would probably be the hardest of his entire life.

3

CAMP ZERO, SZYMANY, POLAND – MONDAY 1.31AM

'MI6?' said Sharp. Such a claim raised more questions than it answered, but he was going to have to park his credulity for a while. 'You've been in American custody for forty-eight hours. Why didn't you tell anyone at Bagram?'

He waited for Malik's eyes to drift up and to the right, the brain's way of looking for information. A pretty reliable "tell" for a lie.

Malik kept his eyes locked with Sharp's. 'I can't trust regular U.S. Army with the information I have. I had to wait until I got CIA.'

Sharp hedged his bets. 'You're going to have to give me more than a few camp names, double-oh seven.'

Malik kicked under the table, his first sign of frustration. 'For the past six months I've been on deep cover in and out of Nimruz. A week ago, I told my contact in London about a credible threat...'

Those two words were like kerosene on a fire to an interrogator like Sharp.

'...a U.S. target, but my source doesn't know where yet. Three days ago, they told me that my cover was blown, and I should get out of Nimruz immediately.'

Sharp said, 'If your cover's blown then you're safe now.'

Malik leaned as far as he could across the table. 'Not from the people who are after me. They're probably on their way here right now.'

'Why would they be after an MI6 agent?'

'The information I have? They will kill anyone, anywhere, to stop it getting out.'

'Who is "they"?'

Malik paused. 'Is this conversation being recorded?'

'You bet your ass it is. Who is "they"?' He flashed his eyes on the table in front of him, then drew a question mark with his finger.

With his finger, Malik drew five letters on the table so that they faced Sharp.

Sharp's eyes narrowed, flashing from the table back to Malik. 'You can't possibly be serious.'

'The nature of my contact's information incriminates certain people like him. People that will do anything to stop that information getting out.'

'But why wouldn't they want to stop a credible threat against a U.S. target?'

Malik laughed despairingly. 'Americans: always so surprised when someone tells you who your enemies really are.'

'If you're stalling, I swear, you won't see daylight for another five years.'

Malik looked up, hearing the distant chopping sound of an approaching helicopter. He was running out of time but he forced himself to remain calm. 'Just one phone call. Article five point four of the Terrorism Cooperative Services Act specifies any friendly intelligence agents must be allowed to make contact with their agency.'

The TCSA had never been made public. Again, code word clearance only. Sharp could have possibly overlooked Malik finding out camp names, but not the TCSA as well.

Most U.S. senators and British MPs didn't know about it. If Sharp made the wrong call it could cause a diplomatic disaster.

He glanced back at the spy hole which was closed again, then took out his phone. 'What's your cryptonym?'

'Tempest,' Malik replied. 'You call William Blackstone at MI6 in London, and tell him that Tempest is blown and he needs to get my handler out.'

'Where is your handler?'

'London. They're in danger too. Please. Hurry.'

Sharp moved away and dialled. Once connected to MI6's European desk, he gave his CIA identification number then Malik's code word.

There was a click on Sharp's phone after he was connected.

From the bed of his countryside residence in Surrey, England, a sleep-drenched voice answered. 'William Blackstone.'

'This is Officer Walter Sharp with CIA. Are we secure?'

'This is a secure line, go ahead,' Blackstone replied.

'Mr Blackstone, I need to confirm the identity of one of your agents. A man under the alias Abdul al-Malik. I've to inform you Tempest is blown.'

There was no answer.

'Mr Blackstone, did you hear me?'

'Sorry, I'm here. I just...he'd gone dark. We thought he was dead. Where is he?'

'He's currently in CIA custody but–'

'Where?'

'I can't disclose that yet, sir. Your agent says he has a credible threat against a U.S. target.'

Blackstone paused. 'Officer Sharp, I'm going to have to put you on hold.'

Sharp shook his head. 'Fine.'

'They're stalling, aren't they?' Malik asked.

Sharp remained stoic. 'Hold tight, Abdul.'

Outside, the helicopter landed, its rotor blades audibly slowing.

Back in Surrey, Blackstone lit a cigarette while he called MI6 Chief Sir Lloyd Willow, who was still up entertaining the German ambassador in his Chelsea townhouse. 'Lloyd?' Blackstone said. 'We've got a problem with Tempest.'

When Blackstone came back to Sharp, he said, 'Officer Sharp, I'm going to get in contact with Langley to arrange Tempest's return. I have to ask that he's kept in isolation until we can debrief him. This is a fragile situation, you understand.'

As if to point out Blackstone's lack of interest, Sharp said, 'He's fine, by the way.'

'What? Oh, of course. Good.'

'He's a tough son of a bitch.'

'It would appear so.'

'I'll wait to hear from Langley.'

As soon as Blackstone hung up Captain Hampton started thumping on the cell door. 'Sir, I think you better get out here!'

Sharp was about to pocket his phone, then decided to leave it on the table.

Malik looked down and smiled sadly. 'It's too late.'

Sharp marched to the cell door. 'You're here under my command. No one's taking you anywhere.'

'You can't stop them. They'll kill me, you and everyone else who has the information...' Malik's eyes suddenly bulged white. 'Hell is empty, all the devils are here.'

Sharp didn't understand what he meant, but there wasn't time to question it. 'Hang tight, Abdul,' he said, opening the door.

Malik looked back to say the one sentence he had been desperate to tell someone the past two days. 'My name's not Abdul.'

Sharp closed the cell door behind him.

Hampton was on edge. He said, 'We've got a bit of a situation here...'

Sharp looked down the darkened hallway at a group of uniformed officials rummaging around in the command control room.

They must have been practically tailing Malik's flight from Bagram to have got here so fast.

As the men turned over desks and ripped out tech gear in the control room, Sharp called out from a distance, 'Hey! What the hell is this?'

They were removing all the Malik interrogation audio files from the command centre hard drive, shifting them onto portable hard drives which were then bagged up. Hampton and Fahran attempted to enter the command but were held back by a soldier in non-specific military fatigues.

Sharp, enraged at the manhandling of his colleagues, charged at the man, who was six four, two hundred pounds – the same height and size as Sharp. The man grabbed for Sharp's wrist. With a few quick flicks of his hand Sharp immobilised him with a deft Hapkido wrist lock called a reverse handshake, sending the man to his knees, his face twisted in agony.

'Who the hell are you, and what are you doing in my command?' Sharp shouted.

The man who looked to be in charge motioned for the others to stay back. 'Walter Sharp. I'm General McNally, I'm with Joint Special Command, JSC. I'm here on direct orders from the White House.'

Sharp had never even heard of JSC. But the three stars on McNally's shoulders told Sharp he should probably hear him out. Sharp let the man go, putting his hands up to show he was done.

The man staggered away, nursing his wrist.

'He's fine,' Sharp complained, as if the man was milking

it. 'If I wanted to break it, it would be broken.'

McNally smirked. 'Only CIA could start a fight in a room full of friendlies.' He was wearing Marine colours, but had no badge identifying him as such; just a plain insignia on his lapel reading 'R01'. A code even Sharp wasn't familiar with.

'General, I don't know what this is all about, but I need this room emptied in the next ten seconds for a secure phone call.'

McNally replied, 'I'm going to be taking over proceedings here.'

'Last I checked, this was a CIA facility, General.'

McNally eyeballed him. 'Don't get cute, son.'

It had been a long time since anyone had dared to call Walter Sharp 'son'.

McNally motioned for the others to leave. He cornered Sharp in front of a plain white poster with an American flag under the words, "THE WORLD IS A BATTLEFIELD." McNally checked his watch. 'As of about five minutes ago, my unit has been instructed to handle Abdul al-Malik's detention.'

'On whose authority?' Sharp asked.

McNally handed him a transfer order. 'He's on the next flight out of here.'

Sharp stared in disbelief at the order. It had been signed by the Chairman of the Joint Chiefs. 'Where to?' Sharp asked.

'An undisclosed location. We leave within the hour.'

An order from the Chairman of the Joint Chiefs was as good as from the desk of the President himself. Failure to obey such an order wouldn't just result in disciplinary hearings, but a court martial and probable dishonourable discharge. If Sharp even attempted to obstruct it, he would end up reassigned as intelligence envoy to Antarctica.

'General...' Sharp began saying, but before he could continue his attention was broken by a shout from Fahran.

He ran down the corridor towards Sharp, and said in Arabic, *'They've locked the door to Malik's cell, sir.'*

'Hey,' said McNally to Fahran, 'I only want to hear English in this compound.'

Sharp answered, 'Then you should go back to Virginia, General.' He paced back to Malik's cell.

Fahran followed behind Sharp, but before they could make it, the door flew open, accompanied by a cry of, 'He's got a gun!'

The three JSC soldiers standing outside the cell pulled their weapons, pointing them at Malik.

Sharp was already running down the corridor, when Malik shouted, 'No!'

A gunshot flashed from inside the cell.

Sharp called to his staff, 'Medic! MEDIC!'

Malik lay on the floor, blood seeping out from a single-shot to his temple. He was perfectly still. A JSC officer checked Malik's vitals: no breathing, no heartbeat.

'He took my gun,' said one of the JSC men, hand at his open, empty holster.

Sharp stared at the gun in Malik's right hand. He thought about how Malik had drawn the letters on the desk with his left. There was no way he'd shoot with his right. Lefties made up barely ten per cent of the population. McNally's boy had guessed wrong.

McNally stood at the cell door, unflustered. 'Okay, nobody touch anything.' He took out his phone and hit a speed dial. 'It's McNally. I need a clean team at Camp Zero.'

While everyone's eyes were fixed on Malik, Sharp pocketed his phone which he'd left on the table.

Everything Malik had said would happen had happened. They'd taken him out. Which meant Malik's contact in London would be next.

Sharp couldn't shake the image of those five letters Malik had drawn on the table.

POTUS.

The President of the United States.

4

GOVERNMENT COMMUNICATIONS HEADQUARTERS
(GCHQ), CHELTENHAM, ENGLAND – MONDAY, 12:59AM
LOCAL TIME

GCHQ, or the Doughnut as the ring-shaped building was affectionately known to its occupants, sat in the heart of the suburbs of Cheltenham. Considering its size, it was well hidden behind suburban estates that took you through an endless network of roundabouts. Unlike its CIA counterpart in Langley, Virginia, that towered over the surrounding forest, GCHQ had a relatively low profile. From a distance it could be mistaken for a corporate call centre.

But inside was possibly the most powerful intelligence and surveillance agency in the world.

Orange alerts for senior staff were reserved for situations that required immediate face to face briefing, and were likely to break soon on national media. Even so, there was no expediting security protocol at the layered entrance. Badge checks were done at the three checkpoints outside the building, where Rebecca's credentials were matched against an internal computer database that was the very definition of unhackable. As much as Hollywood wanted to portray otherwise, such a thing most definitely existed. And GCHQ's employee database was it.

After the badge checks, Rebecca went into what they called the 'tank' (a glass cubicle that locked you inside until your ID was confirmed), which scanned her retinas and fingerprints, then her person, for any hidden electronic devices. She left her personal mobile at the security gate, and checked out her GCHQ-issue mobile that operated on a unique frequency. It never left the premises. Even if someone were to smuggle a phone into the Doughnut it would never receive a signal.

To get to her department – Global Telecommunications Exploitation (GTE) – Rebecca walked down the "Street", a path that looped the whole way around the ground floor, and suddenly it was as if you were in a different building. In between the sofas and bean bags sitting around in 'creative thinking zones', the street had its own Starbucks and other coffee shops (complete with background-checked baristas), restaurants and cafés and newsagents to serve the Doughnut's five thousand employees.

Beyond this sweep of corridors and glass-lined hallways, two floors up, was GTE: the division responsible for monitoring internet and phone traffic for national security purposes.

Outside the double-door entrance to GTE, Rebecca swiped her ID through a scanner, which beeped and unlocked the doors for her. The office spread out the size of a football pitch, eerily quiet except for the low-end hum of air conditioning.

Slightly dimmed night lights made the place feel restful and calm, but that wasn't to last.

Rebecca's boss, and head of GTE, Alexander Mackintosh, paced towards her. Behind him, on a pillar in the centre of the room, hung a sign with the department's unofficial slogan:

DENY
DISRUPT
DEGRADE
DECEIVE

Outside Mackintosh's office, two police detective inspectors from Scotland Yard and a chief inspector were conferring.

The nightshift team, working on computers nearby, had to alter their screens to a generic GCHQ screensaver to avoid broadcasting sensitive material. They might have been the police, but even a chief inspector didn't have clearance for the sort of national security-sensitive material that ran across an analyst's desk on a daily basis.

When one of the detectives went back inside Mackintosh's office, through the open door, Rebecca saw Matthew Billington-Smith – another of GTE's three Senior Intelligence Officers with orange alert status – holding his head in his hands.

Rebecca turned towards Mackintosh, who gestured for her to remain calm.

Only two of the Senior Intelligence Officers had answered the orange alert. Rebecca didn't need to be told.

'How did it happen?' she asked Mackintosh.

He knew that talking around it would only make it harder for them both. 'There was an accident at Moreton House in Pimlico,' Mackintosh said. 'She fell from the balcony. I'm sorry, Rebecca. Abbie's dead.'

An hour later, Matthew's father, director of GCHQ Trevor Billington-Smith, was in Mackintosh's office with the two detectives.

Rebecca and Matthew looked on from their desks, staring ahead, trying to make sense of it all.

Trevor had more than once wagged a finger aggressively

at the ranking detective. Whatever had been levelled at him, hadn't been appreciated by the most powerful man in GCHQ.

Matthew was only five years older than Rebecca, but was already considered one of GCHQ's most impressive talents. He had spent eighteen months as GCHQ liaison to CIA in Afghanistan, but found that he didn't have the stomach for field operations. Matthew was always embarrassed by his double-barrelled surname and felt like he had more to prove, with most assuming he'd been prematurely fast-tracked into his position. They couldn't have been more wrong. Within six months at GTE, fresh out of Imperial College London with a First in Computer Science, Matthew intercepted a Chinese hacker contingent who had sprung some monumental malware on a British telecom giant ahead of a new product launch. If the attack had succeeded it would have cost them hundreds of millions of dollars, and until Matthew came along they didn't even know they had a vulnerability. He coded faster than anyone Rebecca had ever seen. Sometimes she would just sit there and listen to him type. It was like listening to a pianist play a piano with muted keys.

Mackintosh appeared behind Rebecca and tapped a glass of whisky against her arm.

'I don't drink,' she said, still staring towards Mackintosh's office.

Mackintosh offered a glass to Matthew, who accepted it.

'How does someone just fall from a balcony like that?' Matthew asked.

Mackintosh answered, 'The police found two empty bottles of wine in the living room, and it doesn't look like anyone else was there. Two bottles in a girl her size. Accidents can happen three floors up.'

'What do you think's going on in there?'

'They're discussing who's taking on the investigation. Trevor wants MI5.' Mackintosh never called him 'your dad' in front of Matthew, thinking it made a child of him.

'Did she say anything to you, Becky?' Matthew asked. 'Where she was going, what she was doing?'

Rebecca continued staring. It was hard to tell if she was upset or bored. 'I'm not exactly someone people here confide in.'

'Was she seeing anyone?' asked Mackintosh.

Office romances were common in GCHQ, given the stress and nature of the job. It was almost impossible to have a relationship with someone you couldn't talk about work to. Some were second- and third-generation analysts, going all the way back to the Enigma code breakers at Bletchley Park during the Second World War.

'I don't know,' Matthew said, throwing his hands up in frustration. 'Who knows what she got up to. She was always a black mirror.'

Rebecca said, 'She told me she was seeing someone.'

'She never told me that,' replied Matthew.

Mackintosh's back straightened. 'Did she say who?'

'No name,' said Rebecca. 'It was just a casual remark one day. "I'm seeing someone in London but it's complicated." That was the last she spoke of it.'

'When was this?'

'Four months ago.'

Matthew pressed her. 'And you never asked her about it again?'

Rebecca shook her head. 'Her situation held no interest for me.'

Mackintosh asked her, 'What about—'

Anticipating the question, she said, 'She showed no signs of depression in the last three months. No rapid mood swings, loss of interest in work, changes in weight, or reckless behaviour.'

Matthew knocked back the rest of his whisky. 'And they're sure it was an accident?'

Mackintosh leaned forward on his knees. The news had

clearly hit him hard. 'Witnesses on the ground said she was holding a glass of wine, dancing along the window ledge when she tipped over the railing.'

'Do you think that sounds like Abbie?' Rebecca asked. 'A one-night stay for work in London and she gets drunk by herself? So drunk that she falls off the balcony? She was too professional for that.'

Mackintosh flicked through his mobile. 'The papers will have a field day with this: a story about intelligence that we have to comment on.'

'Has it hit yet?' Matthew asked.

'*The Mail Online* has it. "Tragic balcony fall in Pimlico." *The Guardian*'s got it too.'

'Sanctimonious pricks,' said Matthew.

'They're going to enjoy sticking the knife into us after all that Tom Novak stuff. There's no mention yet that Abbie was GCHQ, but they'll have it by morning. The police report's probably being handed over in a brown envelope in front of some all-night burger van as we speak.'

Behind the three, a team of GCHQ Internal Security in black suits made their way over to Abbie's desk. They started disconnecting the leads on her computer and packing up her desk.

Matthew craned his neck to see what was going on. 'Can that not wait?' he complained.

'Protocol, sir,' one of the suits answered brusquely. 'Section thirty-two of internal GCHQ code. All property of deceased agents must be collected for forensics within three hours.'

Matthew got up to pour himself another whisky. He had already poured it by the time he asked Mackintosh, 'You don't mind, do you?'

'Go ahead,' he replied, handing his own glass over for a refill.

Once the internal team had finished, Rebecca woke her

own computer up. It had been on screensaver since she got there. A homicide on government property would necessitate an internal enquiry. Rebecca knew the drill with those by now. She would be asked to hand over hard copies of all recent communications with Abbie. A macabre task. One Rebecca wanted to get over and done with as soon as possible.

When she logged in to her email two new messages were illuminated.

"*From: Abbie Bishop*. <An insurance policy>
Sent: 23.44, 18*th* August 2018."

At first it was sad, like finding an old voicemail from a dead relative on your phone. The timing put it heartbreakingly close to her time of death – Mackintosh said the paramedics had called it sometime between twelve and half past.

Rebecca tried opening the email, then realised Abbie's email had been encrypted using standard GCHQ hardware. But staffers rarely used encryption for internal messages. Whatever Abbie had sent, she only wanted Rebecca to be able to read.

Rebecca decrypted the email using the necessary digital key, then the message appeared:

'Rebecca, I'm sending you this because you're the only one I can trust. I'm afraid I've been keeping a lot of secrets from you for a long time now. Secrets I'm not proud of. It might already be too late to stop it all, but I'm going to try. Tonight could be my last chance. My life is already in danger as it is.

The reason for that should become pretty clear from the files I've attached. The files are password-protected (you'll figure it out), and one is encrypted: it's too sensitive for email – I haven't trusted our system for the last six months now.

I've hidden a key in a README file on the laptop – which I've hidden under a pillow in the bedroom wardrobe here. Input the key and it will decrypt the last file. It's everything you need to prove who's guilty, and who's innocent.

You're not going to like everything you read about me in this. I've been a liar – for a very long time – about any number of things as you will see. Some of it you will understand, some you won't. Once you've read all the files, you will know the full truth.

The files are my insurance policy. Should anything happen to me, you'll know what to do with them. On a long enough timeline, the truth always comes out.

There's only one other thing to warn you about: tell Alexander nothing. HE CAN'T BE TRUSTED.

Your friend, Abbie.

PS. the password: KING OF SCOTLAND - OGLING MONARCH - MOORISH GENERAL - SMALL SETTLEMENT - STORM'

Rebecca forced herself to stay still and not react in any way. She just glanced around the room to check where everyone was. No one was looking.

There was one line that really stood out.

'Should anything happen to me...'

Even without that, Rebecca knew there was something off about the official take on Abbie's death. First, typos: not one error in spelling, grammar, or punctuation. Then the fact that Abbie had had the foresight to encrypt the message. The tone was rational, clear-headed. This from someone who just half an hour later would be so drunk that she fell off a balcony? If it was an accident, why did she think something might happen to her?

The attachment was an untitled folder, password-protected. At a glance, the password clues were as impenetrable as anything she'd seen in a long time. She then reminded herself that Abbie wouldn't have sent her something she couldn't break.

Before she set about cracking it, she opened the second email.

If the first was sad, the second one was downright chilling.

"From: Abbie Bishop. <NO SUBJECT>
Sent: 23.57, 18ᵗʰ August 2018."

'*help*'

That was all it said.

Rebecca instinctively put her hand to her mouth in horror, thinking about the circumstances in which it must have been written.

Then a pop-up flashed at the bottom of her screen.

Rebecca jolted in her seat and took her hands away from the keyboard, as if it had suddenly become incredibly hot.

She glanced towards Mackintosh's office to see if anyone had noticed her reaction, but the blinds were closed.

'***You have one new message from Abbie Bishop. Sent: 01:48, 19th August 2018.***'

Her fingers trembled on the mouse as she opened the email.

'*FIND TOM NOVAK. EVERYTHING DEPENDS ON IT.*'

Rebecca squinted at the screen. *Tom Novak?* she thought. *Of all people, why him? And who the hell sent this?*

It hadn't been delayed in sending, as internal GCHQ emails recorded the time at which messages were composed, as well as the time of sending – both were the same. The email had been written and sent within the last minute from Abbie's laptop.

Rebecca checked the IP address from the email, in case someone had somehow hacked Abbie's email account, but the IP address matched the previous message, and all the others Abbie had ever sent her.

Someone had taken Abbie's laptop from the safe house.

She looked up at Mackintosh, who was across the room with Matthew, their glasses raised.

'To Abbie,' Matthew said sombrely.

Mackintosh chimed his glass with Matthew's, and said nothing.

Camp Zero, Command Control – 2.43am, local time

After Malik's body was taken to the infirmary, and McNally and his men had cleared out, Sharp was left alone in command control, hassling Langley on the phone.

'...I know that, sir,' Sharp explained, 'but this source is credible. MI6 confirmed his status.'

Sharp's superior, Bob Weiskopf, division chief of CIA Counterterrorism Centre, wasn't exactly onboard with Sharp's appraisal of the situation. 'What do you want me to do with that? Put every major public figure in a bunker for the next month?'

Sharp pleaded, 'I'm saying, let's ground POTUS and the veep until we at least know where this is headed.'

'Do you know how many credible threats you've passed to the Secret Service in the last year?' Before Sharp could reply, Weiskopf told him, 'It's thirteen. And how many had legs?' Weiskopf waited this time.

'Zero, sir.'

'You make the boy who cried wolf seem like a goddamn oracle.'

Sharp replied, 'You remember the wolf still comes in the end, right?'

Weiskopf wasn't in the mood for his semantics. 'You've got a dead MI6 agent on your hands, Walt. Find me some actionable intelligence and you'll have my full attention.' He hung up.

Hampton returned from the lockaway where detainees' possessions were kept in evidence. He slumped at the table then said, 'I'm sorry, sir. They took everything of Malik's.'

Sharp pushed his hands back through his hair, trying to contain his frustration. At least in front of Hampton.

'I took Fahran back to his quarters,' Hampton said.

'How is he doing?' Sharp asked.

'He's a bit shaken up. He took this job to get away from executions.'

'Didn't we all,' Sharp replied.

'Is Mr Weiskopf moving on the threat?' Hampton asked.

'He's right. We don't have it.'

'I don't get it. I mean, Secretary Snow is in London tomorrow, right? Can't they beef up security, at least?'

Sharp said, 'He's the United States Secretary of Defense. The only way to beef up his security further is to put him in a tank.'

Sharp's mobile started ringing. 'Jeremy,' he answered. 'What have you got?' Sharp listened intently, then he clicked his fingers urgently at Hampton, pointing at the paper and pen just out of Sharp's reach.

Hampton handed him both.

'Are you sure that's the name...' Sharp said, writing. 'As in *the*...? Thanks, buddy. I owe you.' Sharp hung up, then handed Hampton the paper with a name written on it. 'Get him.'

Hampton did a double take before turning back to his computer. 'What's his involvement with all this, sir?'

Sharp stood over Hampton's shoulder. 'NSA did a comms sweep of the local area from tonight. My guy found an email sent from the middle of a field near the airport. NSA snagged the metadata. It's literally the only email in a fifty-mile radius during that chase. It's got to be the runner from earlier. You'd have thought he'd be contacting someone local. Instead he emails an American journalist. What the hell is that?'

'I don't understand, sir,' Hampton said.

'Jeremy said that the email the runner sent had an attachment, a video file. They can't view it, but they know it's there. It's got to be the video of Malik from the airport. And if JSC and McNally are cleaning shop like I think, they're going to be after anyone who has this video.'

Hampton turned the computer screen towards Sharp, showing the phone number for *The Republic*.

Sharp dialled, then checked his watch. 'Damn. It's nearly nine p.m. there...' He pursed his lips as it kept ringing. 'It's taking too long.' The call went to voicemail. 'Shit.' He hung up, then said to Hampton, 'Get me an editor's number.'

Hampton scrolled as quickly as he could. 'Mark Chang. Senior editor.' Before Hampton could read it out, Sharp had dialled from over Hampton's shoulder.

It rang twice before being picked up.

He was the last person left in the office, and wired on too much coffee. 'Mark Chang, *The Republic*.'

'Mr Chang. This is Walter Sharp with CIA. I need the location and phone number of one of your reporters: Tom Novak.'

Chang, who had a call waiting on another mobile clamped to his other ear, and was rummaging through a foot-high pile of White House press briefings that had covered his desk all day, wasn't exactly paying attention. 'Look, if this is another death threat or marriage proposal, DM him on Twitter like everyone else. I've got an important call on the other line.'

Sharp said in his firmest voice, 'Mr Chang, this phone call is currently being relayed to you via two hundred and forty-eight-bit encryption on three satellites over two continents. All told, this call is costing the U.S. taxpayer around a thousand dollars a second. Believe me when I tell you: this is the most important call you're getting tonight. I'm CIA officer Walter Sharp.' He added, 'I'm guessing you'll remember this time.'

Chang's other call came through, but he hung up on them straight away. 'What can I do for you?'

'I have reason to believe Tom Novak's safety may be compromised. I need his cell number and location.'

Chang fumbled for the other phone – now on the floor – searching for Novak's number, which Sharp wrote down.

After he hung up, Sharp said to Hampton, 'Novak's in Washington. He's got a hearing at Congress tomorrow morning.' He scrolled through his phone.

'Do you want me to call him, sir?' Hampton asked, a little confused why Sharp wasn't.

'We'll get to Tom Novak,' Sharp said. 'But first, I want to find out who this is.' He showed Hampton his phone screen. Sharp said, 'I left it in his cell to see who he'd call. After William Blackstone, there was another outgoing listed at one-seventeen a.m. A call with the international code four four.'

Hampton said, 'British.'

Sharp paced slowly round the room, thinking aloud. 'Say you're an agent in the field whose cover's been blown. You're in fear for your life. You're also in fear for your handler's life. Who do you call?'

'My handler,' Hampton replied.

Sharp said, 'Malik told me his handler was in London. The call he made has the same local code as the call I made to Blackstone. Also in London.'

'Malik tried to warn them?'

Sharp tapped on the number. 'We've got to find this guy.' Sharp's heart found a new gear. He hadn't slept in twenty hours, but he felt wide awake. 'Come on, pick up. *Pick up...*' The ringing stopped, then came the pause he was dreading. 'Voicemail.'

'Is there a name?' Hampton asked.

Sharp squinted slightly, surprised by the well-spoken young English woman at the other end.

'*You've reached the phone of Abigail Bishop. Please leave your message after the beep...*'

5

Rebecca was alone in the office, her desk lamp seeming much brighter in the pale-green night lights above.

Tell Alexander nothing. HE CAN'T BE TRUSTED.

It was all Rebecca could think of, while she tried to work out the angles on Abbie's clues.

She zeroed in on 'STORM' as it was the simplest clue of the five. She had a whole list of synonyms written down – gale, blizzard, hurricane, tempest, cyclone, torrent, assault, uproar – but none of them plugged into the other four clues.

She had been at it for hours, and all she had to show for it was an expanded vocabulary on storms. She threw her pencil down in frustration. She'd tried the elegant solution, now it was time to try something a little less so: a dictionary attack.

It was a program that used over two million words that plugged in as potential password combinations. Deep down, Rebecca held little optimism of it working: it was unlikely Abbie would have picked dictionary words as the password. The hints suggested something more nuanced than that, but she had to try it.

While she let the dictionary attack run, Rebecca turned her attention to Tom Novak. Anyone who had followed the news for the last six months knew his name, and his Wikipedia page was as comprehensive as a famous singer's or actor's, rather than a journalist.

Rebecca searched through it for any connections with London.

"**Thomas Seymour Novak** (born September 12, 1981), is the national security correspondent for weekly news magazine *The Republic*, and author of *The New York Times* bestseller *The Hidden State: How the NSA Steals Elections*, which won the 2018 Pulitzer Prize for non-fiction. He is the son of former *NBC Nightly News* anchor Seymour Novak (August 19, 1949 - January 24, 2014). He lives in Brooklyn, New York."

The pictures showed him accepting his Pulitzer Prize; being interviewed by Wolf Blitzer on CNN; and sitting on stage at one of his many book events.

In Rebecca's line of work, for forging connections between strangers, an analyst couldn't beat what she called the Holy Trinity: Facebook, Twitter and Instagram.

Most of the action was on Novak's Twitter – where he had 275,000 followers. A scroll down the timeline established his posting average was around fifteen to twenty tweets a day. The only mentions of GCHQ were in reference to his NSA story. There was nothing else even vaguely British in his feed.

The online news resource LexisNexis couldn't make any connections either.

If Rebecca wanted to find out more about his relationship to Abbie Bishop, she would have to get closer. Which meant making contact.

Fortunately, security wasn't something Novak mucked about with. On *The Republic* website, at the bottom of Novak's biographical page, was his official email address, a link to his Twitter page, and a link to his IronCloud. Most weeks, Novak received dozens of emails from potential whistleblowers, impressed with the magazine's stance on protecting sources, even when threatened with prosecution by the U.S. government. IronCloud gave sources a safe, encrypted place to leave documents or any type of computer files for potential stories. Even *Republic* journalists themselves reading the materials in drop boxes didn't know who had sent them.

Under the IronCloud link was a line of forty characters, a mix of numbers and letters, broken into groups of four. This was his PGP (Pretty Good Privacy) public key. The 'Pretty' part was a case of severe underselling. After the public key was applied by the sender, it generated a corresponding private key at Novak's end. Intercepting that private key was impossible, and trying to guess the private key using computers was beyond the limits of earthly mathematics. There wasn't enough energy in the world to power a computer for long enough to make it even a possibility.

Rebecca knew better than anyone that there was no way around PGP encryption. Her father had spent years trying – and failing – to.

She signed in to her email. Although the content of the email would be unreadable, NSA or GCHQ would be able to track the metadata from the email. Metadata was information *about* a message: who sent it; who received it; when; and the subject line. So Rebecca knew that she couldn't leave something obvious in the email's subject line. Calling it 'Abbie Bishop' or anything close could raise a flag somewhere. The safest method in the circumstances was to leave it blank.

She typed out her message, '*Abbie Bishop seemed to think we should talk*', initiated Novak's encryption key, then clicked send.

A check on the dictionary attack showed that it was still running, but without success. Realistically it could run overnight – or the next week – and still not work. Covering all bases, she loaded up a brute-force tool she had coded, and used only for emergencies.

It was exactly what it sounded like. While dictionary attacks were methodical and went word by word in different combinations, brute-force attacks were haphazard; random stabs in the dark. The touch Rebecca added was what elevated it above a regular brute-force tool. It overwhelmed a password authorisation system with thousands of requests for access, and while it was busy denying the barrage, one request could sneak in undetected. She called it BACK DOOR because it worked like a burglar sneaking in your back door while you're chasing away people throwing rocks at the front.

Like the dictionary attack it would take time, but at least it was something that could work in the background.

Rebecca pushed her keyboard away as she felt her eyelids get heavy. There were large TV screens on the walls around the office, either showing Google Earth (ready for any computer on the floor to transmit to), or 24-hour news. The ticker at the bottom of the screen read, "*WOMAN FALLS TO DEATH FROM BALCONY OF GCHQ SAFE HOUSE IN LONDON.*"

Now that the news had finally leaked, Rebecca put her head down and drifted into a deep sleep.

It was the same dream she'd had since she was thirteen. Rebecca was lying on her front on the living room floor, doing *The Times* crossword in front of a crackling log fire. She was ten years old.

'Daddy?' she shouted, twirling a pen in her hand. 'Can I have a pencil? I'm not sure about twelve across.'

From his study next door, Stanley Fox replied, 'Then wait until you *are* sure.' He didn't sound his usual bright self. He then added what he always told her when she was struggling with a puzzle, 'Answers don't come to you, Rebecca. You have to find them.'

Rebecca rolled her eyes. 'Thanks, dad,' she mumbled. '"An army rank kept to yourself?" Seven letters...'

She always felt aware of how empty the old Georgian house was with just her and her dad. They would shout things to each other from room to room, their voices echoing around the high ceilings.

Just as Rebecca solved the clue – smiling to herself – she heard a glass smash in the study. Abandoning the puzzle, she found her dad collapsed in front of his blackboard, whisky and broken glass all over the wooden floor. Rebecca kneeled by his side, shaking him as hard as she could. He hardly moved and, after a long exhalation, slurred, 'Private...'

Rebecca leaned back. 'Yes, daddy. I got it.'

As he slept on the floor, Rebecca looked up at his cryptography equations. Ideas were scored out violently, with notes like 'IDIOT' and 'NO NO NO NO NO!' written beside his mistakes. He had run out of space on the board, and simply started writing in pen on the wallpaper.

Unable to move her dad, Rebecca called his closest associate from GCHQ, Sam Sulley, who lived nearby (all the senior GCHQ analysts and officers lived in Cheltenham). After Sam had helped carry Stanley to bed, he promised Rebecca her dad was just fine. He was under a lot of pressure at work.

The next moment the dream had moved forward in time – three years – and thirteen-year-old Rebecca was being held back by Sam while her dad was led out to a white van in his dressing gown and slippers.

'They can look after him there,' Sam explained.

'I don't understand,' Rebecca said.

'He needs some time to rest. I'm going to look after you here until he comes back.'

An orderly closed the back door to the van, which was marked 'Bennington Hospital'. When the door slammed shut, Rebecca woke up.

As she opened her eyes, she found cleaners buzzing around in the background with hoovers. They were the only cleaners in the country that required a three-month background check, full-body scans before each shift for recording, bugging or photographic devices, and the signing of nondisclosure forms saying that anything they divulged about what they heard or saw in GCHQ was punishable under the Official Secrets Acts.

As the office filled up throughout the morning, Rebecca kept staring over towards Mackintosh's office.

Tell Alexander nothing. HE CAN'T BE TRUSTED.

Every conversation they'd ever had, every question he'd asked about Abbie, had now taken on a disarming and sinister taint. What had he been up to? Did he know someone was after Abbie? Might he even be responsible?

Wiping the sleep from her eyes, Rebecca opened her email, looking again at the messages from the night before. She got to thinking about the timing of the messages.

With a flurry of keystrokes she opened a tracer program, which scanned the IP location of the sender. It didn't even require the sending device to still be active: it not only retroactively logged each sending location – like a stamped passport – it logged each location the sender had been in while composing the message.

Whoever the sender was hadn't even tried to cover their tracks. A teenager covering up his internet-porn history would have taken more precautions. It was as if the sender had been holding a big red balloon on a string while in a crowd, waiting for Rebecca to find them.

The message sent after Abbie's fall hadn't been sent from Moreton House, of course, because the police were all over the flat by that time. But the message had been started there. After that, the location kept shifting, but smoothly, incrementally. The time stamps were too fast for them to have been on foot.

She realised they must have been in a car.

And from there, the files were attached, and message sent. Then she had an idea.

She noted the time when the IP locations changed, then pulled up Greater London's CCTV system. One quick call via GCHQ's switchboard to the Metropolitan Police gave her real-time access to all CCTV in their jurisdiction. Such requests from GCHQ were routine, coming through a dedicated caller ID system at the Met's end to speed up the authentication process. She opened an IP/GPS tool on her computer – what looked like a regular computer calculator – and entered the last-known IP address. When she hit 'ENTER' it told her the precise GPS coordinates, 51° 29' 19.5" N 0° 8' 14.3" W., which she then input to the CCTV system. The camera monitoring the approach to the HM Passport Office was the nearest match. Just a few minutes away from Moreton House in Pimlico.

She scrolled the camera clock until it matched the time stamp on the IP tracer, then hit play. The street the camera looked down on was empty, except for an old man walking a dog. Then a black Mercedes 4x4 came haring through the shot, nearly colliding with a taxi at the intersection which had to swerve out the way. She stepped the camera back one frame at a time, until she got a clear shot of the registration plate: 273D101. She played the shot backwards and forwards a minute each way, seeing no other cars. 'Got you,' she said to herself.

She opened up her DVLA access page, then entered the registration plate in the database. After a few seconds of a spinning cursor, it read 'NO MATCHES FOUND.' Although it was a strange configuration, it certainly looked like a U.K. plate.

She called the DVLA. After giving her clearance codes, she said, 'I'm trying to trace a registration, but I'm not getting anything on your database. I'm wondering if it's possibly a dummy plate. It's two seven three delta one oh one.'

The operator didn't even have to search for it. She said,

'You're not going to get anything on that, I'm afraid.' She paused as if it were obvious. 'It's diplomatic issue.'

Rebecca hung forward in her chair. 'Sorry, I'm not familiar with those.'

The operator explained, 'The first three numbers are the country's code, then an X for accredited personnel – like an attaché – or the D you have here for diplomat. The three numbers after the D are a bit like a ranking within an embassy. Those numbers start at one oh one – which is what you have – so they must be pretty important, I guess.'

Rebecca asked, 'What about the code, the first three numbers? What country is two seven three?'

The operator keyed in the code, humming and hawing as if she were checking someone's credit rating. 'Let's see, I always forget these...Two seven three...that's the Americans. Theirs are between two seven oh and two seven four.'

As the operator called out, 'Hello?', Rebecca rocked gently back in her seat and dropped the phone back in its cradle. She tried to get it all straight in her head: someone using an American diplomatic car had been in Moreton House – around the time of Abbie's death – taken Abbie's laptop, then used it to send her an email. But if Abbie was killed for the files on her laptop, why contact Rebecca?

She felt a tap on her shoulder. The sudden contact made her jump in her seat. When she saw who it was she rushed to close down what she had been looking at, but it was too late.

'Sorry,' Matthew said, glancing at her screen.

Regaining her composure, Rebecca said, 'I thought you were at home.'

His face had the drawn look of having been awake only a short while. 'I couldn't sleep. I thought I'd be more use in here.' He clearly looked at the CCTV still of the U.S. diplomatic car. 'What are you doing?'

'Just some DVLA stuff,' she tried to say casually, clicking

the screen away. 'Checking plates on streets near Moreton House. Probably a waste of time.'

Matthew pushed his lips out. 'Better than nothing, I guess. I'm going to go check in with upstairs.' He walked over to the TV screens on the wall where the news was doing its preamble for the Prime Minister's press conference.

Rebecca's mouth hung open, ready to say the words 'I need to tell you something.' But she couldn't. Not until she knew who she could trust.

6

The man had woken up peacefully, a few minutes ahead of his alarm. But, after blinking the blurriness out of his eyes, he became aware of a dark figure standing over his bed. Before he could let out a cry of shock, the intruder whipped a black bag over the man's head, squeezing the bottom tight around his neck, letting no air in. The man gasped, his feet kicking fruitlessly on his mattress.

The intruder – twenty-three – wasn't interested in the man's money, or stealing any of the expensive audio/visual equipment in the flat. The intruder was going to become a martyr.

The Martyr began to smile as the man stopped kicking. As he dragged the body to the hallway, the Martyr thought, *God will welcome him.* He had noticed the Quran and book of Hadiths on the hallway table when he entered. A martyr knew what had to be done in the name of Allah. And some day, in Paradise, *insh'Allah*, his victim would thank him. Of that, and so much else, the Martyr was certain.

With the dead man sprawled on the hallway floor, the Martyr made his way to the bathroom. He washed his hands,

then splashed cold water on his face and through his hair. When he was done, he didn't wipe his fingerprints from the tap, or remove the stray hairs that had fallen from his head. It didn't matter. He would be long gone by the time forensics came back. By the time he was done, everyone would know his name.

The Martyr emptied the dead man's wallet, stopping at one particular form of ID. The name on it was "Riz Rizzaq". The Martyr took out a similar ID from his pocket and compared it with Riz's.

The Martyr nodded appreciatively. His contact had indeed created a flawless copy. The only thing different between the two was the photo.

But the Martyr couldn't leave quite yet.

If the body was discovered too early, the whole plan would fall apart. And killing him any sooner might have raised alarm bells.

So he sat on the floor, next to the dead body, and read from his Quran for nearly three hours. Feeling the power of God's grace upon him.

It was nearly time.

Embankment - 1.41pm

The Martyr's stomach stirred at the sight of armed police covering the tube exits. But they didn't follow him.

He had cut his regular beard, and was now wearing Rizzaq's sleeveless photographer's jacket and a pair of multi-pocket cargo trousers.

Once at Victoria Embankment in Westminster, he approached Cleopatra's Needle. Using a piece of chalk from his trouser pocket, he swiped a horizontal line on the riverside wall between Cleopatra's Needle and the sphinx statue on the right-hand side.

Across the street, three Yemeni men huddled around a map, and saw the Martyr make the sign. One of the three took out a mobile phone and texted the confirmation, "*The sphinx looks to the right.*" The man then took out the SIM, and mashed it with his heel on the ground.

Now no one could call off the Martyr.

Ali residence, central London – Monday, 8.21am

Simon Hussein Ali had been sitting at his study room desk for over an hour, looking out through the bulletproof window at the armed guards patrolling the garden below. He was still wearing yesterday's clothes, save for a change of tie undone around his neck. His eyes stung from being up all night, but under the circumstances sleep had been out of the question.

From the study door behind him twin seven-year-old girls in the uniform of the exclusive Westminster School burst in. Both shouted, 'Daddy!' then each hugged an arm of his.

'Oh no!' he exclaimed, picking them up. They hung from his arms like Christmas decorations as he tried to walk with them. 'I'll never get to work now. I have two little monsters stuck to me.'

'We're not monsters!' they shouted back at the tops of their voices.

His wife Sonia followed breezily behind. 'That *is* debatable.' She kissed her husband on the cheek, looking at his sickly complexion. 'I told them you were still working, so we thought we'd have breakfast downstairs without you.' She mouthed to him, 'You okay?'

'I'm fine,' he replied, trying to be chirpy. He looked over her shoulder, seeing news of Abbie Bishop on the TV.

'Is that going to cause you trouble today?' Sonia asked.

'I expect so,' he answered.

Sonia could see something was deeply wrong with him.

After fifteen years of marriage she knew Simon better than anyone.

'Right, girls,' she said. 'Say goodbye to daddy or we're going to be late for school.'

Simon crouched down to give out hugs and kisses, then stood up to kiss his wife.

Sonia said, 'Remember, I'm out with Victoria until two. Good luck today with the conference.' She kissed his cheek before wiping off the lipstick trace. 'Are you changing your shirt?' It wasn't really a question. 'You can't wear yesterday's shirt. One of the photo editors will pick up on it.'

'I will.' Seeing her about to leave, he said, 'Sonia.'

She stopped at the door.

'Could you come straight back afterwards?'

She nodded, her high hopes for the day already turning to worry. 'Okay.'

Early in his career, Simon had suspected that it wasn't those at the very top who held the real power of deciding matters of life and death. It was those just below the top. He had always pursued the top jobs – head boy, president of the student union, councillor, then MP – because it was what came next. What was expected. There was always something more, something bigger and better. Now he found himself questioning what his entire life had been for if this was where he was meant to end up.

He caught sight of his reflection in the glass door of the cabinet. *An errand boy in a £3000 suit*, he thought. *Not for much longer, though.*

On his desk were two copies of the speech he had been up writing all night, and a letter in an envelope. The letter was written as the sun rose that morning, addressed, "To my successor."

He opened the desk drawer, then closed it. Dissatisfied with the hiding place, he kneeled down, looking at the underside of the desk. Then he heard footsteps bounding up the stairs, dulled by the thick carpet underfoot.

A young man dashed up, past portraits of each British Prime Minister ascending the wall in chronological order, until he was outside the study, facing a recently finished portrait of Simon Ali hanging next to the door.

Ali taped the envelope under the desk, then hastily got to his feet, speech now in hand.

The staffer knocked gently but rapidly on the study door, calling out meekly, 'Good morning, Prime Minister. Secretary Snow is about ten minutes away. Mr Bullock was wondering if you have your speech for the teleprompter?'

The PM opened the study door, his thoughts clearly elsewhere as he looked around the room.

As he shuffled a copy of his speech into his inside jacket pocket, the staffer noticed the curious heading the PM had given his speech: "*My Confession*".

'Churchill never used a teleprompter,' Ali said. 'Please assure my chief of staff that I have not lost the ability to read words from paper.'

The idea of actually delivering such a speech in front of the world's media later that afternoon left Ali in a cold sweat, but also feeling oddly exhilarated. It would be so beautiful, because they would never see it coming: their man on the inside; the one they gifted one of the strongest Tory strongholds in the country to; the one whose ascendency they had so painstakingly orchestrated in the private clubs and smoking rooms of Westminster; whose reputation they had so carefully cultivated with the newspaper reporters they had in their pocket; all the Sunday supplement puff pieces with photos of him in jeans and a sweater; whose every meeting had been choreographed like a Bolshoi ballet; whose every statement had been focus-grouped and polled to death.

They thought they owned Simon Ali, because he always did as he was told.

He had even agreed to drop his middle name – Hussein – to appeal to older, white, swing voters. And with just a few hundred words given to the world's media on a Monday afternoon, the establishment's world was going to come crashing down around them.

7

It was standing room only in Room 2141 of the Rayburn House Office Building. Members of the press and public were pressed tight against the walls, a steady murmur of anticipation spread around the room, awaiting the arrival of Tom Novak – the hearing's main witness.

Congressman Jim Brenner of Oklahoma's first district, and Chairman of the House Judiciary Subcommittee on National Security, looked disdainfully at his watch. A flurry of camera flashes went off in the corridor outside, along with a chant of 'Lock him up! Lock him up!', and supportive cheers.

Tom Novak emerged from the crowd, fighting his way through to the witness desk with the help of a stern cop.

A twenty-seven-year-old man was already sitting at the witness desk, reading briefing notes, unfazed by the hysteria in the air.

Novak unbuttoned his bespoke Tom Ford suit jacket without any hurry, taking a long admiring look around the room before sitting down. 'Good turnout,' he said to himself, taking his phone out. He tapped the man on the shoulder. 'I didn't know my lawyer would have a second chair for this. Do you think he'd mind if I took a quick selfie with the crowd for my Instagram?'

With the tone of a disapproving father, the man replied, '*I am your lawyer, Mr Novak, and yes I mind. Put your phone away.*'

Novak did a double-take. '*You're* Kevin...what was it?'

'Kevin Wellington,' the lawyer said, shaking Novak's hand somewhat reluctantly.

Novak took his seat. 'Sorry I'm late. Pennsylvania Avenue was a car park.'

Kevin steered the microphone on their desk away from them in case it'd gone hot already. 'No you're not, and no it wasn't. I saw you outside giving interviews to CNN and Fox.

'Just getting in some advance spin,' Novak replied.

Brenner punctured the atmosphere with a sharp '*Thank* you' into the mic. He added grimly, 'Now Mr Novak has deigned to fit the United States Congress into his busy schedule, we'll start in two minutes.'

The room ignited in chatter again.

Kevin asked, 'Did you look at my briefing notes last night like you said you would?'

'Kevin Wellington,' Novak said, lingering on the name like he was trying to remember something. 'I never met a Kevin before.'

'Big day for you...'

Novak said, 'They never said they were sending a twelve-year-old to represent me.'

Wellington retorted, 'You fired the last three lawyers my firm assigned to you. The last of which was at ten p.m. last night, so now probably isn't the time for you to get too picky.'

Playing it straight, Novak replied, 'No, I think it's great you're supplementing your paper route by providing defence counsel at congressional hearings.'

With a faint smile, Kevin said, 'Mr Novak, right now you are basically sitting in a court room. The answers you give are going to determine whether or not the committee recommends that the U.S. government bring charges against you under the Espionage Act, which has every chance of landing you in jail for up to ten years. So please. For the love of all that is holy. Can I get you to hunker down? Or are you honestly the only person in this room that doesn't grasp the seriousness of what's about to happen?'

Novak replied, 'No, could you please explain it to me further as condescendingly as you can?'

Kevin let the question hang in the air a moment. He looked over the rim of his glasses, which made him look many years older than he was. 'Normally the phrase "I'm ten times smarter than you" would be an exaggeration, but in this case, it really isn't. It's pretty insane how smart I am. I was editor at Harvard Law Review, and graduated top of my class by three whole per cent. I passed the New York state bar exam at twenty-two, and I am the youngest junior partner in the history of Bruckner Jackson Prowse. That said, my role is extremely limited in these cases. That panel up there can ask you anything they like and I can't raise so much as an objection. They've all been coached for this session for the past four weeks.' He checked his watch. 'We've had about ninety seconds. And as much as you implored my predecessors to, Mr Novak, I'm not here to make speeches on your behalf. I can't help you change the face of democracy. And I'm not in Washington to help you drain the swamp. I'm here to defend you against some very powerful people who want to send you to jail, and destroy the magazine you work for.'

'What do you want me to do then? Novak asked.

Kevin replied, 'You can start by wiping that smug, America-hating smile from your face, or that's what every picture editor will run with on their front page tomorrow. Don't mistake this for a news event. It's PR. Whatever they ask you, tell the truth. If you're not sure how to answer, ask me. These people do this for a living and they're damn good at it.'

'Debating?' Novak asked.

Kevin gave him a cold stare. 'Ending careers.'

From his place at the centre of the fourteen-member panel, Brenner announced, 'Good morning, ladies and gentlemen. This hearing of the House judiciary subcommittee on national security will come to order. We have one item of business today, involving the leaking of classified intelligence from the National Security Agency's databases, and identifying the parties responsible in contravention of the Espionage Act of nineteen seventeen. Mr Novak, would you please stand and raise your right hand.'

As he'd been taught by his father, Novak buttoned his jacket as he stood. His slim, muscular physique was the perfect hanger for his tailored suit, looking more like a male model than a journalist.

After swearing Novak in, Brenner asked, 'Could you confirm your name and occupation, please.'

'My name is Tom Novak. I'm security correspondent at *The Republic* magazine.'

'And you've worked there for eight years?'

Novak said, 'Yes. I've also been shot at on four different continents. I've been on *The New York Times* bestseller list for the last six months, during which time I've been the cover of *Time* magazine. Twice. I also won a Peabody and the Pulitzer Prize for breaking the story that's got me here today. And apparently, according to *People* magazine, I am the thirteenth most-eligible bachelor in America.'

There was laughter and scattered applause from the crowd.

Brenner didn't rise to them, saying, 'Unfortunately for you, Mr Novak, the Pulitzer committee is not considered a legal authority in the United States of America with regards to deciding who has or has not violated the Espionage Act. Nor will your *looks* be taken into consideration.'

Kevin hastily scribbled a note and slid it into Novak's eye line: "DON'T MESS WITH BRENNER."

'Let's get right to it,' Brenner said. 'On February second this year, *The Republic* magazine published a cover story by you titled "The Hidden State: How the NSA Steals Elections". It made a number of far-reaching allegations about National Security Agency surveillance programs. Could you tell the panel how you came into possession of unauthorized, classified material?'

Novak recounted the story of how he had acquired the information that led to his story – which proved to be the biggest intelligence leak in American history – keeping the entire room in the palm of his hand. It had started with an anonymous email sent to him on January 1st. Normally, Novak paid little attention to unsolicited tips on stories as they often turned into nothing. But as he and the source talked through January via encrypted online chat, the source claimed to have 'a treasure trove' of classified material from the NSA.

The source sent a sample of the documents, and they were more than Novak could ever have hoped for. He knew he was into something as soon as he saw the first page stamped in red lettering:

"TOP SECRET//COMINT/NOFORN/"

Communications intelligence. Not for distribution to foreign nationals.

Congresswoman Donna Kershaw of the California twelfth – one of the Democrats on the panel – teed Novak up with a soft question. 'And for the few people in this room and watching at home who don't know, what was in the documents?'

Novak answered, 'They were how-to manuals for NSA operatives in posting fake news or disinformation to social media sites during election cycles. As well as harvesting user profile data. The social media sites gave them everything about these people: where they lived, their age, what movies they watched, what music they listened to, what books they read. Even the contents of private messages. Imagine the NSA having the ability to photocopy the contents of ten million people's diaries without their knowing. That's the scale of it.'

'And what was the response to these stories?' Kershaw asked.

Novak explained, 'In the past, leaks were a storm right from the start, because the sources outed themselves along with the story itself. What hooked other news outlets onto my story was that there had been a massive intelligence leak, and no leaker. Which left me as the face of the story.'

A close ally of Brenner's, Alex Vincent of Texas, asked, 'Mr Novak, is it possible that your source may still be working for the federal government?'

Novak, nonchalant, said, 'They could be sat here in this room right now.'

Wanting to appear as robust as Brenner, Vincent fired back, 'Do you really expect us to believe you don't know who your source is?'

Novak fought hard to keep a smirk from his face. 'Well, congressman, you said in an interview with *Newsweek* last year that you believe the story of Noah's Ark really happened. So, frankly, your disbelief seems a little flexible.'

Even Novak's detractors in the gallery were laughing.

Brenner stepped in. 'I think this would be a good time for a break. Do you have questions at this time, Mr Novak?'

'Just one, Mr Chairman,' Novak said. 'Does the President think going into the midterm elections as the first-ever President to jail a reporter under the Espionage Act will be a good or a bad thing?'

Kevin leaned quickly towards the mic. 'We retract that question, with Mr Novak's apologies, Mr Chairman.'

Brenner was unruffled in his response. 'Mr Novak, I think these days the only profession the American people trust less than politicians are journalists. Whether you like it or not, your work has meant there is a traitor possibly still working with classified material, and we have no idea if they're going to hand that information to a journalist next, or someone in Russia or China, for a very large fee. I'm prepared to go to the ends of the earth to bring that person to justice. Even if that means sending you to jail. Believe me, I'll recommend it.'

Novak was distracted by Brenner's PA sneaking up to the Congressman and whispering a message. Then a number of journalists around the room started getting up and leaving the room, tapping away at their silenced phones. Decorum was abandoned and shocked responses to people's phones sprung up around the room.

Close behind him, Novak heard a woman remark, 'Oh Jesus...' as she scrolled down her Twitter feed.

Brenner raised his hand for a pause. 'Ladies and gentlemen,' he said, 'for security reasons this hearing is adjourned until further notice. The Capitol police ask that you make your way outside in a calm and orderly fashion.'

A stream of armed police officers with helmets and riot gear on burst through the main doors to room 2141. They weren't messing around, marching straight to the committee members at the back and leading them away with some urgency.

A police chief with a megaphone announced, 'Ladies and gentlemen, as a precautionary measure we are evacuating the building. This is not a drill.'

Kevin waited for his CNN app to load while he and Novak made their way out to the corridor.

Kevin fended off some of the press, firing questions at him. 'Mr Novak has no comment to make at this time...'

When they got outside the pavement was packed with people showing their phones to one another in disbelief. Twitter and Facebook had both crashed.

Novak turned his mobile phone on. The first notification he received was an encrypted email:

"Abbie Bishop seemed to think we should talk."

Having never heard of Abbie Bishop, Novak clicked out his inbox without giving it another thought. The next message was from his editor in New York:

"Get back here now!"

Novak asked Kevin, 'What the hell is going on?'

He replied, 'Something's happened in London.'

Entrance to Downing Street, London – Monday 2.34pm

The bright red and orange police vehicles of the Diplomatic Protection Group obscured the entrance to Downing Street in anticipation of the press conference. Although Downing Street was still technically a public highway, and police had no right to refuse anyone entry, the threat of terrorism had necessitated the erection of a secure entrance gate – rather than the line of policemen standing in front of metal barriers that was there in the eighties.

All press with clearance for entry that morning were on a Home Office list presided over by armed DPG officers: Diplomatic Protection Group. The unglamorous work had led to them being pejoratively called 'Doors, Posts and Gates' by fellow police officers, as that was where they ended up standing around.

The Martyr waited in line behind the other members of the press, the credentials for Riz Rizzaq around his neck. His Birmingham accent brought no hint of suspicion to the DPG officer at the gate, and his camera bag was given an intensive check by the Police Search Advisor who handled such duties.

Strapped to the Martyr's chest under Riz Rizzaq's photographer's jacket was a vest filled with plates of explosive, surrounded by a fragmentation jacket. It was this, rather than the actual explosion, that caused the majority of deaths in suicide bombings. Effectively turning the man into a walking, six-foot-tall Claymore mine. The shrapnel inside consisted of ceramic baubles. Although they were lighter than metal ball bearings, they were harder, and – most crucially – evaded metal detectors.

An anti-terror officer walked down the queue with a sniffer dog, the dog being stopped at each person. The Martyr wasn't nervous, even when the dog sniffed around his upper leg, just inches away from the explosive packs. The explosives had been vacuum-sealed behind the ceramic ball bearings for exactly such an eventuality.

After a quick matching of his ID against the records the Downing Street media centre had given the police, the Martyr was waved through the gate. In a matter of minutes, he would be just a few yards away from two of the most powerful men in the world.

The press conference had been due to take place at the Foreign and Commonwealth Office building right across the street – as was standard for press conferences with foreign dignitaries such as the U.S. Secretary of Defense. Standing in the hallway of Number Ten, behind the famous black front door, the PM asked his chief of staff, Martin Bullock, 'Why the change of venue?'

'Sorry, Prime Minister,' Bullock said. 'The Americans wanted something in front of Number Ten. Secretary Snow is just on his way in.'

The front door opened up, letting in an eruption of reporters' questions. Hundreds of camera flashes bounced off the door's glossy paint, before the doorman closed it over again.

Snow and Ali shook hands, enjoying a brief moment away from the press and any microphones.

'How are you doing, Robert?' the PM asked.

Secretary Snow replied, 'Just fine, Simon. Thank you.' He noted the PM's pallor – Ali was practically grey. 'You sure look like you could use some coffee.'

The PM gave his chief of staff The Look.

Bullock knew exactly what that meant. He announced to the various staffers milling around the hall, 'Okay, everyone, back to your desks.' He said quietly to Ali, 'I'm in the other room if you need me, Prime Minister.'

Snow signalled to his staffers to follow suit.

Once the hall had cleared, Ali said to Snow, 'Are you sure you want to do this? It's not too late to back out.'

Snow, ex-military, was resolute. 'The Freedom and Privacy Act, if it goes through, will be the most authoritarian law any Western democracy has ever acted into law. It belongs to the days of the Stasi.'

'Are you really prepared to be despised within your own party, Robert?' Ali asked. 'By your own President?'

Snow replied, 'I've been making powerful enemies my whole life.' He laughed, then put his arm around Ali. He looked deep into his eyes, the way he used to with scared Marine recruits back in the day. 'Are you sure you're alright, Simon? You look like shit.'

'I'll be better when this is over,' Ali replied, already holding his speech.

'You going with hard copy?' Snow asked. 'They had to stick a fork in me when we landed at Heathrow – my head's still in Washington. I'm going with the teleprompter. I can barely give a lunch order without one these days. Do you know the last time I even read a book...'

Ali, zoning out, ended up talking right over him. 'Robert, you should know that I have some things to say out there that are unrelated to our other business.'

Bullock returned to Ali and Snow. 'It's time, gents,' he told them.

Ali pulled Bullock aside, as the doorman opened the front door to another lightning storm of camera flashes.

Bullock looked down at the envelope Ali was handing him – blank on the front, sealed.

Ali had to speak up to be heard over the journalists' shouted questions outside. 'Make sure my lawyer Douglas Robertson gets this.'

Secretary Snow held back on the front step. 'Mr Prime Minister,' he said.

'It's important,' Ali told Bullock.

Confused, Bullock put it into his pocket then watched his boss walk out to Secretary Snow's handshake for the cameras, the press clamouring with their questions.

The Martyr made his way to the banks of photographers and TV journalists already assembled in front of a lectern in the middle of Downing Street. The lectern – adorned with the Royal crest – was set up with two microphones, about five paces from the front steps of Number Ten.

The press talked amongst themselves, expecting another routine press conference. Despite all being in competition, there was much friendly chat and gossip between the various news agencies' political correspondents. Rumours centred on just what Simon Ali was going to announce, given his highly unusual step of not leaking details in advance.

Despite his training, nerves caused the Martyr to fumble a little clumsily with his camera and tripod, drawing some looks from the other cameramen nearby. Only a few feet away, *BBC News* correspondent Sophie Barker was in bemused consultation with her sound assistant.

'Screw it,' she said. 'We'll record audio now and fix it in post. I'm going to kill Riz...'

The Martyr readied himself behind the camera – looking into the viewfinder, as if making final adjustments – preparing the remote trigger in his jacket pocket.

Don't go too early, he told himself.

The front doors to Number Ten opened up to a barrage

of camera flashes and yells of, 'Prime Minister!' from every paparazzo in the three-deep rows.

As Sophie turned away in frustration from the great shots they were missing, she caught sight of her cameraman's ID – Riz's unmistakeable name on it, but not his photo – hanging round the Martyr's neck. She tapped her assistant in the side as the other press jostled for position. 'That guy's got Riz's name on his ID.'

The Prime Minister's security detail from Specialist Protection (SO1) and Secretary Snow's Secret Service agents flanked their men on each side as they approached the lectern.

Sophie pushed towards the Martyr, struggling to get through the crowd.

Ali gripped both sides of the lectern, then looked down for a moment before speaking. 'Normally a speech like this has to be cleared by the Foreign Office, the Treasury, and the intelligence agencies, to check for unforeseen consequences. Whether that be promising to spend money the country doesn't have, or accidentally leaking state secrets. Let me assure you, I am fairly certain what the consequences of this speech will be...'

The Martyr eyed Sophie Barker, now pointing him out to a policeman. As the Martyr slid his way through the press pack, the policeman put a call out on his radio, 'Be advised, we may have a two-twenty entry breach.'

Ali continued, 'None of my advisors know what I'm about to say. If they did, they wouldn't let me say it, because they know it's career suicide. Too often in this country career suicide and telling the truth appear to be one and the same.'

Secretary Snow looked on, as intrigued as everyone else about where Ali was going with this.

Ali's knuckles were white. 'I stand before you today as the Prime Minister of Great Britain and Northern Ireland...' He broke off for a moment.

The Martyr moved to the end of the bank of photographers, where he had a clear run. He took one last look at the policeman, fighting his way through the cameramen and journalists. The policeman wasn't going to make it.

Now was the time. The gates of Paradise were opening.

Ali regained his composure. '...so it is with a heavy heart that I must make a confession...'

The policeman knew what was about to happen as soon as he saw the remote in the Martyr's hand. Too far away to stop him, he called out on his radio, 'Suspect! PM's two o'clock.'

The press nearby turned to look just as the Martyr started his run. As soon as the call went out the police marksmen on the surrounding roofs all turned their sights on the suspect, who looked strangely isolated in the empty space between the press gang and the lectern. The call over their radios changed to, 'Takedown! Takedown!'

The U.S. and U.K. security details on the ground all leapt towards their principals. First priority was to get Ali and Snow as low to the ground as possible.

Those on the perimeter called into their sleeve radios, 'Brace brace brace!'

Ali whipped round to see DPG and SO1 officers lunge towards him from both sides.

The Martyr cried out '*Allahu Akbar!*' Knowing he had got more than close enough for the plan to work, the killer smiled.

The Martyr made it only two further paces before several gunshots hit him. Five were direct headshots, two from the left, one from the right, and two from behind. He was like a pinball bouncing rapidly between two bells.

He had already triggered the detonator.

The blast sent up an orange explosion lasting a second or two. Then a brown cloud mushroomed up the face of Number Ten, blowing out the windows on the entire block. The cloud seemed to swell for a whole minute before reaching its apex, breaking open towards the sky. The camera covering the live feed of the press conference went black.

The armed officers on the roofs threw themselves back to safety. More officers raced from the main entrance, but the smoke was thick and seemed to be taking forever to clear. Was it over? Were there still suspects on the ground? The officers trained their sights on the edge of the smoke where it would clear first. If the blast was a screen for a further armed attack breaching the gated entrance, then it would come in the next few minutes.

Millbank – 2.43pm

Trevor Billington-Smith, director of GCHQ, was in the back of his chauffeur-driven Jaguar XJ, being rushed through the London morning traffic by a police escort. Sitting next to him was MI6 Chief Sir Lloyd Willow.

Billington-Smith was in mid-conversation with Alexander Mackintosh back at GCHQ. 'No, I'm with Lloyd right now. We're on our way to Legoland for a briefing... Don't worry about Tempest. The Americans are tidying up as we speak...'

The iconic Secret Intelligence Services building – Legoland to those in the intelligence community – loomed large in front of them as the car sped down Millbank beside the River Thames.

As they crossed Vauxhall Bridge, Willow turned his attention to the press conference on a TV screen set into the driver's back headrest. He leaned towards Trevor. 'The hell is he doing?' Willow asked. 'He just said he had a confession to make.'

Before Trevor could reply, there was a flash behind and to their left, followed by a short, deep explosion that seemed to come up from the bowels of Westminster. A long boom reverberated off the nearby buildings.

Willow shouted, 'Jesus Christ!', then the TV picture from Downing Street – delayed by a few seconds – cut to black.

Cars on the bridge screeched to a halt as the huge cloud

stretched up over the top of the House of Commons and Big Ben. Drivers got out their cars, watching with awe and horror. Willow stared at the black TV screen, which then cut back to the news studio.

Sir Lloyd could barely talk. 'They just took out Downing Street...'

Billington-Smith shouted to the driver, 'What are you waiting on, man? Put your foot down!'

The frantic call went out over the Downing Street police marksmen's radios: 'Explosion on the ground!'

Police and paramedics ran to where the Prime Minister had been standing only seconds before. An armed officer on the roof overlooking Number Ten called out: 'Can anyone see? Is the Prime Minister down? I need confirmation on the ground!'

An SO1 officer, who had been sheltered from the worst of the blast behind a wall at the press entrance, ran to the side of the Prime Minister's bloodied body. He got on his radio, as he sprinted through the smoke that was churning from police helicopters overhead. 'The PM is down! Repeat, the PM is down!'

The PM's suit was ripped from around his shoulders, his torso riddled with ball bearings, unable to turn his back in time from the blast. It was over before he knew it. He never stood a chance.

A Secret Service agent with a bloodied face – one of his eyes hanging from the socket – crawled along the rubble-strewn ground towards his principal, Secretary Snow. One of the biggest myths about the Secret Service was that they had to swear an oath to die for their charges should the situation arise. But oath or not, the agent had decided he was willing. Even now, feeling his eye touching his lower cheek, he kept dragging himself towards Snow. He called out, 'Mr Secretary...'

Snow's neck had been sliced open down to the windpipe by blast-debris. He had already bled out.

St Thomas' Hospital, a minute's drive over Westminster Bridge, was designated for treating the Prime Minister. At Accident and Emergency reception, the unique tone of the black phone attached to the wall rang out, twice as loud as the other phones. The ring that staff had only ever heard in training. When the head nurse answered, she was told, 'We're code black! This is not a drill!'

Within two minutes the entire ward was cleared. But that was as far as preparations had to go.

Back at Downing Street the SO1 officer stood helplessly as paramedics pulled back from the body of Simon Ali. One medic shook his head at the officer.

On his radio, the officer's voice was heavy, despondent. Slow. What he was about to say had been trained for many times, but never experienced.

'Confirm, all units,' the officer said, trying to summon breath. 'The Prime Minister is dead. We are in a black crash protocol. Repeat. This is a black crash...'

8

Rebecca's phone started ringing. Then the phone across from hers. Then Matthew's, then every phone in the office was going.

Rebecca looked at Matthew in confusion. 'What the hell is going on?' she asked. She picked up her phone which gave a repeating automated response: 'Black crash. This is not a drill. Black crash. This is not a drill...'

Every computer screen went blank – even as some people were typing midsentence – then the words 'BLACK CRASH' flashed up. The TV screens hooked up to Google Earth all changed to the same message too.

A GTE tech assistant came running from the canteen. 'There was a bomb at Downing Street...' As he searched for a working TV channel he was immediately surrounded. Breathless, he tried to explain, 'A guy ran towards the PM, then there was an explosion! That's it. He just...'

'Jesus *Christ*!' Matthew said, watching the news cut back to the studio.

Mackintosh came running down the spiral staircase from the cryptography department. 'What's going on?'

The TV presenter in the studio, who had been anticipating another rote press conference with prepared notes, now found himself having to improvise on the biggest story of his life. 'We're getting...I...' he stuttered. 'We're trying to get in contact with someone on the ground, but there was a huge explosion...' The producer brought in a voice from a mobile phone at the scene. 'We have a cameraman talking to us live from the scene. Robbie, are you alright? What can you see?'

The man could barely be heard over the screaming and sirens all around him. 'There's just...there was an explosion...it's chaos down here. I think...the Prime Minister is down, Michael. He's definitely...' For a moment the reporter lost himself and uttered the words that would be replayed so many times in the coming days across the globe. 'This is a scene of...the Prime Minister is definitely down.'

Mackintosh lowered the volume and raised his hands for everyone's attention. The office turned silent. '*Everyone*! We are now following black crash protocol. Senior Intel, in my office now. Everyone else, I want all our ears open to any chatter on credible threats and FOAs. This is going to take a little time. For now, we're in lockdown. Remember your training. The country's counting on us.'

From the streets surrounding GCHQ, it looked largely like business as usual – this was intentional. From a distance, the changes were subtle but telling: armed guards patrolling the perimeter fence and the HQ entrance were doubled (follow-on attacks – or FOAs – were more likely to come from publicly accessible roads using a 4x4 or small truck of some kind), scouting for possible ram-raid attacks; all visitors to GCHQ were immediately escorted off the premises. No other staff members were allowed in or out.

Black crash protocol extended much further than just GCHQ – through the whole intelligence and security services. Every MI5 agent on U.K. soil was activated by a 'BLACK CRASH' text message, directing them to their nearest substation. All police leave was suspended, all officers recalled. U.K.

airports were closed. Trading on the London Stock Exchange was suspended. Motorway CITRAC signs outside major cities switched to a 40mph limit to avoid dangerous mass evacuations.

Armed police and soldiers kept guard at the busiest public squares and landmarks around the country; three Scimitar armoured vehicles – essentially light tanks – were dispatched outside the main terminals at Heathrow, Gatwick, and Manchester airports.

There were also some subtler elements involved: as in times of national mourning, radio station producers turned on their studios' blue 'obit light' – tested once a week like a fire alarm – to indicate to the DJ some kind of national emergency, or the death of a major public figure. The DJ then cut to the news – interrupting the on-air song if the producer deemed it worthy. For those stations without a news desk or the logistics to run a constant news feed, they cut to pre-approved playlists of middle-of-the-road music, neither too loud nor buoyant. The major TV stations interrupted live programming whenever they were ready, making sure whoever was going on air wasn't wearing bright colours.

Even those on planes weren't left out of the breaking news. Pilots were made aware by U.K. air traffic control of what had unfolded, and made the announcement to passengers.

Even when Princess Diana had died at four a.m., the then Foreign Secretary, who was in the Philippines at the time, got a question on Diana's death within fifteen minutes. And that was in 1997. Now, news, rumour, and hearsay spread even quicker. There was no plan to pull the plug on Facebook or Twitter. In fact, everyone from GCHQ to MI6 was convinced keeping such channels open could be crucial to intercepting FOAs.

No one was in favour of announcing the death of the Prime Minister with a Facebook post or a tweet, but it was clear that any official announcement should be made as soon as possible. There were many draft press releases depending on the situation: terrorism, heart attack, plane crash. The finer details were finessed, then it was sent out to the Press Association. All the major news organisations, TV stations, websites, took their cue from this, confirming the Prime Minister's death.

Anyone standing outside Buckingham Palace at the same time saw the Master of the Household – clad in black jacket, white shirt and black tie – make his way across the red gravel, and pin a black-edged notice to the gates. Without a word he returned to his post inside the palace.

In a world where news was beamed into phones and homes, there was something noble and genteel about the act.

As the news had broken before four p.m., the National Theatre would close that night. All major sports fixtures were cancelled. Cinemas and concerts remained open but were poorly attended.

Several hours after the attack – once Downing Street had been completely tented off from the rooftops down by forensics – the Queen appeared on a live television broadcast from Buckingham Palace. She confirmed the news from behind a lectern in the Throne Room, against a backdrop of red and gold velvet drapes above two red thrones on a dais. Some commentators and op-ed columns would opine in the subsequent days that, if anything, the image only drew attention to the fact that the United Kingdom of Great Britain and Northern Ireland was without an elected leader.

Without any break in her voice or visible signs of distress, the Queen relayed the details mentioned in the press release – sticking to the facts, using few adjectives – then made assurances that the country would grieve, survive, and continue.

Although the United Kingdom had no clear line of succession for Prime Minister the way the United States did for their President, there had always been an idea that Parliament would be able to decide fairly swiftly on an interim Prime Minister.

At least, that had been the plan.

The government's emergency committee, COBRA, was chaired by the Home Secretary Ed Bannatyne. Once the immediate threats appeared contained, and the attack definitely over, talk turned to who would be interim Prime Minister. Bannatyne would normally have been the obvious choice: a senior Party figure who already held high office. Years of experience. But then so had Foreign Secretary Nigel Hawkes. Simon Ali had already announced a General Election for the coming May.

Bannatyne and Hawkes knew that it would have to be brought forward. Which meant that anyone who guided the country through a period of national mourning and inevitable patriotism would be in pole position to lead the party into the election. With neither Bannatyne nor Hawkes willing to budge, it became clear that a vote would have to take place – if for nothing else to reassure a panicking public. The spin doctors also knew that with polls predicting a potential hung parliament at the General Election, any sign of weakness at such a critical time could cripple the party for years.

Conservative Party rules stipulated that party members vote on a leader from a shortlist. Once the party whips realised the vote could go to the wire – literally by a vote or two – senior officials started to worry about the optics of the Tory party squabbling over their leader while the country went to bed without a Prime Minister for the first time since Lord Palmerston died in office of natural causes in 1885.

A compromise was sought with Bannatyne and Hawkes' people: a third contender would be brought onto the shortlist, and they would each whip their supporters to back said third candidate. A neutral, steady pair of hands with no ambitions for the election. A moderate yet respected backbencher with previous Cabinet experience. Someone respected by both sides of the House of Commons. Who, come a General Election, would step aside and let Bannatyne and Hawkes fight out a proper leadership election.

Nigel Hawkes asked, 'And what if they don't step aside?'

No one had an answer to that.

9

By the time Novak reached *The Republic* offices – halfway up a ten-storey sandstone in midtown Manhattan – he felt like he had been on a desert island for the last five hours. His phone had ceased working altogether an hour out of Washington. No texts, calls, email or internet. The airline crew at Dulles Airport almost had to drag him on-board as he sucked up the last dregs of cable news from the TV screens dotted around the gate. The cab driver from JFK had filled Novak in on developments in the hour he'd been in the air.

The Muslim driver – who had an American flag pendant dangling from his rear-view mirror – told Novak, 'Like this job wasn't difficult enough after nine eleven. These maniacs are going to get me killed out here.'

On his way into the lobby, Novak looked up at the building front across the street from *The Republic*. Bastion News – the alt-right website – had unfurled another billboard. Their biggest one yet. 'Bastion News' and their iconic 'B' logo down one side, the words "Honest news for ordinary, decent Americans" underneath. On the other side was *The Republic*'s logo, and under it, "Mainstream media. Fake news."

On any other day the billboard would have caused a stir in the press. Not today.

The office was full, all fifteen staff writers rushed in to file copy for the most up-to-date news for *therepublic.com*. It seemed like almost everyone was on the phone – even the ones typing. The atmosphere was more in keeping with the frenzy of a stock traders' than an upmarket news weekly.

The receptionist told Novak as he rushed past, 'Mark's looking for you.'

Novak, still wearing the suit from his Congressional hearing, tie now loosened, dumped his carry-on case at his desk. Unlike his colleagues, whose desks were covered with books, research papers, random notes written on bar napkins, and coffee receipts, Novak's desk was practically empty. He hadn't been in the office for weeks.

Above his desk was a sign that said, "FACTS or GTFO". Beside that was a picture of Novak as a six-year-old, sitting behind the *NBC Nightly News* desk.

A two-tier plastic tray sat to one side. The top level was marked "Fan mail", the bottom "Death threats".

Novak whipped a sticky note off his computer screen that said, "*Walter Sharp called again – Mark*" with Sharp's number underneath. Novak tossed it in the bin. His attitude to missed calls had always been that if they're important enough, they'll call back.

He was distracted by the TV at the end of the room, the London correspondents for U.S. networks already on the scene. Westminster looked like a war zone in the background, with fleets of armoured police vans sealing off Whitehall, all the way from Westminster Station past the Cenotaph to the Old War Office Building, which Churchill had used as headquarters during the Second World War.

Novak's editor, Mark Chang, appeared beside him. 'We

were watching the hearing on C-SPAN earlier,' Chang said. 'It seemed like you were making a splash, before, you know...'

He gestured at the TV screen. The news ticker scrolling across said: "DEATHS ESTIMATED BETWEEN 50-75".

Novak said, 'Somehow, I don't think I'll be making the news tonight.' He looked over to Chang's office, then to the main conference room ahead, the blinds closed. Novak said, 'Mark, how worried should I be about this meeting?'

Chang replied, 'We need to discuss your future plans. This Bastion thing is becoming a distraction.'

Novak had been waiting to make the speech for days now.

He said, 'Did you see that picture we ran online last week, about the guys who showed up at Senator Haley's rally last week with unconcealed guns on their hips? The story made out like this was some kind of racist intimidation because Haley's black and anti-gun. We then used two thousand words to find different ways of calling these protestors racist. Except what our pictures – which only showed from the waist down – didn't show was that those intimidating protesters were black! And they all had licences to carry. Of course Bastion ran comparison photos with ours, and it went viral as an example of fake news. Don't you see how we lose credibility with shit like that? Bastion News is not the problem here. We are! What kind of editor approves that?'

Mark, looking over Novak's shoulder tried to interrupt. 'Tom–'

Novak hadn't realised his editor-in-chief, Diane Schlesinger, had appeared behind him. She motioned to Chang not to stop Novak, who was in full flight.

He continued, 'I've had three stories killed because it apparently wasn't the right time. Well guess what. No one thought Woodward and Bernstein's timing was right when they started digging around Watergate again.'

Schlesinger had to look down to stop herself laughing.

Novak went on, still oblivious. 'Old news, they said. Done

to death. They buried it on page five, but their editor Ben Bradlee let them keep going. Then they won a Pulitzer Prize and never paid for another lunch the rest of their lives. *That's the kind of editor I need. I need–'*

Schlesinger cast the most recent edition of *The Republic* she had been reading onto Novak's desk. 'Tom, I'm going to stop you there.'

Novak pursed his lips before turning around, trying not to wince. 'Diane.'

She handed Chang a twenty-dollar note. 'I had a bet with Mark here how long it would take for you to get to Woodward and Bernstein again. Mark said thirty seconds, I said two minutes. Looks like I lost.' Schlesinger flicked her long blonde hair behind a heavy, glittering earring. She looked like she'd just walked out of the Chanel shop window down on 57th Street. She had on an elegant black and yellow trouser suit, giving her the look of a queen bee. 'Did you see the Bastion billboard?'

'Hard to miss,' Novak said.

Diane seemed stuck for words. 'I mean...flipping...*heck.*'

'Say what you want about them, they've got balls.'

Mark and Diane exchanged a look, wondering since when Novak was so soft on a conservative news website.

Diane said, 'Henry and I will be in the conference room in ten minutes. Why don't you say hello to Stella before you join us.' She left a trail of a few hundred dollars' worth of perfume tumbling over her shoulder as she left.

Novak looked at Chang. 'Stella who?'

'Stella Mitchell,' Chang said.

'Stella *Mitchell*? What's she doing here?'

'Diane didn't tell you? She's our new Foreign Affairs correspondent. She came over from *The Guardian* last week while you were in D.C.' He pointed to the glass wall of the archive room, where a woman in her early thirties was sitting at a long desk by herself, a desk lamp pointed down on a mass of papers in front of her. 'Also, did you get back to Walter Sharp?'

'Walter...'

'Sharp.' Chang sighed. 'The CIA guy that scared the bejesus out me last night.'

'I don't know the name. Or that anyone under the age of seventy still says bejesus.'

'I sent you like three texts and four emails about it. You need to get that phone fixed. This guy said it was urgent.' He flicked the back of his hand against Novak's arm. 'I'll see you in there.'

Once Chang was gone, Novak fished the sticky note out the bin and put it in his pocket. Sidling over to the archive room he knocked on the open door.

Stella didn't respond.

'Hey. I'm Tom, we haven't met.' The only reason he said his name was in hoping Stella would say with reverence, "I know who you are."

Instead, she said in an impeccable English accent, 'So let me get this straight. Your name is Tom Novak.'

'Yeah,' Novak replied, a little confused, feeling like he'd walked in halfway through his own conversation.

'But you used to publish under Tom Seymour Novak.'

'That was five years ago. How did you know that?'

She lifted a handful of papers. 'Research.'

Novak noticed a pile of *Republic* back issues sitting on the floor under the desk. A few were open at Novak articles, with grammatical errors or certain phrases circled in red pen.

'What is all that?' he asked.

'Everything you've ever had published. It's taken a week, but I needed to know what I was dealing with.' She held her pen up a second. 'Also, I've been eager to ask: are you sleeping with your copyeditor?'

'Excuse me?'

'It was the only explanation I could think of for why they

would let you get away with such appalling misuse of the word "comprise". Second of August, twenty thirteen issue: "the bill is comprised of..."' She broke off, as if the error was glaringly obvious. 'Parts compose the whole. The whole comprises the parts. It should be "the Bill is composed of".'

Novak shook his head and turned to leave. 'I have a meeting.'

'That's funny,' she said, looking up cheerfully. 'So do I.'

Novak set off towards the conference room with Stella trying to catch up.

What struck him about her was her voice. She made every sentence sound like an emergency, and if you were stupid enough to interrupt her you'd miss out on something crucial. On the surface, everything about her was functional: from her versatile grey suit, to her flat shoes, and tied-up hair. But Novak knew plenty about her reporting back in London. You didn't make waves the way Stella did without having some serious talent. Not to mention bravery.

As they passed the copy desk, an editor called to Stella, 'You put a U in colour again!'

Stella replied, 'The Queen once said that there is no such thing as American English: there is the English language and then there are mistakes. Who's wrong: you or the Queen of England?'

'Hey, Kate Winslet!' The editor held her pen aloft. 'This is the only royalty in this office.'

Stella smiled back at her. 'No U in colour. Got it.'

Up ahead, Novak stopped by the tech support desk, handing over his phone. 'Kurt, this thing's acting weird.'

'Acting weird,' Kurt parroted back. 'Hang on, let me Google "phone acting weird" and get back to you.'

'Could you take a look? I've tried everything I know.'

Kurt surveyed the battered-looking phone. 'By everything, do you mean throwing it repeatedly on the ground?'

'Maybe.'

Kurt sighed long-sufferingly. 'Give me an hour.'

As Novak set off again, Stella caught up to him. 'So you don't think you're worthy of using your dad's name, is that it?' she asked.

Novak said, 'It's so readers don't get confused.'

'What's confusing about it?'

'Ask Frank Sinatra Jnr and Hank Williams Jnr how easy it is to make a dinner reservation without getting a comment in return.'

'Do you think people assume that your dad landed you a reporting gig? Because changing your name is never going to convince people like them. Is that why you want to go to jail over your NSA story? I watched your hearing on C-SPAN. Didn't your lawyer warn you not to bait Brenner like that? Was that what the note he passed you said? I bet it was. I bet you twenty...wait, I don't have cash on me—'

Jesus, Novak thought, *does she ever come up for air?*

He paused when they reached the conference room door. 'My dad was watched by two million viewers every night. How the hell do you live up to that?'

'You don't, Novak,' she said, pushing past him. 'You live up to yourself.'

As he opened the door, he realised Stella was following him in. 'This is my meeting,' he said.

She replied, 'This is my meeting too. How about that?' She gave a genuinely delighted smile as she squeezed past him.

The pair found Mark Chang sitting across from Diane Schlesinger, and the magazine's publisher Henry Self.

Fresh from his house in the Hamptons, Self sat ominously in the wings as if no one was supposed to notice him. His attempt at dressing down was a pair of Diesel jeans, a New York Mets cap, and a New York Mets baseball jersey under a $4000 Cifonelli blazer.

Self was by all accounts a playboy, and *The Republic* was his plaything. His father had died of a heart attack shortly before the dotcom bubble burst, leaving behind an eight-figure inheritance for Henry. He set up *The Republic* as a political boutique, where the most distinctive, passionate voices in America could converge. He recruited the finest journalistic talent he could buy (losing himself $1 million a year in the process), and didn't give a damn what anyone thought. Particularly his dad's old friends in the Republican Party.

'Diane, Henry, nice to see you,' Stella said, already familiar with the senior management.

Novak shook Self's hand with just a nod and a half smile.

Self said, 'I caught your hearing earlier.' He rearranged the flaps of his jacket as he sat down. He had the air of someone used to being the most important person in a room. 'Tom, I've paid three million dollars to Bruckner Jackson Prowse to keep you out of jail. Next time, would you be so kind as to listen to the lawyer they've provided you with next time?'

Chastened, Novak replied, 'Okay, then.'

Diane said, 'You are no longer covering the NSA papers, Tom. You're this magazine's most recognisable reporter. We need you back where you belong: asking tough questions, and building stories. The fallout from this Downing Street thing is going to be unlike anything we've ever seen.'

'Downing Street? Diane, I don't know London.'

'I agree. That's why Stella here's going to be your new partner.'

Novak waited for Diane to relent and admit she was joking. When he realised she wasn't, he just smiled. 'Diane, with respect. And this has nothing to do with Stella, who I'm sure is—'

'Is this about sharing your byline?' asked Diane.

Novak thought for a moment. 'I work alone, Diane.'

Stella smiled at the floor.

'Can I help you?' Novak asked her.

Stella said, 'You don't work *alone*. You don't work for Diane. You don't work for anyone.'

'How do you figure that?'

'Okay, then. Could you please list for me the stories you've filed in the last six months?'

Novak turned to Self. 'Henry. You don't go along with this, do you?'

Self said, 'We've got a falling readership, Tom. Bastion is growing every quarter. The only thing propping us up is the ad-spend Diane's bringing in for online. So I ask you: What is it you don't like? That we're asking you to do your job? Or that you have to step out the spotlight for a moment in order to do it?'

Feeling bolshie (but careful to direct it to Diane rather than Henry), Novak said, 'It's funny, because I was never told we had to choose a side. And I think we've changed. I think we've changed because round here we hate Republicans. And we hate this President. But the truth doesn't care whose side you're on.'

Diane laughed. 'Oh Tom, I could fill a book with all those quotes about the truth I've heard down the years. Your father came up with most of them when we were at the *Tribune*. "You don't choose the truth: the truth chooses you." You know why you never hear them now? Because editors back then weren't trying to run a current affairs magazine in a market that's competing with Facebook, Twitter and about a million cat videos. We're competing with clickbait headlines, and ads that are worth more than the...' she fumbled, about to swear, '...*fudging* story underneath it!'

Novak let the dust settle, never afraid of a tense silence. 'Diane,' he said. 'I've never known someone who goes so out of their way not to swear.'

Her eyes narrowed. 'It's a bigger challenge when you're in the room.'

With the most pressing news delivered, Self stood up and

clapped his hands. 'Anyway. That's where we're at.' He looked to Stella and Tom. 'Make big plays, you two. We need to land a big one. And soon.'

Once the door closed behind Self, Diane threw her glasses down. 'What's your problem with London, Tom?'

'There's no story there, Diane. It was a suicide bombing. It writes itself.'

'You're my *security* correspondent. The centre of British political power has suffered a huge, stunning security *failure*. Do I need to make the connection on a wall for you with tacks and bits of string?' Diane rifled through the tower of paper she'd brought with her, and held up a handwritten letter. 'Subscriptions got this the other day. Some little old man from Iowa. Know what it says? "What's happened to Tom Novak? Does he still write for you?"'

'My god,' Novak replied in mock horror. 'People still write letters?'

Stella said, 'I don't understand your reluctance, Novak. There were rumours on the Hill last week about the new Patriot Act getting a reading soon. And the Republicans are already whipping votes for Bill Rand as new Secretary of Defense, which, if it's true, means we should all be out buying canned goods and bottled water right now.'

Novak laughed with exhaustion. 'Let's get one thing straight, Mary Poppins: the only person round here who gets to call me Novak is Martin Fitzhenry. Secondly, you'll never win any awards reporting on a story the entire Western world is on location for.'

'What about Bob Woodward?' Stella said. 'He won a Pulitzer for his coverage of nine eleven, not just Watergate.'

'No, you're right, Stella, because how else would anyone have known nine eleven happened...'

Diane looked to Chang for some support, but all he could do was shrug. Diane asked Novak, 'Is this about you and Bastion?'

Stella waded in. 'What about you and Bastion?'

'Forget it,' Novak said.

'You're not thinking about going across the street, are you? You can't go from *The Republic* to Bastion, Novak. It would be like Jagger leaving the Stones before they recorded *Exile on Main Street.*'

Chang said, 'Nah, it'd be more like Steve Jobs joining Microsoft.'

Novak closed his eyes a moment and felt his temples as if everyone was losing their minds. 'Okay, *first* of all: if Jobs left before he invented the iPhone no one would have cared if he got a job as a greeter at Home Depot. I don't know if you've looked around here lately, but we are not coming up with the journalistic equivalent of the iPhone. Bastion are at least trying. They're disrupting the mainstream media. They're influencing presidential elections. When was the last time *The Republic* could say that? Yeah, they've got some crazies–'

Stella exclaimed, 'Some?'

'But we do too, Stella. And if I *was* Mick Jagger, I wouldn't feel too shabby about moving on after co-writing "Jumpin' Jack Flash".'

Stella said, 'Novak, the NSA Papers was good, but it wasn't "Jumpin' Jack Flash" good. Get over yourself–'

Diane slammed her hand down on the desk. 'Enough!' She turned to Novak. 'Tom. You're not freelance. You have a contract. Or like Henry said, you can resign and pay the rest of your retainer to Bruckner Jackson Prowse on your own.'

Novak thought of an old saying of his dad's: "You can have the story you care about, or the story people are interested in. But you can't have both."

'I'll take your frustrated silence as a yes.' Diane turned to Stella. 'Are you going to keep him in line?'

Novak said to himself, 'No, that's fine. Pretend like I'm not even here...'

Stella waited until he made eye contact with her again. 'I have every confidence in him,' she answered.

'Tom, Stella: you're on a flight to London tomorrow morning. Heathrow should be open again by then. Let's aim for three thousand words for dot com by Friday, five thousand for print in a week.' Schlesinger put her glasses back on.

As Chang, Novak, and Stella reached the door, Diane called out, 'Tom. A moment.'

He felt like his high school English teacher was keeping him back after class.

'I know why this Bastion offer appeals to you,' Diane said. 'Two-fifty a year isn't nothing.'

Novak added, 'Plus stock options.'

Her smile was all steel. 'We're sinking, Tom. I know you know that. And right now, Bastion looks like a pretty good life raft. But out of three houses, Henry just sold two and re-mortgaged the third to keep the lights on around here. If he finds a generous bank we might have six months.'

He didn't show it, but Novak was stunned. He had no idea things were that bad.

'You belong here,' Diane said. 'You can turn this place around. Yeah, we make mistakes, but we hit more than we miss. You know that. You're not going to win any Pulitzers across the street. You know that too. But that's not what you want anymore, is it.'

'My dad didn't get into the media for ideals, Diane. It was a job.'

'Yes, in the *end* it was. But he didn't start out that way. And certainly not when he was your age. You want to talk about fire? I watched Seymour Novak storm into board meetings and demand resignations over a misattributed photo credit.'

Novak replied, 'And the last fifteen years of his career involved a live hour of filmed narcolepsy in front of five million people every weeknight. He was thirty-eight when he went to NBC. I'm thirty-six, Diane. Fires go out.'

Diane said, 'Fires can be relit.'

Novak shook his head.

'You're a great writer,' she said. 'But Bastion will butcher your copy, and when they realise you're not the right-wing hatchetman they want you to be, they'll throw you overboard when some twenty-five-year-old alt-right vlogger with half a million YouTube subscribers comes along.' She paused, wearing the look Novak's mother used to have when he did something disappointing. 'You've already made up your mind, haven't you?'

Novak took a beat. 'Stella's been here a week. This isn't just about the London story, is it?'

Diane had never lied to him. She wasn't going to start now. 'I think you need to focus on some basic journalism for a while. Find your chops again.'

Novak nodded. It was the answer he had feared. 'You'll have three thousand words by Friday.'

As Novak opened the door, Diane added, 'Tom. I know I might be asking a lot, but try not to use the words "massive government conspiracy" at any point.'

Stella was waiting on the other side of the door, holding a sheet of paper. 'Hey. I didn't mean for that to get so...'

'Stella,' he sighed, 'kick my ass or make nice. I don't care which, but pick one.'

Stella handed him the paper. 'Wires from AP. You'll never guess who they've made interim Prime Minister.'

Novak looked at the wires for a moment, then said, 'You're right. I've never heard of her. Who the hell is Angela Curtis?'

10

It was no secret that, like many private technology firms, GCHQ had many ex-hackers on their payroll. A lot of hackers made a point of attacking only government sites in order to show off. A peacock hack, they called it. Strutting around in the gaping hole of security vulnerabilities, waiting for someone to notice their signature. Many hacks are done for money, but what a hacker wants most of all is credit. Mostly from other hackers: the only people who can appreciate the complexity of what they've done. The only credit Rebecca wanted was from the recruiters at GCHQ. She had gone the 'white hat' way: a hacker who points out vulnerabilities in order to fix it, rather than exploit it for personal gain like 'black hats'.

Ultimately, to GCHQ, hacks were like puzzles. And if a hacker happened to be the best puzzle solver then GCHQ wanted them. If you proved yourself like Rebecca had, they would give you the biggest puzzle in the world to play with.

They called it ECHELON.

The system had once been for military and diplomatic communications only, but since 9/11 it had been adapted to collect data on any phone call GCHQ wished. The data didn't even need to be recorded in real-time. Searches could be back-dated by up to thirty days: seeing what numbers a target called, and when and where they took place. A potential gold-mine in the aftermath of a terror attack. Not to mention the biggest violation of privacy in the history of telecommunications. All of it now legal.

Rebecca's dictionary- and brute-force attacks were still running on her computer, coming up blank. If she couldn't access the files Abbie sent her, it was going to be almost impossible to figure out what she had been doing in London in the first place. Rebecca couldn't rely on the American diplomat emailing again, so the only other angle she could work was Mackintosh. And if she was to get access to his computer, she'd have to get creative.

In his afternoon briefing, Mackintosh gave an update on MI6 and MI5's progress to a packed room of GTE analysts and technicians.

Mackintosh had just declared that he wanted a list of every text and instant message sent in the hours preceding the attack. He said, 'Rebecca's going to explain how we can do this.'

Rebecca, sitting at the front with Matthew, went to Mackintosh's computer which was hooked up to the projector screen on the wall. She typed in "5,000,000".

'That's how many texts are sent each hour in London,' she said. 'We only need to narrow those five million down to the Westminster area. Bombers like this can't operate alone. There will have been some kind of confirmation message from the bomber to the rest of a sleeper cell. They wouldn't risk meeting, but I'll bet there was visual contact made at some point. The Paris attacks, Boston bombing, Brussels, Madrid, they all had these things in common.'

Rebecca wasn't the most confident presenter, but her reputation was enough to keep the room in the palm of her hand.

She went on, 'We have to widen our search to around three hours before the bombing. So, how do we narrow down those messages sent in one of the most populous areas in London? We can discount all messages ending with an "x", or anything with "love" in it. Bombers use blank, anonymous codes – something prearranged. And they don't waffle, so ignore anything longer than one hundred and sixty characters – the length of a standard SMS. I'd also bet the house on them using English.'

Rebecca deleted "5,000,000" and typed in "3000-5000".

'It'll be hard, but if we can narrow it down to that – which I think is more than realistic for an area and time frame like this one – split between us in ops, that's only a thousand messages each. The language of the confirmation message will be stiff, a non sequitur. The cell will ask something like, "Is your bag packed?" and the bomber will reply, "The trees are green and the sun is shining." Ironically, the more they try to remain anonymous the more they stand out.'

Mackintosh stepped forward. 'Out there, somewhere, is an active terror cell. We can't build virtual fingerprints on any of them until we get that text.'

While Mackintosh spoke, Rebecca took a stapler and rested it on the ENTER key.

As the room cleared, Rebecca was the last to leave. On her way past, Mackintosh caught her arm. 'Becky, a word...I know I'm expecting a lot from you so soon.'

'We worked in the same office together,' she said. 'Let's not pretend like we were sisters or something.'

'If I'm expecting too much, you can tell me.'

As long as he seemed more pliable than usual Rebecca took a shot at upping the ante. 'I was thinking...with Abbie gone, Matthew's now the only senior officer in GTE authorised for STRAP Three material. I thought you might need more cover in that area the next few days...'

Mackintosh shifted weight from foot to foot. 'Rebecca. I appreciate the work you do here. As does the Director. But you're twenty-five. Matthew is an exceptional case, and he's still three years older than you. Your own father didn't make STRAP Three until he was thirty-one. And he was the best cryptographer GCHQ has ever had.'

Rebecca nodded. 'I understand.'

'I remember your interview notes,' Mackintosh said. 'We never had a candidate asking about STRAP Three access at a preliminary interview before. Why is it so important?'

Rebecca was angry at herself for making her position so obvious. Searching for a convincing lie, she said, 'It's the highest clearance there is. And I want to be the best.'

'Patience,' Mackintosh said, checking his watch. 'I've got a briefing on the third floor, but I'll be back for the evening rundown.'

Just as Rebecca had hoped.

He took his briefcase and shut his office door behind.

Rebecca returned to her desk, thinking about the stapler still resting on the ENTER key, stopping Mackintosh's computer from timing out while he was gone.

Rebecca sat in the canteen doing *The Times* cryptic crossword in pen. Between clues she flicked in and out of her email inbox, even though she had desktop notifications on. Still nothing from Novak. She needed to get his attention.

She typed: '*We need to talk ASAP. Abbie Bishop's death wasn't an accident.*'

She highlighted the text then changed it to plainscript before encrypting it. Then she hit send.

As she was about to return to her crossword, the dictionary- and brute-force attacks finished up: no successful password found for Abbie's files.

Rebecca tilted her head back to stretch her neck. She had such little time on breaks to try and get somewhere with the password, she was forcing it, thinking too hard.

The news was muted on a large wall-mounted TV at the end of the room.

Rebecca pulled over a copy of *The Post* newspaper from a neighbouring table, recognising the exterior of the safe house in a photo above a report on Abbie. When she saw the headline, Rebecca picked the paper up in astonishment: 'Tragic balcony fall of GCHQ officer linked to MI6."

Mackintosh hadn't mentioned anything about the story. Plus, it was *The Post*, which was better known for its pictures of topless models and extensive celebrity coverage rather than intelligence scoops.

The report would have been rushed out to make the print deadline – even so, it mentioned details that the reporter, Dan Leckie, couldn't possibly have found out in the three hours between Abbie's death and his deadline.

"The intelligence officer, who died after falling from the balcony of a GCHQ safe house in Pimlico in the early hours of Monday morning, has been named as Abigail Bishop..."

Rebecca skimmed it, her heart racing.

"... sources that link her to an MI6 operation called Tempest... The Foreign Office has issued a statement saying that 'it is government policy not to comment on security matters.'"

Rebecca slowly put down the newspaper.

Tempest.

She took out her notes from earlier, where she'd written all the synonyms for STORM. The word Tempest now seemed to light up the rest of the clues. They were all synonyms. With that in mind, now there were few possibilities she could think of for SMALL SETTLEMENT other than hamlet. Once she had that, the others fell like tenpins.

She scribbled them down:

"KING OF SCOTLAND > MACBETH.

OGLING MONARCH. Ogled > leer. Monarch > King. KING LEAR

MOORISH GENERAL > OTHELLO

SMALL SETTLEMENT > HAMLET

STORM > TEMPEST'

She grabbed her laptop which was still open at the password window, then typed 'William Shakespeare' and hit ENTER.

The window refreshed – PASSWORD ACCEPTED. Then a new window appeared:

"Hell is empty. And all the devils are here."

A list of files unpacked rapidly, then siphoned into a single folder named 'AB'.

She clicked into the folder, opening the first document. It showed a passport-type picture of Abbie from what looked around five years earlier. Her hair hadn't quite grown out of the conservative bob she wore throughout her Trinity College, Cambridge days. What struck Rebecca most was how wide and bright Abbie's eyes were, a look that was to slowly dim over the next five years.

Rebecca was familiar with the nature of the document. She'd seen plenty of them in her time.

It was an MI6 personnel file.

She moved on, scrolling down the page.

'Name: Abigail Bishop. Start of employment: 2nd April 2009...'

Rebecca did some quick maths.

Two years after Abbie joined GCHQ.

The rest of the personnel file only obfuscated things further. Her date and place of birth were different to the ones Abbie had told Rebecca. Was she from Nottingham like she had told her, or from somewhere called Hadley Green, as listed with MI6? Was she twenty-two when she joined GCHQ, or twenty-four? Rebecca had always thought Abbie looked older.

The other files were arranged chronologically – MI6 briefing papers on Operation Tempest, which was to be spear-headed by an agent whose name was redacted. They must have been the principal agent, as the same size of black bar cropped up on every page, multiple times.

It was then Rebecca realised *The Post* had been dead-on with their story: Tempest was a genuine MI6 operation. Which could mean only one thing: someone was leaking them classified information. But why leak it to *The Post*? Surely somewhere with some clout like *The Guardian* or *The Times* – somewhere with recognised political influence – would be more credible?

Rebecca looked at the time on the TV. She should have been back ten minutes earlier.

She closed her laptop then hurried out of the canteen, clattering into two GTE colleagues at the door. She mumbled an apology, before hurrying back to the main floor.

Although Mackintosh's office had glass walls on the side facing the GTE open-plan office, Rebecca was respected enough that her presence there wouldn't raise many eyebrows. Except from Matthew, who would know there was no need for her to be in there alone. Once he was out the office, then she'd be able to access everything on Mackintosh's computer. That would require something of a diversion though.

When she returned to her desk Rebecca tapped into the MI6 mainframe, where there was a shared intranet for file-sharing on current cases – they called it Homeland.

As it was a shared space, when files were requested it didn't show who made the request. The request was uploaded by the relevant personnel, then downloaded by someone with the proper clearance.

'Matt,' Rebecca said.

Matthew took out one of his earphone buds – he was listening to recorded phone calls on the ECHELON system. 'Yeah?'

'There's a request on Homeland for Abbie's personnel files. That would normally be Alexander's remit, wouldn't it?'

'Yeah, I can do it, though. Give me a sec.' He clicked to Homeland. 'Yeah, I'll need to go up to List X room. It's STRAP Three.'

'Oh sorry,' she said, doing her best impression of someone apologetic.

Matthew stood up. 'That's alright. It's just up the stairs. I need a break from listening to jihadi voicemails anyway.'

Rebecca smiled at him as he went past. 'Cheers.' As soon as he was gone, she clicked into Homeland and quickly deleted the false request she'd just made. Then she went casually but quickly to Mackintosh's office carrying a DVD and a memory stick.

She took the stapler off the ENTER key, then tapped into Mackintosh's personnel comms files.

GCHQ kept a meticulous log of phone calls in and out, and emails from every server.

There wasn't time to look through the files, but even a quick scroll through Mackintosh's inbox showed messages with the subject: "Abbie Bishop (NOFORN)", meaning no foreign nationals were to be given access to the memo. It was also marked as STRAP Three security clearance.

It meant that all of Abbie's movements on her desktop computer that Internal Security had taken away would leave no trace of what she'd actually been accessing, creating or sending. A ghost user, they called it. Like someone walking across snow and leaving no footprints. Whatever Abbie was working on, someone had given her clearance to work in total secrecy. Which meant that the files sent from Abbie's laptop would be the only evidence left of Operation Tempest.

Rebecca clicked into Mackintosh's burn box: messages that had already been deleted. On a regular computer, deleted messages were more like hidden messages. With some inventive programming, and if you knew where to look, deleted items could still be found. A GCHQ burn box went one step beyond that: the process was meant to be failsafe. But Rebecca had found a way. She started up a program of hers from the memory stick called PHOENIX, which resurrected deleted messages.

Such was the beauty of modern data, nothing was really gone forever: everything left a trace.

As flash drives weren't allowed out of GCHQ, she fished out a blank DVD (a CD would be too small for such a large cache of documents) to copy as much material from the hard-drive as she could fit on the DVD: 4.7GB. More than enough space.

As the files wrote to the DVD, Rebecca kept watch on the GTE office door, waiting on Matthew arriving back any second. Then she noticed the red dot next to the clock at the bottom corner of the screen turn green.

Mackintosh had logged in remotely from his tablet.

The blood drained from her face as she tried to think of a valid reason for being on his computer. An MI6 agent would have a prepared answer, or be able to blag something convincing on the spot. Rebecca had nothing but blind panic. If he checked the cameras facing his office after suspicious activity, she'd be history.

If she ejected the DVD before it had burned she'd lose the lot, and she might not get another chance to copy the material again.

There would be a lag of about ten seconds between what was shown on screen – the window showing a massive cache of files being copied onto a disc – and what would appear on Mackintosh's tablet.

Rebecca's feet tapped rapidly on the floor as the time remaining – five seconds – threatened to overlap with the lag time.

The moment the window cleared, Rebecca ejected the disc and snapped the drive tray shut. She stared at the home screen.

Had he seen any of her activity? There was no way of knowing.

Rebecca took her memory stick and disc back to her desk, just as Matthew reappeared.

As Matthew passed her desk, he said, 'That was weird. I couldn't see anything.'

'Really?' Rebecca said. 'I'm sure if it's important they'll raise it again.'

Matthew looked over at Mackintosh's office, seeming to linger on something.

Rebecca realised she'd left the door slightly ajar.

Matthew didn't say anything, but he'd noticed it. Of that, Rebecca was sure.

When the office quietened down later, Rebecca put the DVD into her own computer and wrote a cryptonym on to it. If anyone tried to open it, the files would crash and break into meaningless random code. She wrote 'Windows 10 Boot Disc' on the disc in black marker, then slid it into the drive of her personal laptop. No one was going to bother making a trusted officer boot up a laptop with what looked like a basic boot CD on the way out the door.

This is it, she thought, looking down at the open disc tray. *Am I really going to walk out of here with STRAP Three intelligence? In the eyes of the law that's espionage.*

Normally a civil servant who unearths malpractice or

corruption can benefit from whistleblower protection under the Public Interest Disclosure Act. But for those in the security services – MI5, MI6 and GCHQ – The Official Secrets Act 1989 couldn't have been clearer: whistleblowers had no protection.

But Rebecca knew that if she wanted to find out the full truth about Abbie's double life with MI6, Tom Novak, and Tempest, she would have to take a risk.

She checked that no one was looking, then closed the laptop tray with the disc inside.

11

It was already dark when Angela Curtis was driven from Buckingham Palace in her armoured, bombproof Jaguar XJ Sentinel having accepted the Queen's commission to lead the government. Her convoy was led by motorcycle riders of the Special Escort Group, and two black, unmarked Range Rovers.

'I told you she doesn't like me, Rog,' Curtis grumbled, reaching for her mobile.

Roger Milton, her special advisor sitting opposite, asked, 'What makes you say that?'

'She didn't like me when I was Home Secretary, and she actually seems to like me even less as PM.'

'Name me a PM she did like.' Milton's face was lit up by his phone screen.

'Churchill and Harold bloody Wilson,' Curtis replied, trying to see Milton's phone. 'What's happened while we were in there?'

'They've set the COBRA meeting for later tonight,' Milton said. 'But first you're going to have to do a press conference. The party's worried it'll look like a coup, getting sworn in by the Queen then dashing off to bed.'

'Does anyone honestly believe I'm going to sleep tonight? Ten hours ago I was a backbencher. Now, because two cabinet ministers couldn't resolve their own pissing contest, they've handed me the keys to Number Ten.'

'You know they don't actually give the Prime Minister keys.'

Angela Curtis swallowed hard. It was the first time he had called her that. 'Figure of speech, Rog.'

Milton said, 'We don't know what the country thinks about anything to do with you. You haven't had any polling done since you were Home Sec.'

Curtis stared out the window, her eyes glazing over at the thought of being responsible for all the people now walking the streets. 'I just keep thinking of Simon's wife and those little girls. What the hell must they be going through.' Curtis snatched for the grab handle above the door, as the car swung a hard left onto the Mall. 'Christ, I'm never going to get any work done in this thing.'

In the long walk down the corridor to the Cabinet Meeting room, Milton handed Curtis some final notes. 'Remember, no smiling,' he said.

'I'm too terrified to smile,' she replied.

After some photos, the room was cleared of the press and the meeting started with a minute's silence for former Prime Minister Ali and the other casualties.

'I know that for many of you sitting here today, I am not your first choice for this job,' Curtis began, the only one standing. 'So, let me spare us all the fatuous statements of having "more that unites us than divides us" and all the other crap one might say at a moment like this. We can save that kind of talk for the press.'

Milton scoured his notes. 'She's off page already,' he whispered to an associate.

'I expect a number of you in this room think the reason I'm standing here is because Simon Ali and many others were murdered this morning. But I'm also here because of a man named Thomas Hobson. For those of you who don't know, Hobson was a hostler in Cambridge in the sixteenth century. Over time he acquired a reputation, that the only horse he would ever offer a customer was the one nearest the door. Whether I like it or not, I am Hobson's Choice. I was voted in to act as caretaker until the General Election, nothing more. The only reason Ed and Nigel's people got behind me was because Ed and Nigel don't want to become electoral poison by having a public leadership battle in the aftermath of a national tragedy. They've put aside personal ambition for the good of the country. At least for another six weeks. Let's be honest, I'm standing here because everyone in this room – and quite a few outside it – knows I will never win a General Election. Not in six weeks, six months, or ever.'

Milton clasped Curtis's notes to his chest and tried not to grimace too openly.

Silence prickled across the room. No one could believe Curtis had actually dared to tell the obvious truth.

She went on, 'But if you think for a second I'm only here to warm this seat until then you are all sadly mistaken. We're going to find out who's responsible for this barbaric attack, and we're going to bring them to justice.' Curtis spread her hands across the table in front of her, leaning forward with a look of strength and determination no one in the room had seen from her before. Her voice seemed to have welled itself several feet underground. 'Wherever these murderers have come from, wherever they've been, or wherever they're going, we're not going to come back at them with coalitions, poems, hashtags, charity concerts, knee-jerk suspensions of civil liberties, internment, or a police state. We will be true to our ideals as British citizens, and we will defend the values that give us our moral authority. We will not have murder on the streets of

London, or Manchester, or any other city they seek to terrorise in the name of Allah, or whatever nihilistic, Bronze Age superstition they use to dress up their hatred for women, homosexuals, liberty, justice and democracy. Let's not kid ourselves about what we're dealing with here. I don't need a full investigation or MI5 to tell me we're not dealing with a new sect of Anglican suicide bombers.'

The atmosphere was too heavy for laughter, but the room seemed to appreciate the levity.

Curtis's voice began low, steadily rising as she took in the nodding heads and looks of support she saw in front of her. Coming to a defiant crescendo, and the loudest voice anyone could recall in the Cabinet Office.

'We've been here before. We came together before. And we're going to do it again. We're going to bury our dead. Our friends. Our colleagues. Associates. We're going to mourn them. But we will not wait another day before we bring the roof of their poisoned house down upon these perpetrators, and drive them back to the gates of hell itself!'

The entire Cabinet were already on their feet when Curtis finished with, 'This is Great Britain! We've beaten fascists before, and god help me we'll beat them again!'

The room erupted with applause and slaps on the table, ministers waving their papers to wild cheers of 'Hear, hear!'

Down the corridor, some of the waiting press were startled by the noise. They had never heard a roar like it from the Cabinet Office.

When the room emptied, the press swarmed around the door. In the scuffle, and cries of questions, no one noticed Curtis passing a Dictaphone she'd had in her pocket to a reporter. The reporter exchanged a knowing look with her, then disappeared with the next major news cycle in his hand.

Milton escorted Curtis from the Cabinet Room, through the

paparazzi throng to the press conference. Through a fixed expression, he mumbled caustically to her, 'When the hell did you write that?'

Curtis waved away demands for comment on the meeting. 'I just said what I was feeling. You never forget your lines that way.'

Milton wondered where *this* Angela Curtis had been all his political life. She was like a different person.

He struggled to keep up with her. 'If only the press knew what happened in there...'

She knew that the speech and its reception would play well in the media.

Milton asked, 'What did you pass to Harrington?'

'What are you talking about?'

'No one else might have noticed, but I did.'

'Harrington and I go way back.' She smiled fractionally at Milton. 'Don't worry about the Cabinet meeting story. It'll get out eventually.'

The door leading into the press conference came into view down the hallway.

Milton said, 'Angela, nothing can prepare you for the chaos of what's behind that door. The Home Office has nothing on what's out there. There's going to be yelling and shouting right from the first question, and you're going to be blinded by flashes. Keep your eyes on the back of the room or the flashes will blind you, and you'll end up looking blinking and terrified.'

'Chaos, flashing, back of the room.' She exhaled. 'Okay.'

'What do you say when they ask about the General Election?'

Curtis took the speech from him. 'Our first and only priority right now is keeping the people of this country safe.'

He held her shoulders. 'This is the most important press conference of your life.' Then he let go.

'Really? That's the last thing you're going to say to me?'

Milton could tell she was ready.

A Downing Street civil servant nervously put her hand out to Curtis, showing her the way to the press room. 'They're ready for you, Prime Minister.'

'Remember,' Milton added. 'It's not just an attack on London and Great Britain, it's an attack on all civilised people, everywhere.'

The door opened and camera flashes went off all around the room. What seemed like every journalist in Britain was on their feet, microphones and phones poised to record, launching landslides of questions at her.

Standing at the lectern, seeing only the whites of the press's hungry eyes, the realisation hit Curtis that there was an entire country hanging on her words.

After a pause for the room to settle down, she said, 'Her Majesty the Queen has asked me to form a government and I have accepted.'

Live coverage of the press conference played on the video wall of the Cabinet Briefing Room before the emergency security meeting.

Foreign Secretary Nigel Hawkes and Home Secretary Ed Bannatyne, although seated next to each other, had their chairs pointed at forty-five-degree angles away from the other.

While the security agencies huddled in a familiar clique, Bannatyne whispered, 'We've got a bit of a problem.'

'You don't have to tell me.'

'She looks...' Bannatyne couldn't find the words.

Hawkes found them for him. 'Like a Prime Minister?'

'I've never seen a PM get a standing ovation like that. Not in Cabinet.'

Hawkes showed Bannatyne his phone, logged in to Twitter. 'Patrick Harrington from *The Mirror* has got a recording of her speech.'

'What? How?'

'I don't know. But it's everywhere.'

The headline read, "Curtis gives rousing first Cabinet speech to standing ovation."'

Hawkes said, 'So much for unelectable.'

When it came to taking questions, Curtis fended off the usual procedural questions about the bombing investigation, deflecting ably when she didn't know the answer. A grubby-looking man, unshaven and tie done up like an afterthought, called out, 'Dan Leckie from *The Post*.' The journalists around him seemed to scowl at his presence.

'Prime Minister,' Leckie said. 'Do you have any further information about Abigail Bishop?'

'I'm sorry,' Curtis replied. 'I'm not in a position to confirm casualties yet.'

'She wasn't a casualty in the bombing...'

Curtis glanced over to the wings while Leckie kept talking.

'She was an intelligence officer who was found dead at a GCHQ safe house on Monday night. My source tells me she was working for MI6.'

Milton brushed his hair back with his hand, their signal for "no comment".

Curtis showed no signs of irritation. 'I know you've been serving at her Majesty's pleasure for the past year, Dan, but you've obviously forgotten it is government policy to neither confirm nor deny the identity of any individual working for intelligence agencies. It would be wrong for me to comment further.'

Leckie persisted, shouting over the next round of questions coming from all sides. 'What can you tell us about Operation Tempest?' But he was drowned out by reporters calling out more questions on the bombing.

12

THE REPUBLIC OFFICES, NEW YORK – MONDAY, 1.11PM

Novak, Stella, and Chang had decamped to Chang's office. Stella was checking the *Reuters* wires for updates on London, while waiting for replies from her contacts in the U.K. Foreign Office. Novak was distant and uninvolved, toiling with his laptop. The screen was oddly pixelated and flickering, like a TV receiving a weak signal. He could barely read the emails in his inbox.

While on hold with another reporter, Chang held his phone against his chest whilst giving out directions. 'Stella, what do we know about the bomber? Has he ever been on a watch list? A no-fly? Where did he pray? If so, are there any radical preachers there? Does he have siblings? Are they in custody also? What countries has he been to in the last five years? What's his radicalisation history? This is going to work a little differently to what you were used to at *The Guardian*. Diane's got a three-tick system here, so you'll have to sit on things a little longer than you're used to.'

'I can do that,' Stella said absently, reading through the wires. She seemed to have found something interesting. 'I left London with a ton of unreturned favours.'

Chang said, 'Also, what's the latest in Whitehall? Any friction between U.S. and British intelligence? Tom: who's going to be a thorn in the administration's side on the new Patriot Act? Also, what's it going to be called? Republicans are good at naming things. The Freedom Act.'

Stella added, 'The Death Tax.'

'One of my favourites...' Chang went back to his phone call. 'Hi, Greg? Give me one more minute.' He held the phone against his chest again, his face dropping when he saw Novak's inattention. 'Tom?'

Listening to Stella and Mark bouncing ideas off each other made him want to be there even less. He sat staring at the email he'd received a week ago from Bastion News CEO Nathan Rosenblatt:

'Hi, Tom. Thanks for the drinks last night. I'm really excited about you coming to Bastion News. If you think your profile's big now, wait till you come here. I'm going to get you on Fox, MSNBC, CNN, Colbert, Couric. I'm going to make you a star. And a star deserves a star's pay as you'll see from the contract I've attached. Have your people look it over and get it back to me. Talk soon, buddy.'

Rosenblatt wasn't lying about a star's pay. The contract was a yearly salary of $250,000.

There was a postscript, though, that Novak hadn't paid much attention to at the time. Now, after Diane's advice, he kept coming back to it.

'PS. I had an idea for your first piece: an expose of your experiences inside the mainstream media. We can call it "The End of The Republic"? Think about it.'

Novak moved the cursor over the Reply button, but was wavering over the keyboard.

Chang asked, 'Are you listening, Tom?'

Novak closed the email. 'Sorry. Laptop trouble.'

Stella turned the wires monitor to face Chang. 'Have you seen this?'

After a quick scan of the opening paragraph, Chang said, 'Congratulations Stella, you've found the one non-story happening in London right now. A woman threw herself off a balcony.'

'It's the balcony of a GCHQ safe house.'

Chang looked at the report again, from *The Post* in London. Initially intrigued, he corrected himself with a shake of his head. 'No, Stella. I want British intel on the bombing.' He went back on his phone. 'Hang on, Greg...'

Stella said, 'The report says this woman was an MI6 spy.'

Exasperated, Chang got on his phone. 'Greg, can I call you back? Thanks.' He hung up then tossed his phone on his desk. 'Can we keep our focus here, people! Jesus, it's like shepherding cats. Now, look—'

Before Chang could get any further, Martin Fitzhenry burst in, holding out four new pages.

'Fifteen hundred on London, as requested, Mr Chang,' Fitz said, passing the pages over.

Chang took it, then checked his watch. 'I gave you the brief thirty minutes ago.'

'It would have been five minutes earlier but I got a little tangled tracking down a Thomas Jefferson quote.'

'What was the quote?' asked Stella.

Fitz held out his hand. 'Stella Mitchell, as I live and breathe. Martin Fitzhenry, pleased to meet you. Novak, you lucky swine. How did you poach her from *The Guardian*? One of the best writers they had.'

Novak grumped, 'Diane brought her here. Nothing to do with me.'

Beaming at meeting one of her idols, Stella said, 'Pleasure to meet you.'

From the age of twenty-five, Fitz already had the reputation of a Fleet Street legend, with a prodigious output in books, newspapers, magazines and essays (not to mention prodigious input of alcohol and cigarettes). Since making the transatlantic switch in the late eighties, Fitz had been the quintessential English-writer-in-New York.

He could routinely knock back three or four drinks at lunch and still bash out fifteen hundred flawless words, that placed an event that only happened that morning in immaculate political and cultural context. In five years of editing him, Chang had never found so much as a misspelling or solecism.

Novak said, 'He's our occasional guest features editor. In baseball terms, it's like having Roger Clemens as a relief pitcher, bottom of the ninth.'

'There are at least three things about that sentence I didn't understand.' Stella said.

Fitz explained, 'What dear Novak means to say is, this is a sunrise-sunset publication. It hires people starting their careers, and those, like me, who are on the back nine. This way our generous benefactor, Mr Self, gets some cheap young talent fresh out of Harvard, and...' Fitz motioned for her to fill in the blank.

'I never went to university,' Stella said. 'When I was twenty I was covering crime for the *Birmingham Courier*.'

'I thought so,' Fitz said. 'Your work has the discipline of the old school.'

'What do you make of Angela Curtis?' Novak asked.

Fitz deferred. 'I think Stella's probably your man on that.'

Eager to prove herself, Stella said, 'It's a sideways move, but it makes sense. Bannatyne and Hawkes cancel each other out in a leadership vote, and the Tories can't afford to look indecisive. I knew her when she was Home Secretary. The papers got pictures of men arriving late at her flat and leaving early in the morning. All it took was three different men over the course of six months, and the scarlet letter was painted on her door. The public thought they were okay with a single woman in her early forties being in government who was as promiscuous as any man her age. The polls suggested otherwise. The party threw her to the wolves, and she was out at the next cabinet reshuffle. She once told me if she'd been married when she was thirty, she'd have been PM.'

'She's in it now,' Fitz added, making for the door with a cigarette in his mouth waiting to be lit.

'Fitz,' Novak called out. 'You never said what the Jefferson quote was.'

Fitz turned around. 'He said, "If choosing a government without newspapers, or newspapers without government, I should not hesitate a moment to prefer the latter."' He sensed his friend was hurting in some way. Something in his eyes, his unusually slumped posture. Trying to buck him up, Fitz said, 'After a day like today, there's no other reporter I'd want in London more than you, Novak.' He knocked on the door frame, like he was physically punctuating the end of his sentence.

Novak smiled back. He was grateful for the compliment, but he didn't truly agree with it.

As Fitz exited, Chang tried to get back to where he was. 'As I was saying. Now that–'

Then Kurt knocked on the open door. 'Sorry to interrupt, Mark.'

'Okay. I *actually* give up...' Chang threw his phone down on his desk in despair.

Kurt said, 'I kind of need Tom to come look at this.'

He and Stella followed Kurt to his desk, where he had the back off Novak's phone. They gathered around it like it was a body on an operating table.

Kurt angled his laptop screen towards them. 'I ran a diagnostic, and at first it seemed fine. But when I rebooted it, all the web browsers crashed. Then my malware program started going crazy. So I unhooked the phone, and it stopped and the web browsers all came back.'

'What does that mean?' Novak asked.

'There's a virus on your phone.'

'On my phone? Is that even possible?'

Kurt gave the sort of dismissive snort only a tech-head could give. 'It's unbe*liev*ably easy. But it does require someone physically having the phone and connecting it to the infecting laptop. How long has it been like this?'

'Like, two days? But I'm having the same problem with my laptop as well now.'

Kurt took it from Stella and hooked it up to his own laptop. In a matter of seconds, the malware program started flashing that a threat had been detected. 'Interesting,' Kurt mumbled. 'Same virus.'

'What does it do?' Stella asked.

'Nothing too dangerous. It's not there to steal data or files, it's what they call an irritant. Just kicks you off the internet whenever you try to use it. It's the sort of virus that wants the user to know something's in there.'

'Like the computer equivalent of a heavy-breathing phone call?' Stella offered.

'Kind of,' Kurt answered. 'There are different versions of it. Some of them are pretty cool actually. There's one that makes your screen shake so you can't read anything, and–' Kurt froze as the screen went black. He tapped furiously on the F8 button. When that didn't work, he tried random keys on the keyboard. Nothing. He dragged the mouse pad. Still nothing.

'What is it?' Stella asked.

'It's just died,' Kurt said. 'No, wait...' He saw a small underscore appear in the top left corner of the screen, blinking. Then words started typing themselves. 'Whoa!' Kurt pulled his hands back. 'I'm not doing that.'

A basic networking font appeared on the screen for a few seconds:

"*Thought is free*"

The cursor blinked, then moved down a line, writing,

"*Hell is empty. And all the devils are here.*"

A few seconds later the black screen disappeared, and the laptop came back to life as if nothing had happened.

Kurt reached for his phone, slack-jawed. 'Cathy?' he said in a mystified tone. 'You better get up here.'

Novak asked him, 'What's going on?'

Kurt stared at him in bemusement. 'I have *absolutely* no idea.'

Stella waited with Novak at his desk while Kurt and Cathy ran more checks on the laptop and phone. Stella couldn't resist passing him her *Reuters* printout.

'As long as we're waiting here,' she said, 'maybe you could take another pass at this.'

Novak took a quick look then tried to hand it back. 'I know you just got here and you're eager to make a splash, but trust me: a woman falling off a balcony isn't the story that's going to do it.'

Stella refused to take the paper from him. 'You don't think that merits further investigation?'

Novak reluctantly kept reading the report. After a few lines his heart felt it had moved a few inches nearer his throat. 'Abbie Bishop...'

'What is it?' Stella asked.

'I got an email this morning from someone saying they were a friend of this woman. And that Abbie thought we should talk.'

Stella asked, 'You've never heard her name before? You never had a contact at GCHQ?'

'No one,' Novak answered. 'Though I'm sure they know plenty about me.'

Stella bundled her laptop into Novak's lap. 'What are you waiting for? Write back to them! We could get out ahead of *The Post* on this.'

'Okay, okay,' Novak said, reaching for the keyboard.

'Um... Tom?' Kurt appeared, holding Novak's phone up like it was about to detonate.

'What's wrong?' Novak asked, signing into his email.

'I'm sorry, I didn't mean to pry. I was copying out your saved contacts to your new phone when an email came through. I think you should read this.' Kurt handed him the phone before backing off to his desk.

After reading it Novak showed the phone to Stella.

"We need to talk ASAP. I have proof Abbie Bishop's death wasn't an accident."

'That's it,' Stella said, hauling Novak to his feet. 'We're leaving for London...' she pointed firmly at the ground, '*tonight*. We're finding this woman.'

Novak nodded. 'You got a go bag?

'Of course,' she replied.

'Get it.'

Kurt left the laptop on Novak's desk. 'You also got an email from an Artur Korecki? Looks like there's a video attachment.'

Novak said, 'Thanks, Kurt.' He didn't recognise the name, and he was too busy getting ready to leave to take any notice.

On a story like Stella's, there was no time for hanging around luggage carousels, so carry-on luggage only was essential. Novak's tech was always the same: phone, laptop, chargers. Clothes: cotton Oxford easy-iron shirts, two ties (one black, one navy), smart/casual black brogues which could be worn with either suit or casual trousers. Everything for the city had to be versatile enough to cover formal and informal events. You never knew where you might end up: anything from an embassy dinner, to sitting about a Westminster press office or a hospital waiting room for several hours.

Novak and Stella met each other with their bags back at the centre of the office, ready to go.

Stella asked, 'What do we tell Mark?'

'I don't know,' Novak said. 'But you better think of something quick.'

Chang was walking briskly towards them holding his

phone. From a distance he said, 'I told you to call that guy.' He sounded angry then realised they both had go bags. 'Where the hell are you going?'

'What guy?' asked Novak.

He covered the mouthpiece then yelled, 'Sharp! Walter! CIA! How many times?'

'Shit,' Novak said, remembering the note in his pocket.

Chang passed him the phone. 'Take the damn call so I can actually move on with my life.'

Novak turned his back on the others to answer. 'Tom Novak.'

The voice on the other end was all business. 'This is Walter Sharp, I'm with CIA. I hear people in the background. I need you to move to a room where we can talk alone.'

Novak moved towards Chang's office, lowering his voice. 'Are you the one who put this virus on my phone and computer—'

'You have a virus on them right now?'

Novak shut the door. 'Yeah, my tech guy is working on them.'

'Tell him to shut them down. Shut them down *right now* and take out the batteries.'

Novak waved for Kurt's attention behind the floor-to-ceiling window looking out to the office, pointing frantically at the laptop and making a "kill" gesture across his throat. 'What is this?' Novak asked. 'What's going on?'

'I think that virus is designed to give them your location.'

'Give who my location?'

'The men who are hunting you, Mr Novak.'

'What are you—'

Sharp spoke clearly, trying to alert Novak to the danger without panicking him. 'I need you to trust me, Mr Novak. I believe you may be in possession of a video file. A video certain people will do anything in their power to retrieve. I need you to follow my instructions. Do that, and I'll try and keep you alive long enough to figure this thing out.'

Video file. Novak looked in horror at his laptop, remembering the email with a video attachment.

Sharp asked, 'Do you know a man by the name of Artur Korecki?'

'Oh, Jesus...Yeah. There's a video...'

'Don't say anything more, Mr Novak. This isn't a secure line. We need to get you out of there.'

13

Angela Curtis received a standing ovation from the men waiting for her in the secure Cabinet Office Briefing Room.

In attendance: Head of the Metropolitan Police Sir John Pringle; MI6 Chief Sir Lloyd Willow; MI5 Chief Sir Teddy King; director of GCHQ, Trevor Billington-Smith; Foreign Secretary Nigel Hawkes; and Home Secretary Ed Bannatyne.

'As you were, gentlemen,' she said, taking a seat at the head of the table. She thought, this must have been how Maggie Thatcher felt. 'Where are we?' she asked.

Sir John Pringle stood in front of the video screen. 'Prime Minister, we're now in a position to confirm the name of the bombing suspect. We received this video an hour ago.' He signalled for the video to play. It showed a young British Asian man, wearing a military jacket over civilian clothes. The man spoke confidently and without aggression. 'My name is Abdullah Hassan Mufaza, and tomorrow I will detonate an explosive device at Downing Street and, *insh'Allah*, kill Simon Ali, for perpetrating attacks on Muslims all around the world. He has denied the true message of Allah, and for this he will be slaughtered.'

Pringle stopped the video. 'He goes on to cite the policies

of the British government in the Middle East, and an incessant stream of quotes from the Quran.'

'Where did the tape come from?' Curtis asked.

'His wife, Fawzia, is a Somali national with British citizenship. She found it on their kitchen table this evening, sitting on top of a Quran. She's being questioned in the high-profile suite at Paddington Green, but it doesn't look like she knew what her husband was doing.'

'Do we release this?' Bannatyne wondered aloud.

'No way,' Curtis said. 'We made that mistake on seven seven. We're not distributing propaganda on his behalf, but release stills of his face. We need everyone who knew this man to be talking to us.'

'I could leak it to the BBC,' Hawkes offered.

'No,' Curtis said. 'A closed-door Foreign Office media briefing. That way everyone gets it at the same time. It'll have more impact and we won't piss anyone off by looking like we're playing favourites.'

Bannatyne flashed his eyebrows up at Hawkes at how cannily Curtis was playing it.

Curtis asked. 'Is there a history here that we missed?'

Everyone at the table deferred to Sir Teddy King's decades of experience with anti-terrorism at MI5. 'He's a cleanskin, Prime Minister,' King said. 'We had no intelligence on him, no history of radicalisation. No known connections.'

'Was there any suspicious online activity?' Curtis asked.

Trevor Billington-Smith of GCHQ fumbled through his notes. 'There may have been something, let me see...'

The others exchanged troubled glances. It was well-known in Westminster that Trevor was not the most technically astute for a GCHQ Director. Typically a position taken by a civil servant, Trevor was more of a political appointee.

Sir Teddy King stepped in. 'We haven't seen evidence of suspicious online behaviour, Prime Minister. I will say, though, that you don't get your hands on the sort of materials required for a bomb like this without help.'

'How the hell did he get into Downing Street in the first place?' Curtis asked. 'The entire country assumed we would have made that place impregnable.'

Pringle switched the screen to a picture of a Downing Street press pass for a BBC employee. 'The man in this picture is Riz Rizzaq, a BBC cameraman. His body was found at his flat in Hackney two hours ago, in what we thought was a burglary-gone-wrong. We found this.' Pringle switched to a shot of a charred press pass with Rizzaq's name on it, but a different photo in it. 'It was practically at the gates of Downing Street. A reporter at the scene, Sophie Barker, has given a statement that her cameraman, Mr Rizzaq, didn't show up as planned for the press conference. She later saw the bomber, identified as Mufaza, wearing this ID.'

'They killed Rizzaq and stole his ID,' Bannatyne said, as if that were the end of the matter.

'But how did they get Mufaza's photo on Rizzaq's ID?' Hawkes asked.

Pringle switched to a scene-of-crime photograph of Rizzaq's wallet. 'They didn't. It was still in his flat when officers arrived.'

Sir Teddy summarised, 'If it looked like Rizzaq had been robbed for his ID, it could have blown their plan. They wouldn't risk a hand-off on the morning of the bombing. And if it was taken any earlier, it would have raised a red flag at Downing Street.'

Curtis looked to Trevor Billington-Smith. 'It's GCHQ who make these cards. Can they be copied or faked?'

Trevor took off his glasses, looking a little lost. 'I must admit, Prime Minister, I'm not entirely familiar with the process.'

'If I may, Trevor?' asked King. 'It's important to understand, Prime Minister, you can't just cut out a photo and replace it. The entire card is seamless, like the ID page of a passport. Then there's the watermark which, to the naked eye, appear as simple blue lines. But when you magnify a few hundred times, it reveals a complex, unique number string assembled by GCHQ cryptographers.' He zoomed in on the charred ID, revealing a number string. 'There is simply no way Rizzaq's card could have been copied, and certainly not on the morning of the attack. Forensics are in no doubt about this. The technology required is not in the public domain.'

All eyes fell on Curtis to draw the daunting conclusion. 'Teddy, are you saying that the press pass Mufaza used was genuine?' She looked to Trevor Billington-Smith. 'There's a mole in GCHQ?'

Trevor looked like a man who knew his career was dangling by a thread. 'We think so.'

As Foreign Secretary, GCHQ fell under Hawkes' responsibility. He said, 'GCHQ screens employees for nine months. How is this possible?'

Trevor was a picture of anguish, but trying his best to keep it together. 'We have somewhere in the region of a thousand-plus analysts who have access to classified software. It's a complex system.'

Curtis asked, 'What about the other cell members? Are we close to tracking them down?'

Sir Teddy said, 'The bomb was certainly not assembled in Mufaza's flat. Its complexity, the conditions required for handling the materials...I'd say we're looking for at least another two or three people.'

Curtis paused, trying to think of a plan. She said to Bannatyne, 'I want a DSMA-Notice issued on that detail about the press ID. Tell the news editors if anyone prints it, the British government will own their paper before the first editions hit the pavements.'

Trevor said, 'GCHQ has already been combing through mobile phone records from this morning and lunchtime to track down the remaining suspects. I've got our best people at Global Telecoms Exploitation division on the case.'

'Lloyd,' Curtis said, trying to figure out why her head of MI6 was present, but yet to speak. 'Are we looking at foreign suspects?'

Sir Lloyd Willow cleared his throat. 'All our channels are open, Prime Minister, but this is looking like an entirely home-grown plot, unfortunately. There's another situation we need to make you aware of.'

'Oh good, because this was all rather dull so far...'

Sir Lloyd passed Curtis a file marked "HVT". 'Late on Sunday night CIA took custody of a high-value target by the name of Abdul al-Malik. He was arrested at a checkpoint, making for the Pakistan border out of Afghanistan.' The video screen changed to the CIA mug shot of him. 'After a routine interrogation Malik was shot during a struggle in his cell. Suicide, the Americans are saying.'

'I don't understand,' Curtis said.

Willow hated having to say it. 'He was one of ours.'

'He was British?'

'It's a good deal worse than that. He was MI6.'

'Excuse me?'

'He'd gone dark for several weeks. We thought he had been killed, then CIA alerted us they had him.'

'Where?' Curtis asked.

Hawkes said, 'Some Abu Ghraib hellhole, knowing that crowd.'

'It's a, uh...' Willow tried to put it delicately. 'It's a black site, Prime Minister. We don't have the full facts yet, but it seems Malik might have turned.'

'A double agent,' said Curtis. 'For who?'

'That's still unclear. The Americans say they're investigating the shooting.'

'I want the CIA Director on the phone after this.' Curtis

caught herself in the speed of her own calculations. She turned to Hawkes, thinking he knew best. 'Can I do that?'

Sir Lloyd said, 'Normally best to let CIA matters go through me in the first instance, Prime Minister. There are certain intelligence matters we're not fully ready to share with CIA yet.'

Curtis examined the HVT file. 'This says he was working on an operation called Tempest. I just got a question about Tempest linking it to the death of this GCHQ officer, Abigail Bishop.'

Willow said with more than a little embarrassment, 'We don't know where he's getting that, Prime Minister.'

Bannatyne said, 'I don't see why we can't just revoke Leckie's press credentials.'

'Because this isn't Moscow?' Curtis replied without looking at him. She waved the HVT file at Willow. 'This is precisely what High Court injunctions are for. Or are we saving them up for a free coffee the next time a journalist wants to out a classified operation during a live press conference?'

A chill came over the room.

'Sir Lloyd,' Curtis said, 'how did Leckie even find out this operation existed?'

'I've no idea, Prime Minister,' Willow replied a little too honestly.

Curtis surprised everyone by slamming her hand down on the table. 'I don't want to hear that anymore! Lloyd, Trevor, for Christ's sake clean up your house.'

Willow and Billington-Smith hadn't expected to feel the weight of the new PM's wrath quite so early. They each replied, 'Yes, Prime Minister.'

'And I want hourly updates on these other cell members. If you'll excuse me, I have a Home Office briefing, then I need to find out where exactly I'm going to be sleeping tonight.'

. . .

Willow and Hawkes shared the lift down, standing at opposite sides. It was the first time the men had been alone since before the bombing.

Hawkes snapped, 'I thought your people were monitoring journalists.'

Willow gazed up at the floor ticker, unperturbed. 'No one takes *The Post* seriously.'

'How the hell did someone like Dan Leckie slip through the net?' Hawkes asked.

'The problem with nets, Nigel, is that they're full of holes. And our net has about sixty million people in it.'

'Well, someone is leaking classified information to the creep.'

Willow's face stiffened, standing back against the lift with his arms folded. 'Don't worry about Dan Leckie. He'll be writing freelance for the *Norfolk Gazette* this time next week.'

Hawkes said, 'His story's still out there. Angela Curtis won't let this just drift away. She was a nightmare when she was in the Home Office. She's going to be ten times worse running the shop.'

'You said you could control her.'

Hawkes countered, '*You* said you could control Simon Ali and look at what nearly happened. Christ knows what he was about to say if that bomb hadn't have gone off.'

Willow replied, '*Listen* to me. The Right Honourable Angela Curtis doesn't understand that it benefits no one to let this get out. It's easy demanding full exposure of the truth when you're on the backbenches. But once Curtis has spent a few weeks seeing exactly how the sausages are made she'll back down.'

Seeing the lift one floor away from ground, Hawkes hit the "Stop" button, and the lift jarred to a halt. 'Are you not worried that whoever is leaking this stuff isn't on our side? We need to find them. *Quickly*.'

Willow nonchalantly reached over and started the lift

again. 'Our man at GCHQ is in control of the situation.' As the doors opened, Willow stepped out first. 'Oh, and Nigel.' He looked back, as serious as Hawkes had ever seen him. 'Don't ever talk to me like that in front of the others again. The things I could do to you are *disgusting*.' As he turned he mumbled, 'I hate when politicians try to do politics.'

14

Officer Sharp checked his phone while waiting in the corridor outside the briefing room. Sharp could hear distant footsteps somewhere, the corridors now sparsely populated at this hour. Only the extremely dedicated or those being punished by manning night desks were left. Being summoned to Langley for a ten o'clock debriefing was not a good sign. Night debriefings were only ever called when extreme secrecy was required.

Bob Weiskopf, division chief of CIA's Counterterrorism Centre, called Sharp into the briefing room from behind the closed door. When Sharp entered, Weiskopf gestured for him to sit in the empty chair at the end of a long mahogany table, with a harsh fluorescent tube light hanging over it.

Unaccustomed to wearing a tie, Sharp pulled at his shirt collar. A quick survey of the room told him why they'd scheduled so late: at the end of the table was CIA Director George Millar, looking grim as he took the battery out his phone; opposite Sharp was Weiskopf, and three strangers in dark suits conferring and passing notes to each other, no visible ID hanging from their jacket pockets.

One of the strangers nodded to an assistant standing by

the video wall at the end of the room. A profile of what little details they knew about Abdul al-Malik filled the screen.

'Coffee?' Weiskopf asked Sharp.

Sharp said, 'I'm good,' but kept his gaze fixed on the strangers.

Director Millar leaned forward and the room hushed. 'This was already a long day before London happened, and it's going to be a long night. Let's get things rolling.'

Weiskopf took his cue. 'Walt. We thought it would be a good idea to have a proper sit down. About what happened at Camp Zero.'

Sharp pointed with his pen at the unidentified men, talking to Weiskopf as if the men couldn't hear him. 'They can't be NSA because we're on government property and they'd have their badges on display. And seeing as they're two seats down from the Director of CIA, and no one has yet told me what any of this is about, perhaps these gentlemen can identify themselves.'

They were around Sharp's age, early forties, and had the grizzled, humourless expressions of men whose careers had floundered on desk jobs. Sharp had met plenty like them in his time: budget men, policy men, and the closest they had come to combat were tersely worded memos to the Pentagon. Men who thought they could ascend the company purely by saying 'Yes, sir' to every request.

Weiskopf tried introductions. 'This is Baxter, he's—'

'We're with the General Counsel's office,' Baxter said.

'I thought we were to discuss the investigation into the death of Abdul al-Malik?' Sharp asked. 'What does that have to do with the CIA's legal advisor?'

'Quite a lot, agent,' Baxter replied.

'I'm an SSO,' Sharp corrected him. 'Specialized Skills *Officer*. I'm not an agent.'

Baxter raised his palms to gesture no offence intended.

Weiskopf said, 'There is no official record being taken

here. This meeting does not exist, nor will it ever exist. All the men in this room are code word clearance or higher.' He clasped his hands together. 'We just need to clear a few things up. Informally. You understand.'

Things felt far from informal to Sharp.

Baxter explained, 'The General Counsel's office has been asked by Director Millar to go over some of the details about the death of Abdul al-Malik in Camp Zero.' He had a reedy voice and rakish build. His neck fit his fifteen-inch collar with room to spare. With one look, Sharp could tell Baxter had never done so much as a pull up in his life. Sharp couldn't understand a man like that.

Baxter said, 'You've made a number of serious accusations against JSC and General McNally in particular, with regards to the events of that night.' Distracted by Sharp's continuing wandering eye, Baxter asked, 'I'm sorry, is there a problem?'

Sharp pointed at the screen where Malik's details were. 'Who wrote up that profile of him?' he asked.

'I did,' Baxter said.

Sharp replied, 'Okay.'

Wondering what the issue was, Baxter said, 'I'd like to play a recording taken from the prisoner's cell two nights ago, but unfortunately the tapes seem to have disappeared. Do you know anything about that, Officer Sharp?'

Sharp was as surprised as anyone. He thought McNally would have been desperate to use them against him in some way. 'JSC took them. Ask General McNally.'

'You are aware that those recordings are CIA property. If you have them-'

'I don't have them! And if you're going to insist on asking each question twice, this is going to take a while.'

'Would you care to tell us what Malik told you?'

Sharp paused. 'I'm not willing to disclose that information at this time.'

'Not *willing*?' Baxter said, incredulous. 'Would you care to explain why?'

'Because I'm not under subpoena, this is not a deposition, I have not been read Miranda, and I'm not sitting in front of a grand jury.'

Weiskopf put his hand out for calm. 'Okay, settle down. No one's talking about grand juries here...'

Baxter took out a record from his file and laid it on the table. 'This is an email you sent to Congresswoman Donna Kershaw of the House Judiciary Subcommittee on National Security. Could you tell us why you sent it?'

Sharp replied, 'I would have thought that was pretty obvious to anyone who read it.'

'You asked her to open a murder enquiry,' Baxter said, as if the severity of such an act were obvious. 'Of a prisoner at a classified overseas facility.'

'The congresswoman has clearance for classified material like everyone else on that committee, which regularly holds closed-door hearings on all manner of classified articles.' Sharp clarified, 'I did not name the facility, nor the victim.'

'You sent the same email to each member of the committee,' Baxter said. 'We're sitting here because some of them are concerned you're going to leak this to *The New York Times*. You know how the President feels about leaks.'

Sharp maintained perfect composure, but inside he wanted to rip Baxter's head off. 'I've never leaked anything in my life, sunshine. I've got twenty years in the field. I passed sniper school when I was twenty-five, and have thirteen confirmed kills. Do you have any idea how hard sniper school is? I've been awarded the Intelligence Medal of Merit, a Bronze Star Medal for valour, and the Marine Corps Achievement Medal. What have you got? Five years in private practice and two in the stationery cupboard?'

Weiskopf made a half-assed intervention. 'Walt...'

Baxter passed across a printed copy of Sharp's phone records. 'Why did you call SIS in London?'

'MI6,' Sharp said derisively, taking the log. 'No one calls them SIS in the field.'

'Why did you call them?'

'Malik said he was one of their agents.'

Baxter smirked at Weiskopf, then looked back at Sharp. 'And you believed him?'

Sharp said, 'Malik referred to two different code word CIA locations, as well as the TCS Act. Not to mention a cryptonym that was accepted by his MI6 London station chief William Blackstone.'

'Where?' Baxter asked. 'On the tapes no one has?'

'That Malik was MI6 is not even up for debate.'

Baxter smiled. 'Do you have any thoughts on that, Bob?'

Weiskopf answered, but he didn't look happy about it. He knew he might be about to bury one of his most loyal and respected agents. 'Blackstone told myself and Director Millar that he confirmed to you Malik was once MI6, but had been disavowed. He says this was communicated to you at the time. Also, that Malik should be considered highly dangerous and a suicide risk if captured.'

'That's impossible,' Sharp said, taking out his phone. 'Take my phone, give it to NSA. They'll have recorded the damn phone call.'

'Your phone's encrypted, Walt,' Weiskopf said.

'Bob. Right after the call, we spoke about it.'

Weiskopf shuffled awkwardly in his seat. 'Maybe in the heat of the moment...with Malik's outlandish claims – the credible threat, the MI6 claim, and you'd been working long hours – you might have misunderstood Blackstone.'

Sharp wasn't about to turn on his own boss in a room with strangers, so he said nothing. He knew it wasn't Weiskopf's fault. Someone at MI6 had given him a stacked deck. Now

Sharp couldn't work out his next move. He hadn't prepared for this.

Baxter, glowing at this turn of events, pushed a file with the letters "HVT" stamped on the front across the table towards Sharp. 'MI6 sent this to us this morning. If you turn to the bottom paragraph of page three, they highlight concerns Malik had quote "gone off the reservation." Page four concludes Malik as high-value and should be brought in.' He looked wearily at Weiskopf. 'They just never got around to telling us.'

Weiskopf added, 'Our special relationship seems to be more of a friends with benefits situation these days.'

Sharp couldn't believe what he was seeing. 'They're disavowing Malik?'

Director Millar decided it was time to step in. 'I spoke to Sir Lloyd Willow earlier.' He turned to the others. 'And if you really want to piss him off, forget the Sir when you call.'

Everyone laughed. Except Sharp.

Millar said, 'He said Malik had been dark for nearly a month. They're convinced he turned.'

Baxter sat back and folded his arms, wondering what Sharp's story would be now.

Millar added, 'Malik's got rogue agent written all over him.'

'What about Secretary Snow?' Sharp asked.

Baxter flicked through his notes. 'Did Malik specify a credible threat against London?'

'That's not the—'

Baxter kept the heat on. 'I have your report here. You said he referred constantly to a U.S. target. He was trying to throw you off the scent of an attack in London. Can't you see that, Officer Sharp?'

'You think Secretary Snow was just a coincidence?' Sharp asked.

Director Millar nodded his permission at Weiskopf.

'MI6 have a video confession from the bomber,' Weiskopf said, flicking to a still from the video. 'The target is made explicit: it was the British Prime Minister. Secretary Snow's not even mentioned on the video. Just some very convenient collateral damage for them.'

Millar said, 'I'm looking at the report here and Malik's got you tied in knots. Giving you code word clearance intel and cryptonyms – which an agent in his position would have. He convinces you he's for real, sets you off on the wrong path, then he kills himself before anyone can untangle his story. The Downing Street cell had help from somewhere. Malik must have been one of them.'

Sharp wouldn't even look at Baxter anymore. He held his finger out at Weiskopf. 'I want it on record–'

Baxter gestured at the lack of note-taking going on. 'There *is* no record here.'

'– on *record*, that there's something highly suspicious about General McNally and JSC's actions in Camp Zero two nights ago.'

Baxter tapped his pen on the table. 'You're carrying a truckload of nitro glycerine on a very rocky road, Officer Sharp. That's a three-star general you're talking about.'

Sharp could sense his career hanging in the balance, so he decided to go all in. 'I want to know why a three-star general showed up in the middle of the night, carrying orders from the Chairman of the Joint Chiefs, demanding I hand over my detainee, and why not even half an hour later my detainee winds up dead in circumstances that can *politely* be described as suspicious. Agent Malik was on to something, and whatever it was, both JSC and MI6 wanted it covered up.'

When Sharp was done, a heavy silence fell across the table.

Director Millar, looking to wrap things up, took a long, deep breath. 'Walter. Listen to me now. You were a good Marine, you were a good sniper, and your whole career you've been a damn good SSO. And a smart one. Twenty long years. There's a decent pension at the end of that rainbow too. Don't start making mistakes now. There will be no Critical Incident Report into Malik's death, which will be ruled accidental. The details classified. As far as the Agency's concerned, there will be nothing on your permanent record.'

'I don't follow, sir,' Sharp said.

'Bob,' Millar said.

Weiskopf looked reluctant. 'It's not a suspension,' he said. 'We're just taking you out of the field for a little while. But you gotta stop sending the emails, Walt.'

Millar put the period on proceedings. 'That's all. Dismissed.'

Sharp stood up and buttoned his jacket. 'Sir.' As he walked to the door, and while Weiskopf and Millar conferred at the front of the room, Sharp stopped behind Baxter, then leaned down and pointed to the video screen. 'That's not his name.'

'I'm sorry?' Baxter said.

'His name isn't Abdul.' Sharp loosened his tie on the way out.

Once Millar and Baxter were alone, Baxter asked, 'What do you think?'

Millar used a remote to switch off the video wall that still had Malik's mugshot up on it. 'There's nothing about this that doesn't stink.'

'The Brits are leaving us holding the bag.'

Millar leaned back and sighed towards the ceiling. 'Sharp is right. It's win-win for them. They deny Malik, and now he's our mess. I've got to hand it to them. MI6 played this beautifully.'

'What else did Lloyd say?'

'They'll bury the Malik thing if we do too. Nobody wants this out there. Especially Goldcastle.'

'Surely they knew going into this there would be a few stumbles along the way.'

'Stumbles, Baxter. Not falls.'

'What about this Polish guy with the camera?' Millar asked. 'Korecki. Is he going to be a problem?'

'As your deputy legal advisor, I'd recommend all you know is that we're handling it.'

'And Novak?'

'He's got nothing.'

'I don't want to see a picture of Malik's face on the front page of *The Republic*.' Millar stood up and walked towards the door. 'If I do, it's your ass.'

15

Rebecca had been ploughing through ECHELON data for nearly seven hours, her share of the hundreds of thousands of text messages sent in the Westminster area in the hours leading up to the bombing. From somewhere across the office someone called out, 'Does anyone know the capital of Belarus?'

'Minsk,' Rebecca replied as fast as someone would answer "What's the capital of France?".

'Who do we go through for their intel? Romania?'

'KGB,' Rebecca said, her mind wandering to the DVD she'd hid in the drive of her personal laptop. 'Good luck with that,' she mumbled, having experienced the intractability of the Belarus security services in the past.

Mackintosh had returned from his briefing, and was in his office prepping for the evening rundown: GTE senior staff's summary of the day's activity.

Rebecca kept waiting to be summoned by Mackintosh and questioned about activity on his computer during his absence. But it appeared that she'd got away with it.

After hours of scrolling through lines of text – black words against a white background – Rebecca's vision held traces of the colours each time she looked away from the screen.

Sitting there, using technology that cost millions to create, using decades of research and development, she felt like she was back in her family home, lying on the floor with her puzzle book. Listening to her dad working in the next room. There was no other feeling than that brief moment of realisation, that the puzzle had been solved. Her joy lasted precisely as long as it took her to walk from the living room to her dad's study, and wait for his judgement on how hard the puzzle had been. He would say, 'Good.' Then he would turn the page and point to an even harder one.

There was always another puzzle.

About to turn away from the screen to give her eyes a rest, Rebecca noticed a text message that met her first criteria: semi-broken English.

Rebecca felt like someone trying to toss a coin and land on heads ten times in a row: the first heads is a good start. But there is so far to go it's hardly worth getting your hopes up.

Until she realised it met the second criteria too: a non sequitur.

Now she was cooking with gas.

Then criteria three: no reply to the text.

"*The sphinx looks to the right.*"

It was just what she was looking for. A textbook go code.

She edged forward in her chair, dialling into the FAIRVIEW system. It brought up the origin and selling point of every mobile phone number in the country. With a retailer's location Rebecca could pull up CCTV in shopping centres or on nearby streets, then run facial recognition software. In a matter of a few hours Rebecca could have a picture of at least one of the suspects. With a bit of luck one of the terror cell members, other than the bomber, made the purchase, then photos could be circulated, and foreign intelligence agencies consulted on who their suspects are.

'I've got it,' she said. She stared at the screen, almost disbelieving what she was seeing.

Matthew got slowly to his feet. 'Are you sure?'

Rebecca printed the mobile phone data and passed it to Matthew.

He read the message to himself.

Rebecca said, 'There's no reply and no context before it.'

He broke into a smile as he passed it back to Rebecca.

She shouted to Mackintosh. 'Alexander! I've cracked it!'

All across GTE heads suddenly bobbed up into view from behind computer screens, eager to find out what Rebecca had done this time.

Her body felt made of air as she took the data to Mackintosh who had now come out his office. Rebecca felt like she was running to her dad's study all those years ago. She passed him the ECHELON printout.

Mackintosh asked, 'What about the mobile?'

'It's a burner,' Rebecca answered. 'Bought from a newsagent in Stoke Newington eight days ago.'

He wouldn't allow himself even a smile yet. 'What about CCTV? Tell me there's something.'

Rebecca couldn't stop grinning. 'There are two HD cameras covering both sides of a pedestrian crossing over the road. I checked the map. The newsagent's in a cul-de-sac. Whoever bought the phone will be on at least one of those cameras.'

'Bloody hell.' He looked up and finally smiled. 'We've got it.'

As it approached two a.m., the GTE staff relented to their exhaustion after a sixteen-hour shift. They shuffled out slowly, yawning but buoyed by their success. The night team was now in, following up on Rebecca's CCTV leads.

Someone looked back at Rebecca still sitting herself. 'Shouldn't we tell her to call it a night?' she asked.

Someone answered, 'She's always here after midnight.'

Mackintosh and Matthew made their way out together.

'Don't stay too late,' Mackintosh told her. 'It's been a big day and I need you fresh tomorrow.'

'Yes, boss,' Rebecca said, saluting him with her pen.

She relaxed a little in her chair as she heard the main doors swoosh shut. Other than the "Action On" night team working in a separate block down the hall – monitoring GCHQ systems and worldwide news bulletins, twenty-four hours a day, to take immediate necessary action should the country come under sudden attack – Rebecca was left on her own. Now she was finally free to follow up her lead on the black Mercedes from the U.S. embassy.

With the car being diplomatic issue, the DVLA had nothing they could give Rebecca. She'd have to get a little creative.

She tapped into the National Data Centre's number plate recognition technology. Using over eight thousand cameras on British roads, the NDC captured nearly thirty million number plates every day, along with their time, date, and location.

Rebecca logged into the NDC, navigating to its tracking page. Under the vehicle tab, she entered 273D101 into the 'Registration plate' field. The window listed plenty to do with the car itself (manufacturer, model, date issued to U.S. embassy), but nothing about any human personnel related to the car.

She clicked instead to the 'Live tracking' tab. After a few seconds loading, a grid map of a small section of central London appeared. To the right was a list of cameras where the number plate had last been scanned. The locations of the cameras were scattered all around central London.

Then Rebecca saw the time stamp against the camera scans.

The journey began forty-two minutes ago on Upper Brook Street: the nearest main street to the U.S. embassy.

The last scan was only thirty minutes ago on Praed Street.

There were a number of places there that got Rebecca's attention. Namely, proximity to Paddington Station. But she could see from the listings that there were dozens of cameras closer to drop-off points for the station that would have picked the car up.

The Moroccan consulate on Praed Street was a possibility, but that didn't feel quite right to Rebecca. No extradition treaty with the U.K., and no pedigree in intelligence.

She clicked into maps and zoomed in on the street, dragging across, looking for landmarks. That's when she saw it: The Frontline Club on Norfolk Place – *the* media hotspot in London for journalists of the crusading variety, with an emphasis on international affairs.

Have they broken the password on Abbie's laptop, and now they're going to leak the files? Rebecca wondered.

She clicked on 'Update user' then ticked 'Live remote monitoring updates'. Now any time the Mercedes was snapped on registration plate recognition, the details would be sent to Rebecca's computer.

Before she logged off, she had a thought.

As the diplomatic car had a 'D' plate for diplomatic staff (and legal immunity), Rebecca wouldn't have access to a list of U.S. embassy personnel. Unless she wanted to hack the embassy. Which might have been possible, but would leave a trace.

She clicked back to the search menu. Under 'Date' she selected 'All', bringing up every log of the car. Rebecca scanned down the extensive list to find recurring camera locations. The one that came up most was a turnoff for Holland Villas Road – a quick check on the map showed what looked like an extremely expensive street of Georgian villas, with security cameras mounted on iron gates on most of the driveways.

The traffic camera scan was every weekday morning between half seven and quarter to eight, then again at seven or eight at night.

Holland Villas Road had two streets on either side, both with busy crossroads on them. And cameras at each. But the embassy car had never been scanned there. Which meant the car could only have been travelling down one road all of those times: Holland Villas Road.

For the first time that day Rebecca smiled.

The cameras had given her the vehicle and workplace of whoever took Abbie's laptop from Moreton House. Now she knew where they lived.

10 Downing Street, London – Monday, 11.11pm

Technically, now that Angela Curtis had formally announced her premiership to the country, Sonia Ali had no claim to Downing Street, or any other official residence of the Prime Minister. But Curtis had insisted that Sonia and the children be taken to Chequers, where the Ali family could grieve in peace for as long as they needed.

Curtis stood in the bedroom doorway with her laptop under her arm, taking in the scene. It was all so suburban and normal. Although an aide had quickly packed a bag for Sonia – once the building had been deemed safe – the sudden end to the Ali tenure meant that upon entering the Prime Minister's bedroom it was still filled with the Alis' personal belongings. Framed photos sat out in the dresser; the duvet only half-made; discarded makeup wipes and lipstick-marked tissue paper still on Sonia's dresser; a tie Simon had changed out of at the last minute was still strewn across the bed. Curtis couldn't bring herself to touch any of it.

She moved through to the study instead. Like the

bedroom, it was situated at the rear of Number Ten facing the garden, and had been shielded from the blast. Some of the secretaries' rooms, Junior Lords' room and upper offices were out of bounds, their windows blown through. The iconic front façade would need extensive repairs.

Curtis opened her laptop on the desk. Bizarre as it was, she felt like she'd missed all the news. She'd been given every fact the authorities had on the bombing – type of explosives used, the casualties, other possible threats – but had been sheltered from bigger picture things like the mood of the nation.

She cruised the news websites to get a sense of how it was all playing. Under photos from Downing Street, editors had mostly used the same photo of Curtis from her press conference: her expression defiant, hand raised like a swinging sword. She had to admit to herself: she looked like a Prime Minister. The press seemed to be of the opinion that she sounded like one too.

She didn't even feel guilty about her trick with Harrington's Dictaphone. Come the time, he'd be rewarded with the first sit-down interview with Britain's new Prime Minister. More often than not, the press was the enemy. But sometimes they were crucial allies.

The early coverage was glowing, both for the party, Parliament as a whole, and for Bannatyne and Hawkes, both trumpeted as having put country first.

But deeper down in comment sections, and on Twitter, one question was gaining traction. What was Simon Ali about to confess to? In the immediate aftermath, it had naturally been forgotten about. Curtis knew that it wouldn't stay that way, though.

Twitter – as she expected – was rife with speculation under the *#AliConfession* hashtag: he'd had an affair; he'd swindled his finances; he was leaving Islam; he was going to swap parties at the next election... It was endless. All of them faintly ludicrous. Curtis couldn't help but wonder which of them might be true.

As she crossed her legs under the desk, she felt her thigh brush something loose, then tumble down against her leg. There was an envelope lying on top of her foot. The front of it said, "To my successor."

Curtis knew the author before she even opened it. She had seen plenty of documents with his handwriting over the years.

It was unmistakably Simon Ali's.

It began, *"If you're reading this, then you have won the general election. Congratulations.*

"After my confession I assume the backlash against the PM following me will be substantial. I'm sure I've made an already hard job harder still. For that, I apologise. You do, however, have an opportunity now. To make a clean break with the past.

"God only knows where I've ended up by the time you read this. Disgraced? Without question. In jail? Possibly. Dead? More than likely."

A chill ran up Curtis's spine.

"Should anything happen to me, there are a few things you should know. Firstly: do not trust Nigel Hawkes, regardless of your party. I'm sure my speech will have finished him off, but I don't want to take any chances.

"And secondly: if anyone from Goldcastle ever contacts you: JUST SAY NO. They'll be the death of you.

"Sincerely, Simon Hussein Ali."

Curtis couldn't move.

The letter made it sound that even the darkest theory on the internet about what he'd done wasn't even close to the reality.

As Curtis's imagination started running away from her, a knock on the study door took her by surprise. She quickly turned the letter over.

Milton stood at the door, slightly out of breath. 'Sorry, Prime Minister,' he said. 'I thought you should see these. GCHQ has found a mobile linked to the bomber.' He brought over a large photo emailed from Cheltenham two minutes earlier. 'They managed to get this picture.'

It was a high-resolution image of two suspects, one of them carrying a newly bought pay-as-you-go mobile.

'Have they ID'd them yet?' Curtis asked.

'MI5 think they might have names for you within the hour,' Milton replied.

Curtis stared at the photo in wonder. 'How on earth did they find this?'

Milton threw his hands up. 'They're GCHQ.'

'Do me a favour. Find out who it was. I want to tell them well done.'

'Of course. Also, housekeeping are about to clear out the bedroom for you—'

'No, really,' Curtis said, 'I can just go home.'

'Prime Minister, you can't go home. We need to keep you somewhere...' He trailed off, knowing what she'd say.

'Safe?'

'Yes, well... We can't have the Prime Minister getting hounded by photographers leaving a semi-detached in Shepherd's Bush every morning. We'll leave that to the leader of the opposition.' He'd been with Curtis long enough to know when something was on her mind. Something beyond the immediately obvious. Something he didn't know about. 'Let's just get the country through this. Tomorrow's papers have all been very generous.'

Curtis nodded absently. 'What's all this Dan Leckie stuff I got at the press conference?'

'He's trying to make some noise on his comeback tour.'

'We're sure this Tempest thing is a dead end?'

'Sir Lloyd Willow assures me MI6 have it under control.'

Curtis nodded at him. 'Good job today, Roger. Go home and give your kids a hug. There's a lot of parents not coming home tonight.'

'I will. Thank you, Prime Minister.'

Before he could leave, Curtis said, 'Actually. One other thing. What do you know about Goldcastle?'

'The consultancy? Not much. I heard they did a sterling job for Simon Ali. They're an American outfit though. I can get a memo together in half an hour?'

Curtis waved it off. 'No. It's nothing. Go home.'

'Goodnight, Prime Minister.' Milton left.

That morning, Curtis had left her small flat off Portobello Road, her career grinding to a halt. Now she'd been thrust into a role she'd thought had long since passed her by. Yet there were conflicting feelings of guilt and horror about the atrocity that had put her in her new position, and the astonishing opportunity she now had. It was hard to go to bed not thinking about the polls. By morning she might be as high as 90% approval.

Left alone in the study, it all hit Curtis at once. She knew her history: she'd replaced the first British Prime Minister to be assassinated in office since Spencer Percival in 1812; GCHQ had a mole working in league with a terrorist cell; an MI6 spy had died in CIA custody; another had died in dubious circumstances across the city; and she had to deal with it all herself.

10 Downing Street was a lonely place to occupy without a spouse or partner.

Curtis took a cigarette lighter from her bag and picked up Ali's letter. Even without the rest of the speech, if the letter got out it could cripple the party. Maybe it was the thought of her polling numbers and the upcoming election, but something told her to hang on. That the letter might be valuable at some point. Particularly with its mention of Ali's acrimony towards Hawkes.

She tucked the letter away inside her personal Westminster diary, then called Milton.

He hadn't yet made it out the back exit of Downing Street. 'Yes, Prime Minister?'

'Sorry, Roger,' she said. 'I need you to find some information for me.'

'Of course,' he replied.

Curtis paused. 'Get me everything you can on Abbie Bishop.'

'Of course.'

'And Roger. Do it quietly.'

16

Novak sat on the end of the bed in his ground floor room of the squalid Mayfair Motel just off I-78 Express. His concerns about the cleanliness of the place would have to be put aside for at least one night.

After grabbing his go bag, Novak changed taxis three times on his way to New Jersey. He developed a crick in his neck from looking over his shoulder most of the way from Manhattan.

The Republic had used the Mayfair in the past as a secret interview spot for sources, politicians, and even the odd Hollywood celebrity. Chang had sent Novak off with instructions to email him every two hours, or he would send over a private security officer to check on him. No one else in the office – except for Stella – was to know what was going on.

There was one knock then two fast knocks on the door – a previously agreed pattern. Novak kept himself half-shielded behind his door as he answered. 'I thought you already left for London,' he said.

Stella barged past in a soaking wet brown mac, carrying a bag from a nearby Seven Eleven. 'I got them to bounce me to a later flight.' She put half a Twinkie in her mouth as she spoke. 'I've got doughnuts, beef jerky, and potato chips.'

'So no actual *food*, then?' Novak asked.

She finished off her Twinkie while she shuffled off her mac, shaking the rain off it. 'There were more Twinkies in the bag when I left the store. Sorry about that.'

Novak stayed standing, ignoring the food.

Stella went to the bathroom, then emerged with a towel wrapped like a turban around her head. She sat down on the bed. 'In the taxi on the way over "Jungleland" by Bruce Springsteen came on the radio. Is that the best saxophone solo you've ever heard or what? I'm not normally a saxophone kind of gal, but phew!'

Novak knew she was trying to take his mind off things, but it wasn't working. He paced slowly across the room.

She took out a DVD case from her handbag and held it out. 'Kurt managed to extract the video.'

'That dude's a genius.' Novak took the DVD to the player under the TV.

Stella unravelled the towel and hand-dried her hair. She had a wide, cheeky grin on her face – from knowing something Novak didn't.

'What's on it?' he asked, waiting on the disc loading.

From under the towel, Stella answered, 'You know how you stopped getting emails a day ago? Kurt thinks the video is the reason.'

'What?'

'He said it was hidden away in some obscure temp file made by the virus. Like someone's been looking after the video.' Stella looked around in vain for somewhere to put her wet towel, then tossed it onto the bed. 'Kurt thinks the hacker's actually been trying to protect you. Monitoring your incoming traffic. They hid the video away to stop whoever's after you from seeing it.'

Novak asked, 'But if the hacker's worried about my safety why not just delete the damn video?'

'Trust me. You're going to be glad he didn't.'

Novak pressed play.

The video started off shakily, with stray strands of long grass blowing in front of the camera, as if from a hiding spot. The camera trained on a small white Gulfstream jet, taxiing to the end of the runway. Artur zoomed in on the tail number, N511GA, whispering narration in English as he filmed. 'Okay, guys. As you can see the plane is now stopped, and hopefully we'll get a shot of something, or someone, from inside in a minute.'

As the stairs unfurled from the side of the plane, four men in combat gear took a man in an orange jumpsuit – hooded and shackled – down the stairs.

'Is this what I think it is?' Novak asked, his body rigid with anticipation.

Stella shushed him. 'Wait.'

Once the plane's engines stopped whirring, Artur halted his narration. He zoomed in on the shackled man, who stopped halfway down the steps, raising his head as if gulping for air through his black hood. One of the four handlers seemed to understand the man was struggling, and reached for his hood, but another put a hand on his forearm to stop him.

'Wait for it,' Stella said.

After some discussion the handler took the prisoner's hood off for a moment. The shackled man turned his head to the sky, taking in as much air as he could. He squinted as the stair-case lights beamed up at him, giving Artur a perfect shot of the prisoner's face.

The prisoner looked in his mid-thirties, with oddly short hair for a supposed radical. Light stubble, no beard. And a vague Middle Eastern look that could have placed him in any of a dozen nationalities.

At the top of the stairs, a middle-aged man in a navy suit and dark tie, was on the phone. He held his wrist up to his mouth, talking into his radio. In a swift flurry the prisoner's hood was thrown back on, and he was hustled into the back of the Mercedes. The livery on the side said, "*Stare Kiejkuty*".

'What language is that written in?' Novak asked, squinting.

Stella said, 'Polish. It's a restricted military facility. A suspected CIA black site since two thousand and five.'

In the video, five more agents came charging down the stairs, weapons now drawn and fanning out towards the perimeter fence. Artur's camera shook, then began the nauseating judder of him running with the camera pointed at the ground. Somewhere behind him were American voices shouting at him to stop. The clip ended with Artur desperately panting for air as he ran.

Then it cut to black.

Novak kept staring at the screen. It was several seconds before he moved, backing away from the TV.

'How do you know this guy?' Stella asked.

'He's just a young Polish guy. He would email me links to his YouTube page, and ask for interviews with me. Shit about secret governments controlling the world and UFO sightings. He kept saying I was the reason he wanted to become a journalist, so one time I wrote back and wished him well. It was harmless, I didn't want to shut the guy down.' Novak shrugged. 'He just seemed lonely. I hadn't heard from him in a few months.'

Stella took out her mobile. 'We have to take this to Diane.'

Novak replied sharply, 'We can't take this to Diane.'

'Why not?'

'What do we have? We don't know who that prisoner is, who owns that plane, where it is now, what's going on – nothing."

Stella said, 'You're telling me that's not video of a CIA rendition flight?'

'I'm telling you what we have that's a printable story. Diane Schlesinger will never go to press with this. She had twenty years at *The New York Times*: it's on the record and it's double-sourced. We don't have half that.'

'But if we find Artur, that's one source. And you're meeting your CIA guy tomorrow.'

Novak said, 'A veteran CIA agent, go on the record over this? You're dreaming. Our *story* – the one our editor's given us – is the Downing Street attack. Artur Korecki will already have disappeared into the same rendition program he uncovered. The CIA's going to lock this guy up for the next twenty years.'

'I don't know,' Stella said. 'It looked to me like he had a pretty good head start. Plus, he knew that terrain. He would have been the only one knowing where he was going.'

'It's possible,' Novak conceded. '*Maybe.*'

Stella laughed in frustration. 'Novak, I wanted to work for *The Republic* because I thought they had the bravest reporters. Diane *headhunted* me. I told her I would come on one condition: that I get to work a story with you. I wanted to see what the guy who broke the NSA papers was made of.'

'Then you should have looked elsewhere,' said Novak, stepping away from her.

'What do you mean?'

'It's time for me to move on.'

She sighed in disgust. 'Bastion?'

He said, 'Yeah.'

'I thought that was just contract negotiation bullshit. To drive your price up.'

Novak laughed desperately. 'There's no money, Stella! Henry's remortgaging houses. He'll be selling office furniture in six months just to keep a working phone line up.'

The news hit Stella like she'd walked out in front of a bus. 'Then why the hell did Diane take me on?'

Novak scoffed. 'Because they really need you. And they *really* don't need me.'

'Are you crazy?' said Stella. 'In the last year you were responsible for the most popular issue of *The Republic* ever printed. You kick-started a debate on privacy and social media that no one wanted to have before. You raised the profile of the magazine, and made it more money than ever before. Where's it all gone?'

Novak replied, 'The magazine's been running a loss since Henry started it. The money the NSA story made has barely made a dent in the accounts. What little *has* been made has gone straight back into my legal case, fighting a story that can't stand up.'

Stella had heard plenty of downbeat statements from Novak since she arrived in New York, but this was of an entirely different order. 'Why can't it stand up?'

Novak flashed her a knowing look. 'Please. I saw the rings you made around the NSA papers issue.'

'That was just—'

'No, it wasn't just *grammar*, Stella! I saw what you wrote. Inconsistencies. Doubts about my source.'

'I was thinking out loud. You know what it's like when you vet someone else's source: you pick at loose threads. And you pull on them until they give.'

'That's for someone's reporting,' Novak said. 'You did the same to my hearing testimony.'

Stella couldn't think of anything to say.

'I saw it,' Novak admitted. 'You did a good job hiding it under an old issue but I saw it. You printed a copy of my congressional testimony that morning. Ask me the question you wrote in the margin.'

It took Stella a moment to gather her nerve. 'Did you lie about how the NSA papers were leaked to you?'

Novak nodded, then said, 'Yes. I lied.'

In the moment, he felt the weight of a year-long lie leave his shoulders.

Stella was almost afraid to ask. Actually hearing him admit it was more shocking than she'd imagined. 'How did it go down?' she asked.

Novak stared into his hands. 'I was a junior reporter that had been handed a job at *The Republic* because Diane Schlesinger used to work with my dad. I made some decent stories in my twenties, won some minor awards, but no one who mattered knew my name. I came to Washington and I was nobody, working the most boring process stories. Every day, I was a glorified stenographer. Then one day there was an NSA briefing, and when the press room cleared I found a memory stick on the floor. I sat there for ten minutes on my own waiting for someone to come back for it. While I was waiting, I plugged it into my laptop, and I realised the biggest story of the decade had fallen out of the sky.'

Playing devil's advocate, Stella asked, 'What if someone accidentally dropped it, then once *Republic* printed the documents they were too scared to come forward?'

Novak replied, 'The first file on the drive was a "README" with instructions about how to read the files securely.'

'What about the pull quotes you used in the story about the leaker's intentions?'

Novak was clear-eyed and telling the truth. 'Everything after that was as I described. The memory stick had a tracker, and I was later contacted by the source. That was it.'

'Why the hell did you lie?'

'Whoever left the stick there, left it for someone random. I didn't intercept anything. I didn't think...'

'Didn't think what?'

'I didn't think I'd get as much credit if everyone knew it was luck. So, I came up with a cover story. Then I took it to

Mark, who showed it to Diane. Six months later I was on the cover of *Time*.'

Stella shook her head, trying to clear it. 'I think your lawyer is going to be earning that retainer pretty soon.'

'Why's that?'

'Let me put this the way a government prosecutor will: Mr Novak, if there are two memory sticks sitting on the ground in front of you, one of which has been dropped purposely, the other by accident: how can you tell which is which?'

Novak bristled at the point. 'Stella, it was right in the middle of the room. No NSA personnel walked through the media gallery, and would never have been assigned seating amongst–'

'To professional reporters like you and I, yes, that's obvious. But to anyone else, the prosecutor's introduced doubt: has Tom Novak published classified material without the aid of a whistleblower?'

Novak asked, 'Do you really think that's a distinction the public cares about?'

Stella retorted, 'It's a distinction the federal government cares about. Without that material coming directly from an NSA or Pentagon whistleblower, the leaking of the intelligence is on *you*. And there aren't any legal protections for that. That's why the government prosecutes whistleblowers and not reporters.' She then added, 'Normally.'

Feeling dire about his position, Novak tried to change tack. 'Stella, that story could have landed in the laps of fifty other reporters much more talented than I am. So yeah, I'm going to Bastion because I'm not what everyone thinks I am. I'm not a journalist. I'm just trying to earn a living.' The weight of this admission seemed to have taken something out of Novak. He sat down on the end of the bed, exhausted by it all.

If he was expecting praise for his admission, he couldn't have been more wrong.

Stella said, 'That's bollocks, Novak. You know your problem? You want to be like your father: popular, inoffensive, and wealthy.'

'There are worse things to be in life, Stella.'

She stood in front of him, leaning on her knees to stay in his face. She wanted him to look right into her eyes. 'I read those *Republic* articles you wrote before the NSA papers. On conflict diamonds; embedded in Fallujah; lobbying in Washington... The guy who wrote those, I'd walk into fire with. Because that guy knew exactly what he was doing.'

Novak looked away. 'I think you're easily impressed.'

Stella said, 'I think my last four boyfriends would agree with you. But look at all the shit you shovelled at the NSA. For months on end. What did they ever do?'

'Well,' Novak said, 'they're forcing me to give up my source – who I clearly don't know – and if I don't the U.S. government's going to send me to jail.'

Stella wasn't swayed. 'That's long after the story got out, to send a message to other leakers, not reporters. You could do *Dateline*, *Fox and Friends*, and *Larry King* one after the other and go home afterwards without having to switch cabs. Artur Korecki sends you one video from a field in Poland, and suddenly you're hiding out here like Frank Pentangeli?' Stella made her way to the mini-bar, and took out two vodkas. Both for herself. She didn't bother with a glass. 'Nathan Rosenblatt just wants to hurt Diane and *The Republic* by taking you away.'

'Do you think I don't know that!' Novak snapped. 'Do you think I've not been around long enough to know I'm being played? But I've got to go somewhere with a future for me.'

Stella opened one of the vodka miniatures and necked it. 'Well, when you realise we're onto something a little more important than your career, let me know. I'll be over on this side of the room, drinking. A lot.'

Novak turned back to the TV, and started Artur's video over.

17

With the sort of day she'd had, Rebecca should have been wiped out, longing for her bed. Instead, she charged into her flat, heading straight for her computer, resolved to an all-nighter.

The DVD with Mackintosh's files was booting up by the time she realised she was still wearing her coat, standing over the keyboard. All the letter keys were faded, but the space bar and Ctrl buttons (most-used by programmers) were especially worn, like the spot where a drumstick has repeatedly landed on a snare. She threw her coat off, dropping it straight to the floor, then sat in front of the screen. Little did she know that everything she thought she knew about Abbie Bishop was about to be turned upside down.

She started with the now-decrypted files Abbie sent her. It soon became clear that Abbie hadn't been lying when she wrote to Rebecca that she might not like what she found out about her. The facts were undeniable. Abbie's entire GCHQ history was laid out on the screen.

Abbie had joined GCHQ in 2007 – only a year before Rebecca, but in that year Abbie had seemingly made about five years of progress, and had already been granted STRAP

Three clearance after her first six months. It was unheard of. It had taken Rebecca – who had been the very picture of a model recruit – three years to advance to that level. Someone, somewhere high up in GCHQ or in the government, had been pulling strings for Abbie almost as soon as she had arrived. Fast forward to 2009 and things got murkier.

Abbie had left a digital trail to a bank account in her name, into which exactly £5000 was deposited every month for the last nine months. Now the account was flush with £45,000. Not bad for a civil servant.

In Rebecca's eyes it had all the hallmarks of a slush fund – or some kind of bribery, maybe even blackmail – except Abbie hadn't touched a penny of it. No withdrawals, and no other deposits. There had been some inventive accounting going on, but Abbie had circled all the linked accounts that traced the cash going into her account from 'The Goldcastle Group'.

Rebecca searched online for the name, finding a slick-looking website for a political consultancy firm. Its homepage boasted the logos of mostly American political campaigns: the current U.S. President's, Secretary Robert Snow's. It also, surprisingly to Rebecca, had the logo of Simon Ali's General Election "Britain First" campaign. The Party had kept that one quiet.

"Data is what we do" said the website banner. Below it, various blocks of text with sharp graphics announced: "We know how to find voters, and make them yours. We are a global leader in political consulting, with a unique focus on voter data. We have supported over one hundred campaigns in twenty different countries. Our speciality is in the United States, where we played a pivotal role in Presidential, state, and congressional elections."

Rebecca didn't understand why Abbie would have been receiving money from such a source. Whatever the reason, Abbie had kept it secret for a long time.

Rebecca kept searching and found a document that

appeared to be exactly what she needed: 'Operation Tempest – STRAP Three eyes only.'

A file explaining exactly what Tempest was and who was involved.

She clicked to open it, but her heart quickly sank.

A window opened in the centre of the screen: 'PLEASE ENTER THE DECRYPTION KEY THEN CLICK OK.'

Of course, Rebecca thought. Abbie told her she had encrypted the most important files and left the key on her laptop.

The key was 128 characters long.

Knowing how impossible it would be to break the key without Abbie's laptop, Rebecca moved on to Mackintosh's files.

When she'd copied the files from Mackintosh's computer, it had copied all the root data associated with the files too. It only took two minutes for her OPEN WINDOW program to scan for the most frequently used phrases associated with certain documents that had been password-protected.

Mackintosh may have been in GCHQ, but even he wasn't above one of the cardinal sins of digital protection: using the same password for multiple items. He'd grown lazy with the wealth of documents in his possession, and assumed he had little to fear from internal security breaches.

Rebecca did 'Select all' on the files, had OPEN WINDOW assign the same password to every file, and sure enough every one of them unlocked.

Now she could do keyword searches on everything inside the files. Names, places, dates. She had it all.

She looked first for 'STRAP Three'. It wasn't pertinent to exposing whatever Mackintosh might be up to. She just wanted to see what she was dealing with.

Her excitement quickly turned to trepidation at the words at the top of the first file:

Top Secret STRAP Three document.

'Okay...' she said through a long exhalation, knowing the gravity of what she was looking at.

Even the different font it was written in compared to STRAP Twos set Rebecca's fingers tingling.

There were memos inside from the Prime Ministers' personal secretaries; minutes from Cabinet briefings, with follow-up emails from Secretaries of State, all swearing and bickering with each other; personal opinions on foreign heads of state; and transcripts of personal phone calls.

Browsing through the other files it became clear that Mackintosh had access to the sort of material that would leave a newspaper editor salivating. On a few pages Rebecca saw mentions of incidents that would have been front-page news for at least a week, and another that would have been worthy of a prominent MP's resignation.

Rebecca took a moment to gather herself. There wasn't time to screw around and get seduced by gossip.

She needed to find any material on Abbie.

There was nothing immediately obvious. The first thing to come up when searching 'ABIGAIL BISHOP' was a dossier on a young MI6 agent called George Abassi.

None of the material was redacted and had 'Highly Classified' digital watermarks on every page. There were British army generals who weren't authorised to read the dossier, let alone Rebecca.

The agent's picture showed a young, light-skinned British Asian. The eyes were wide yet blank, giving nothing away. He looked neither cruel, nor gentle. There was no smile. His DOB gave his age as thirty. Under his real name, it listed various aliases the agent had used throughout his missions. The last of which was Abdul al-Malik.

Skipping to the end of his bio, it was noted that Abassi was 'KIA 7th December 2018 during Operation Tempest.'

Killed in action.

She drummed her fingers on the tabletop. 'Only on Sunday night. Tempest again...'

Wondering why the file had been caught in a search for Abbie, Rebecca was about to click away, when she saw a single line at the bottom of Malik's profile:

'AGENT CONTACT: Abigail Bishop.'

She had been secretly running an MI6 agent for more than a year.

On a hunch, Rebecca tracked down the same encrypted Operation Tempest file Abbie had sent, but Mackintosh's version required a key as well. She thought it telling that for all the indiscreet, politicised, and highly sensitive material on his hard drive, the only encrypted files all related to Tempest.

If anything, it made her even more determined to press on.

Rebecca sorted the list to 'Date modified', then most recent at the top.

The first was a template document for creating an ID card. Namely from the U.K. Press Card Authority. In the top-right corner was a BBC logo. The name was, 'RIZ RIZZAQ – TV CAMERA OPERATOR'. The only thing missing was the accompanying photo.

Although the BBC had their own ID cards for clearance on BBC property, when attending outside events with any kind of police cordon or secure entrance, the police only accepted valid U.K. Press Card Authority passes. It was the media's equivalent of a driving licence. And it had just as many security features: various holograms, raised lettering, raised tactile pattern, Optical Variable Ink feature which changed the colour of the UKPCA logo from blue to gold when the card was tilted, and a ten-digit alphanumeric code. In short, they were completely impossible to counterfeit. The cards were produced by the same manufacturer that made U.K. driving licences and credit cards, all made on secure units that were protected like prisons. The cards were made from a central database, supplied by certain 'gatekeepers' of the industry: BBC, Sky, the NUJ, ITN among others.

Rebecca knew that she was looking at no fake. It was the root document for a new U.K. press pass, which could only have come from one place.

Mackintosh had hacked the card manufacturer's database.

A quick Google of Rizzaq brought up numerous reports on his murder, blamed on a home invasion.

Rebecca said to herself, 'Why would Mackintosh have the root document of Rizzaq's press pass?'

When she searched Mackintosh's files for 'RIZ RIZZAQ', she got her answer. There was a PDF among the files called 'Press ID final draft'.

As soon as she opened it, Rebecca's stomach flipped. The pass had Rizzaq's name on it, but it now had a photo added. Not of Rizzaq's kind face, and soft eyes, but of the slightly steeled, hollow expression of Abdullah Hassan Mufaza.

For a moment, all Rebecca could do was sit and stare at the screen, her mouth covered by a slightly trembling hand.

This can't be right, she thought. She pushed her chair back, and walked circles in her living room, trying to unwind and disassemble any possible reason for Mackintosh to be in possession of such a document.

Was it a theoretical what-if to demonstrate how Downing Street security could have been breached? Or perhaps Mackintosh had mandated a red team hack (where GCHQ operatives try to hack the very systems they've made) to prove the UKPCA was vulnerable to outside hacking?

There was only one thing that could maintain Mackintosh's innocence: the date the file was created.

If the file had been created after the Downing Street attack, then it was conceivable Mackintosh had just been experimenting with some graphics – perhaps to see how easily a terror cell might have made a forgery. But the ID was in a unique GCHQ file format called a RIG, which were totally impenetrable. Any attempt to edit them would be as convincing as changing the name on someone's passport by cutting out letters from a newspaper.

Even though Abbie's final email to Rebecca had warned her Mackintosh couldn't be trusted, it was a stretch for Rebecca to accept any notion she'd been working for years with someone capable of colluding with the sort of people who had attacked Downing Street.

She returned to the computer. Then, with half-averted eyes, she right-clicked the file and selected Properties. When she saw the date, she whispered, 'Mack. What the hell have you done?'

On the screen, the tab said, 'File created 1/12/18. File last modified 1/12/18.'

Two weeks before the Downing Street attack.

18

Stella was asleep on the bed with two mini-bar empties by her side. After a twenty-hour day, that was all it had taken to finally wipe her out. She was on her side, tucked in a corner of the double bed, her back to Novak.

He was sitting with the clean laptop Kurt had given him. The email from Nathan Rosenblatt was up on the screen, and had been for some time now.

Novak had muted the TV and put in subtitles for CNN, so Stella could catch some much-needed sleep before her red-eye flight to London.

The Washington correspondent on Capitol Hill stood in the shadow of Congress – the American flags on top at half-mast. '...what I've been hearing throughout today from various White House sources is that the President thinks the Downing Street attack warrants, quote, strong consideration for fast-tracking the new Freedom and Privacy Act, which is now being touted by Republicans on the Hill as the Patriot Act for the post-NSA papers era.'

The alarm on Stella's phone went off. Still face-down on the pillow, she patted around the bed hoping to find the phone without having to lift her head.

Seeing her struggle, Novak turned the alarm off for her.

Stella groaned as she sat up. 'Is that safe?' she asked. 'Being online?'

Novak replied, 'Kurt put a Tails operating system on the memory stick. It bounces my internet connection here from one server to another, all over the world. Nothing gets in, and nothing gets out. It would take weeks to unravel the connections. It would be like trying to unknit a sweater the size of Nebraska.'

A beep came from the laptop.

When Stella got up out of bed, she saw Rosenblatt's email on Novak's screen.

A notification window had popped up at the bottom right of the screen.

"You have one new OTR message."

OTR (off-the-record) was an encryption program that allowed secure communication online. For journalists who needed to contact high-value sources without NSA tracking, it was essential. It was like instant messenger, except it kept no record of messages, and as soon as one message appeared the previous one deleted itself. And not in the still-leaving-a-trace-behind sense. The OTR server had no facility for recording data. If you didn't read it with your own eyes, it was gone forever.

Elated, Novak said, 'It's him!'

'Who?' Stella asked.

He signed in to OTR as fast as he could, then clicked on the waiting message. '*Him.*'

Stella said, 'Okay, I still have no new information since my last question.'

He showed her the message waiting for him:

Artur.K: Trust no one.

Novak said, 'In OTR you can set security questions. Mine to Artur was what do you always end your emails with?' Novak beamed. 'He's alive!'

Stella put on her glasses and checked her watch. 'Bugger. My flight is in ninety minutes.' She ran to the bathroom whilst brushing her hair. 'What's he saying?' she shouted.

Artur.K: You have to help me.

Novak typed out a reply. 'He says he needs help,' he shouted back.

Tom.Novak: It's OK, Artur. I got your video. Where are you? Are you safe?

Stella threw cold water on her face while barking instructions. 'Tell him you want to meet. But don't call it an interview. It'll freak him out.'

'Thanks, Stella,' Novak mumbled. 'I've only been doing this fifteen years.'

Artur.K: I'm fine.

Novak sighed in relief.

Tom.Novak: thank god.

Artur.K: But Artur is in trouble.

Novak's stomach lurched. 'Shit...'

Stella had the tap running and couldn't hear him.

Tom.Novak: Where's Artur? Who are you?

Artur.K: Please help me.

Novak called back to her, 'Stella.'

She could tell the weak way he said her name that something was wrong. She stood in the bathroom doorway, drying her face with a towel. 'What is it?'

'It's not Artur.'

'What?' Stella marched to the laptop, grabbing the screen and pulling it towards her. 'How can it not be him?'

Novak took the laptop back.

Tom.Novak: Who are you?

Artur.K: My name is Wally Bartczuk. I am Artur best friend.

Tom.Novak: How did you sign in here and know his security question?

Artur.K: He give me passkey and security answer before. In case something happen.

Tom.Novak: What was he doing at the airport?

Artur.K: I am night watchman at Szymany military airport. I tell Artur about recent arrivals. American crew. Passengers taken to Stare Kiejkuty.

Tom.Novak: The CIA black site?

Noticing the leading question, Stella warned him, 'Tom. You know you can't use that if he confirms.'

Novak said, 'I'm not looking for confirmation, Stella. I just need to know what he knows.'

Artur.K: That is what they say here. The Polish Biuro help the Americans. They tell us what to do. To delete flight logs keep no records say nothing. They pay me 500 zlotys every time plane comes in. Last Sunday night I tell Artur another plane is coming. He want to film for his youtube channel TruthArmy. The plane land and I do not see him again. Police come to his house arrest his mother and give wanted for Artur. But he not home. His mother tell me Artur come home but ran off before police catch him. I have not seen or heard him since Sunday night.

'Jesus,' Novak said. He looked at Stella, sensing they now had a real story. 'He's still on the run. We could still find him.'

Tom.Novak: Do you have any idea where he might be Wally? Where he might go? Maybe a friend's house? Or a relative.

Artur.K: Artur do not have other friends.

Stella was running around frantically for the rest of her things. 'Ask him how he knew to contact you.'

Tom.Novak: How did you know to contact me?

Artur.K: The Biuro take me in for questioning. Ask me who is Tom Novak. They ask me many times. I must know Tom Novak. Where is he? I tell them I do not know because it is truth! They say Artur email you Sunday night. When they let me go I find your name in Artur OTR contacts.

Stella said, 'If he doesn't know where Artur is or where he might go then he's useless to us.'

Novak was taken aback at Stella's ruthlessness. Her old London politics were still alive and well. That system of ditching anything and everyone who can't help your story.

'I can't just wish him good luck, then sign off,' Novak said.

'You're going to have to,' Stella replied, balancing on one foot at a time as she put on her shoes.

Artur.K: I am scared.

Tom.Novak: It's going to be ok Wally. Don't tell anyone about this.

Artur.K: I do not have family. Parents gone. Artur is my only friend.

Tom.Novak: I'm going to find Artur. don't worry

Artur.K: How much trouble am I in?

Tom.Novak: Keep your head down. Talk to no one. You haven't done anything wrong.

Stella stood in the door, holding her carry-on luggage aloft. 'I have to go,' she said in apology.

'Hang on,' Novak said, raising a forefinger.

Tom.Novak: I'll talk to you again soon. Use Artur's log in so I know it's you.

Artur.K: I will. Thank you my friend.

When Wally signed out Novak shut his laptop. The exchange had clearly got to him. On top of everything else, he now had another stranger in Poland on his conscience.

Stella raised her arms, frustrated at the situation. She said, 'I'm sorry, but I have to go. And you're going to have to decide whose team you're on, Novak.'

'Yeah, I know,' he said.

She gave him a quick hug – one armed, in half-profile. As she opened the door she recoiled from the pouring rain.

Outside the bar across the street, a fistfight had spilled out onto the road, halting the oncoming traffic. She looked back at Novak as she raised her coat collar, speaking above the car horns. 'Jungleland,' she said.

Novak smiled.

'Best sax solo ever,' she called out. And with that, she was gone, running across the flooded parking lot.

Once she was in a cab, Novak closed the door. He looked around the empty room. A faint trail of Stella's perfume was still in the air.

He sat on his bed, turning things over in his head. He had never felt like such a fraud. He'd been up to his neck on stories in the past. Namely the NSA papers, but that was all on him. Only Novak had dealt with the source, no one else. Now he had Stella, Artur, Wally, Chang, Diane, and Henry all relying on him – to protect them, to build their careers, to write a story, or just to help them stay alive.

It was all too much. He hadn't asked for any of this, and he resented the hell out of it.

He pulled up his email from Rosenblatt. He could taste the money, imagine the opportunities, feel the freedom. The offer was right there. He couldn't work out what was stopping him.

Whenever anyone asked Rosenblatt why he called his media company Bastion, he told them it was because he thought of himself as a man who maintained principles of freedom and liberty from big government. But there was also a part of him that liked the idea of having a news site named after a way of being able to better attack your enemies. As far as he was concerned, he was at war with the mainstream media. That was why he wanted Novak. Deep down, Novak knew Rosenblatt didn't want him. Rosenblatt just didn't want Diane to have Novak.

Then Novak got to thinking how right Stella was: all the shit he threw at NSA. News cycle after news cycle, he hammered them. The worst they ever did was subpoena him nine months later. Now some kid from Poland sends him a video, and suddenly he's getting warnings from the CIA and has to hide out in a cheap motel. It didn't make sense.

Novak might have felt like a fraud, but the part of him that made him want to be a reporter in the first place also wouldn't let go of something: he had to know the truth.

He started hammering out a reply.

'*Thank you for your offer, Nate. But The Republic is where I belong.*

'*PS. Don't bother getting anyone else to write that piece on "The End of The Republic". We're just getting started.*'

Once he hit send, a notification in the bottom of the screen flashed up.

"'*Abbie's death wasn't an accident. Yours won't be either.*' — *From Rebecca Fox.*"

As soon as he saw Rebecca's name he put his hands to his head. Officer Sharp had scared the shit out of him so badly in New York, he forgot he had been about to reply to Rebecca's last message.

He reached out as quickly as he could for the trackpad on his laptop, then clicked the window. She had used his PGP key to send an encrypted email.

In OTR, her username was already illuminated on his friends list. She was online and waiting.

Tom.Novak: I'm sorry. I was about to reply earlier but got sidetracked.

He figured sidetracked explained it as well as 'hiding out in a fleabag motel in Jersey on the advice of a rogue CIA agent.'

Tom.Novak: Do you really have evidence Abbie Bishop was murdered?

Rebecca.Fox: Official government records. STRAP Three Clearance, Top Secret.

Tom.Novak: I assume I don't need to point out that giving me such information is a violation of the UK Official Secrets Act, and you could be jailed for disclosing even the documents' existence.

Rebecca.Fox: Yes.

Novak puffed out his cheeks. *Good*, he thought. He didn't have time for hand-holding.

Rebecca.Fox: Downing Street isn't what everyone thinks.

Tom.Novak: What do you mean?

Rebecca.Fox: There's been collusion at very senior levels. I can't say any more until you've seen the documents.

Tom.Novak: Can you suggest a safe way for me or one of my colleagues to view these documents?

Rebecca.Fox: OK. When can you meet?

Tom.Novak: I'm in the States for at least the next 24 hours. Or my colleague Stella is in London for a few days if you'd want to meet her?

There was a pause of around five seconds that felt like five minutes. Novak didn't notice he'd tensely clasped his hands together. He was also holding his breath.

Rebecca.Fox: Set it up.

Tom.Novak: BRB...

Without thinking, he grabbed the new phone Kurt had given him and dialled Stella, who was running through Newark Airport's Terminal B towards the closing British Airways gate.

She managed to answer whilst running. 'Yeah?'

As Novak recounted the email, Stella reached her gate. She made frantic apologising and just-two-more-seconds gestures to the flight attendant. 'Okay, follow it up, but Novak I *have* to get on this plane and my boarding pass is on my phone, which is currently pressed against my ear!'

'Okay, okay,' Novak said. 'I just need your PGP key. Can you text it to me before you take off?'

Stella turned away from the attendant, covering the receiver and lowering her voice. 'If they let me on the bloody flight, then yes!'

'Great. I'll get back on OTR. I'll call you after the meet tomorrow.'

Then, a sense of unease came over Stella. Something about how his phone reception had been drifting in and out. 'Novak. Where are you calling me from?'

Novak froze at the other end as he realised his error. 'The new cell Kurt gave me.'

'Hang up now,' Stella demanded. She clicked off, saying, 'Shit!' to herself. She apologised to the attendant, then took off her shoes. Carrying both in one hand, she ran as fast as she could along the jet bridge to the plane. She'd be the last passenger to board.

Novak stripped off the back of the mobile and tore out the battery as fast as he could. He threw the phone down on the bed then froze.

It was hard to change the habit of a lifetime. He regularly made upwards of fifty phone calls a day. Like most modern journalists, the only time he wasn't on a phone was when he slept or was at a funeral.

'It's okay,' he reasoned with himself. 'You didn't give away any locations.' He paused. 'But they could be watching her phone, so you gotta get out of here. Act quick. Don't panic. Just go.'

He returned to the laptop, his quivering fingers making typos on almost every word, making him double back with vicious stabs of the delete button.

Tom.Novak: Rebecca ive got to go. Emergency. OTR later, ok.

He didn't even wait for a reply. He shut the laptop and flung it into a bag along with everything else.

He dashed to reception to check out, explaining to the manager, 'Sorry, man. Change of plan.'

The manager – big, black, gold rings on several fingers, wearing a Brooklyn Nets basketball jersey, reading a dog-eared Elmore Leonard novel – raised his eyebrows like he expected backchat. He had a strong South Jersey accent – his Rs much harder than North Jerseyites. 'Ahmma still charge you the whole night. We don't got an hourly rate here.'

'No problem,' Novak said, putting down a hundred-dollar bill for a room that cost thirty-nine.

The manager put his book down and inspected the note carefully.

Novak said, 'I was thinking, if you kept the change you could forget me if anyone came asking.'

The manager pouted with a slow nod. 'I can dig that,' he said.

Novak kept his head down as he pounded the streets. He needed a new motel at least two miles away that took cash and didn't need ID.

NSA Headquarters, Fort Meade, Maryland – Monday, 9.10pm

On the seventh floor – Domestic Data Analysis – of NSA's black-glass headquarters, a junior analyst, no more than two weeks into his job, had been given a list of eighteen phone numbers to have on real-time scan throughout the night. He wasn't told any names and wasn't shown any warrants. The persons listed had committed no crime, had made no threats to do so, yet this twenty-year-old analyst would record any and all activity on those phones: every conversation, text message, even when the phones were switched on or off, and the exact location of each phone pinpointed to within ten feet.

At the NSA's new $1.5 billion Utah Data Centre, one of its supercomputers tagged one of the analyst's numbers, lighting it up on his screen.

He fumbled with his phone before dialling his superior. 'Mr Lewis. I've got one, sir.' He paused, pulling up the connected phones' locations. 'She's got a call received at Newark Airport...coming from New Jersey...' He zoomed in tighter on the map. 'Near the Mayfair Hotel.'

Lewis asked, 'Who's calling her? Do we have it?'

'Unknown number, sir. We don't have it.'

'I want that phone's location pinged every ten seconds. You hear me? And get me audio on that call.'

'Um...' the analyst wasn't sure how to say it. 'Can I do that, sir? It's just...um. My clearance here says metadata only. I don't have authorisation.'

'Listen, son. I'm your authorisation. Now get me the damn audio.'

The analyst noticed the flashing dot on the Mayfair Motel

had disappeared. 'Wait, sir. I've lost the signal...' Knowing he could refresh a signal even on a phone that was switched off, he gave it a shot. 'Trying to ping it now...' He got nothing. 'No, sorry, sir. It's gone.'

Lewis clicked off to listen to playback of the phone call. It couldn't have been clearer than if Stella and Novak had sat in a recording booth with mikes hooked up. When it was through, he called a number for CIA, Langley.

'Jeff Waters, Counterterrorism,' came the answer.

'Jeff, it's Lyndon Lewis at NSA DDA,' Lewis said. 'I've got a call from our guy tonight.'

Waters asked, 'Do you have anything we can move on?'

'He's arranged a meet with someone tomorrow.'

'Okay. Let's get a black team up. CT wants Novak and the asset in the next twenty-four hours.'

'Will I tell them capture?' Lewis asked.

Waters answered, 'My orders are this is a national security Priority One. It's capture or kill.'

19

Even though it was still dark out, once Stella ascended the staircase to street level at Westminster tube station, she could see the devastation of the bombing from as far back as Parliament Street.

Streetlights were on and the light from dozens of forensics lamps leaked across the road. Past the police cordon at the Cenotaph, Whitehall was still littered with debris, marked with small red cones to be examined by forensics. The smallest fragment could provide a critical clue as to where the attackers sourced their materials.

Stella sheltered from the spitting rain under the archway linking the Foreign Office to the Treasury.

As the Foreign Office building had been declared safe, police allowed a phased re-entry, first on the King Henry side. The Whitehall side was still too much of an active crime scene.

Stella finished her double-shot espresso, trying to shock the jetlag out of her system. The loss of time from eastwards jetlag always hit her harder than westwards. She had landed only an hour earlier, barely time to drop her bag at the chain hotel Chang had booked her in. Still, it felt good to be back where Stella regarded as home.

In New York, she hadn't figured out the angles like she had in London. She could barely find her way around Manhattan let alone the other boroughs. Now that she was just dropping by, it was time to call in a few favours.

She knew her contact's routine from her days at *The Guardian* where she first made a name for herself – largely thanks to said contact. It was a quid pro quo relationship: in return for inside information on Foreign Office policy, Stella gave him a heads-up on any ministers briefing against the government. Behind the seemingly united front for the press was a constant battle being fought over Treasury budgets; Ministers squabbling over who wanted to appear on *Newsnight*; ambitious backbenchers seeing opportunities to raise their profile; juvenile feuds that were barely above the level of a school playground. Ministers were like bickering child actors, all haggling for screen time: the only real currency left in modern politics.

A man with a pile of the day's newspapers under his arm – the front pages carrying pictures of smoke rising from Downing Street in the aftermath – came past the Foreign Office archway, not noticing Stella.

She called out to him, 'Charlie Fletcher.'

He put his head down and upped his speed. 'Not today, Stella, I'm late.'

Stella set off in pursuit. 'You're exactly on time.'

Not wanting to draw attention by having a conversation fifty feet apart, Charlie stopped.

'Are you alright?' she asked. 'It must have been scary down here.'

He said, 'I've got three researchers from international development in the hospital who were at a window overlooking the press conference. They'll live. Just.'

Stella asked, 'How are you finding life on the other side of the ropes?'

'The pay's better, and I don't break the law as often as I used to.'

Charlie was barely into his forties. Since leaving journalism, he'd become convinced that his £31k salary, Savile Row suits and Foreign Office personnel pass amounted to being the same as James Bond.

Stella had been on the politics desk during Charlie's stint as Features Editor at *The Herald*. There had always been rumours about phone hacking going on during her two years there. Features always seemed to find celebrity stories that no one else had.

Charlie faced daily harassing demands to find raunchier, sensationalist copy, no matter the cost. Finally, one of Charlie's reporters had been caught out when they hacked a story too far, one of Britain's most beloved actors, and the actor sued. Despite the hacking having been sanctioned from the top down, the only one to be convicted was a single reporter. For appearances, Charlie stepped down from his role at *The Herald*, but only after the chief editor put in a kind word for him at the Foreign Office. Just three months later, he was working for Nigel Hawkes, and *The Herald* folded after nearly 100 years in circulation.

Stella started working her angles. 'Has there been any word from overseas intel yet? Word is, this Mufaza is a cleanskin.'

'No one has anything,' said Charlie. 'Until last week he was just a carpet cleaner no one knew anything about. This is the world we live in now.' He leaned in, speaking quietly. 'His wife says he had been growing more radicalised over the past few years. Attending mosques with militant imams, watching Anwar al-Awlaki speeches online.'

'Do they know how he got access to Downing Street?'

He shook his head. 'I don't have anything on that yet.'

Stella didn't look convinced.

'I don't,' Charlie insisted.

'What about Ali's speech?' Stella asked. 'Someone must have a copy.'

Charlie pulled back with a roll of his eyes, like she'd asked for something impossible. 'Stella...'

'Oh, piss off, Charlie. Like you're not desperate to tell me you know.'

'Twitter knows more about that than me. The speech wasn't green lit by the Foreign Office, and it wasn't sent to the teleprompter.' Seeing that she was about to interrupt, he added, 'Stella, I swear to god, the only person who knew what Simon Ali was about to say is lying on a slab under armed guard in the St Thomas' Hospital morgue.'

'Is this how it's going to be then?' asked Stella.

'How what's going to be?'

'You seem to be forgetting our last meeting when I agreed not to report on your boss's rather dubious expenses claims. Foreign Secretary, the Right Honourable Nigel Hawkes MP.'

He was on the back foot now. 'For which we are *both* very grateful.'

'And for which I got absolutely nothing back.' Stella tried to frame it in language he would understand. 'I get you off, then you roll over and pretend you're asleep. Is that it?'

A colleague of Charlie's shouted to him from the front steps of the Ministry.

'Be right there!' Charlie answered. He spun Stella away from the man's view. 'One name. Riz Rizzaq.'

'Who's that?'

'A no one who's about to be someone.'

'Charlie–'

'A BBC cameraman found dead in his flat Monday evening. And that's something the Home Office will never give you. Are we even?'

Stella thought about it. 'You should use a different hair

pomade, Charlie. That one runs in the rain.' She turned and hailed a taxi, leaving Charlie feeling at the globs dripping from his hair.

In the taxi, the ever-aware Stella clocked a black Audi with two men in the front that had been tailing her since Great George Street.

While the taxi stopped in traffic, Stella moved towards the driver's partition. 'Excuse me. How long has that black car been behind us?'

'I was just thinking that,' the driver replied in his thick South London accent. 'Been there since Embankment, he 'as.'

Coming all the way into Hackney, it was too far to be a coincidence.

Stella sat in a café around the corner from Shoreditch Police Station, tucking into the full English breakfast she'd been dreaming about all across the Atlantic.

An overweight man in his fifties came in, wearing a black leather jacket that was too long for his stubby arms. 'The usual, Tina,' he wheezed. While he waited at the counter, he glanced over his shoulder at Stella sitting in the corner.

The café was quiet after the morning rush.

When he sat down at her table with a groan, Stella gestured at his jacket with her knife. 'Midlife crisis already, Sidney?'

He knew Stella too well to be offended. 'Only twenty quid down Harrow market. Dolce and Gabbano.'

'It's Dolce and Gabbana,' she said with a mouthful of sausage.

'That's not what the label says.'

'You always were a man who knows a bargain.' Stella slid one of the café takeaway menus across to him.

He lifted a corner of the menu, seeing five £20 notes inside. 'Seems quality to me.' He put the cash into his inside jacket pocket, where his police detective ID was hanging, then slid an envelope back to Stella.

The ID named him as "Detective Sidney Vickering".

'This place hasn't changed much,' Stella said, sweeping up the envelope.

'The only place round here what hasn't,' Sidney said. 'I mean look at them.' He drew Stella's attention to two men chatting on the street. One with a handlebar moustache, and trousers that stopped well above his ankles. The other had a long, manicured beard, and wore yellow dungarees. 'Is that what a man looks like these days, Stel? Bloody hipsters. You know they opened a bloody shop that only sells cereal. These knobs are paying a fiver for a bowl of Lucky Charms what'll cost you three pound a box in the Yankee bit at Tesco. It's not the city I grew up in, Stel.'

Stella wanted to get on. 'How sure are you this guy was killed by the bomber?'

Sid replied, 'Sure enough that MI5's taken it out our hands. Who gave you the heads up?'

'Someone who knows as much as you.'

'That so?' Sid nodded. 'He doesn't know what else I've got for you. I guarantee that.'

'Tell me it's not black stockings again,' Stella said.

He leaned a little closer, stale cigarette breath wafting across the table to her. 'We found a body on the banks of the Thames this morning at low tide. About half a mile from Parliament.'

Disinterested, Stella said, 'I'm on foreign affairs for the Yanks these days. But I can pass it to someone else.'

'Trust me. You'll want this one for yourself.'

'What's the MO?'

'Male, white, late thirties. He had a phone on him but no ID. Didn't even have labels on his clothes. Single shot in the forehead, double-tap in the chest. Killed sometime Sunday night into Monday morning. Professional job. *Very* professional.'

Stella started gathering up her things. 'Give it to someone at the *Mail*. I'm not being sniffy, Sid, but drug and gangland killings are too small for me.'

'It's not gangland. They don't come into Westminster.'

'Who's the victim?'

'We don't know yet, but his fingerprints are on record.'

'He's got form?'

'Not with us.'

'What records then?'

'What if I told you his record's classified and I can't get access. Would that still be too small for you?'

Stella sat back again. 'I'm listening.'

The waitress put down the detective's breakfast and coffee. 'There you go, Sid.'

'Ta.' He waited for the waitress to leave before saying, 'All I know is he's ex-GCHQ.'

'GCHQ? That would be two of their own killed the same night.'

He ate his breakfast messily, chewing with his mouth open. 'You talking about Abigail Bishop?'

'I'm following up on that story. Accidental death, or maybe even suicide.'

He smirked.

'You know different?' Stella asked.

'According to the final autopsy, Abigail Bishop fell off a balcony after necking two bottles of wine. But the first autopsy, before MI6's doctors started poking about the place...' He purposely trailed off.

'You mean MI5 surely?'

'Nope. Six. Swear on me mum's grave. Started invoking anti-terror legislation and national security.'

'But MI5 handles domestic.'

'All I know is, before they showed up, her blood levels were normal. Could have driven an ambulance that night, she could. Both copies of those autopsies are in there with the other geezer's.'

'And what about the other geezer? You think it's a coincidence two GCHQ employees died the same night?'

'That's what we're starting with.'

'Can you get me into the evidence room? I need to see that phone.'

Sid dipped some toast into his egg yolk. 'I'll text you.'

'And no one else is getting these autopsy reports, right? From what I hear the Met's got its own eBay profile these days.'

'It's a seller's market, Stella, but for you I'll make an exception.' He looked up at her optimistically, as he wiped egg yolk from his mouth with a napkin. 'You back for long? Thought you might fancy a drink later.'

'Another time, Sid,' Stella said, putting her cutlery down, breakfast unfinished. 'You should use some of that money to take your wife out.' She raised her eyebrows warningly at him.

'Worth a shot,' Sid said with a grumble.

Stella chuckled as she got up. On the way out the door, she mumbled to herself, 'Creep.'

Stella stopped at the end of a path leading to a modern apartment block overlooking the rare greenery of London Fields. She looked back down the road at the underground station sign, and numerous buses blocking up the main road. 'Good access,' she said quietly to herself. Someone could be in Whitehall within half an hour if they timed the trains right.

The piles of fresh flowers at the front door told her she had the right place, but to be sure, she checked the address against the note Sidney had given her: "Residential address – Riz Rizzaq."

Spotting a postman descending the inner stairwell, Stella quick-stepped down the path, rummaging in her bag as if looking for keys. She caught the door just as the postman was exiting. Stella gave an exasperated laugh at him, 'Forget my head one of these days!'

The postman smiled politely.

Once safely inside the lobby, Stella made her way confidently up the stairs – like she belonged there – listening out for any neighbours. In the second-floor stairwell she looked down at the residents' parking area, as a battered red Ford Escort pulled in. When the driver got out, whistling in a trying-too-hard-to-be-casual way, Stella hid behind the landing door.

Trailing behind the Escort, a black Audi puttered into the car park too. The same as the one that had followed Stella earlier.

Neither of the two men inside got out.

Stella peered down to the ground floor, seeing the top of the man's prematurely balding head as he made his way inside. As the front door clattered shut clumsily behind him, he muttered, 'Shit.'

He was wearing a wrinkled suit, which looked like it had been slept in. His demeanour screamed paranoia, looking around in the most unsubtle of ways.

Stella listened to his footsteps getting closer to the second floor. She was sure there was only one flat the man was bound for. She stepped back, hands poised at chest height as the landing door opened. Before the man realised what was going on, Stella grabbed his left arm and twisted it up his back, turning his wrist inward, which sent him straight to his knees in agony.

'Why are you following me?' she demanded. 'One lie and I break your wrist.' She tugged his wrist a little more to let him know she was serious. She could smell the previous night's lager on him.

The man cowered. 'Bloody hell, Stella. It's me!' He tried to turn around, giving an embarrassed smile, despite the pain etched on his face. 'It's Dan.'

She let his arm go then pushed him away with her knee. She stared at him in incomprehension. He had aged a lot in the three years since she had last seen him. 'Superhack? Why am I not surprised.'

'Nobody calls me that anymore,' he said, feeling his arm.

To everyone else he was Dan Leckie.

Stella said, 'There I was thinking you spent your days hiding under rocks.'

Leckie struggled to his knees, flexing his arm to check for damage. 'Her Majesty's been putting a roof over my head the last few months.' He had the voice of a Cockney wideboy.

Stella made no attempt to help him up. 'I thought they gave you a year.'

'Good behaviour,' he said, grinning with crooked, nicotine-stained teeth. There was something gormless about him. Like he should have been at the nearest dog track ripping up losing tickets. Now he was up close, Stella remembered his pinhole eyes and tiny mouth. His suit was too big for him, and the trousers were two shades of grey away from the jacket.

Stella asked, 'Where does stalking fall in your parole guidelines?'

'Stalking?' he asked, as if mystified by the accusation. 'I'm an honest citizen again.'

'Well, your tradecraft needs finessing, Dan. My cab driver was on to you as far back as Whitehall.'

'What are you talking about?'

'The black Audi outside. That isn't one of yours?'

Leckie laughed. 'You think I've got the bangers and mash for an Audi? Give over, will ya.'

Stella peeked out the balcony window. 'Looks more serious than police.'

'I thought you was in New York.' He made "thought" sound like "fought". 'You covering Downing Street?' He started walking down the hall. He knew where he was going.

Stella followed. 'The only story in town.'

'You think so, eh?' He took out a "bump key" and a small rock hammer. The bump key had specially fashioned grooves and cuts, to fit the maximum depth of the keylock. Dan slid it in like a regular key, then readied the hammer.

'What are you doing?' asked Stella.

Dan hit the bump key, which drove the key pins into driver pins, and unlocked the door. 'Piece of piss these new builds,' he said. He opened the door, standing aside to let Stella in first.

Stella hung back. Breaking and entering hadn't exactly been on her resume at *The Guardian*, but she didn't see that she had much choice.

Dan went straight to the living room, opening up cupboards and drawers. 'Six months away. I tell you, I missed all this. Duckin', divin', snoopin'—'

'Hacking?'

He smiled. 'That's all in the past, Stella.'

She took out the police report, moving slowly from room to room as she pieced the evidence together.

Seeing the report, Dan shouted, 'Nice one.' He rifled through paperwork in a drawer: piles of bills and bank statements. 'I know this constable down Bethnal Green, young guy. He charged me fifty. How much was yours?'

Stella didn't want to let on that he'd got his for half the price of hers. 'Same.'

He laughed. 'Liar. You forget I sat across a desk from you for two years. I can tell.'

She was uncomfortable swanning around a dead man's flat with him. 'Why don't you tell me what this is all about.'

'It's all in the report. Murder made to look like burglary. Bomber steals Rizza's ID–'

'It's Rizzaq.'

'Whatever...steals his ID, gets into Downing Street, blows the gaff up. End of. But the Home Office has got an injunction out on that little detail.'

The pair froze as a neighbour next door rattled their keys. Dan put a finger to his lips.

At the sound of the door shutting, Stella whispered, 'I'm leaving.'

Dan chased after her.

When Stella got outside, the black Audi was gone. She looked from one end of the street to the other, then realised she didn't really have a plan for where to go next.

Dan twirled his keys on his finger as he went to his car. 'You know your problem, Stella? You don't know how to chase a real story. This is the real world, not Whitehall politics. That copper's wasting your time.' He stood by the passenger door he'd opened for her. 'Your editor will thank me.'

On any other day, Stella would never have trusted him. But he was clearly onto something. 'This better be good,' she said, getting into the passenger seat.

Dan smoked a constant stream of cigarettes as he drove across the City.

Stella waved in front of her face and rolled her window down, choking on the smoke.

He slammed on the brakes and blasted the horn, as a taxi stopped in front of him, 'Ah, you wanker...'

Stella prodded at an empty can of Carling by her foot. She nudged it out of the way, turning up her top lip in disgust. The dashboard was caked in nicotine ash and dust, unboxed Oasis and Arctic Monkeys CDs piled around the gear stick, the floor a bed of old newspapers, betting slips, Ginster's pasty wrappers and Coke cans. A pillow had been jammed up against the back seat and door, and a light blanket stretched out across the seats. *Is he sleeping in here?* Stella wondered, starting to feel sorry for him.

He was practically purring as he handed Stella another police report from his glove compartment. Smoke pumped out his mouth and nose as he spoke. 'You're interested in the wrong murder investigation.'

Stella read the report's title. 'Abbie Bishop. I saw your article on the wires.' Not wanting to give away how keen she already was on the story, she said, 'You didn't mention murder anywhere in the report.'

Dan said, 'That was before I spoke to a certain pathologist forty-five minutes ago.'

Familiar with Metropolitan police reports, she went straight to the detective inspector's comments on the crime scene. "She had somewhere in the region of fifteen units of alcohol in her stomach."

'That's about two bottles of wine,' Stella said.

'Look at the other report underneath, then look at the times.'

Stella switched pages. 'These were printed at the same time.'

'The one I got first was from the pathologist. Only trace amounts of wine found in the blood. Barely half a glass.'

'Maybe it took longer to show up and they redid the report.'

Leckie shook his head. 'Nah, because look...' He passed her another file of photos taken from the scene of the safe house. 'The bottle on the table. It's nearly full. And the glass has barely been touched.'

'She drank another bottle.'

'Nope. Police report lists that only one full bottle was found.' He looked at Stella. 'Who drinks a bottle of wine, then takes the empty downstairs to the bin before drinking another one?'

'You think it's more likely that someone changed the autopsy report?'

Dan said, 'There were no bottles in Abbie Bishop's bin, or any of her neighbours for that matter. And the council hasn't done a pick up yet.'

Stella was impressed with his thoroughness. This wasn't the same Leckie she had once known.

'They want it to look like an accident or maybe suicide,' he said. 'But it ain't. I bet you all the lager in London.'

Stella lowered her window. Judging by the smell in the car, it seemed Leckie had already drank all the lager in London.

'That's something else they've changed,' he added. 'I spoke to the copper who was first on the scene. He tells me he heard glass smashing, then a scream.'

Stella scanned down to that part of the report. 'The French window was broken.'

'Exactly,' he said. 'Who jumps through a window before throwing themselves off a balcony?'

'You think someone threw her off?' Stella asked.

Dan replied, 'I think someone threw her off, and the police are covering it up. Whatever it is, GCHQ are up to their necks in it. They're stonewalling me.'

Stella continued inspecting the discrepancies in the two reports. There was no denying it: solid, credible, hard-copy evidence. 'This is good stuff, Dan,' she said.

He felt a swell of pride, but was careful not to show it. 'Yeah, cheers.'

She laid the police report on her lap. 'The problem is. You and I both know you didn't get this story legitimately.'

Dan didn't react. He just stared straight ahead.

Stella continued, 'I think in a desperate bid to shoot your-self back into the big time – and every editor's phone contacts

– you found some dirt on someone. Something from your previously unpublished greatest hits. And that's enough to get you on the right track, but we both know you're way out of your depth on this. I saw how you got shut down at the Downing Street press conference. You need me, or this story you're betting your big comeback tour on is going to end up at the bottom of a filing cabinet marked "No One Gives a Toss".'

Deep down, Dan knew this was all true. 'The way I look at it, Stel. I'm giving you everything I have. What do I get in return?'

'The other half of your story: a man who washed up dead on the banks of the Thames this morning.'

'What's the link?'

'He was an old GCHQ colleague of Abbie Bishop's.'

'Two dead GCHQ officers within a few days of each other?'

'Actually, the body's been in the water just over a day, which means they were both killed the same night.' Stella could see him turning it over in his brain, how they could be onto something good.

He took a moment to consider. 'Alright, Stel. Deal.' He put his cigarette in his mouth to free up a hand from the steering wheel.

She shook it. 'Deal.' She held onto his hand. 'Provided you stop calling me Stel.'

Dan laughed. 'Another deal.' He took a long congratulatory drag. 'You know what the beauty of this story is? No one else will be able to put it together.'

'Let's not get carried away, Dan. We're not the only journalists capable of putting money in an envelope. What makes you so sure?'

'No one else has what I have.'

Years of being able to sniff out trouble told Stella something else was going on. 'Dan. How did you find out about Operation Tempest? And if I think you're lying to me I'm getting out this car at the next red light.' She reached for her seatbelt clip – ready to bail – to show she was serious.

'Okay, okay. Don't be dramatic.' He paused. 'The thing is...' He grimaced slightly as he tapped another cigarette out the pack. 'It's a little bit dodgy.'

Stella sighed. 'Why am I not surprised.'

20

Novak's search for a new motel after his Mayfair evacuation had kept him up most of the night, getting only two hours sleep. By the time he got on the 108 bus from Newark, over the New Jersey Turnpike and the Hudson River to Port Authority, he was almost on his knees. His eyelids burned. Everything around him felt far away.

Keeping tabs on anyone who might be following him through the bus station was a nightmare. Novak's heart rate spiked when anyone standing on their own was looking even vaguely in his direction. With the passengers waiting for the 8th Avenue subway cramped together on the platform, one man kept creeping into Novak's peripheral vision. He was wearing a backpack and an NYU sweatshirt, and kept a mobile phone to his ear but didn't seem to be doing much talking. He had been following Novak since Port Authority.

When Novak emerged from the stairs of the dingy 1st Avenue station, he made a diversion across the street to a hotdog vendor. From there, he kept tabs on the NYU guy crossing over to East 14th Street. Novak wondered, *If he's going to NYU, why didn't he get the subway to 8th Street instead of going too far then having to walk back?*

The man made a right towards a tenement, sprinted up the front stoop and went inside. Novak relaxed a little, and put his uneaten hotdog in the bin.

The Village Cinema on the corner of East 12th and 2nd already had a small line outside for their day-long "70s Conspiracy Thrillers" festival. Mostly older couples, and young men sipping coffee from takeaway cups. Novak noticed two of them had got the Starbucks barista to put their names on their cups as "Woodward" and "Bernstein".

Ordinarily this would have made Novak smile, but he had other things on his mind. Namely, the most important dead drop of his life.

He approached the ticket booth. 'I've got a reservation for *All the President's Men*. The name's Walker.'

The clerk checked the reservation. 'It's not a busy screening. You can sit where you like.'

Novak passed him a twenty. 'I'll be fine, thanks.'

He'd reserved a seat at the back for a reason.

Once in the theatre, he found his seat – third row from the back, five seats in, tight up against the wall. The Village was perfect for Sharp's requirements: a cinema that wouldn't be too busy, but not so quiet that Novak stood out.

Before the lights dimmed Novak did a quick scan of the theatre. No recognisable faces.

Sharp had told Novak to watch at least the first half hour of the movie, but that point passed. An usher was sitting on a stair in the aisle nearest Novak, knees pulled up to his chest, immersed in the movie. Novak was right in his eye line. Where Sharp had made the dead drop.

Novak could almost feel the envelope burning a hole under his seat, but he wasn't sure he could reach down for it without raising the usher's attention.

Not wanting to look behind, Novak waited for the screen

to go dark as the first scene with Deep Throat came on. While the screen showed a long pan around a dark underground garage, Novak reached under his seat. He quickly slipped the envelope into his jacket pocket, then waited a few minutes. He ducked out the row, just as Ben Bradlee gave his speech to Woodward and Bernstein, about the future of the country depending on their story.

As Novak paced up the aisle, the usher whispered, 'You're going to miss the best part.'

Novak replied, 'I've seen it before.'

Facing the ATM outside the cinema doors, Novak opened the envelope. The note inside said, "*Tompkins Square Park, Temperance Fountain – 11.30am. Catch the ball.*"

Novak checked his watch. He was already late. Now he had to run six blocks in five minutes to make it in time.

His legs felt stiff and, after barely a block, he was already getting out of breath. The cool air did nothing for his rising temperature. It was a tension-sweat. Hot under the arms. His rapidly beating heart working like a train furnace, churning out ever-hotter blood around his body. He could have stripped to his underwear and still felt overheated.

Hidden away amongst the typical East Village tenements, with fire escapes zigzagging up the front, Tompkins Square Park appeared like a deep green oasis in the middle of the Village. It was like a mini Central Park, with pick-up basketball games; shredded guys in vests doing calisthenics on pull-up bars; and mothers with prams taking mid-morning strolls. Autumn was robbing the trees of their leaves, the sun arrowing through gaps in the branches. The air was cold and clean and crisp.

Novak wiped beads of sweat from his forehead, slowing to a walking pace and recapturing his breath. When he reached the Temperance Fountain as instructed, he did a slow three-sixty of the area, looking for anyone carrying a ball.

That was when Novak saw him: a jock carrying a double-strapped backpack, wearing a tight long-sleeve baselayer under a retro Patrick Ewing Knicks jersey, bouncing a basketball. His arms and shoulders bulged underneath the baselayer. He looked more like a football wide-receiver than a basketball player.

When the man was close enough to Novak, he bounce-passed the ball to Novak.

Officer Sharp pulled Novak into a half-handshake/half-hug move. While their faces were close, Sharp said, 'Just two guys shooting the shit, hanging out. Give me the ball back and sit down with me.' His accent was soft Midwestern. He led Novak over to a bench with a clear view of the park entrance.

Novak sat down, trying not to look nervous.

When Sharp sat down, he kept up his cheerful smile but spoke quietly. Taking in Novak's oxford shirt and black brogues, he said, 'I told you to dress sporty.'

'I'm sorry,' Novak said. 'It was all I had in my go bag.'

'Why are you late? Were you followed?'

'No, I...I thought for a moment there was maybe someone.'

'Describe him to me.'

As Novak started scanning around the park for the NYU guy, Sharp bounced the ball.

'Don't look for him,' Sharp said. 'Describe him.'

'White. Short black hair. About six feet, grey NYU sweater, backpack.'

'Okay.' He held the ball. 'I'm Walter Sharp, CIA.'

'Tom Novak.'

'I need you to sit back and try to relax, Tom. So far, you've done fine.' He pronounced it 'fan', with an easy-going, folksy charm. 'You weren't at your apartment last night.'

Novak said, 'You told me not to stay there.'

'Exactly. That means you're listening. Which means you have a good chance of making it through this thing.' He added, 'You can smoke if you want.'

Novak didn't bother asking how he knew. He just smiled and lit up.

Without making eye contact, Sharp asked, 'Where did you stay last night?'

Novak answered, 'A motel in Newark.' He snorted half a laugh. 'Then another motel in Newark.'

In an instant, Sharp's tone turned from friend to interrogator. 'Why two motels?'

'It was just a precaution,' Novak said unconvincingly, a nervous hand drifting up to his forehead.

Sharp told him, 'Stop touching your face.'

Novak put his hand down.

'Something must have made you think the first motel was no longer safe. What happened?'

Novak looked sheepish. 'I got a break in a story, so I called my colleague. Stella.'

Sharp looked down into his hands. 'When I said no phone calls, was I unclear in some way? You of all people should know that.'

'It was a new phone,' Novak said. 'The first call made on it. It couldn't have been longer than thirty seconds.' He thought harder. 'A minute, max. How could anyone know it was me?'

'Don't you get it?' Sharp said, barely restraining his frustration. 'They don't find you by tracking *you*. They find you by tracking your primary connections: your editor, your colleague, your family.'

Novak felt it necessary to correct him. 'I don't have any family.'

'Known contacts, then. They see a call come into Stella's

phone, they don't know it's you. But now they're going to track every call you make on that phone until they're sure.'

Novak nodded. 'I know. I screwed up.'

'You got lucky. Don't rely on luck ever again. Get rid of the phone.'

Getting frazzled by Sharp's intensity, Novak said, 'Okay, I will.'

Sharp had a quick look around. 'Reach into my bag and take out the black folder with a map wrapped around it. Keep the map behind it and open the folder.'

Novak did as he was told.

Sharp sat back as if soaking up the sunshine, looking out over the park rather than at Novak. 'What I'm about to tell you is off the record. For background only. That black folder you're holding is a CIA prisoner transfer request from Bagram to Szymany Airport, Poland.'

Taking a beat, Novak said, 'Officer Sharp, before we go any further, do you acknowledge that you're showing classified material to a journalist?'

Sharp said dryly, 'Deniability is not that high on my priorities, Tom. I'm way past that.'

Novak clarified, 'It's so neither of us perjure ourselves if we're ever asked about this meeting in a court of law.'

Sharp said, 'I've got twenty years with the company, Mr Novak. This is the first time I've leaked anything in my life. I'm not exactly jumping for joy doing this, but there are lives at stake.'

Novak read the name of the prisoner in the transfer request. 'Abdul al-Malik. He's the guy in the video from Artur?'

'Yeah,' Sharp replied. 'He was detained near the Afghan-Pakistan border on suspicion of terrorism. He was brought to my CIA facility–' he raised a hand, 'don't bother asking where – and during my interrogation, he told me he was an MI6 agent. When I called MI6 with his code word they confirmed his identity. Malik went on to tell me he had uncovered a credible threat against a U.S. target, and because of this information his life was in danger.'

'Who from?'

'He knew we were recording audio of the interrogation. So he drew five letters on the table.' Sharp took out a piece of paper and wrote the letters on it, then showed it to Novak.

POTUS

Sharp asked, 'Got it?'

After Novak nodded, Sharp took a lighter to the paper, then dropped it to the ground. When it was charred completely, he stamped it out.

Novak was as sceptical as Sharp had been. 'Why would an MI6 agent think that the President wanted to kill him?'

'I don't know. But after fifteen minutes, a JSC unit arrived with a demand from the Chairman of the Joint Chiefs of Staff – answering directly to the President of the United States – that I hand Malik over to them. Believe me when I tell you: this goes all the way to the top.' He took the folder back and put it in his bag.

'Where's Malik now?' Novak asked.

'While I was out the room, JSC tried to move Malik from his cell. At which time, Malik, who was starving and sleep-deprived, somehow managed to steal a gun from a Navy SEAL, and shoot himself in the head. The official verdict will be accidental homicide. It was an assassination, Mr Novak.'

Novak looked down. 'Jesus...'

'Malik said this thing,' Sharp continued. '"Hell is empty, all the devils are here."'

Novak lifted his head. 'Say that again.'

Sharp repeated, '"Hell is empty, all the devils are here." I looked into it. It's from *The Tempest*. Does it mean anything to you?'

'My laptop,' Novak said. 'That same quote appeared on

the screen back in New York. It was like they knew I was watching it.'

Sharp said, 'Definitely not JSC. They don't play games like that.'

'Officer Sharp, I've worked in security for seven years now, and I've never even heard of JSC.'

'Turns out, they've been running black ops all over the Middle East, North Africa, Europe, South America. They go anywhere they please, and every year they're handed a blank cheque from the President that says "I don't want to know" on it. They're completely off the books, answerable only to their CO and the President.'

Novak asked, 'Why would they want Malik dead?'

Sharp said, 'I think JSC were helping MI6 clean up something to do with an operation Malik was involved in. Something I can't get near. It's all classified STRAP Three by the British.'

'I'm not familiar with their classifications,' Novak said.

Sharp explained, 'STRAP One is the kind of intel British political aides are always leaving on memory sticks on the subway. STRAP Two is the kind they interrupt a Prime Minister's meeting for. If it's STRAP Three, they wake up the Prime Minister in the middle of the night. MI6 are now denying Malik was theirs; that he had gone rogue and resisted calls to come in.'

Novak could see their play. 'Take him out, then disavow him. And now they're coming after me.'

'The British will clean house after this. All the other records on the U.S. end have already been destroyed. No Critical Incident Report has been filed. And JSC stole all the tapes of Malik's interrogation.'

Novak could see the bigger picture now. 'Artur's video is the last piece of evidence Malik existed.'

Sharp said, 'I have friends at NSA that tell me every resource they have is going into recovering that video. They have no idea what's at stake, of course. If they destroy all evidence of Malik, no one can prove there was ever any conspiracy. Everything and everyone related to Malik is being taken out. Malik, Secretary Snow, and Prime Minister Ali are all dead. Unfortunately, it doesn't end there.' Sharp reached into his pocket for his phone. 'After I called MI6 I left my phone with Malik. As I hoped, he used it while I was out the room.' He showed Novak the call log. 'He called this number. A woman in London called Abigail Bishop.'

Novak was dumbfounded.

Sharp didn't have to ask if he had heard of her. 'How do you know her?'

'A contact mentioned her in an email. Then my colleague Stella saw the wire report on her.'

Sharp said, 'Malik told me that his handler was also in danger. He tried to warn her, but his call must have come too late. I assume your source was acquainted with Miss Bishop in some way.'

Novak didn't answer.

'Sorry,' Sharp said, realising Novak was too much of a professional to out his source.

'I need to tell you something,' Novak said cagily. 'My source thinks there's been collusion with senior British officials in the Downing Street attack.'

Sharp nodded. 'It's possible.'

Novak couldn't believe how casually Sharp was taking it.

Sharp said, 'You have to start asking yourself: why would someone with information on a credible threat against a U.S. target be killed by U.S. forces? Aided and abetted by MI6. Meanwhile, the British Prime Minister was about to read a confession to something on live network TV.'

Novak paused. 'Unless someone wanted that credible threat to be realised.'

Sharp nodded as if to say *Now you're getting it.*

Novak said, 'My colleague, Stella, is following up the story in London. Do you think they'll go after her as well?'

'That depends on what she finds,' Sharp said. 'I'm just trying to keep you alive, Mr Novak. Honestly? I didn't expect you to make this meeting.'

In a way, it was the scariest thing Novak had heard Sharp say so far.

Sharp went on, 'They killed Miss Bishop at a GCHQ safe house, they took out Malik in a secure CIA facility, and got the British to cover for them. Tom, you might think because you've printed a few strongly worded articles in a magazine that you know all about taking on the military industrial complex. But believe me, whatever it is they want to stop you from finding out, they will do what*ever* it takes to stop you.'

'What do I do?' asked Novak. 'Hide out in motels the rest of my life? Start covering sports?'

'If they just wanted to kill you it would be done by now.'

'What would you do?'

'If I were you?' Sharp smiled wryly. 'We got a saying doing surveillance: Keep your head down, and don't keep your head down. You got to know who's around you. Who's been ten paces behind you the last three blocks. And you've got to do it without them knowing you've seen them. Don't remember jackets. They're easily changed and often reversible, especially at this time of year. Look at their shoes. It takes too long to change shoes.'

Novak took out a reporter's flip-notebook, about to write in shorthand.

Sharp stopped him. 'The hell are you doing, man?'

'Making notes. It's how I remember.'

Sharp shook his head. 'Notes aren't going to help you out in the field. You're going to have to get used to a different style. And quickly.'

'Try me,' said Novak.

'We're talking dolphin surveillance. Now you see them, now you don't. They go out in force. They're big, they're visible, and they want you to know they're onto you. To make you feel like you've got the upper hand. You turn a street corner and they're gone. I've been on the wrong side of a dolphin team before, and it messes with you. Paranoia increases, your body language makes you more visible. You start seeing the enemy every-where. So you gotta stay calm. Then you've got your waterfall team. It's resource-heavy and expensive, but that isn't an issue for these guys. New York blocks are ideal for a waterfall. As soon as a surveillant passes the rabbit – that's you – they double back, crossing streets. Then they rejoin the stream of traffic coming your way, in a change of clothes. One time in a jacket, the next in a t-shirt. Like I said, you gotta look at their shoes.'

Novak nodded, a little overwhelmed.

'Your best bet?' Sharp said. 'Meet the source who emailed you about Abbie Bishop.'

'It's already in motion.'

'There's a lot of very powerful people who are going to try and stop you getting this out. Are you prepared to risk your life for this story?'

Novak was resolute. 'I'm ready.'

'You've done it before.'

Sharp nodded. 'How much cash do you have on you?'

Novak said, 'I don't think my contact is after money.'

'No, for you,' Sharp replied. 'Nothing's going to be more toxic for you than leaving a trail at ATMs or, worse yet, card payments over the next few days. What's your max?'

'Eight hundred.'

'Take all of it. Keep it in separate rolls of fifties in different pockets so you don't draw attention to yourself. Shopkeepers remember guys who pull out five hundred bucks for a pack of cigarettes.'

Novak's head was spinning. 'You know, I haven't been the kindest reporter to the CIA the last few years.'

Sharp had heard him say it before, and he couldn't stand it any longer. 'Not for nothing, Mr Novak. But we never use the "the" with CIA.'

'Fine. What I don't get is, why are you helping me?'

Sharp said, 'They killed a foreign intelligence agent on my watch. A friendly. A man I said I would help. That might not be a hill of beans to you or anyone else, but in my line of work friendly intelligence agents look out for one another. Now the company's hanging me out to dry.' Sharp stood up and got both straps of his backpack on. 'You're not the only one who cares about the truth, Mr Novak. Of all the things worth fighting for in this world, the truth's a pretty good one.'

Novak looked down at his forgotten cigarette, the ash long and unbroken all the way down to the filter.

Sharp started bouncing the basketball. 'If you need to contact me again I've added you to my OTR contacts. I'll be leaving the city tonight. Stay safe.' He wandered back towards the park entrance, slipping seamlessly into a crowd of guys who had just wrapped up a game at the courts.

The city was as loud and alive as any other weekday at noon, but Novak couldn't hear any of it. He found himself walking nearly twenty blocks towards Lower Manhattan, putting together the pieces of what Officer Sharp had told him.

The President of the United States. Implicated in something like this.

As Novak found himself on the narrow one-way streets in Little Italy, he felt like he was surrounded by suspicious characters. All the yellow cabs. People on phones. Beat-up old vans with blacked-out rear windows. He couldn't take it.

Seeing a 'Free Wi-Fi' sign on a small Italian diner on the corner of Mulberry Street, he swooped in, taking a booth in the back corner. Novak's mental checklist told him everything about the place was ideal: it was a place he had never been in before; as he was using public Wi-Fi he would be on a network with no associations with his name or IP address in any way; and judging by the two other customers on tablets and smart-phones, he wouldn't stand out using a laptop.

The waitress offered Novak a pot of coffee, but he didn't think stimulants were what he needed right now. It was only at the mention of a menu that he became aware of how empty his stomach was. He needed real food. He ordered the Italian Special hoagie at the counter.

'Cash or card, hon?' the waitress asked.

'Cash,' he replied, laying down a ten-dollar bill.

While the waitress rang it up and got his change, Novak looked up at *Fox News* on the TV, cutting to breaking news of terror cell arrests in England.

The grill chef shouted to the kitchen, 'Hey, Frank, they got those pricks in England.' He then turned to Novak. 'Sorry about the language, my friend. But these guys...' He motioned at the TV in disgust.

'No problem,' Novak replied, noticing a picture above the grill station of a girl in her early twenties standing on the steps of the London School of Economics.

The grill chef was joined by a pot washer – all glaring eyes, towel tossed over one shoulder – neither exchanging any words.

The *Fox* correspondent stood outside what remained of Downing Street. '...the U.K. Home Secretary Ed Bannatyne, is refusing to comment on the specific intelligence that led them to this terror cell. But my sources in government are calling this a major win for GCHQ, the U.K. version of our NSA.'

The news ticker said: 'Death toll estimated around 75 people...Deadliest terror attack in British history...'

The other chef patted the grill chef on the back. 'Hope they rot in hell,' he said, before returning to the kitchen through the swing doors.

'His little girl,' the grill chef explained to Novak. 'My

niece. She was standin' outside the gates at Downing Street when it happened. She's lucky to be alive.'

'I'm glad she's okay,' Novak said, unable to think of anything else to say.

The grill chef passed Novak his hoagie on a plate. He squinted slightly, then pointed his tongs at Novak. 'Hey. Ain't you that guy?'

Novak replied, 'No.'

'You know, the guy. Who did that NSA story.'

Ordinarily, Novak would have loved being recognised. He would have come back behind the counter, had his picture taken with the grill chef and the rest of the kitchen crew, then put it on Instagram to show that he was still a regular guy, who did regular things like eat hoagies in Little Italy. Somewhere inside him, that desire was no longer there.

'Not me, man,' Novak answered, picking up his plate.

The scrolling newsbar on the screen changed to breaking news.

The reporter on the Capitol steps said, 'Thanks, Katie. I have been speaking with a number of sources this morning, and they're all telling me retired four-star General Bill Rand is expected to be announced later today as the President's nominee for Secretary of Defense. As with all cabinet appointees, General Rand will require Senate approval by a simple majority, and so far – at least from the Senators I've spoken to – this nomination is expected to sail through. As General Rand has been retired for more than seven years, he doesn't require a congressional waiver in order to serve. However, there are a number of Senate Democrats concerned about the President adding a third military appointee to his cabinet...'

Novak set up in a corner of the room, so his laptop screen faced a blank wall behind his banquette. Last thing he needed was a constant parade of staff looking over his shoulder, or –

worse – members of the public using restrooms. It also allowed him to scope out anyone entering the café.

He plugged in his Tails operating system from his memory stick, then logged into OTR. When he left Caspar's later, he would be leaving no trace of himself behind.

One username was waiting on his OTR safe list: *Rebecca-.Fox*. He clicked on it, and almost immediately a message appeared:

Rebecca.Fox: What the hell happened to you?

Tom.Novak: I'm sorry. I had to leave my motel. And there was no wifi at the second place.

Rebecca.Fox: You're in hiding, or being followed. Which is it?

Novak stopped for a few moments, trying to work out how she knew.

Tom.Novak: Hiding. How did you know?

In no time, Rebecca's reply appeared. He had never seen anyone type so fast.

Rebecca.Fox: You were staying at a motel, and judging by the time you bailed on our OTR chat last night, I'd say you were somewhere in the Eastern Time Zone. Can't be Washington or you'd have been in a hotel.

Novak started to smile.

After a brief pause, more appeared.

Rebecca.Fox: Which really only leaves New York, and if you're staying in a motel in New York then you must be hiding from someone, because you posted a picture on Twitter six weeks ago of the view from your living room window, which clearly shows the Williamsburg Savings Bank tower, which means somewhere near Brooklyn. And you haven't moved since that picture was taken because your Twitter-post locations are exactly the same. Which means you have no need to be staying in a motel in New York state unless you're being followed, or you're hiding.

Novak, who'd been about to take a bite of his hoagie at the start of Rebecca's post still had it held there at his mouth. He put it back down, unbitten.

Tom.Novak: OK. That was pretty cool.

Rebecca.Fox: I'm not trying to impress you. If you're in danger, then I am too. So you need to tell me why you left your first motel.

Tom.Novak: I'm investigating a link between Abbie and a member of the British intelligence services who died in suspicious circumstances the same night as her. When you told me about your new information last night I wanted to run it past my colleague Stella. So I called her cell. As soon as I realised I could be tracked by doing that I got out of there.

Rebecca.Fox: If I had your number right now I could ping it to within sixteen feet of your current location. That's close enough to bundle you into a van without much fuss. You can't take risks with that. If your other story is linked to Abbie in any way, then I'd say you have some very serious people after you.

Tom.Novak: Is there anything else I could do to secure myself?

Rebecca.Fox: Pick good passwords is number one. The most popular password for the past five years is "123456". Second place? "Password". People are morons.

Tom.Novak: I'm good. I'm also using Tails from a memory stick to hide my connection.

Rebecca.Fox: That's smart, but in certain circumstances it can actually make it easier for people in my line of work to find you. People hiding their connections on public wifi services is a sign of someone with something to hide. OK, they can't see anything you're up to on that connection but it gives them a starting point. That's often all we need. If you go into a store and tell the security guard you're going to steal something but he won't see you do it, he at least knows you're a thief.

Tom.Novak: What about OTR? I've always just taken experts at their word that it's safe. Can't NSA hack anything?

Rebecca.Fox: Only in stupid action movies or books. The NSA doesn't have super computers that break code faster than mathematics allows. That's the beauty of it. The security agencies are limited to the same mathematical rules as everyone else.

Tom.Novak: An annual budget of $10 billion doesn't stack the odds in their favour?

Rebecca.Fox: The numbers are always in favour of those encrypting over those decrypting. Say you use 64-bit encryption key, imagine a *corridor with 64 doors. Behind each door is either a 1 or 0. To decrypt, you have to figure out the exact combination of 0s and 1s behind all 64 doors to break the key. A good programmer would take about a full day without sleep to break that key. Say you added a 65th door. With key encryption, you're not just adding a single extra door to check on its own. You have to check door 65, but also the 64 others all over again. Now imagine going from 64-bit to 128. It's an exponential nightmare. So yeah, we're safe here.*

Tom.Novak: They're saying GCHQ is responsible for catching the terror cell. Anything to do with you?

Rebecca.Fox: We don't take victory laps here.

Novak couldn't work out if he'd offended her or not.

Rebecca.Fox: Let's get to business. The night Abbie died she emailed me 100s of files. I think they might be useful to you.

Tom.Novak: What have you got?

Rebecca.Fox: Sending now.

Novak's laptop pinged a notification:

"IronCloud has received a new file ready for download for *tom.novak@therepublic.com*. Enter your key to decrypt file."

Rebecca.Fox: Tell me when it's open.

Once the file opened, Novak realised he was looking at top secret British intelligence: a dossier on the man Artur had videoed.

Tom.Novak: It's open.

Rebecca.Fox: I have evidence Abbie was working covertly as that agent's handler for MI6. Whatever he and Abbie found out during Operation Tempest, I think Simon Ali found out too. And he was killed before he could tell anyone about it. That file's just a tiny taste of what you can expect. Stella gets the rest on a memory stick when we meet in person.

Tom.Novak: When and where?

There was a pause.

Rebecca.Fox: Tomorrow. 12pm. Hatchards, London. I'll be browsing the crossword books.

Tom.Novak: I'll set it up. But I need your help with something.

Rebecca.Fox: What?

Tom.Novak: There's a video file NSA is trying to track from a contact of mine. It would really help him if you could find out how close they are to finding him. If they haven't got him already.

Rebecca.Fox: What's his name?

Tom.Novak: Artur Korecki. He's Polish.

Rebecca.Fox: Leave it with me. And tell Stella I'll see her tomorrow.

Before Novak could reply, *Rebecca.Fox* disappeared from his messenger window.

21

Leckie's street-level flat on Lambeth Road was sandwiched between an alleyway leading to a cement back garden filled with old car tyres, and a flat whose door opened straight out onto the pavement.

Empty beer cans rattled against the inside of the front door as Leckie let Stella in. She couldn't believe the squalor he was living in. She also couldn't help but feel a little responsible for him ending up there – even if all she'd ever done was tell the truth.

Leckie went straight for a battered old laptop in the corner, which Stella noticed was hooked up to a landline telephone under a table.

'Sorry about the mess,' Leckie said.

'It's okay,' Stella replied, hugging herself against the draft coming from the door and the windows.

Outside, traffic passed by so close it sounded like it was actually in the room. There were piles of paper everywhere, notes written on betting slips, bus tickets, folders, document wallets, printouts...

There were a number of old photos of the same girl around the room, and some couple-selfies of her and Leckie.

'Your girlfriend?' Stella ventured, picking up a photo. The frames were the only things that had been dusted in the room.

Leckie set up the laptop speakers. 'Ex. Natasha. She took off when I got sent down. I haven't heard from her since.'

'Where was this taken?' She showed him one of the photos.

A plaintive smile came across his face. 'That's a place near Loch Lomond. You know it?'

'Never been.'

'It's called Conic Hill. Natasha used to go there when she was small. One Friday night we just threw our stuff in the car and drove north all night. We listened to the Beach Boys. We talked about...I don't know. Everything. When we got to the top of that hill... That was when I knew, you know.' He shrugged. 'Didn't work out in the end.'

'You didn't just lose your job.'

'True. Still...no hard feelings about you testifying and all that.'

'Dan. If there had been any other way... At least you got in with *The Post*.'

'Not really. This is a one-story contract. It's a cattle market in there.'

'You're freelance?'

Dan wiped the laptop screen down with his cuff. 'I almost single-handedly took down the biggest-selling tabloid in the country. No editor's going to put me on their books after a phone hacking charge.'

Stella gestured to his Journalist of the Year 2012 award on the wall. 'You'll always have that.'

'That's a laugh,' Leckie said. 'When I got sent down they rescinded the award. Said it was gained through illegal means. I kept it anyway. Some dick on Wikipedia edited it out my entry, though. Like I was Lance Armstrong or something.'

'Is that why you're hacking again?' she asked.

Dan placed the laptop aside. 'I'm starting all over again

like some poxy staff writer. Have you any idea what that feels like? After those years at the top, the office parties, having celebrities, footballers, MPs calling me, begging me to take a story. To living like this? I used to have a beautiful three-bedroom gaff in Clerkenwell. Pool room, everything. I just need one break, Stel. But it needs to be big, and it needs to be soon.'

'Who have you hacked, Dan?'

'See, I know this guy, right–'

Stella had heard that sentence from Leckie many times before. 'No,' she said, 'we're not down the pub. Tell it to me straight.'

'He was on background.' Dan paused to light a cigarette. 'Charlie Fletcher.'

'Why am I not surprised,' Stella said.

'He says, have I heard about this Cabinet minister who's been banging this civil servant chick. So Charlie gets me his mobile, and I dial into his voicemail.'

'You hacked a minister's phone? Dan, you're still on parole.'

Leckie clicked through to the relevant files on the laptop and turned the speakers towards Stella. 'What you're about to hear is that little break I need. And after this, *I swear*, I can go straight.'

Stella perched on the end of the sofa arm. 'Go on then.'

Dan pressed play.

"Message - First...August...two twenty...a.m.

FEMALE: Hi, it's me. [long pause followed by a sigh] Just lying in bed, thinking about you. Again. When can I see you? I hope it's soon. I saw you on the TV tonight. You looked so handsome. Thank you for wearing the tie I got you."

"Message - Third...August...five oh five...p.m.

FEMALE: I got the files you wanted. They're way worse than you thought. Call me when you can."

Stella was growing impatient. 'Dan, can we get to the point...'

He shushed her as the next message played. 'I want you to know, that what you're about to hear, I promise you, is genuine. Okay?'

Stella gave a shrug of low expectations.

"Message - Seven...December...ten...thirty-one...p.m.

FEMALE [out of breath, panicked]: You've got to help me! Tempest is blown...They know everything, Nigel... [she starts to cry] You've got to help me get out of here—"

The message ended.

Stella stared at Dan in disbelief. She asked, 'Is that what I think it is?'

'It's the last phone call Abbie Bishop made before she was killed.'

'Who's Nigel?'

Dan shook his head. 'Listen.' He played another track, a much earlier one.

"Message - Twelve...August...nine eighteen...p.m.

MALE: Good evening, my darling. I'm just finishing off Cabinet notes, so I'll send a car for you about ten. Oh, and I was thinking...wear that black dress again."

Stella knew the voice anywhere. 'Bloody hell.' She stared in disbelief at the laptop. 'The minister is Nigel Hawkes.'

She pushed herself off the sofa arm and paced the room, rushing her hands through her hair.

Dan said, 'They'd been at it about six months. They talk on another track about how they met at some American embassy thing.' He smiled, overwhelmed. 'Do you get why I can't handle this on my own?' He looked like a man with no legs who had been told to run.

Stella's phone buzzed with a text: *'Westminster Public Mortuary. Side entrance. 1pm. - Sid.'* The extra fifty she'd put in his envelope was now looking like value for money.

Putting her phone away, Stella asked, 'What else do you have?'

'The rest will give you everything,' Dan replied. '*Everything.* Hawkes is up to his neck.'

Stella nodded. 'Get me the other recordings, and I'll give you the other half of your story. Deal?'

Dan looked around the room. It wasn't as if he had a lot of options. He grabbed his car keys off the table. 'Alright. I'll even throw in a bonus meeting with someone tomorrow. You're going to want to talk to them.'

Stella followed him outside. 'Who?' she asked.

Dan pulled the house door shut with a clatter of the letter-box. 'The man who heard Abbie Bishop's last words.'

Streatham House, London Bridge – Tuesday, 11.12am

Although the British press was still known as Fleet Street, all the major newspapers had long since departed the area for plush new buildings across London. *The Post* had been the first to move out in the eighties: the Fourth Estate's glory days when almost every paper circulated at least a million copies a day.

The paper had been bought over by the international media conglomerate News Media Group thanks to sweeping deregulation laws, despite NMG also owning another tabloid and a broadsheet – amounting to ownership of a third of the entire U.K. newspaper market. The group had become so powerful, any potential Prime Minister had to curry favour with them.

After the phone hacking scandal that brought down *The Herald* – where Stella and Leckie first cut their teeth with the big boys – *The Post* had managed to survive. Though its sales took a hit at the time, the public's memory quickly faded. After being on the right side of popular opinion with Simon

Ali's General Election win, it was like the whole scandal had never happened. *The Post* was soon back to knocking out daily sales in the millions like its heyday – sales that bankrolled *The Post*'s gleaming, glass-fronted HQ, Streatham House, overlooking London Bridge.

The man behind it all was Bill Patterson.

Patterson's ascendency had been nothing short of meteoric. He had left school at sixteen without a single qualification, then started work as a bicycle messenger. Now at age fifty-two, he was chief editor of the U.K.'s biggest-selling newspaper.

In the lobby Leckie asked Stella if she was sure she wanted to join him, reminding her she still had a lot of enemies in the newsroom.

Stella said, 'I'm not leaving your side until we have those recordings.'

They shared the lift with ten other reporters – mostly men – returning from what was either a very early liquid lunch, or the end of a very long night. Judging by how often they brushed at their noses, it appeared alcohol hadn't been the only intoxicant consumed.

To get to the newsroom floor they passed a wall covered in the most famous *Post* front pages: Michael Jackson's death; Princess Diana's death; MP sex scandals; Saddam Hussein's capture... Then there was a glass cabinet filled with the various prizes the paper had won over the years: Scoops of the Year; Best Column; Best Sports Writing... *The Post* had won the lot. In the centre was its most recent addition: Newspaper of the Year.

The three receptionists were young blonde women, each of them on the phone, explaining why a particular reporter wasn't available. On each side of the newsroom were tables

grouped together for the various sections of the paper –
Showbiz, Politics, and Sport dominated in terms of size.

It was often said that tabloid reporters could get hoisted
into broadsheet work, but never the reverse. As Stella followed
Leckie down the newsroom, the long-standing enmity between
tabloid and broadsheet was clearly alive and well.

Someone muttered to her, 'Scab bitch.'

Stella didn't react.

What did take her by surprise was their response to
Leckie.

'Awlright, Superhack,' someone said from behind a laptop
screen in a mock-Cockney accent, followed by a few cackles
from nearby.

Leckie, holding a keyring with about twenty keys on it,
deflected as best he could. 'Always a bit of banter in here,' he
said to Stella with a grin. He turned to the rest of the newsroom and announced, 'Superhack's back!'

'I thought you said no one called you that anymore,' said
Stella.

Some balled-up paper was thrown at him.

He batted it away. 'Get out of it,' he said, forcing a laugh.

It came across to Stella like the bullied child's attempts to
laugh along with their tormentors. He swaggered the rest of
the way, making out like he was notorious.

Leckie's desk was at the farthest back corner, next to a
long counter where extra packs of printer toner and paper
had been left. Along with a week's worth of recycling, all of it
loose.

Leckie was no longer smiling. He swiped the desk clear,
causing a clatter as dozens of empty Coke and Red Bull cans
hit the ground. Chuckles broke out around the newsroom.

All that was left on the desk was a ten-year-old desktop
computer and a landline phone. Both covered in dust.

Leckie knew exactly what was going on. 'After I got put
away, management became a bit stricter with certain, shall we

say, "research methods" that had become pretty routine in here.'

'They're mad at you because you got *caught*?' Stella said.

'As far as they're concerned, I spoiled the party. Now everyone's got to be more careful.'

Stella leant against the desk and turned her back to the newsroom, which had noticeably quietened since their arrival.

Dan switched the computer on, then crouched down to the bottom desk drawer, his keys at the ready. 'I put the other recordings on a little memory stick in here,' he said, then he froze.

'Don't you keep a lock on it?' said Stella.

Dan dropped the keys then opened the drawer. 'There was last night.' He ruffled through the drawer, then emptied its contents onto the floor. No memory stick in sight.

'Right,' he said, 'we officially have a problem.'

Behind them, there was a rapping of knuckles through the closed venetian blinds on the Perspex window of the editor's office. A Scotsman's brusque shout followed. 'Leckie! In here! Yesterday!'

'Right there, Bill,' Leckie replied soporifically. He turned to Stella. 'Don't worry. I'll find it.'

The editor's office blinds twitched, revealing only a pair of bloodshot eyes leering at Stella. 'You too, darling,' the voice added.

The office was filled with the smoke of about fifteen cigarettes. Something Patterson seemed oblivious to, as he looked over the layout for the evening edition. 'Glad you decided to grace us with your presence,' he said.

'Sorry, boss,' Leckie said. 'Been chasing a few things.'

Patterson looked up. 'What is *she* doing in my newsroom?' There was a kind of lethargy to his anger, the kind only extremely powerful people can get away with and still be menacing.

The last time Stella and Patterson had been in the same

room together was in front of a Commons Select Committee hearing on phone hacking.

Leckie replied, 'She's helping me with Abbie Bishop.'

Patterson slowly tapped the ash off his cigarette. He said to Stella, 'Do you feel safe because there's a room full of people out there? Trust me, love, if I knocked you out right now you wouldn't get one witness in that newsroom to come forward.'

Stella replied, 'You seem to have mistaken me for your first wife, Bill. I always wondered: the hundred grand you settled that case for, was that a hundred grand for each black eye you gave her, or for both?'

'Off the record,' Patterson said, 'it was worth every penny. Sit down, the pair of you.'

Behind Patterson's desk was a hanging picture of Simon Ali at Patterson's wedding – Patterson's fourth and most recent earlier in the year.

'So,' Patterson said. 'Abbie Bishop.'

Leckie lit a cigarette and crossed his legs as he exhaled, trying, and failing, to look relaxed. 'It's moving. Baby steps.'

'Baby steps,' Patterson mumbled to himself. 'You know why I want you? Because Dan Leckie always knows what the punters want. They like watching the football down the pub with a nice cold pint; they don't give a fuck about Africa, the markets, or their wives; and they think anyone who doesn't look or sound exactly like them is either a poof or a terrorist. The punters don't give a fuck about some posh bird who topped herself. They want to read something that makes them proud to be British. They want to read about politicians putting Britain first. Downing Street's on fire, the government's on its knees. Why the fuck would I pay you for baby steps?'

Dan said, 'The story is solid, but if I'm going to bring it all together I need my memory stick back.'

'What are you talking about?'

'Come on, Bill. It was in a black metal box in my desk. Who has it?'

'Well, fucking hell, let's see. You left it in your desk, where you never are, surrounded by bloodthirsty tabloid hacks who would do anything for a story, and who blame you for them being treated like criminals for the last year.' He paused. 'They blame *her* mostly, but you're up there too.'

'Look...' Stella began, trying to rescue the situation.

Before she could, Patterson interrupted. 'He said you were covering London now. So you must be working for a foreign paper. What is it?'

'*The Republic*,' Stella said.

Patterson applauded. '*The* fucking *Republic*, ladies and gentlemen. Now *there's* a publication absolutely *no one* gives a fuck about. Where can you even buy that over here? What does it sell a week? Oh, I'm sorry. You don't count sales, you measure on a fucking moral compass, don't you.'

Stella couldn't resist taking the bait. '*The Republic* is probably the most influential news magazine in the States. How many world leaders do you see reading *The Post*?'

'Oh fuck off, darlin',' Patterson said. 'They don't read *The Post*, but when I call them at ten o'clock at night they fucking well answer. You and your sanctimonious muckraking for months on end: you might have the snarl of a T-rex, but you've got as much reach. We fucking *entertain* people at this paper. What have you ever done? Except bang on about a bunch of pompous arseholes' right to privacy. They're not complaining about their privacy when their new film's coming out, do they? No, they don't give a fuck about privacy then. I get their agents on the phone, begging to get their fucking clients' mugs into my Showbiz section and make it look like it's not a paid advert, which it fucking well is. Go on, get out of here, the pair of you.'

Stella didn't move.

Leckie too. 'What about my memory stick, Bill?'

He went back to his emails. 'Go fill out a form at lost property, like I give a fuck.'

'He's bullshitting, Dan,' Stella said, holding firm. 'He's listened to the recordings, but he wants them himself. Right, Bill?'

Patterson completely ignored her. 'The things is, Dan – it's not working out. I don't see this story coming together without the recordings.'

'You're firing me?' Leckie said in amazement.

Patterson took out a piece of paper from his drawer without having to search – it had been prepared earlier with the help of some NMG lawyers. He put on his glasses, which still failed to give him any sense of sophistication. 'Quote, "you the Author, Daniel Leckie, warrant that the work submitted under this agreement may be terminated at any time..."' He peered over his glasses. He knew the rest well enough to recite from memory. '"Any violation of this renders the Author's contract with News Media Group null and void. And all materials collected during said contract shall belong to News Media Group." Your own contract, Dan. Which you signed.' He slid the contract across his desk for Leckie to see.

The air had gone out of him. Dan's shoulders slumped. 'You sat in that chair a few weeks ago and told me you could get me my old job back if I brought in a big story. Something juicy. Your exact words. And that I should use any means at my disposal.'

'Did I *tell* you to hack someone's phone?' Patterson asked.

As much as Stella knew it was still going on, she couldn't believe it was taking place right in front of her. After all the headlines, all the scandal, the public outrage, the angry MPs, the committee findings and hand wringing: nothing had changed.

'That's what I love about the hypocrisy of liberals,'

Patterson said. 'You rail against phone hacking, but as soon as it's a story you want like Abbie Bishop then suddenly it's okay. You,' he pointed at Stella, 'actually teamed up with the very guy that you helped send down. Welcome to the darkside, Miss Mitchell. You're officially a hypocrite like the rest of us.'

As they made for the door, Patterson called out, 'Let me know if your memory stick shows up. It would be terrible luck to lose anything important on it. Or indiscreet.'

Only then did Stella notice it wasn't just Simon Ali that was in Patterson's wedding photo. Nigel Hawkes was there too.

'You made back-up copies, right?' Stella asked as they walked back through the newsroom.

Leckie exhaled heavily. 'The last recording happened barely two nights ago. I've not had a chance.'

'Good move,' Stella said. 'Really smart, Dan.'

Before they reached reception, someone shouted, 'Hey, Dan! I thought we could get a beer sometime. I left you a message on Hugh Grant's phone but you haven't replied yet.'

The entire newsroom erupted in laughter. For once, Dan didn't laugh along.

In the sanctuary of the lobby, Stella and Dan took a timeout by the lifts.

'What do you think he's up to?' Stella asked.

Dan had his hands on his hips, staring at the marble floor. 'Sitting on it so he can do his own story? Or maybe Hawkes got to him.'

'How though?' Stella asked.

Dan had nothing. He looked bereft. 'This story is all I've got, Stel. I'm not quitting. Not yet. They'll have to kill me.'

Stella set off for the exit. 'Come on,' she said.

He chased her through the carousel door. 'Where are we going?'

'Westminster Mortuary,' Stella replied.

. . .

As they crossed Lambeth Bridge, Stella checked her side mirror. Immediately she got a sinking feeling. A black Audi snaked out from behind a taxi, nearly colliding head-on with a double-decker bus in the opposite lane.

Stella said, 'That car's back again.'

'Are you sure it's following us?' Dan asked.

The Audi accelerated suddenly, tailgating Leckie's Escort with a threatening rev of the engine. Close enough to give a nudge at any time.

'Yep,' Dan said, looking into the rear-view mirror, 'they're following us.'

Stella grabbed her seatbelt as Dan jumped a gear to accelerate.

The Audi followed easily, purring in comparison to the Escort's clapped out engine. The end of the bridge was on them in no time, and Leckie prepared to dive right down Embankment.

'Go left,' Stella said, raising her voice to be heard over the engine's effort.

'Westminster's right!'

'We have to lose them first.'

'Bugger it.' Leckie lurched left, cutting off a taxi to dive through an amber light. The Audi followed, busting through a clear red, nearly poleaxing a motorbike coming from Millbank.

Seeing traffic stalled up ahead, Leckie swung left into the bike lane, blasting his horn at the cyclists who had to take evasive action towards the pavement.

Both cars tore down Millbank beside the Thames, half on the pavement, half in the bike lane.

Leckie knew there would be little scope to lose a tail around the busy Wandsworth Road, and the next set of lights at the crossroads ahead were red. Traffic from the right was just setting off, led by a red double-decker bus.

Leckie floored it, shouting, 'Hold on!'

They charged out, barely squeezing ahead of the bus. Their rear bumper glanced the side of the bus. The nudge gave Leckie the help he needed to make the ninety-degree turn at speed.

The Audi had tried to follow, but the bus now blocked its passage.

As the Escort screeched onto the much quieter road of Bessborough Gardens, the Audi was boxed in, a cacophony of car horns coming from all angles. The Audi barrelled backwards, shunting the car behind out the way, then did a three-point turn to pursue the Escort. With its superior acceleration the Audi made up the gap in no time.

Leckie scoured for a turnoff but there was nowhere to go. The Audi kept accelerating, barging the Escort's bumper at an angle, trying to knock it off the road.

'Christ. Just pull over, Dan!' Stella shouted, clinging onto the handle above the door.

Before Dan could do anything, a black Mercedes 4x4 M-Class with blacked-out windows came haring up alongside the Audi.

'There's two of them now!' Stella cried, noticing the distinctive registration plate of the Mercedes.

It turned sharply right then back left, ploughing into the back of the Audi, sending it into a tailspin.

Dan let out a euphoric laugh at their fortune, looking in his rear-view mirror as the Audi sat stricken across a traffic island. The driver tried in vain to get going again, but the wheels were lodged under a bollard.

The Mercedes then sped off in the opposite direction, tyres squealing.

'Jesus...' Leckie gave a burst of terrified laughter as he realised they were safe.

Stella turned around in her seat, managing to get a picture of the Mercedes' registration plate on her phone.

Leckie alternated quickly between the rear-view mirror and the side. 'I thought we were toast. Who the hell was that?'

Stella checked the photo she'd taken. 'The Merc was a foreign plate. The Audi was definitely British.'

Leckie turned down the nearest side street off the main road. 'Looks like someone's decided to help us.'

22

Novak was walking briskly down Mulberry Street, trying to ignore his hunger pangs from the smell of fresh pizza emanating from the deli windows. Then he clocked a silver sedan puttering by across the road. Far too slow a pace for New York midday traffic.

Novak slowed, then stopped a passer-by for directions to Grand Street subway, knowing he'd be pointed in the direction of the sedan. Now he had an excuse to look over at the sedan, following the man's pointing arm. The passenger flicked his head away too late. He knew Novak had made him.

It was the same guy who had been wearing the NYU sweater. He was now in a white shirt and tie.

Novak thanked the man for directions. The man shook his head as Novak took off in the opposite direction to where he'd just been pointed. With some luck, Novak thought the NYU guy might back off now he'd been spotted. It was worth a try.

As Novak continued on, his gaze darted from one side of the street to the other. As his paranoia grew, all of Sharp's advice receded further into the background. Sharp could single people out to focus on, but Novak didn't have that talent. It took years in the field to learn what to look for.

Novak's mistake was in trying to keep tabs on anyone and everyone. His mind became a fog of one-liner physical descriptions, and an endless stream of images of shoes.

Then it happened. A familiar pair of shoes from a few minutes ago. The man had been in a dark green army surplus jacket, but his brown boots had looked too clean for the rest of his outfit. Unscuffed. And Novak had just seen them again.

Novak kept on walking. His pulse quickened, making him want to run.

He turned onto a rundown stretch of Grand Street. As soon as he was around the corner, he ran as fast as he could, zigzagging through the lunchtime crowd. Novak had no idea what he was going to do, but when he saw a homeless man sat in front of a disused hardware shopfront, he decided to take a shot at something.

Crouching down in front of the man, Novak figured he had about thirty seconds tops.

The homeless man was in his sixties. His face tanned with deep forehead cracks, his years on the street marked like rings on a tree. He had rolled his socks up over his trouser bottoms to stop rats crawling up them in his sleep. After that happens the first time, you never let it happen again.

He had on an oversized, filthy denim jacket, and a trucker hat from 'Betty's Diner – Georgia, USA'. His handwritten cardboard sign read, "Colonel Michael J Baker. 11th Armored Cavalry Regiment. Vietnam vet on hard times. Any and all help appreciated."

Still checking both sides of the street, Novak said, 'Excuse me, sir. I have a favour to ask and I don't have much time. If you were to let me borrow your jacket and hat, and I got you to walk once round the block, I'd give you five hundred dollars. But you need to be out of here in about ten seconds.'

Having never been a drunk or druggie, Colonel Baker's reflexes were sharp. He passed Novak his cap, hoisted the jacket straight over his head, then held out his hand.

Novak shoved an uncounted bunch of fifties into Baker's hands, then said, 'If that's short, I'll pony up when you get back. If it's too much, you can keep it.'

Without a word, Baker put the cash in his trousers and set off around the block.

Novak whisked the jacket and cap on, recoiling from the putridly sharp smell. Before he sat down, he knocked his shoes off and sat on them. They were too clean and new to be out on display. Novak turned the jacket collar up, pulled the cap low, and the Colonel's blanket over his lap to hide his clean trousers. He stared down at the pavement and waited.

All he saw were pairs of shoes. One woman dropped some change into the old coffee cup.

Then a pair of shoes he remembered stomped by.

Brown boots. Unscuffed. Versatile.

Sharp had been right: the man didn't have time to change shoes.

The steps were brisk and determined as they went past Novak.

He counted slowly to thirty, then checked to see if his tail was still in sight – he wasn't. The silver sedan was farther down the road.

Novak hid himself in profile behind the shop inlet. Down the road, his tail crossed at the lights, then jumped back in the sedan.

Once they were gone, Novak finally relaxed.

Rather than leave the Colonel's jacket and cap – not to mention his cup of change – unattended, Novak waited a minute for him to return.

The Colonel sat back down at his spot, putting his jacket and cap back on. 'You're the weirdest son of a bitch I ever met out here,' he said. 'And this is New York.'

'You've no idea what you did for me, just then.' Novak put his hand out to shake. 'Thank you, Colonel.'

Baffled, the Colonel shook Novak's hand and said, 'You too.'

Once Novak got on the subway to Brooklyn – on an empty car – he checked his cash. He'd given the Colonel six hundred dollars. He was glad at the thought of helping him out, but it was cash he might badly need in the next twenty-four hours.

He reached a quiet residential street lined with over-hanging trees, and brownstone townhouses. Park Slope, Brooklyn: one of the most sought-after locations in the city.

For Novak, it was about a safe haven. Someone he could trust.

He knocked on the door, not knowing if there would be anyone home. He hadn't called ahead.

A man wearing a bathrobe and smoking a cigarette answered. 'Novak,' Fitz said, breaking into a smile. 'You never said goodbye yesterday. I thought you'd be in London by now.'

Novak slipped off his shoulder bag. 'I'm in trouble, Fitz.'

When Novak had brought Fitz up to speed on his morning of dead drops, secret meetings and diversions, Fitz took a long plaintive look at his empty whisky glass.

'The problem with alcoholics,' he explained, 'is they spend all their time worrying about that first drink. That's why I say, get it out the way early in the day. The fourth and fifth drinks of the day are much more enjoyable.'

Fitz freshened his own glass at the bar – which was well-stocked.

He had been there an hour and Novak still had a full glass. Lost in thought he put it down on the oak coffee table. 'There's one thing I can't get my head around,' said Novak.

'What's that?' Fitz asked.

'Malik knew of a credible threat against a U.S. target. Yet he claimed it was the President that wanted him taken out.'

'All Presidents have kill lists these days,' said Fitz.

Novak asked, 'But why would he want a threat against the U.S. to get through? His own Secretary of Defense died in that attack.'

'Maybe that was the President's plan,' Fitz said. 'I heard that Robert Snow was going to London to announce his opposition to the Freedom and Privacy Act.'

'That would be like the Secretary of Agriculture coming out against farming equipment.'

'I saw a copy of the latest draft of the bill three days ago. It makes East Germany look like Disneyland. It was going to be my lead story until Downing Street happened. It's not that much of a stretch to believe that the President had Snow killed.'

'You're drunk,' said Novak.

'True,' Fitz agreed. 'But tomorrow morning I will be sober, and I will still be right about the Freedom and Privacy Act.'

Novak laughed.

'What's next?' Fitz drained his glass.

'I need to figure out a way to get to London that doesn't raise any flags.'

'My boy, your life has turned into a Robert Ludlum novel.'

'Yeah. And when my passport flags up at the airport, it'll be *The Novak Idiocy*.'

Fitz waited for Novak's laughter to fade. 'I was glad to see you reject Bastion's offer.'

'How did you know?' Novak asked.

'That twenty-four-year-old twerp at the *Times* who always wears bowties just tweeted that he's the new Bastion News security correspondent. I wonder if he knows he was second choice.'

'Better him than me.'

Fitz slapped Novak on the top of the arm. 'As long as you want to stay, my home is your home.'

Later, Fitz was in his downstairs study giving a webcam interview to early-evening *Fox News* on the Downing Street bombing. Novak could hear him from upstairs in the spare room. He kept the picture on but the sound muted as he signed into Darkroom.

Ever since Novak's NSA story highlighted that both NSA and GCHQ had the ability to tap into any webcam and switch on any computer microphone, developers had rushed to find a more secure video chat facility. Darkroom had become the techies' favourite, and was doing for video chat what WhatsApp had done for secure texting. End-to-end encrypted, NSA and GCHQ-proof video chat.

From downstairs, Novak could hear Fitz:

'I for one think it's now very much in the public interest to learn what exactly Simon Ali was about to confess to. This was a very hastily arranged press conference, and until four days ago, his meeting with Robert Snow wasn't even on the books...'

Novak closed the door over a little as he called Stella on Darkroom.

Stella was walking down a quiet London street in the dark when she came on. 'Novak. Man, am I glad to see you.' Thinking he was staying in a rather plush hotel, she asked, 'Where are you?'

'I'm at Fitz's. He's downstairs doing a video interview right now.'

Getting to business, Stella said, 'You're not going to believe what I've got over here.'

'I was going to say exactly the same thing,' Novak replied. He could make out someone lingering beside Stella. 'Who's that with you?'

Stella looked to her left. 'That's Dan.'

Leckie pushed himself into frame and said, 'Alright, Tom.' He then said to Stella, 'I'm going to get some chips. You want anything?'

Stella declined.

Once Leckie was gone, Novak asked, 'Who the hell is he?'

'He's an old colleague from *The Herald* days.'

'*The Herald?*' Novak said. 'Hang on. That's the one they convicted?'

'Yep. It was my testimony that helped put him behind bars. In fact, I didn't just testify, I left the paper and joined another paper's crusade against them.'

'Now you're working together?'

'He's got valuable information, Novak. We need him. But you better tell me what you've got before he comes back.'

Novak said, 'The prisoner from the plane was called Abdul al-Malik. He was arrested on suspicion of terrorism. And he was MI6.'

'Was?'

'A few hours after Artur's video was taken, a black ops team showed up, and Malik ended up shot. They say suicide. Sharp says they took him out. Thing is, earlier, Malik had made a phone call to Abbie Bishop.'

Stella was stunned. 'Are you serious? What's their connection?'

Novak replied, 'She was Malik's handler. Abbie was working for MI6. Of all the people he could have phoned, he phoned her. Think about it. They're thousands of miles apart, and they both end up dead the same night? The day before Downing Street?'

'You think Downing Street, Abbie and Malik are all connected?'

'Stella, I'm ready to take this to Diane already.'

'Let's not get ahead of ourselves.'

'What have you got?' asked Novak.

'More confirmation that Abbie Bishop was not entirely who everyone thinks she is.'

'How so?'

'Dan has some voicemail recordings.'

Now Novak understood why Leckie was involved. 'Stella, we can't use hacked voicemails for this.'

'Hang on—'

'For *anything*. Are you mad?'

'But as a means of getting us on the right track. We don't have to use them. Without them we'd never have known she was having an affair with Nigel Hawkes.'

Novak froze as the name sank in. 'My god.'

Stella said, 'There are messages between them going back six months. Dan says there are other recordings, but his editor won't give them up.'

'Why not?'

'He's friends with Hawkes. He's not going to let them get out.'

'What are you going to do?' asked Novak.

Stella replied, 'We're working on it.'

'What about Abbie's post-mortem?'

'The police are still treating her death as accidental.' Stella put on her editor hat. 'What's solid is that I've got both tox reports on her. The first said she was stone-cold sober, and the second said she could barely stand up. And I ran the doctors' names on the second report. They're in-house MI5.'

'MI5 verified their identities?'

'I didn't need to. Even MI5 doctors need U.K. medical licenses. Their names are on public record on the General Medical Council's website, which lists them as Classified.'

'Nice catch.'

'Before Dan gets back, should I float some things that might be a little outside the box?'

'How far outside the box?' Novak asked.

Stella said, 'Foreign Secretary has affair with intelligence analyst. She finds out more than she should have, blackmails Hawkes, then he has her killed.'

For once in his life, Novak felt like he had to be an editor. 'Okay, I think we need to start a little bit closer to the box. Speaking of which: I have a source inside GCHQ who wants to meet tomorrow. I'm going to send you an OTR about it.'

'Okay,' Stella said. 'But Novak, a car tried to run us off the road earlier. We're fine, but whatever we're onto is clearly sending up flares. I don't know how many more people we should be bringing into the fold here.'

'Funny,' said Novak. 'I was going to tell you the same thing.'

'What do you mean?' Stella asked.

He paused. 'You said you helped put this Dan guy away. Now he's just out of jail and he's handing you sources for free?'

Stella hesitated. 'He really needs this story. You think he's up to something?'

'Possibly.'

'He's coming back over,' she said. 'Before I go, I need to tell you about the mortuary.'

Novak asked, 'What about it?'

'The police pulled a body out of the River Thames. An old GCHQ colleague of Abbie Bishop's. They found a phone along with the body in the river. There was a number in the call history the guy called several times last week. I still can't get my head around it.'

Novak was distracted by something on the TV. 'Sorry, Stella,' Novak said. 'One second.'

The right half of the screen where Fitz had been had gone black, as if the studio had lost the connection with him. Except Novak couldn't hear Fitz talking downstairs. The anchor was struggling to get a response. Pressing her earpiece, she said, 'Can you hear me, Martin...'

Novak lowered the phone, and wandered out onto the landing. He didn't want to call out in case Fitz was still on air.

'Novak?' Stella repeated. 'Did you hear what I said?'

As he peered over the staircase banister, he whispered, 'I've got to go...'

Stella tried again. 'I said the calls were made to–'

Novak hung up, just as he saw a man wearing brown boots and dark clothes striding out of Fitz's study towards the living room. He was holding a handgun by his side.

Novak crouched by the banister, looking back at the TV that was still playing. Had the man downstairs heard it?

A cacophonous blast started from the stereo in the living room. Stravinsky's "Rite of Spring" that Fitz was listening to earlier. Its tense chugging strings put Novak even further on edge. Whatever the man was going to do next, he didn't want the neighbours hearing.

The man strode back into the study, then dragged Fitz – with a clear plastic bag over his head – under the arms into the living room. Fitz kicked his heels at the parquet floor, leaving black streaks behind. He was running out of oxygen and losing strength.

Novak dialled 911. He whispered, shielding the mouth piece. 'There's an armed man in my friend's home. It's 23477 Hawthorn Avenue, Park Slope. Repeat, he's armed.'

The operator paused. 'Sir, we got a call already for this address. The ambulance and police are on their way...'

What the hell? Novak thought. *Who called that? And why an ambulance?*

There wasn't time to discuss it. He hung up, then grabbed his backpack with his laptop and the files Sharp had given him earlier. He clung to the wall as he edged down the hall, keeping the backpack tight to his chest.

Some books and a drawer were tossed towards the living room doorway. There was no exit on Novak's side of the building: the only way out was through the kitchen or the front door. Both of which the intruder had covered. In any case, he couldn't leave Fitz behind.

The man was shouting at Fitz, 'Give me the asset's location and I give you oxygen!'

Novak crept down the stairs. He could only see as far as the hallway by the front door. Peeking into the living room he saw the intruder – the NYU sweater guy who had been following him earlier, now plus a baseball cap, and a scarf wrapped across his face – tearing Fitz's drawers and cabinets apart. He went back to Fitz to let air in, then tied the bag back up. Fitz was prostrate in the armchair, legs stretched up, hand clasping fruitlessly at the bag.

Novak knew that if he tried to be a hero, he could end up getting Fitz killed. But he also couldn't just stand by and watch his friend be tortured for something Fitz knew nothing about.

The intruder called out, 'Tom Novak! I know you're up there. Tell me where the asset is and your friend lives.'

Novak was almost relieved that he could bring about an end to Fitz's suffering.

'Please,' Novak answered, holding the bag out first from around the doorway. He had to shout to be heard above the music. 'I'm unarmed.' He kept his eyes down as he entered the living room. 'I haven't seen you. Just take the files and leave my friend. Please. He's not involved in any of this.'

The intruder stepped towards him, pointing his Glock 19 at Novak's face. 'I want the asset. Where's the asset?' He was American.

'I don't know about any asset. There's no one else here, I swear.' Novak threw the backpack over to the intruder and put his hands up.

He dragged the backpack closer with his foot, but wasn't satisfied with just that. 'Tell me where the asset is and this is all over.' He turned the gun on Fitz. 'Or he dies.'

Fitz was no longer kicking his feet, he drifted into unconsciousness.

At a loss at what else to do, Novak put his hands up higher. 'Please! I don't–'

As the intruder prepared to fire, the lights went out and the stereo shut off. The entire house was thrown into darkness and silence. Then there was a flurry of heavy running steps from the kitchen, then a scuffle broke out next to Fitz. The intruder groaned as he was knocked back against the book-cases, sending books falling all over him.

The man held the intruder from behind, arms locked around his neck, cutting off his airway. The intruder dropped his gun to pick up a hardback book, then sent it whirling into the man's face. Now the two faced each other. With the gun out of sight in the darkness, the intruder grabbed a wrought iron fire poker, and swung it viciously at the man. Novak tried to get to Fitz.

The man warned Novak, 'Stay back.'

Novak knew the voice. It was Walter Sharp.

Instead of backing off, Sharp grabbed a cushion then marched straight towards the intruder. Sharp absorbed the impact of the poker using the cushion. Then he grabbed the poker handle, and flicked it back across the intruder's windpipe. He went straight to the ground, gurgling for breath.

Sharp kicked the poker to safety then checked the intruder's pockets.

Novak scrambled towards Fitz. He whipped the plastic bag off then dragged him to the hallway.

'Bloody hell,' Fitz wheezed, coming back to life. 'Next time...' he spluttered, 'you're staying in a hotel.'

Novak exhaled in relief, but it was too soon for laughter.

Sharp put Novak's backpack over his shoulders, covering the intruder with his Beretta 92. It wasn't as good as a Glock for concealed carry, but in twenty years Sharp had never been let down by a Beretta.

'We've got to go,' Sharp said calmly, guiding Fitz and

Novak out. 'He'll have a backup team outside and the police will be here soon.'

'That was you who called the ambulance?' Novak asked, helping Fitz to his feet.

'Either way one of the three of you was going to need an ambulance. We need the police for cover against the backup team.'

'Backup team?' said Novak.

Sharp looked the pair up and down. 'You got everything?'

'Yeah,' Novak replied.

Sharp and Novak ran out into the night, while Fitz struggled a little behind. Sharp saw a black van pulling up at one end of the street, two police cars and an ambulance at the other. At the police's request the ambulance hung back.

Seeing the police draw their weapons, Sharp shouted, 'Down down down!' He shielded Fitz and Novak as they ran for cover behind a bank of parked cars. Shots were fired from the black van, bullets shattering car windows.

'What are they doing?' Novak yelled.

'They think one of you is the asset,' Sharp replied, waiting for a pause in the shots. He wasn't about to fire his weapon in a dark residential street at a target over one hundred yards away.

'What asset?' asked Novak. 'I offered him the files!'

'They don't want the damn files.'

The intruder emerged from Fitz's doorway, stumbling slightly and holding his throat. He had his Glock pointed at the three men. 'Where is the asset?' he yelled.

The police came in waves of three officers down the street, hiding behind trees as they shouted demands for a show of hands.

The intruder shouted again. 'Where's the asset? Where's Artur Kor—'

One of the policemen shot the intruder in the chest. There was no time to muck about with shoot-to-wound. In movies, shoot-to-wound seemed easy and obvious when you wanted a suspect in custody. In practice, shoot-to-wound was almost impossible. Regular motor function was still possible up to thirty seconds after a heart stopped beating, and a shot in the shoulder was no guarantee of survival.

The police shouted 'Suspect down!' and moved in. As the black van made a frantic U-turn and sped away, Sharp led Novak down the avenue, in the opposite direction from the police. Fitz couldn't keep up.

Novak shouted back for him, but Sharp pulled him on.

'He needs oxygen,' Sharp tried to explain. 'He can't come.'

'That's fine with me,' Fitz wheezed, sitting up against the front wheel of a shot-out car, holding his chest.

Sharp told him, 'Keep your hands up and shout that you're unarmed.' He smashed a car window with the handle of his gun, then unlocked the door from the inside. Novak dived in the passenger side, then Sharp shoved his head down as the police fired at them.

Sharp dipped his head as glass from the back windows sprayed all around him. He barged the cars in front, and then the back, to make space to get out.

'Fitz...we've got to go back for Fitz!' Novak kept shouting.

Sharp gunned it down the street. 'The medics are there. There's nothing more we can do.'

Novak kept calling for Fitz.

Sharp could tell he was going into shock. 'Look at me!' he said. 'Breathe. You're safe. He's safe. Listen to your breathing.'

Once they made it out the suburbs, Novak started to calm down. 'Who the hell was that guy?'

Sharp said, 'Possibly private military.' He reached over with a free hand and patted Novak down, pulling his jacket open. 'Are you hit?'

'I'm good.'

'Lucky I was tracking you.'

Novak scoffed. 'Yeah, lucky. That's what I feel right now.' He put his head in his quivering hands. 'Thank you,' he said finally.

'We need to get off the road,' Sharp said. 'We'll be safer on foot.' He pulled over outside a deserted car park, surrounded by a chain-link fence near Franklin Street subway.

As they descended the stairs, Sharp said, 'Looks like we're in this together now.'

23

WESTMINSTER PUBLIC MORTUARY, LONDON – TUESDAY,
THREE HOURS EARLIER

Detective Inspector Sid Vickering slouched against the bonnet of his Vauxhall Astra, finishing the last inch of a cigarette.

He had a pear-shaped torso which, with his stumpy legs, gave the impression he might topple over at any moment. He stood up as he saw Stella and Dan approaching.

Vickering ushered them in through the side entrance. 'This way,' he said.

'This is Dan, by the way,' Stella said. 'He's helping me with my investigation. I hope that's alright.'

'Suit yourself,' Vickering replied without turning around.

'Nice to see you again, Detective,' Leckie said.

Vickering corrected him, 'It's Detective Inspector now.'

The mortuary had been refurbished a few years ago, and was now a slick modern setup, all glass doors and brushed steel interior. It also had the capacity to deal with up to one hundred bodies at a time.

Vickering led them to a room filled with silver drawers – gleaming like a Michelin-star kitchen.

He pulled one of the drawers open, revealing a dead body

lying on a metal tray. 'Like I said. Single shot in the head, double in the chest.' The body was still drying out – the stench rising up.

Vickering couldn't even smell death anymore. He said, 'The bullet entries suggest he was lying on the ground when he was shot. Probably knocked out. His time in the water's made it difficult for forensics.' He unfurled an evidence bag containing a patch of woollen jumper with a dark red spot on it. 'SOCO found this on a jumper he was wearing. They ran the blood and it isn't his. But it turned up a match they received only the day before.'

'Whose blood is it?' Stella asked.

Vickering glared at her. 'Abbie Bishop's.'

'I'll be buggered,' Leckie said.

Always seeing the objective-journalist angles, Stella asked, 'What are the chances of cross-contamination between the two bodies?'

Vickering said, 'You mean, what are the chances a forensic pathologist carried some of Abbie Bishop's blood over fifty feet from one body to the next, in the most tightly controlled forensic facility in the country?' He tried to be charitable. 'None.' He wandered to the doorway, checking for approaching footsteps.

Stella said, 'Either he was in Abbie Bishop's company at some point...'

Leckie concluded, 'Or his killers were. Maybe they planted it on him. Either way, that's DNA proof linking her to another murder.'

Vickering returned to the drawer, closing it over. He said with irritation, 'Abbie Bishop's death is being ruled accidental.'

'Not the first time round,' Leckie retorted. 'I've got a pathologist's report that says Abbie Bishop was sober the night she died.'

'This isn't my shout,' Vickering said.

'What if we could convince you?' asked Stella.

'Okay, then. Convince me.'

'I need something first.'

'Like what?'

Stella said, 'The ID of the man in the river.'

Vickering grumbled. 'His name's Goran Lipski. He was ten years with GCHQ before he was sacked for a number of security breaches. The details of which are classified.' He folded his arms. 'What do you know?'

Leckie said, 'Abbie was shagging the Right Honourable Nigel Hawkes. For the last six months.'

Vickering stared back. 'Gee, I wonder how you got that.'

Leckie laughed.

Vickering turned to Stella. 'I'm disappointed to see you keeping the company of pond life, Stella.'

'I did my time,' Dan said. 'Which is more than I can say for a number of your colleagues. There used to be a time when hacks and coppers could get along. As long as we paid our bills on time.' He took out a wad of twenty-pound notes and held them out. 'We'd like to see Lipski's phone.' He paused before adding, 'Detective Inspector.'

Vickering pushed Leckie's hand away with disgust. 'Come on,' he said, leading them outside.

Back at the station – under a constable's guard – the evidence room was tightly secured. All the confiscated guns and drugs from all the London boroughs ended up in there, waiting in evidence bags to be farmed out to the various courts. Many a dirty cop had earned unplanned bonuses making things disappear from that room in the past.

Vickering took out the box of evidence bags taken from the Thames site where Lipski had been found. Glancing over his shoulder every few seconds, Vickering said, 'The techs have already checked it: the water killed the phone. I don't know what you think you're going to find.'

After putting on a pair of latex gloves, Leckie took out the SIM card and slotted it into Stella's phone.

'Didn't you hear me?' said Vickering. 'It's been in the water for two days.'

Leckie said, 'The phone's dead, but a SIM card can survive a forty-degree wash.' He handed Stella the phone, the glowing screen lighting up his smile. 'See, it's fine.'

Stella, also wearing gloves, scrolled through the SIM's contents: the phone book, text message inbox, and call log. All empty.

'What kind of "tech" doesn't know SIM cards are practically bombproof?' Stella asked.

Vickering replied impatiently, 'They said it was dead. They were professionals.'

'Who were they?'

'MI6.'

Leckie and Stella shared a look.

Stella asked, 'And an MI6 tech told you there was no usable information that could be extracted from a SIM card that had been in water?'

Vickering said, 'That's what they told me.'

'They're either incompetent or lying.' Stella kept scrolling through, then showed Dan a number. 'It comes up a lot last week.'

'Call it,' he urged her.

Stella hit the call button.

Vickering wandered away, muttering to himself, 'Waste of time...'

As Stella waited for an answer, somewhere in the room a distant ringing started.

Vickering froze.

Dan said 'What the—'

Stella shushed him. She lowered her phone to get a better

handle on the location of the ringing. 'It's in here.' She followed the sound towards one of the locked drawers. 'It's coming from in here.'

Vickering scrambled with the keys. When he unlocked the drawer, the ringing got even louder. He held the phones next to each other. Stella's number was on the incoming call screen.

'Nice one,' said Dan. 'So whose phone's that?'

Vickering paused, rechecking the files. 'But that's...' He didn't understand. 'That's being held for Counter Terror.'

Stella carefully took out what else was in the drawer with the other phone.

The evidence bags had the empty boxes of burner phones bought at a newsagent; an Oyster card for the London underground; street maps of Westminster with handwritten notes on them; surveillance photos of Riz Rizzaq.

Stella said, 'Sid. Who owns this phone?'

Vickering had turned white. He could barely get the words out. 'It was in the house used by the Downing Street bomber cell.'

24

Artur Korecki had been running all evening as if his pursuers
had their gun sights trained on him, and might shoot at any
moment. Lactic acid in his legs burned so deeply and intensely
he could barely lift his feet. The wet underfoot had sapped his
energy, and now he couldn't swallow oxygen fast enough to
replenish his starving muscles.

He'd run over boggy marshland, through a maze-like
forest – like something out of *The Lord of the Rings* – and
crossed rivers that went as high as his chest. Now darkness had
fallen, he deemed it safe to finally rest, sheltering under a tall
bush. His denim jacket was tattered and covered in mud from
two nights sleeping rough in the countryside. His extremities
ached from the cold. He didn't even have the energy to
breathe warmth into his red raw hands.

The first night out, near Lake Walpusz, a military vehicle
approaching had forced Artur to take evasive action. He had
jumped off a cattle-crossing bridge into the freezing water
thirty feet below. He had timed dipping his head under the
water as the truck got closer, taking forever to pass. When
Artur emerged – shaking like someone was shoving him back
and forth by the shoulders – he was convinced he was going to

die. Even in his battered state, he had remembered reading that the best way to survive a fall into freezing water (as wrongheaded as it seemed) was to take off all your clothes. Once you were out of the water, the real danger was the cold being held in your clothes, not in the air. He had sat down, then started digging up dirt and covering himself with as much of it as he could. It was amazing how much warmth could be found in the ground.

By morning his clothes were almost frozen stiff. But he had survived. That was all that mattered.

Rhododendron bushes had been his makeshift shelter through the previous night's rain, driven in sideways by a stiff wind. His swift escape from home had left him ill-equipped for rough winter nights. All he had were the clothes on his back. The laptop, spare phone, flash drive and passport in his backpack appeared to have survived in the sealed plastic bag he'd put them in – but those items didn't seem much use to him now. At least he had thought of grabbing his passport. Without that, his plan would never work.

As Artur emerged from the woods, he found a clearing at a bend in the Omulev River where a car had parked up. It was a beaten-up old Volvo, with two male teens inside, passing a bottle of vodka and a joint back and forth.

The clearing was a few hundred metres wide, and Artur was convinced that as soon as he stepped out the of shrubbery the *Biuro* would surround him. He also knew he might not get another chance to escape: he hadn't seen or even heard a car for hours.

He snuck up on the car from the rear, keeping low, his breath stuttering out his mouth with nerves. Inside the car Pink Floyd's *Dark Side of the Moon* was playing loudly, the two occupants in the pushed-back front seats, stoned and singing along to "Us and Them".

Artur tapped gently on the window, 'Excuse me. Please, can you help me?'

The driver was the less stoned of the two and heard Artur first. 'What the hell, man?' He cleared his long hair out his eyes and rolled his window down. 'Hey. What's up?'

Artur stayed crouched by the driver's door. 'Please. I need help. I'm being chased by the *Biuro*.'

The passenger, stoned out his head, croaked, 'You're shivering, man. Get in.'

Artur climbed into the back seat.

The passenger passed him a blanket, 'Take this,' threw back some chocolate and crisps, 'eat this,' then held the joint out, 'and smoke that.'

Just thankful for a soft seat and warm air, Artur tilted his head back in relief. He took some chocolate, but declined the joint.

'What do the *Biuro* want you for?' the driver asked.

'To give me to the Americans,' Artur said.

'Shit, man. That's all you had to say.'

The passenger said, 'I was just saying, man…it's the new world order. The world police.'

The driver started the engine. 'Where do you want to go?'

'As close to Gdańsk as you can get me.' Artur emptied his wallet and handed his cash to the driver. 'I'm sorry, but this is all I have.'

The passenger pushed Artur's hand back. 'No need, man.' He then changed tracks to the opening bass riff of "Money". 'We got Floyd, some weed: a road trip to Gdańsk…'

They stayed on backroads until Artur reckoned it was safe to take the E77 – the inter-Euro motorway – explaining his situation on the way north.

As they pulled up in downtown Gdańsk they exchanged handshakes through the driver's window. 'I don't know how to thank you,' Artur said.

'Stay alive, dude,' the driver said. 'That's all you gotta do.'

'I'd offer to take your names and phone numbers so I can repay you some time, but if I get caught, I wouldn't want you guys to–'

The driver wouldn't hear of it. 'It's cool.'

Artur passed him a note. 'Can you do me one last favour? Get this to Waldemar Bartczak. He lives in Szymany. His address is on the back.'

The driver took the note. 'I can do that. Peace, Artur.'

'Yeah, godspeed,' the passenger added.

Artur knew it was a risk, but it felt like one worth taking. With no other safe means of contacting Wally, his hand felt forced.

He wandered into the night, staying out of the dim lights that lined the avenue leading towards the Golden Gate in the historic part of the city. He didn't know where he was going to sleep that night, except that it wouldn't be under a bush.

The passenger asked the driver. 'What'd he write?'

The driver looked at the note:

'Wally – I made it to Gdańsk, thanks to some friends. You can reach me on my 'other' email address. Stay off the phone. Tell Novak I'll be on a bench in front of the waterfall at the Berlin Pariser Platz every day until he gets there. Stay safe.'

25

A scan of a photo of Stanley Fox slowly zoomed in and out on Rebecca's screensaver. It had been there for the last three hours after Rebecca clicked out of Mackintosh's files.

She had rested her head on her arm next to the mouse, then drifted in and out of microsleep: her eyes still closed, but every few minutes she jolted into consciousness again. Her dreams were a blizzard of Mackintosh and Abbie's files, draining any pretence of rest from her sleep.

She was woken by her mobile ringing, still in her jacket on the floor. The caller ID was not a good sign: 'Alexander Mackintosh – Work'.

'This is Rebecca,' she said, barely masking her lethargy.

'Rebecca, it's Alexander. I know it's your day off, but I need you to come in. Just for an hour.'

She waited for him to elaborate a little, but nothing came. Acid swirled in her stomach.

Mackintosh said, 'My office at eight.' It wasn't a question. He hung up.

Rebecca, still holding her phone, said quietly, 'Shit.'

Before she left her flat, she uploaded the stolen files to her IronCloud, then threw all her discs and memory sticks and hard drives into her microwave. A thirty-second nuke was enough to wipe all data from them.

At the front door she looked the place over, wondering if she would ever be back.

The walk to GCHQ was a blur to her. Mackintosh had never sounded so grim. And if it was a work emergency she would have been pinged with a colour-coded alert. Had he been on to her long? If she hadn't agreed to come in, would the police have descended on her flat? She was probably being tailed right now. *No point looking for them*, she thought. For the possible arrest of a GCHQ officer, they'd send someone good. Too good to be spotted in Cheltenham rush hour in the dark.

Rebecca had seen GCHQ operatives arrested twice before. They always did it in the building. Nice and quiet, with nowhere to run to. Those were for minor offences, though. Rebecca was under no illusions: there was nothing minor about what she'd done.

At each checkpoint at GCHQ exterior, Rebecca expected a pair of armed officers to come up behind her, then that would be it. She'd be history.

But at each stage she sailed through as usual, until she got to GTE.

The blinds in Mackintosh's office were open just enough to show a male figure with his back to the window.

Mackintosh beckoned Rebecca into his office from a distance away. He looked on edge. Nervous. Two things he rarely was.

'What can I do?' Rebecca asked Mackintosh. Her pace slowed as she approached his office, realising the man with his back to her was GCHQ Director Trevor Billington-Smith.

'Come inside,' Mackintosh said.

After flashing a brief smile, Trevor picked up Mackintosh's

phone and quickly dialled an outside line. 'Yes, we're ready,' he said.

Rebecca looked at Mackintosh to get a read on the situation. He winked at her, which only confused her more.

Trevor held the phone out to her. 'It's for you,' he said.

Rebecca tentatively took it. 'Hello?'

The voice at the other end said, 'Miss Fox...'

Mackintosh and Billington-Smith looked pleased with themselves, smiling at Rebecca.

The voice continued, 'This is Angela Curtis. I wanted to convey the government's immense gratitude for your sterling work this week. Trevor's told me all about it.'

'Thank you, Prime Minister,' Rebecca managed to say, widening her eyes. Now that she could finally relax, exhaustion hit her like an avalanche.

'I also understand you were colleagues with Abbie Bishop?' Curtis asked.

'Yes, I was,' Rebecca said. She couldn't help but notice Curtis's tone had shifted. She sounded conspiratorial.

'A terrible tragedy,' Curtis added.

Rebecca waited to see what she was getting at.

Trevor squinted at Mackintosh, wondering what was being said.

Curtis said, 'You're Stanley Fox's girl, aren't you?'

'Yes, I am.'

'He was a great man. He would be proud to see you continuing his work in national security.'

'Thank you.'

'I've been looking into you, Rebecca. I need to talk to you about Abbie. Alone. I need someone I can trust.'

Rebecca didn't understand why she was the one Curtis was talking to. Could she not trust the upper echelons of her own GCHQ?

Curtis went on, 'My secretary will contact you tonight to

arrange the details. Now smile and nod, and tell me thank you for my time or something.'

Rebecca smiled and nodded. 'Thank you very much for your time, Prime Minister.'

'Rebecca: I talk only to you on this. And you talk only to me. Is that clear?'

'Indeed. Thank you, Prime Minister.'

After Curtis hung up, her secretary came on the line: 'Thank you for your call, Miss Fox. You can now hang up the line.'

Rebecca hung up, her head in knots.

'Sorry about the cloak and dagger,' Mackintosh said. 'Trevor thought it best to keep things quiet.'

Billington-Smith said, 'I know I should toe the usual line about it all being a team effort. But we couldn't have caught the cell without you, Rebecca.'

'Thank you, sir,' she replied.

'You've done a huge amount,' Mackintosh said. 'All by yourself. Haven't you?' The smile he added at the end only made it feel more threatening. 'I'd say no one really knows the half of what you've been up to.'

Rebecca tried not to swallow hard. 'It's a team effort, sir,' she said on the way out.

The smile slid from his face once Rebecca had gone.

Before Rebecca left for the day – and before the morning shift's start at eight – she signed into the JWICS (Joint World-wide Intelligence Comms System). The system was an intranet for United States intelligence agencies, and which certain areas of GCHQ were granted special access to.

She then dialled into the shared NSA database which listed all Tier One Protocols: the most important actions taking place in the agency across the globe. The list ranged from most-wanted lists in cybercrime, to tracing agents and assets that had gone dark.

Near the top of the list for all Eastern European agents was a 'Black Capture' listing (someone who can be pulled off the street and bundled into a van) for 'ARTUR KORECKI'.

Anyone other than Rebecca would have been impressed at the depth of their searches – and how close they'd come to capturing him. Analysis of his YouTube videos had found several occurrences of filming near Jezioro Sasek, a lake that NSA had managed to identify thanks to GEOPOINT, which scanned the location from several angles in the videos. Based on the data – size of the lake, height of mountains in the distance, the surrounding landscape – they were able to identify it. It was like Google Maps on steroids. A local NSA asset had made a pass at the location late on Monday morning – missing Artur by mere minutes before he had disappeared into woods and continued his way northwest.

Since then, NSA's trail had gone cold.

Artur's listing had the picture from his *Dowód osobisty* national ID card that everyone over eighteen in Poland by law had to have. Some stills of him from YouTube identified the clothes he was last seen wearing.

After some brief biographical details cribbed from his *Dowód osobisty* (DOB and home residence) it noted 'of particular interest is any activity involving video files made by the suspect'.

A link took Rebecca to the search parameters of the video. The search was doing a real-time sweep of all the data NSA and GCHQ and the other Five Eyes agencies had hoovered up since Sunday night, looking for any video files that were active in any way – being emailed, posted on YouTube, Twitter or forums.

The search was catching a lot of hits. Mostly from Twitter and Instagram, whose video content most closely matched the search parameters. But with NSA's processing power, if Artur felt it was safe to post his video on some conspiracy theory message board, the metadata could give away his location.

In networking terms, what Rebecca needed to do was about as complex as changing your relationship status on Facebook.

What made it possible was her knowledge that intelligence requests for Tier One Protocols weren't made by investigating agents: they were made by entry-level graduate agents who weren't ready for the field. It was glorified data entry. They just happened to be dealing with classified intelligence.

All Rebecca had to do was click into 'Edit search'. In the field for video file size she decreased it to between thirty and fifty megabytes, and shortened the video length to between thirty seconds and a minute. Such broad parameters would result in a huge increase in how many files NSA quarantined. The search could be running around for days before someone realised they were looking for the wrong kind of file. Given the insane workloads and level of information changing hands between departments, let alone other agencies, Rebecca knew it was doubtful anyone would ever notice.

She logged out and set off quickly for the station. Her train to London would be leaving in less than thirty minutes.

26

It was after midnight London time when Stella got the call from Mike Chang that there had been a shooting at Martin Fitzhenry's. That was when Novak's sudden departure from his Darkroom call made unsettling sense to Stella.

Chang didn't know much except Fitz had been taken to Mount Sinai hospital with a suspected heart attack. All Fitz had said was that a man had helped Novak get away, and had probably saved both their lives.

According to Chang, Diane Schlesinger was ready to set all of New York alight to find Novak, but everyone was clueless as to where he was. Only the unnamed saviour knew that.

Henry Self had been prowling *The Republic*'s office in his gym clothes and sneakers, having been interrupted during a late-night touch-football game in Central Park. He had already enlisted the NYPD Commissioner and a senior agent-friend in the FBI within the hour to help with the investigation; such were the people in Self's mobile contacts.

Stella spent the rest of the night tapping up old contacts for information on the Downing Street bombing cell. But no one – not the Met and certainly no one at Whitehall or MI5 –

was giving out any names, or any details whatsoever about the cell. She made phone calls until well past midnight.

As for information on Goran Lipski, all Stella could find on him was a mortgage from the early nineties in his name. After that, Goran Lipski joined GCHQ, then disappeared off the face of the earth.

Even Dan got in on the act, making calls until the battery on his mobile ran out.

He and Stella decamped to his flat for the night rather than a hotel. No one knew Dan's address, except for the Bulgarian landlord he paid in cash each week. Dan's place at least had a bathroom window they could escape out.

The Alamo bar, Walworth, London – Wednesday, 10.11am

Stella straggled behind Leckie, who strode confidently into the pub. The Alamo on a midweek morning was not exactly Stella's scene.

Men who had gone to the bookies at eight – and whose losing streak started at five past – sat at small round tables of their own, staring reflectively into their pints of lager.

At the far end of the pub, by the pool tables, a lone young man was breaking off – sinking two stripes as he did so. He was drinking the remnants of a protein shake. Stella noted his gym bag on a chair beside the pool table.

'There's our man,' Leckie said, leading the way.

After sinking three balls on the bounce, the man said, 'You must be Dan Leckie.' He potted another ball. 'And this must be Stella Mitchell.'

His handshake was firm. He wore jeans, but smart, slim-cut ones, with a snug black v-neck tee. He clearly worked out.

He had just turned twenty-five, a rookie PC on £22k a year.

Dan introduced him. 'Stella, this is Leon Walker.'

He added, 'Constable Leon Walker.'

'Drink, anyone?' Dan asked.

'I'm good, thanks,' Walker said.

Stella just glared at him.

'You're up early for your day off, constable,' Stella said. 'Or are you late shift?'

'I thought Mr Leckie had explained,' Walker said, placing his pool cue back on the wall stand. 'As of yesterday morning, I'm currently on administrative leave.'

'Why?' Stella asked.

'For continuing to investigate the Abbie Bishop murder case after I was told not to.' He took a seat with his back to the door. He didn't want anyone seeing him talking to reporters.

Stella sat across from him and took her notebook out. 'For now you're just on background,' she said, as Dan returned holding a pint of lager. 'Your name won't appear in any stories I write.' Stella glanced at Dan. 'We write.'

After a sip of lager, Dan said to Walker, 'Tell her what you told me.'

Walker finished his protein shake, then said, 'I was coming to the end of a pretty uneventful beat – the bling beat they call it. Pimlico. So there's a lot of money around. Lots of quiet residential streets. Beautiful cars. On Sunday night I was twenty minutes from the end of my shift, when I turned onto Moreton Place. There was a group of seven gathered around a porch step. The men were in black tie, the women in ball gowns. Me? I'm half-Jamaican, living in a tower block. This is my aunt's pub. I grew up in places like this. So I found it hard not to stare at them as I went past – I couldn't help it. Then I realised there was something not quite right about them.'

'Like what?' Stella asked.

Walker said, 'I can't say for sure. It seemed just like they were...acting.'

'What happened?'

Walker said, 'From a balcony four floors up, about a hundred yards down the road, I heard glass smashing followed by a woman's scream. In the moonlight I saw a woman falling from the balcony, before landing on a silver Aston Martin DB9, setting off its alarm. Naturally, I was straight on the radio for an ambulance dispatch while I ran towards her. I climbed onto the bonnet of the car and checked the woman's vitals. She was still breathing but her head had deep lacerations. She was trying to say something, so I leaned real close and told her to hang in there.' He broke off, reliving the moment. 'I tapped her cheek to stop her eyes shutting. But after that she was gone. I administered CPR. By the time the ambulance came, Miss Bishop had been dead two and a half minutes. The paramedic asked me if I saw her jump. I'll tell you what I told him: all I saw was her *fall*.'

Dan egged him on, smirking. 'Get to the good bit.'

Walker said, 'While I was taking statements from the eyewitnesses, this metal shutter of the residents' underground car park opened up. A black Mercedes M-Class with blacked-out windows charged up the ramp onto the street. Then it sped off.'

Dan and Stella looked at each other, both thinking the same thing: Lambeth Bridge.

'Did you get a look at the registration?' Stella asked.

'All I could tell was that it looked foreign,' Walker replied.

Stella looked at Dan, who nodded his approval.

'What did the witnesses have to say?' Stella asked.

'That's where it gets interesting. I took statements from all seven. When I was done, guess who showed up to secure the scene?'

'Who?' Stella asked.

'MI6.'

Stella squinted slightly. 'I don't understand. You mean MI5, right?'

'I was shown ID by the investigating officer. Even still, it's my first homicide, so I radioed the station who confirmed they got the call. These guys were MI6.'

Stella said to Dan, 'Like they handled the Lipski crime scene.'

Walker turned his palms up. 'It wasn't like I was in a position to argue. When I asked what was going on, they told me the crime scene upstairs was part of a GCHQ safe house and I didn't have authorisation to enter it. What got me in trouble was the next day, when I tried to follow up with the witness statements. Only one of the seven saw anything. She told me Miss Bishop stood on the ledge a moment, then threw herself off. Except there are a few problems with that statement. First: the broken French window that leads to the balcony. I clearly heard a smash, followed immediately by Miss Bishop's scream as she fell. Why would she throw herself through the window first?'

'There was no mention of suicide in the final police report,' said Stella.

Walker nodded vigorously. 'Only accidental death, right. What about the scream? She didn't scream on the way down. She screamed before she started to fall. Those aren't the only problems.'

'What else?' asked Stella.

'The witnesses all showed me driving licences and passports. But when I got to the station, none of their details checked out. Not a single working phone number. So I ran their names through the Electoral Register, the DVLA, Inland Revenue: everywhere. Not even birth certificates. It was like those seven people never existed. When someone found out about the searches, the Chief Superintendent suspended me. Failure to follow orders, he said. It's weird.'

'I don't understand,' Stella said, unacquainted with police rank.

'Administrative leave for a first-year rookie PC, you're lucky if it's the cleaner that handles your paperwork. For the Chief Superintendent to get anywhere near this is like getting the Home Secretary to come round to deal with a noisy neigh-bour. It's unprecedented protocol.'

Dan certainly had an idea. 'Unless he was under orders from someone higher up the chain to snuff out any problems.'

So far Stella liked what she had heard. Not because Walker was telling her things that confirmed her theory, but because he was believable. With any possible source Stella always asked herself, why are they talking to me? What might the other side of their story be? How authoritative a source are they? What proof in documentation do they have? But most of all, Stella always looked for passion: a lack of it.

In her experience, people who were passionate about a story were rarely the most reliable. They magnify facts that fit their theory, and ignore anything that doesn't. Walker was different. He was self-effacing. He didn't try to attach the definitive to things he didn't know. Stella now had to set about poking holes in the very theory that would make a great story.

She turned back a page in her notes. 'Constable Walker, if these witnesses gave false names, who do you believe them to be?'

For the first time, he hesitated. 'Ms Mitchell, it might not seem like it, but we're in the same game. We can both know certain things to be true: that the only other witness to Miss Bishop's death directly contradicts what I saw and heard. And that witness is not only wrong, she's a liar with a fake identity. The only reason for those witnesses to be there was for a premeditated plan to murder Miss Bishop and control the scene afterwards.'

Stella said, 'But we're not in the truth game, are we, constable? We're in the evidence game. The what-we-can-prove game.'

Walker added, 'And all I can prove is the identification those witnesses gave me was entirely fake.'

'Do you have any documents to prove that?'

Walker said casually, 'I've got a picture of one of the witnesses.'

Dan flicked Stella's leg with the back of his hand. 'Told you he was up to it,' he said.

Walker explained, 'She gave me her passport for ID, but I was suspicious of how new it looked.'

Stella said, 'How new it looked?'

'See, whatever their cover was, they didn't think it through. I'll bet it was arranged last minute.'

'What makes you say that?'

Walker seemed to think it was obvious. 'She was standing about in Pimlico wearing a dress that cost, easy, four figures. The passport had been issued three years earlier, but it was pristine. Someone in her position would travel at least twice a year. That passport's not been in and out of luggage twice a year for the last three years. No chance. So I took a picture of it on my phone.'

Stella was still trying to remind herself Walker was a rookie.

'That's why I'm speaking to you,' Walker said. 'I need you to find that woman. You find her, you find who the conspirators are. Then you know who had Abbie Bishop killed.'

'Can you send me a copy of the picture?' Stella asked, holding her phone out so he could read her number.

Walker texted it to her. 'I don't care about the suspension,' he said. 'What I care about is my dignity. My honour. Have you got any idea what a suspension on a rookie cop's sheet looks like five years down the line? I should have been the last black man in Britain to want to join the Met. Trust me, I've good reason. But I did it because I want to make it better. I'm talented, I know. And I'm smart. A lot of people might think the smart thing for me to do here is come back to work in two weeks and shut up, but I can't do that. They knew what was going to happen to Miss Bishop, and they sent me on that beat because they thought I wouldn't cause a fuss. Wouldn't ask any questions.'

Stella remembered something from earlier. 'You said Abbie tried to say something.'

'Yeah,' Walker said. 'I thought she was trying to tell me someone's name, someone to call. I've seen a few people die in my time. That was the first time I've had anyone quote Shakespeare to me.'

'Shakespeare?' Stella said, getting a rush of adrenaline. She knew what she was hoping Walker would say.

'Yeah, I looked it up afterwards. "Hell is empty. All the devils are here."'

Dan, who had been in mid-sip of the last of his pint, suddenly choked a little.

Walker continued, 'It's from *The Tempest.*'

All Stella could picture was Novak's laptop and the same words appearing on the screen.

Walker said, 'I'm doing this because you're the only ones who can investigate this properly. I'm relying on you now.'

Stella stood up and offered her hand. 'Thanks for talking to us, Constable Walker. If you think of anything else that might be important...'

'You're stealing my lines now,' Walker said with a smile.

Once Dan and Stella got outside, he asked her, 'What d'you think then?'

Stella said, 'Let's go through the list for an unauthorised source, shall we? One: What's his motivation? He's not out to hurt the force, or incriminate anyone. Actually, in speaking out, the only person who's been hurt is him. Two: what's the other side of the story? So far, lies or silence. The only evidence for suicide or even accidental death have all been faked – the witnesses, Abbie's tox report, sealing off the scene to independent sources. Three: is he in a position to know what he claims? Of course. He's a policeman who was first on the scene. And four: does he have documentation to back up his story? Yes. He has the picture of the witness which we can now trace.'

'Solid as a rock,' Dan asked. 'I'd go to print tomorrow, if we could.'

Stella knew they were still a long way from that. 'I've heard that quote before. Hell is empty, all the devils are here. Or seen it anyway. It came up on Tom's laptop in New York. When it had a virus on it.'

'That can hardly be a coincidence,' Dan said.

'Like you choking on your pint when Walker told us, you mean?' Stella said. 'You've seen it too, haven't you.'

Dan didn't see the point in pretending otherwise. He seemed to be an open book to her. 'I heard her say it. Abbie Bishop.'

'What?' Stella halted. 'When?'

When he realised she'd stopped walking, Dan stopped too. 'One of the recordings. The stolen ones. Abbie was telling Hawkes that if she ever used that phrase he should raise an alarm with MI6. It was a code that she was in danger.'

'She said all this in a voicemail?'

'Not quite. It was a normal conversation.' He started walking again. Hands in his pockets.

Stella pulled him around. 'I thought you only accessed voicemails,' she said.

'I lied,' Dan said. 'I had Hawkes' phone tapped as well.' He tried to protest. 'It was so easy, Stel. I couldn't *not* do it!'

She couldn't believe how quickly their story was coming together and falling apart at the same time. She said, 'If nothing else you're proof that jail is no deterrent to reoffending.'

'Are you actually mad at me?' he asked.

'How perceptive,' she said.

'This is a massive lead.'

'It's a massive lead that's massively useless,' Stella exclaimed. 'What happens when my editor asks how we know that that phrase was a warning code and what it means? How can we *print* it? *The Republic* isn't *The Herald* or *The Post*, Dan. We can't listen to voicemail, then fake a bunch of research notes so it looks like we got there legitimately.'

'Why not?' He honestly didn't see the problem.

She grabbed his arm. pulling him on towards Elephant and Castle tube station.

Dan thought Stella was done with the argument.

Then she said, 'If we *were* going to use them, how would it work?'

27

The red-stone detached house in the middle of Archer Street had first appealed to Sharp due to its excellent visibility from both the deep porch-front, and fenced back garden. The nearest neighbours were a healthy toss of a baseball away, which meant he would be left in peace, and be able to keep tabs on any unscheduled visitors.

Being in CIA so long gave Sharp a unique perspective on real estate: what made for a good property didn't always ensure the greatest privacy.

When the real estate broker had enquired, politely, as to Sharp's occupation, Sharp told her he was in insurance. Which wasn't altogether a lie. Insurance of sorts. This was prior to her running Sharp's credit rating, which when it came back told her she needn't have worried. The house had been on the market for $415,000. Sharp paid cash.

He had been left a healthy inheritance by his father who had sold his drill bit company to the U.S. government in the eighties. He had died soon after, still not really knowing what his son did for a living. Sharp's mother had died in childbirth, and he had no other living relatives, which made him the perfect candidate for CIA.

Now Sharp found himself sharing his house with another occupant for the first time in his nine years of living there.

Novak woke up to the sound of clanging metal and grunting somewhere downstairs. He had slept deeply – deeper than he had done in months: the comedown from last night's adrenaline and feeling safe for the first time in three days.

He stopped halfway down the stairs, finding Sharp in the centre of what was once a dining room, pounding out bench presses with cast iron plates rattling on a barbell with each repetition. The rubber mats that covered the floor were all doused in white splotches of salt from old sweat.

In the light coming through the front-door window, Novak noticed how wrinkled his clothes were – especially his white Oxford shirt which he'd slept in. It was freezing outside, but Sharp hadn't felt it necessary to put on the radiators.

Sharp grunted his loudest as he grinded out the last few reps in his fourth set, planting the bar back in the rack with a crash.

Novak picked up the pile of newspapers on the hallway table: *The New York Times*; *The Wall Street Journal*; *Le Monde*; *The Guardian*; and the latest edition of *The Republic*. 'You must have a gold card for your newsagent,' he said.

Sharp stood up and towelled his face. 'He orders them in special for me. Not much demand for *Le Monde* around here.'

He wore a stringer vest, which he believed was the only way to lift. He was big, but also extremely cut: his body fat was comfortably under ten per cent, low enough for chiselled abs. He grabbed a khaki vest and threw it on.

'Any word about Fitz?' Novak asked.

Sharp replied, 'He's at Mount Sinai Hospital,' Sharp said, removing plates from the bar. 'He's stable and talking, according to your editor. I told him you're alright, but you're going to be out of contact for a while till we work this thing out.'

Novak clocked the weight of the plates Sharp was removing: he had been benching three hundred pounds for about ten reps a set. Novak could barely do half that. He was too embarrassed to tell Sharp that he also lifted. Novak had muscle, but Sharp was like the north face of the Eiger in comparison.

Sharp said, 'I might look like a military grunt, but I'm not such a yahoo I don't know who Martin Fitzhenry is. I've got four of his books over there.'

Novak looked at the impressive book cases lining the entire west side of the room. 'Have you read all these?' he asked, picking out random psychology books from the shelves with titles like *Extreme Ownership*; *Discipline Equals Freedom*; *The Art of War*; *Influence – The Science of Persuasion*; *The 48 Laws of Power*.

Sharp made his way to the kitchen, finishing the last of his water on the way. 'I try to keep my ratio eighty per cent read, twenty unread. I'm away from home too much.'

Sharp wasn't like the other CIA agents Novak had met before. His French must have been pretty good to read *Le Monde* (it seemed somehow appropriate that no American newspaper had thought to include 'World' in the title), and his interest in literary fiction took Novak particularly by surprise.

Sharp dropped piles of fresh fruit into a blender along with whey protein powder and finely milled oats. His post-workout breakfast. 'You must be hungry,' Sharp said.

'Um...' Novak paused, looked at the whirring blizzard of fruity porridge in the blender. 'You got any Pop Tarts or something?'

Sharp stifled a laugh as he drank straight from the blender jug, taking half of it in one go. 'I can scramble some eggs.'

Novak took a seat on the barstool at the breakfast counter. 'That sounds good.'

During the lull in conversation that followed, Novak tried

to work out if he could now ask the questions he'd wanted to the night before. When they were on I-87 heading north out of New York City, driving deeper into the serene pine barrens of Albany County, and they were just two guys from different walks of life on a highway in the middle of the night.

Sharp cracked some eggs into a frying pan and stirred them up.

'I really want to thank you again for last night, Officer Sharp,' Novak said. 'Me and Fitz would both be dead right now if it wasn't for you.'

Sharp just nodded. 'What would you like to ask, Mr Novak?'

'Sorry?'

'You're flattering me – which is fine, I guess. But you think that if you've massaged my ego a little I won't mind a tough question so much.' Sharp looked over his shoulder. 'We're off the record, so go ahead.'

'I've always wanted to ask someone involved in CIA rendition: how do you know you're not torturing an innocent person?'

Sharp's automatic responses kicked in. 'The United States does not torture,' he replied.

Novak laughed. 'Are we playing *that* game? Come on. Malik was sent to you like hundreds of others. Are you going to tell me he was the only innocent that the CIA has tortured?'

'We make more than we miss,' he said.

'How would anyone know?' Novak asked. 'The White House has censored every report into CIA torture programs. You've got gangsters turning informant on their rivals to get rid of them. Now the White House itself is using it to eliminate its enemies. What do you think Malik knew that was so dangerous he was assassinated?'

Without checking with Novak first, Sharp dropped a dollop of hot sauce into the eggs. 'It's not for me to say.'

'A contact at GCHQ sent me Malik's file. Will I tell you a little about the man you were about to torture?'

Sharp said, 'I think we both know you're going to anyway.'

'He was born into a deprived area in London to Syrian-born parents. He was such a gifted student he secured a no-fee bursary at Eton College. Trust me: that is rare. He was a star of the debating team. He left Oxford with a First Class Honours degree in Politics, Philosophy and Economics. Everyone in Malik's circle thought he'd be destined for politics. Instead, believing he was in debt to the U.K. for giving his family asylum, he applied for an army intelligence posting. His application found its way to MI6, who were looking for someone with brown skin, familiarity with Arabic and an ability to mix with different social classes.'

'That's prime candidate material right there,' Sharp said.

'He sure was,' replied Novak. 'Malik was in the field as a case officer at twenty-four. He had station chief written all over him. Maybe even a council associate or diplomat. Top brass were grooming him for political positions. Instead he turned down two promotions to stay in the field, because he knew his knowledge of the Levantine dialect of Arabic would be crucial to the success of MI6 black ops in Western Syria. He went to places no one else in their right mind would want to go. He did it out of a sense of duty.'

Sharp had stopped stirring the eggs. 'What was his name?' he asked, looking away.

Novak said, 'George Abassi.'

The only sound in the kitchen was of food sticking to the pan.

'You think the President has the right to order the murder of someone like that?' Novak asked.

Sharp went back to the eggs. 'It's not for me to say.'

Novak couldn't work out if Sharp was uncommitted or being evasive.

Novak said, 'Why?'

'Because I swore an oath to defend the United States constitution against all enemies, foreign and domestic. And to obey the orders of the President and the orders of officers appointed over me.'

'What happens if a person you believe to be a domestic enemy is also the President?' Novak asked.

Sharp slid Novak his plate of eggs across the marble counter. 'It's not for me to say. That's why the constitution protects a free press.'

'If you went on the record with me,' Novak could already see what Sharp thought of the prospect, 'as an unattributable source. To keep me on the right track...'

Sharp said, 'I've given you deep background already. You're *on* the right track.'

'I can't go to press with deep background, and you know it. You're the only person who can confirm Malik existed. MI6 have total deniability.' Novak was only mad because he knew he'd rushed into it. Now he might never get Sharp onside. He picked at his eggs with his fork.

'You can't always get what you want, Mr Novak,' Sharp said. 'The Rolling Stones wrote a whole song about it.'

'Either way, I can't stay here,' Novak said. 'I need to find Artur.'

'Isn't the video enough for your story?'

'It's not about the story. It's about a kid from Poland who's risked his life to tell the truth against the most powerful country in the world. It's more than I ever did.'

Without realising it, Novak had spoken to that part of Sharp that he – and everyone else who ever served as a U.S. marine – valued most.

'*Semper fidelis*,' Sharp said. 'That's why you want to find Artur.'

Novak nodded. 'Always faithful.'

'How are you going to find him?' Sharp asked in such a way that Novak could tell he was already on-board.

Novak said, 'I got an OTR message this morning from a buddy of Artur's. He's going to be at the Berlin Pariser Platz every day at midday until I get there.'

'Pariser Platz. Shit.'

'What's wrong?'

'It's a bad place to meet undercover.'

'Isn't it a busy square full of tourists?'

'It's also surrounded by overlooking buildings with a ton of windows that can see all points of the square. A busy taxi rank, from what I remember. Plus the square full of tourists isn't a good thing. It's very easy to blend in to that if you're tracking someone. For our purposes, Pariser Platz is about the worst you could do if you're being followed.'

'Our purposes?'

'I didn't bring you out here for some country air, Tom. We're in this together now.'

Novak said, 'I can't get a message back to him. If I want to save Artur, Pariser Platz is all we've got.'

'Then we'd best figure out how to do this thing without being followed.'

'How do we do that?' asked Novak.

Sharp went to his pantry cupboard and took out a cheap phone with its battery detached. After sliding the battery back in, he said, 'I call in a favour from an old friend.'

28

Piccadilly at midday two weeks out from Christmas was as busy as Rebecca expected. An entire workforce all seemingly given the same hour to run out and buy a sandwich and a coffee, then with the added hassle of a never-ending stream of Christmas shoppers and tourists, lost in their maps and cameras and phone screens, or staring slack-jawed at the famous Piccadilly Lights video billboards.

Rebecca's meeting place was Hatchards: Britain's oldest bookshop. Founded in 1797, it was a testament to the endurance of books that it still flourished while countless book chains had fallen by the wayside over the years.

Rebecca had chosen it for her fond memories of browsing the cavernous corridors with her dad. She had been too young to know the difference between a good book and a bad one. She just loved the smell, and the tactile difference between all the old hardbacks. The carpets felt like walking across someone's living room.

When she got to the crossword books, she immediately recognised Stella and Dan from the pictures she'd pulled online. There weren't many of Stella, but there were plenty of Dan: infamy always brought more search results.

The pair were doing a decent job of being inconspicuous, Rebecca thought. Although Dan looked like he'd been dragged in there against his will: hands stuffed in his jacket pockets and not a hint of interest on his face.

Rebecca stood next to them for a moment, then took a book off the shelf, flicking through the pages. 'Did you take the battery out your phone, like I said?'

Stella glanced at Rebecca. 'Before we got the Tube,' she answered.

'Show me.'

Stella showed her the separate pieces, thinking that was that. Instead, Rebecca took them from her and put them in her pocket.

'What about him?' Rebecca asked, indicating Dan.

'He didn't bring his phone,' Stella said.

Rebecca shelved the book and continued to browse. She kept her voice low. 'Everything we talk about here is off the record.'

'Fine.'

Although the shop was busy – Christmas book-buying was well under way – the corner Rebecca had chosen left them in peace and free to talk.

Stella took a book down. 'This is Dan. He's helping me with the story.'

'That's lucky,' Rebecca said. 'He seems to know more about all this than anyone at GCHQ.'

'I have my ways,' he said, grinning.

Rebecca looked him up and down. 'Don't think because you managed to crib some intelligence from a phone hack that you have any idea what you're dealing with.' She rummaged in her pocket, then placed a memory stick into the open pages of the book Stella was holding.

Stella calmly pocketed it. 'What's on it?' she asked.

Rebecca waited as an old woman walked past holding a basket of books. When the woman was gone, Rebecca said,

'I'll give you the short version, but if you're going to print any of this you'll need the documents to back it up.'

Rebecca shelved her book then wandered to the more secluded corner at the Drama section.

Stella gently followed. When Dan came as well, Stella put her hand to his chest and said, 'Wait here.'

He stayed where he was, grumbling to himself.

Rebecca waited for Stella to join her, then gave her back the pieces of her phone. 'By all appearances,' Rebecca said, 'Abbie Bishop was employed by GCHQ. Even down to her income tax and national insurance records. But two years before she joined GCHQ she was hired by MI6.'

'To do what?' asked Stella.

'As far as I can tell from her documents, MI6 sent her in to spy on GCHQ.'

'Why would MI6 want a spy in GCHQ?'

'That's the question,' said Rebecca. 'She was being paid each month by something called the Goldcastle Group. I think it's related to the political consultancy that did work for Simon Ali in the last General Election.'

Stella said, 'I remember reading a *Politico* article on Goldcastle. They were using computer algorithms to target political ads on social media in American Senate campaigns. But I thought they were a British firm.'

'They are,' Rebecca said. 'They seem willing to work anywhere provided it's for right-wing candidates. They've focussed mainly on the U.S. so far because that's where all the money is. But they've helped get right-wing candidates elected in Italy, Hungary, Argentina and Australia.'

Stella pursed her lips. 'Using online data to target voters has been going on for a few years now. What's different about this?'

Rebecca did a quick shoulder check to be sure no one was close by. 'This isn't just mining publicly available data, or filling out online questionnaires. They're using data on U.K. citizens' internet browsing histories and non-public social media posts and messages, all collected illegally by GCHQ, and passed on by Abbie to Goldcastle.'

'The government has repeatedly said GCHQ only collects data on terror suspects.'

Rebecca tilted her head at what she saw as Stella's naivety. 'GCHQ haven't stopped. NSA hasn't stopped. They just lobbied for new laws to legitimise it all. Last year Trevor Billington-Smith, director of GCHQ, told a closed-doors Commons Select Committee he wanted to quote "collect it all. Every click. every search". At my station in Global Telecoms Exploitation, that's exactly what they let us do. I can own your entire life in under an hour, and I don't even need a warrant.'

Stella asked, 'What was Abbie actually doing for MI6?'

Rebecca replied, 'She was assigned as handler to an agent called Malik, whose job was to root out potential threats from Syria bound for the U.K., and report back to their MI6 superiors: William Blackstone and Sir Lloyd Willow. Then Abbie discovered neither Blackstone nor Willow had followed up on what Malik had termed a credible threat.'

'Why wouldn't they follow up?'

'I don't know,' said Rebecca. 'But Malik couldn't have been clearer about the threat the cell posed.'

'You're talking about a massive intelligence failure, the likes of which the U.K. or any other major Western country has never experienced before.' Stella felt like she needed a moment. 'Can I see those documents?'

Rebecca did a shoulder-check on both sides. 'It's all on the memory stick. Speaking of which: don't put that into any computer you own or work with. You need an air-gapped laptop to look at those files. Brand new, never connected to the internet, and will remain that way until you're done with this story. I've given you more than enough so far, so let's get to it.' Rebecca rolled her wrist in a discreet "hurry up" gesture.

Stella said, 'I'm going to list a number of details Dan and I know. You don't have to confirm anything verbally. If you're familiar with them, say nothing. If you're not, take a book off the shelf.' Stella took a subtle look round to check no one was nearby or approaching. 'Abbie was having an affair with Nigel Hawkes.'

Rebecca slowly took a book down off the shelf. 'Go on,' she whispered.

'Abbie's last words were "hell is empty. All the devils are here." A warning code that she was in danger.'

Rebecca took another book off the shelf.

'An ex-GCHQ agent, Goran Lipski, was murdered the same night as Abbie. He had fragments of Abbie's blood on him.'

Rebecca took another book.

'Last week, Lipski made several phone calls to members of the Downing Street bombing cell.'

Rebecca stared at the shelves, stunned.

'Shall I move on?' Stella asked.

Rebecca took another book.

'That's it,' Stella said. 'That's everything we have so far.'

Rebecca kept looking at the shelves. 'Abbie wrote that phrase to me. Hell is empty. It came up with her files on Tempest.' Rebecca put one book back on the shelf. 'Do you have any reason to suspect Abbie was killed because of her affair with Hawkes?'

Stella said, 'I'm sure he would have been eager to keep it out the papers. But I haven't seen anything that suggests Hawkes is involved with Abbie's death.'

'The money she was receiving each month,' Rebecca said. 'If she was blackmailing Hawkes, he might have been rinsing the money through Goldcastle. To keep his fingerprints off it.'

'Or maybe someone was paying Abbie to stay close to him.'

'Either way, someone could have wanted rid of her.' Rebecca put another book back. She still had two.

'Are you familiar with this guy Lipski?' Stella asked.

'We never worked together,' Rebecca replied, 'but I talked to him a few times. If you ever had a technical issue you were always sent to Lipski. It amused him, how much smarter he was than everyone. He loved getting one over on the guys at Five and Six. He said they didn't respect his work. That they were too busy breaking down doors, wanting to save the day.'

'When did he leave?' asked Stella.

'He was fired six months after I started,' said Rebecca. 'There's been a lot of cases of GCHQ officers spying on boyfriends or girlfriends, small stuff.'

Stella raised her eyebrows. 'That's small stuff?'

Rebecca said, 'In comparison, Lipski had been using the ECHELON system to spy on politicians, finding out they got the Met to drop drink-drive charges or something, then black-mailed them afterwards.'

'Politicians actually do that?'

'You wouldn't *believe* what these people get away with. They were doctoring friends' kids' exam results, fast-tracking relatives up NHS waiting lists, that kind of thing. With Lipski they could never prove the money trail. So they cut him loose for misappropriation of intelligence software. A fireable offence, but nothing criminal. I haven't heard his name since.'

Stella looked around to check on Dan. He was wandering the aisle, head down like a bored child.

Stella wondered aloud, 'What if Lipski found out Hawkes was having an affair, then tried to blackmail him?'

Rebecca seemed bothered by something else. 'Lipski might have been a crook but I don't buy that connection between him and the Downing Street bombers. Bent? Absolutely. But he wasn't an ideologue. And he certainly wasn't a mercenary.'

'Does GCHQ have anything on the bombers that would explain it?' Stella asked.

Rebecca paused. 'This won't get leaked to the papers until tomorrow, so the information's embargoed until then: two are from Birmingham, and three others are from Manchester, all in their early twenties, all British-born. They corresponded largely through dark web chat rooms used by European jihadis. All cleanskins.'

'No zealot like a convert,' Stella said.

'In Islamic terrorism, converts are always the most keen to impress,' Rebecca explained. 'They might not be able to recite as many of the hadiths, but give them some Claymore mines, a bag of nails, and a remote detonator and they'll show you how much they believe.'

Stella said, 'Lipski's blood on Abbie's clothes and his phone calls to the bombers...that's a connection between Abbie and Downing Street.'

Rebecca put another book back on the shelf. 'Lipski isn't GCHQ's only link to the bombing.'

Stella unconsciously leaned a little closer.

'I have files that prove a rogue senior officer at GCHQ created the ID necessary for Mufaza to gain access to Downing Street.'

Stella couldn't believe what she was hearing. 'Rebecca, are you saying someone in GCHQ has worked to facilitate the murder of the British Prime Minister?'

Rebecca answered calmly. 'That's exactly what I'm saying. I also have a contact – someone senior in Downing Street – who will only discuss Abbie with me, rather than the director of GCHQ or anyone else there.'

'Could I talk to your source?'

Rebecca smiled, and put another book back on the shelf. Leaving her holding one.

Stella thought she'd try her luck again. 'When you say senior at Downing Street, how senior?'

'*Very* senior,' Rebecca replied. 'With the files I've given you you'll have nearly everything I have.'

'Nearly?'

'There's one file Abbie thought was too dangerous to send unencrypted. She put the decryption code on her laptop, which was stolen before she could get it to me.'

'The other files are classified?'

'All of them are STRAP Three. You'd be wise to only publish this in the States where there's no law against publishing classified material. You could end up doing more jail time than your new partner.'

'We're a long way off thinking about printing anything yet,' Stella said. 'Frankly, if we all survive the week we'll be doing well.'

'What do you mean?'

'Last night a shooter broke into Martin Fitzhenry's house where Tom was staying. It seems he managed to escape – where to no one knows yet. But Fitzhenry's in intensive care.'

'Has something happened to you and Dan too?' Rebecca asked.

'Someone tried to run us off Lambeth Bridge yesterday. We only got away with the help of another car.' Stella took out her phone. 'Can I show you?'

'Quickly,' Rebecca replied.

'It had a foreign plate.'

Rebecca only needed a glance at it: 273D101. 'That's not a foreign plate. It belongs to someone diplomatic in the U.S. embassy. I tracked that car to the safe house on Sunday night.'

Stella said, 'That makes sense. Dan found the police constable who was first on the scene at Pimlico. He saw that same car speed away moments after he found Abbie. He's convinced the only witnesses were planted there by British intelligence.' Stella passed Rebecca her phone, showing the picture of the witness. 'This is one of them. Do you have a way of identifying her?'

Rebecca handed the phone back ruefully. 'She's internal affairs at MI6.'

Stella's face lit up. 'You *know* her?'

'She came to see Abbie at GCHQ earlier this year. Now she's helping mop up her murder.' Rebecca paused, glancing at Dan, who was being offered help by a bookseller.

Dan waved him off.

'You can't trust anyone,' Rebecca said, her gaze holding on Dan. Then she put her last book on the shelf.

'That diplomatic car,' Stella said. 'If it's so heavily implicated in Abbie's murder, why were the people in it yesterday so eager to help Dan and I?'

'There's only one person who can answer that,' Rebecca said. 'You have to find that U.S. diplomat. You find them, and you find the people responsible for this. The details are on the drive. The rest is up to you.' Before Rebecca turned to leave, she pulled out a book on cryptic crosswords, leaving it jutting over the edge of the shelf. 'Try the one on page fifty-seven. It's a tough read. Keep it to yourself.'

Stella watched her leave, then looked back quickly at the shelf.

Tired of aimlessly wandering, Dan came back to Stella. 'We good, yeah? We got it?'

'We got it,' she said, distracted.

'Good. Let's go.'

'I'm going to buy something,' Stella said. 'It'll look better if I buy something.'

'Whatever,' Dan said. 'Get you outside.'

Once he was gone, Stella took the book off the shelf and turned to page fifty-seven. Rebecca had sneaked it onto the bookshelf earlier. She'd written a message for Stella in the boxes.

Thirteen across, five letters:

'DANIS'

Intersecting with five down, seventeen letters:

'DOUBLECROSSINGYOU'

For fourteen across – using the C in five down – she'd written:

'CHECKHISTEXTS'

29

DON'S SHOOTING RANGE, OUTSKIRTS OF ALBANY, NEW
YORK – WEDNESDAY, 11.30AM

Novak had his window down as Sharp drove them along I-90 in his Toyota Landcruiser. The Pine Bush near the edge of Schenectady county was one of the biggest pine barrens in the world, and the smell of fresh pitch pine and bear oak mingled in the cold air with black huckleberry, and sweet fern on both sides of the interstate. It only got stronger when they pulled off onto Route 155 towards Don's Shooting Range.

A cloud of yellow dust looped up behind them on the dirt road.

The Landcruiser may have been one of the toughest 4x4s ever constructed, capable of charging through a deep river, but the passenger seat wasn't giving Novak the easiest ride of his life.

He bobbed up and down on his seat at each pothole Sharp struck. After a while he was convinced he was hitting them on purpose. Weeds and overgrown grass sprouted up through the centre of the road where car tyres never reached.

Sharp had to shout to be heard over the noise of the engine coming in through the open windows, and the rougher terrain away from 155. 'Between you and me. Did you ever meet your source?'

'On the NSA story?' said Novak. 'No, never. Could be dead for all I know.'

'You wouldn't tell me even if you had, right?' Sharp smiled at him.

Novak smiled back. 'No.'

Sharp added, 'I saw some clips of your hearing. That was a gutsy move you made there. For what it's worth, I think it was a great story.'

'It's a *good* story,' Novak insisted.

Sharp was baffled. 'You understand that great means better than good, right?'

Novak laughed. 'Journalists have this thing when they talk about a story. Good means like it's rock solid. That it can stand up to any level of scrutiny.'

'Huh.' Sharp thought it over. 'I kind of like that.'

'Who is this guy?' Novak asked.

'A buddy of mine from sniper school.'

'Is he still serving?' Novak asked.

'He quit after a few tours in the Middle East.'

'Iraq?'

Sharp paused, thinking how to phrase it. 'A country we never officially declared war on.'

Novak would have bet the house that Sharp was talking about Yemen. Drones had taken out a lot of enemy combatants there, as well as plenty of innocent children and families, but Novak had heard whispers of Spec Ops in Yemen that went terribly wrong around 2008.

'He's been running this place ever since.' Sharp added, 'Invite only.'

There were distant pops and bangs at the end of a dirt road. Sounding faintly like gunfire.

'The thing is,' Sharp explained, 'Don's a little touchy about strangers. It'll probably be best if you wait in the car.'

Novak replied, 'Should I be worried?'

Sharp pouted, thinking it over. 'He's not a big fan of the

federal government, so I'd stay away from that. I'm a rare exception because he knows me.'

Novak didn't exactly feel full of confidence.

When they pulled up, Don was on the front step and looked like he'd been sitting there for years. An old rocking chair was set up with a well-worn cushion on the seat, and a scoped AR-10 assault rifle leaning against it. A sound choice when you're looking to hit targets coming down the dirt road and get off multiple shots quickly. Don Marshall was a man very much prepared for anything.

As Sharp got out the car – raising his hands as if under arrest – Don called out:

'The President wants to find out who be best at apprehending criminals. So he sends in CIA, FBI and the LAPD to catch a rabbit in the forest.'

Sharp started to smile. Don always started their meetings with a joke.

Don went on, 'CIA goes in first. They interview all the other animals in the forest and turn them into informants. They torture all the plant life, and after a month of investigations they done concluded the rabbit don't exist. Next the FBI goes in. They don't do no research, and after a few days they just burn down the forest, killin' every animal, but they refuse to apologise because they say the rabbit had it comin'. Last to try is LAPD.' Don came down the steps. 'After an hour they come out with a raccoon that's half beaten to death and the raccoon is yellin', "Okay! I'm a rabbit, I confess!"'

'I think CIA comes out of that one best, if you ask me.' Sharp said, then embraced his old friend.

Don still had the strong frame that made him a tough Marine, but also the slight paunch that arrives on a man in his late forties who sits around a shooting range all day. If Novak didn't know about the military background, he would have said Don was a sure-fire redneck.

He was wearing a t-shirt with a hammer and sickle coloured by stars and stripe, under the slogan "TAXATION IS THEFT".

After briefly conferring out of Novak's earshot, Sharp turned back to the car and waved Novak to come out.

Novak opened his door reluctantly and walked towards the front steps. 'Pleased to meet you, Mr Marshall,' Novak said, putting out his hand.

'You here to collect taxes, son?' asked Don, quizzically turning his head a little.

While Novak struggled to construct a sentence, Don's straight face cracked into a grin. He flicked his hand at Novak's stomach. 'Only the feds call me Mr Marshall. Any buddy of Walt's calls me Don.'

Sharp winked at Novak as they followed Don inside.

After the hallway, the house became open-plan, revealing a huge, unofficial survivalist's store: there were piles of canned goods, batteries, boxes of Mayday survival bars, dynamo chargers, military fatigues.

And guns. Lots and lots of guns and ammunition.

'Walt tells me you're in a hurry,' Don said. 'We'll get right to it. I got anyone's back who's looking to evade the federal government.'

Out back was the shooting range, nearly five hundred yards long – the longest in the county. Which meant Don had acquired a very loyal customer base, mostly made up of local military personnel in between tours of duty. There were what sounded like four or five people shooting, but Don didn't seem worried about any interruptions.

He led Novak and Sharp to a photo booth set up in the corner of the room. 'Alright,' Don said, looking Novak up and down. 'Lose the sport jacket.'

Novak took off his Massimo Dutti blazer, worried at what might become of it.

Don then looked carefully at Novak's face, specifically his now-thick stubble. 'When you goin' be travellin'? Tomorrow?'

Novak turned to Sharp for direction.

Sharp said, 'Later today.'

'Damn.' Don rummaged through a drawer, then produced an old pair of hair clippers with lots of loose hairs around the blades. 'Get on it.'

Novak took the clippers. 'For my face?'

Don sighed. 'Son, if you show up at the airport lookin' exactly like your passport, exactly like last night when the cops saw you, with exactly the same hair, and exactly the same clothes, then I've gone wasted my lunchtime here.' Don brushed at Novak's stubble with the back of his forefinger. 'Takin' this off will clean you up. Then all's we got to do is trim down that hair some and we're good to go.' Don turned on the clippers, which buzzed like a lawnmower, then passed them to Novak.

Novak emerged from the photo booth, clean-shaven, dressed down to his white t-shirt under his dusty Oxford shirt. As Sharp waited for the roll of pictures to emerge, Don pushed Novak into a chair and started on his hair with the clippers.

'You're not going to go too deep, are you?' Novak asked.

'Deep enough,' replied Don.

When he was done, Novak's hair was cropped to about half an inch. The whole thing was over in a few minutes.

Don handed Novak a filthy old barber's brush. 'Clean up,' he said, then went to a cupboard drawer which revealed a small safe. He took out a handful of passports, all in slightly different shades and states of wear. He was careful in examining each one, picking just the right one for Novak.

'College lecturer...' he said to himself, opting for one with more wear and an earlier issue date.

Novak corrected him, 'Actually, I'm a journalist.'

Sharp mumbled, 'Don't worry about it.'

'Back in twenty minutes,' Don said, before disappearing into his workshop.

The door had been closed over slightly, but not all the way. Novak's journalistic curiosity got the better of him, and he sneaked a look where Don was working: hunched over an old wooden workbench, with a magnifier on an adjustable arm, picking and cutting and snipping with the sort of precision tools favoured by model makers.

Sharp pulled him back. 'He doesn't like to be disturbed.'

When Don finally returned, he handed Novak the passport he was about to pay a thousand dollars for.

Upon opening it, Novak had to remind himself it wasn't the passport he had been carrying around for the last eighteen months. Until he looked at the name, DOB and everything else that used to be his own. As far as passport control would be concerned, Novak was now Jeremy Webb, born three months after Tom Novak.

'Nice work, Don,' Novak said, shaking his hand.

'You're welcome, Mr Webb,' replied Don with a laugh. 'The haircut's inclusive in my charges, by the way.'

Novak took out five hundred dollars, withdrawn from a gas station ATM on the way to Newark: a ploy to make it look like they were headed south when the withdrawal flagged at NSA later. They had then double-backed towards Don's.

Novak wrote out his Paypal details on some scrap paper and handed over the cash.

'What exactly are you going to do with this?' Novak asked.

Don answered, 'See, I sign into your Paypal account using a VPN going through San Francisco. Then I buy a bunch of survivalist goods with your account which make it look like you on the west coast and settin' up to hide out for a while. By the time NSA works out you ain't there, you be half way across the Atlantic under a passport they ain't lookin' for. That's a little obfuscation extra in Don's Disappearin' service

I'm throwin' in for my buddy here.' Don put his arm around Sharp. 'I swear to god, CIA be the only thing keepin' this country from fallin' apart, brother.'

Sharp smiled. 'If there's one thing we still do well, it's getting assets out of hostile territory.'

30

Rebecca made her way down Vauxhall Bridge Road towards Pimlico just as a heavy rain shower began.

Now that she'd passed on everything she had on Abbie and Matthew, she felt a sense of completion: she'd taken things as far as she could. Now it was up to Stella and Novak to finish it and get the truth out there.

That didn't mean she was able to relax yet. She knew it could still be hours before she knew if she'd been followed to Hatchards or not.

Most pedestrians were walking in the opposite direction to Rebecca, umbrellas opened or coat collars held up against the downpour. The pavement was at a standstill thanks to a long line of French students – all wearing the same red cap, and horribly underdressed for the weather – cowering from the rain.

While she waited to pass them, Rebecca noticed a man in a smart tan mac about a hundred yards away. Even from such a distance he appeared to be holding Rebecca's gaze.

He seemed to only have eyes for her, and unfazed by getting soaked.

As Rebecca passed the French students, the pavement

cleared and there was no one between her and the man. She shifted to the left side of the pavement to move away from him, but he drifted over to the same side too.

He made no attempts to avoid colliding with her. Rebecca braced herself and closed her eyes momentarily. Would she be stabbed? Shot with a silencer? Or bundled into the white van idling across the street on a double red line?

He gave way slightly at the last moment, gently brushing her shoulder. Enough to knock her off course a little.

'Pardon me,' he said politely, barely looking at her.

Rebecca recognised him. It was Roger Milton.

She kept walking, seeing the van across the street drive off in the opposite direction. She was still turning the encounter over in her mind when she reached Belgrave Road, marking the start of plush Pimlico: white and cream Georgian terraces with pillared doorways lined both sides of the road.

The rain had subsided when Rebecca heard a ring coming from one of her coat pockets. Except her mobile was in her bag with the battery taken out.

The ring was unfamiliar to her, too. A basic early-Nokia tone. She reached into her right pocket where inexplicably there was a mobile phone. It was no ordinary phone. It had no keypad, and there were only two buttons: a green one for answer, or a red one to hang up.

Rebecca had heard of but never seen one before. A Hannibal phone, that protected voice and data up to the level of Top Secret. It looked like the sort of old mobile you might find in a cash converter store, but with an ISDN card inside, that scrambled and encrypted the voice of the user.

Rebecca answered it. 'Hello?'

A woman said, 'Rebecca. I'm glad to have found you. It wasn't easy.'

'I'd have questioned how it was even possible,' Rebecca replied.

'You know who this is, I assume?'

'I do.' Rebecca looked around once more. There was no one nearby. 'I'm sorry, I don't know what I should call you.'

'Call me Angela,' she replied. 'I'll keep this brief because this isn't an ideal situation for either of us.'

Rebecca couldn't concentrate being out in the open. It wasn't the sort of conversation she wanted anyone else hearing. She ducked down a staircase to a windowless basement to get off the pavement.

'You can believe me when I tell you the phone you're holding is untraceable,' said Curtis. 'We can both speak freely here. I've seen the files on Miss Bishop – there's only so much they can keep from me here. Do you believe MI6 was involved in her death?'

Rebecca relished the opportunity to say it out loud. 'I do.'

'That was what I feared. I've seen evidence that GCHQ is involved too.'

'The press pass?' Rebecca asked.

'Yes.'

'I've seen it. I have the original documents it was created from.'

'Rebecca, I need to know who created it.'

'Alexander Mackintosh.'

'Does he work for Goldcastle by any chance?' Curtis asked.

Rebecca hesitated. 'I'm afraid he's GCHQ.'

'So he's the mole,' said Curtis, more to herself than Rebecca.

'You know about Goldcastle, too?' asked Rebecca.

'I know enough. I've seen records that show Abbie was being paid five thousand dollars every month by Goldcastle into a secret bank account.'

'How did you find that out?' Rebecca asked.

Curtis smiled coyly. 'I'm the Prime Minister, Rebecca. I still have *some* access.'

'What else did you find?'

'She was stealing user data from GCHQ's systems. Personal data on U.K. citizens collected from social media sites and web browsing. Which I'm sure could have proven very useful to a firm like Goldcastle.'

'You don't need me, then.'

'I might have the security clearance,' said Curtis, 'but I don't have physical access to the systems necessary to find out what I need to know. I need you to investigate for me.'

'Prime Minister, I'm not in a position to–'

'I just updated the BIGOT list. As of ten minutes ago you have been granted STRAP Three clearance for all British intelligence systems.'

The BIGOT list contained all the various clearance levels of classified personnel. There were a number of theories as to where the term BIGOT came from. The most popular theory proposed that it was the codeword for Operation Overlord, the British Invasion of German Occupied Territory. The list of personnel cleared to know the details of Overlord were known to be on 'the BIGOT list'. Over the years, the name had stuck.

Curtis said, 'No one else knows about this except you, me, and Roger Milton. Use your clearance wisely, Miss Fox.'

'I don't understand, Prime Minister.'

'There are no moves I can make on this. I'm just the caretaker around here. I can't summarily fire the directors of MI6, GCHQ and the Foreign Secretary without triggering a monumental PR disaster, and an almost immediate motion of no-confidence from the House – which I would certainly lose. I could be put in jail for telling you what I know. I need you to find out why Simon Ali would have been so scared of Goldcastle.'

Rebecca was taken aback, not so much at Curtis's vulnerability, but how nakedly she expressed it.

For a moment, Rebecca didn't think of herself as talking to the Prime Minister. She simply said what she thought her own father would have said to her at such a time. 'I don't claim to know much about politics, but I remember when everyone thought you were destined for Downing Street. Before the tabloids turned on you.' Rebecca couldn't help but become impassioned, even if it meant Curtis hanging up on her. 'I know you're scared, but we're all scared! Look at what happened when we left the country to be run by the people we thought knew best. We've never been more isolated, or mattered less to the rest of the world. When this is all over, we're going to need someone to lead us out of this darkness. Who's going to build us back up again, not tear everything down. Because if the people responsible get away with this, then there's a good chance our democracy will just be something that Churchill used to talk about. Something they have to remind kids about in history class.' Rebecca added, 'We need a Prime Minister. The country needs you.'

There was a long silence at the other end.

Rebecca thought at first that she'd gone too far. She'd allowed emotion and the rare intimacy Curtis had granted her to get the better of her judgement.

Curtis finally spoke. 'Goran Lipski,' she said quietly, giving little away of how Rebecca's speech had affected her. 'He's the key to all this now.'

She hung up.

Rebecca set off for Moreton House with a renewed sense of purpose. Finally, after the thousands of overtime hours, she had been given the STRAP Three clearance she had craved since she joined GCHQ. And though it opened up all sorts of possibilities for getting to the truth surrounding Abbie's death, Rebecca couldn't help but think how it might illuminate the past.

Hyde Park, London – Wednesday, 12.56pm

It was a quiet time of day for the park. Its use as a shortcut to Paddington from Central London wouldn't become busy until five.

Stella often wondered why more journalists didn't hang out in the park in early evening: away from the bustle of Westminster, it was often your best bet for cornering a junior political operative and getting a useable quote. Stella had exploited this little-known secret many times over the years.

Stella and Dan stayed off the paths, cutting across the long, wide fields, where it was easier to scope out any possible tails in the open space.

Dan had been crowing all the way since Piccadilly.

'Did I not tell *you*, Stella Mitchell,' he rejoiced, so caught up he completely forgot they were supposed to be walking London quietly. 'And everyone said my Abbie Bishop story was bollocks.'

Stella shushed him and gave his jacket a tug. 'It was stolen bollocks we couldn't use until Novak set us up with her. Let's not get ahead of ourselves. We've got the U.S. diplomat to find now.'

Dan pulled out his phone, and for once Stella wondered what he was doing.

'Who are you texting?' she asked, trying her best to sound casual.

Dan replied, 'Just work.'

'What do you mean work? Patterson fired you.'

He slipped the phone back into his pocket, his speech jittery and nervous. 'I think the paranoia might be getting to you, do you know that, Stella Mitchell. I'm just texting and you're all like what's going on, who you talking to? You need to chill...'

For someone so experienced at lying, Dan was surprisingly bad at it. Now Stella was replaying all the moments she'd seen him texting since they paired up, and wondered what he'd been up to the whole time.

She at least knew Rebecca was onto something.

Once they were out of the park, Stella bought a cheap laptop from a Tesco in Bayswater. She convinced Dan they were better sticking to somewhere with smaller streets where a persistent tail would stand out more. There was also a Premier Inn there that Stella had used once before to interview a confidential contact. It would give them somewhere safe to base themselves for a day or two with an internet connection.

Stella also needed to send Diane the first draft of her Downing Street piece – which was going to be difficult, as she'd done no work for it, and was about to present her new editor with an entirely different story than the one she'd been told to get. Stella knew that if she and Novak didn't land the Abbie story in a big way, her career in New York would be over before it had started.

Stella had known plenty of young British reporters who went over to New York, thinking everyone would be swept up by the quaintness of their accent. After a few editorial meetings and the novelty had worn off for everyone, they realised they were in the same shitfight for stories with every other reporter in town.

For Stella, failure wasn't an option.

She and Dan spent the next few hours sitting at a cheap bureau in their hotel, poring over the contents from Rebecca's memory stick on the new laptop. After half an hour with the files from Matthew's computer, Stella reckoned there was enough material for at least four career-ending front-page stories – if *The Republic* were inclined to print salacious gossip from MP's private emails and Whitehall memos.

The trouble began in the early evening, after Stella had sent her first draft of the story to Mark Chang's IronCloud.

Dan could hardly contain himself, reading the contents of Matthew's hard drive. He kept on and on about how he'd found his ticket back to the big time.

Stella was already tense, waiting for Mark's imminent and probably irate reply to her rushed draft. She finally had to tell Dan, 'You do realise that the material isn't yours. It's *The Republic*'s. And they won't print a word of this stuff.'

'Are you crazy?' he exclaimed. 'Why would they not want this?'

'Because the gossip in there is nothing compared to the access we'd lose on actual major stories in the future. We'd never get another story – not so much as a quote – from anyone in Westminster or Washington as long as I lived. There's an unwritten etiquette to this sort of thing that's more important than the Chancellor thinking the First Lady drank too much when he visited Camp David last year.'

Leckie lit a cigarette, then ripped it angrily away from his lips. 'That's all very nice, Stella. But I've got an overdraft that's growing by the day, and a career that's got the long-term prospects of a hedgehog crossing the M4. Not to mention...' He trailed off.

'What?' asked Stella.

His face was etched with pain. And fear. 'Forget it. You wouldn't understand.'

After taking a can of lager from the minibar, he retreated with it to one of the twin beds, lying on top of the duvet with his shoes on.

While Dan sulked, Stella's phone buzzed silently with an encrypted text from Rebecca back in GCHQ:

'*Confirmed by my Downing Street source: Abbie was stealing data from GCHQ. Possibly for Goldcastle? Also: Dan sent the following messages just after our meeting: "Got the pen drive. Minted stuff. My price just doubled, mate."*'

Stella replied: '*Who's he texting?*'

Rebecca: '*A mobile currently in Streatham House.*'

The headquarters of *The Post*.

Stella's heart sank. She had wanted so badly to believe in him.

Stella: '*Were any texts sent to Bill Patterson?*'

Rebecca: '*Yes. A few messages to the same number in recent days were directed to someone called Bill. He's selling you out to the Post. You have to stop him, Stella. He'll poison this entire thing and the truth will never come out.*'

Stella felt so stupid. Falling for his Cockney-geezer schtick, and, worse still, feeling sorry for him. All because they had once shared a desk for a few months. Now she'd endangered the whole story.

What got to her most was the feeling of having let Novak and her editors down. There was only one thing she could do.

She packed up the laptop and drive and put it in her shoulder bag: if she left either of them in the hotel room, Dan would be making copies of everything before she'd left the car park.

Without looking up from his phone, Dan asked, 'Where you off to?'

Stella tried to wipe the disgust from her tone. 'I need to talk to a contact.'

He kept texting. 'What contact?'

'A private one.'

'Can you bring back pizza?'

Stella opened the door. 'I'll see what I can do.'

While she waited for the lift, Rebecca texted again:

'*This just sent. Dan: "Stellas gone out on her own. We should ditch her now. We've got enough for our own story. Republic's still a few days away from publishing." REPLY: "Keep her on the hook until she finds out who had this Abbie bird done in." DAN: "Then I get my tapes back?" REPLY: "Then you get your tapes back + ££. Bill."*'

Stella got into the lift and, once the doors closed, rammed the heel of her palm into the wall. 'Bastard!'

31

THE REPUBLIC OFFICES, NEW YORK – WEDNESDAY, 9.16AM

Mark Chang's morning had been so busy it felt like lunchtime already. Fitz's Downing Street piece – '*It Doesn't Feel Like We're Winning*' – written from his hospital bed, had gone viral following news of his shooting. Syndicated news channels wanted Chang as a talking head for their evening news later. A few nationals had even requested access to Fitz at the hospital.

That was all about to seem like small fry in comparison to what was coming.

Less than a minute earlier, he'd forwarded Stella's first draft to Diane. The next thing he heard was Diane in the next office shouting, 'Flipping *heck*!'

Moments later his door flew open.

Diane remonstrated as she marched across the room. 'Is she serious? I came back from the hospital to see Fitz for this? Someone with her connections, and on a major terror attack she can barely cobble together fifteen hundred words? She should be sending me four thousand so we can start arguments over what to cut! This is a process story.'

'To be fair,' said Chang, 'that's sort of what we gave her.'

'I could read this anywhere, Mark. I already have in yesterday's *Times*.'

Chastened, Chang nodded. 'I know.' He took a breath and turned his laptop around. 'She also sent this.'

Diane lowered her reading glasses from her forehead. As she read, by the end of paragraph four her mouth started to hang open a little. 'When did this all happen?'

'Sunday night.'

'And Stella has tapes?' asked Diane, always craving sources.

'She's heard them. She's got them.'

Mark waited until Diane was finished reading.

She took off her glasses. 'This could be really good.'

Mark still seemed edgy. 'If we get one thing wrong, though...'

Diane nodded. 'It could put our lights out. The litigation alone... You and I could be sitting in depositions for the next eighteen months. Meanwhile, the bank forecloses on the rest of Henry's property, then we no longer have a publisher. Then we're up for sale, and we're all out of a job.'

'Sounds about right,' Mark deadpanned.

'And where the expletive is Tom Novak?' She went to the open door and called out to the office, 'If anyone speaks to Tom Novak, I want you in my office, and golly help you if you're not out of breath from sprinting.'

There was total silence except for phones going unanswered in the background.

'Good,' she said, then turned back to Mark.

'He's off the grid,' Mark answered. 'I had Kurt try to track his phone, any kind of web presence. He hasn't posted on Twitter, Instagram, anything.'

'If this is a Bastion News thing, I swear to...'

'Didn't you hear?' said Mark. 'Rosenblatt hired some new kid instead.' He tapped into his phone to find the story on a media-insider blog.

'Great,' said Diane. 'Now I've got a reporter working for me because someone beat him to another job.'

'No, no, look...' Mark showed her the story. 'Novak turned them down.'

Kurt knocked gently on the open door, scared of interrupting. 'Excuse me. I thought you'd want to see this. It was in our IronCloud.' He brought over his iPad.

Diane read the message aloud for Mark's benefit. '"Sorry for the lack of communication lately. Whatever Stella sends you is for real. I'm working on the back-end of it and will have a draft ready in the next few hours. But I need a day or two to find a source and get them on record. Without them, nothing else I have will stand up. Tell Diane she was right, and tell Henry the bank can go..."' she paused, 'I'm not saying that. "Eff themselves. If we're going down we're not going down without a fight." It's from Tom.'

Mark smiled. 'He's back.'

Diane handed Kurt his iPad. 'Thanks, Jimmy.'

He stopped, thinking about correcting her, but Mark waved to him to let it go.

Diane swept her hair back, taking a second to think. She was in the zone now. 'Tell Stella I want a draft,' she wagged her finger, 'and it's *just* a draft, okay? We don't know what this is yet until we have something more definitive that links Tom and Stella's parts.'

Chang said, 'She's close, I can tell.'

'Get her closer. Then we start stress-testing sources.'

Chang was already dialling Stella's phone. He waved his pen at Diane. 'Thanks, boss.'

On the way back to her office Diane subtly fist pumped to herself.

32

Traffic had been slow through the tolls on the Massachusetts turnpike, as commuter traffic filled the roads.

'You're telling me this now?' Novak exclaimed, rubbing a hand over his newly cropped hair.

Sharp, at the wheel of his Landcruiser, couldn't help but laugh. 'How did you think I was going to get you through customs and passport control? Facial recognition software will log you the second you walk into the terminal and NSA will own your ass.'

'What the hell are we...' Novak threw his hands up.

'Going to do?' Sharp explained, 'The usual methods require two things we don't have: time and cash.' He paused. 'Having given it a lot of thought in the last twelve hours, I've decided you should join CIA.'

Novak waited to see if Sharp was joking.

He wasn't. 'You're going to be an expert witness in a military tribunal at our base in Camp Lemonnier in Djibouti. At least that's what I'm going to make it look like. We need to get you to Berlin, but flying direct is a bad idea. You can't risk that. So we fly you to Schiphol in Amsterdam, then instead of Djibouti you drive to Berlin, find Korecki, get him on record, meet up with Miss Mitchell in London, secure all your sources and contacts somewhere, write your story, blow this thing sky high, all without the knowledge of the most powerful intelligence agencies the world has ever known. Then we all go home. Easy.'

'Yep,' Novak replied, a feeling of dread washing over him. 'Easy.'

Sharp hooked his hands-free onto his ear, then hit a speed dial on his phone. 'This is Walter Sharp, ID seven one three Yankee nine nine Alpha Zulu. Requesting secure line, please...' After a brief wait, Sharp was connected. 'Hey, Sharon, it's Walt. Look, I need a plane pass for Boston Logan and I need it within the hour. I just got a major break in a case... Sure, the name is Jeremy Webb...'

After he got confirmation, Sharp hung up then started dialling another number – not speed dial this time.

Novak asked, 'All I need is this passport, and I'll be up in the air?'

'Me too,' said Sharp. 'It's CIA's plane. I can't send you up there alone. Getting you out the country's the easy part. The tricky part is what we do when we get to Amsterdam.' He put his hand up as he got an answer. 'This is Walter Sharp requesting an open rendition transfer at Schiphol.' Without missing a beat, he added, 'The prisoner's name is Jeremy Webb.'

Ordinarily, Sharp's plan would have been simple enough if Novak was only flying domestically. The Transportation Security Authority (TSA) – the agency of Homeland Security that secures airports – was only interested in the protection of commercial airliners. Despite the damage an errant private plane could potentially do to a metropolitan area. But as soon as international borders were concerned, on either private or commercial aircraft, the TSA wanted to see your ID, and it wanted to search your luggage. Except in Novak and Sharp's case, all that mattered was that the TSA believed Novak's passport looked legit. No flight operator would be matching up names to a passenger list. Technically, the flight operator was Walter Sharp and CIA.

CIA kept planes ready to go in several major airports on the east coast – the west coast, less so. The challenge at Boston Logan was that private planes, whenever grounded, had to be secured by armed guards at all times. CIA's solution was to outsource this security to a private local contractor who mostly used ex-Spec Ops and -U.S. Army. Otherwise known as Pension Patrols.

Sharp and Novak cleared security without a hitch, thanks to Don's fake passport. They may have lacked boarding passes, but that was what a CIA badge was for. A simple follow-up call from TSA to Langley revealed no problem, confirming SSO Walter Sharp as escort for a CIA-protected witness from Boston Logan to Amsterdam Schiphol. He might have been on administrative leave, but his booking credentials hadn't been touched: Sharp could arrange an official CIA charter flight from and to anywhere in the world.

Flying to Schiphol was the perfect ruse for Sharp, as it happened to be the main European airport link to Africa. Just what a customs official might expect for someone apparently on his way to Djibouti.

The pilot was already doing his pre-flight checks when they reached the runway. He didn't even know he was flying a plane for CIA. He was just a hired hand like so many other private plane pilots out there.

Novak was feeling pretty good about things as they taxied to their runway.

The brief wait with nowhere to run to or hide, brought a rare moment of peace for the two men. Novak slid down his seat a little, watching the sunset shimmering past Deer Island over Massachusetts Bay.

The sunset didn't seem to hold much interest for Sharp, who tilted his seat back and closed his eyes. How easily the old habits kicked in. When at rest, he extracted every second of recovery he could from it.

'What do you think you'll do when this is over?' asked Novak.

Sharp kept his eyes closed when he spoke. 'That depends if I'm still alive at the end of it. I'm as much a target as you are now.'

Novak waited to be asked reciprocally, but Sharp wasn't interested. Forcing the issue, Novak said, 'I think I'm going to–'

His eyes still closed, Sharp simply talked over him. 'I had this sniper mission once – I can't tell you where. I had to crawl through marshland to set up a shot of over seven hundred yards. The target was a particularly bad son of a bitch, who had evaded capture for the last three years. He'd set himself up in a little shanty hut in the woods. Our intel said he was going to clear out the location by the end of the week, and god knows when we'd find him again, so I was damned if I was going to be the one to lose him. But the marsh had this grass, was real tall, and it waved all over the place if you so much as looked at it. It took me two days to crawl three hundred yards. And at the end of it, I executed the shot, one to the chest, and another to the head on the way down. I tell you it was a thing of beauty.'

Novak shook his head in wonder. 'That's some going.'

Like he had done since he was a child, Sharp ignored the compliment. He had never heard a compliment that made him a stronger person. 'I was able to take the shot because when the time came I was ready. My old tutor at sniper school once told me, never stand when you can sit, never sit when you can lie down, and when you're in a combat situation never stay awake when you can sleep.' He opened his eyes and leaned a little across his armrest towards Novak. 'It's only going to get more dangerous now. The second we stop appreciating that, the weaker it makes us.' He tilted his seat even further back, and shoved a pillow behind his head. 'Worry about the future tomorrow.'

Some seven hours later, the pilot woke both Sharp and Novak with a message that they'd entered European airspace. Sharp had been asleep the entire flight. Novak had been restless, waking with a start what felt like every five minutes.

Sharp released his safety belt and made for the overhead compartment.

Having heard his phone call about Jeremy Webb's rendition, Novak had an idea what was about to happen. Sharp hadn't felt it necessary to ask Novak's permission. It was clear: it was this way, or no way.

Sharp took down a plain black holdall and took out a pair of handcuffs and a black hood.

Novak asked, 'No orange jumpsuit?'

'We don't do that in Europe anymore,' Sharp replied. After putting on the handcuffs, Sharp whisked the hood over Novak's head. 'Resist the urge to talk,' he told him.

As they landed at Schiphol, Sharp kept a lookout for the *Royal Marechaussee* – otherwise known as KMar, the Netherland gendarmerie that dealt with military policing – who would be waiting on the tarmac. Ordinarily the Dutch MIVD (their version of CIA or MI6) would have taken on duties coordinating with a rendition flight of a CIA prisoner, but Sharp had deliberately left his request too late for the MIVD to respond, knowing they would double-check with Langley that everything was above board. The less experienced KMar would be glad just to come along for the ride and play at spies for the night. They talked about CIA like they were celebrities, with much more expensive and advanced gear than KMar would ever have. It was like pulling some kid off a municipal golf course and asking them to caddy for Tiger Woods for a day.

KMar were handed an order that came direct from Langley to MIVD headquarters in Zoetermeer near The Hague, who dispatched a team from MIVD's Amsterdam office. CIA wouldn't realise the plane had been chartered for another week. Authorising charter flights was way below the pay scale of people like Bob Weiskopf, or any other superior of Sharp's. CIA ran somewhere around fifty flights a day in the very definition of the word "worldwide". On the plane side, they were in the clear.

Things got a little trickier at immigration.

Sharp's protected-witness story was fine back in Boston, but a CIA agent bringing an American witness onto Dutch soil required paperwork from the U.S. embassy. Paperwork Sharp didn't have.

What Sharp knew, however, was that the U.S. government had a secret agreement with the Netherlands – as well as Italy, Spain and Belgium – that meant they would never have to reveal any prisoner details in a rendition – a take-it-or-leave-it demand of a secret Congressional treaty with the E.U. Immigration would simply check Sharp's credentials with the U.S. embassy in The Hague, who would tell the Dutch he had a valid accreditation and was to be let through.

Which is exactly what happened.

Sharp walked Novak off the plane at an isolated section of Schiphol's runway three, where two KMar guards were waiting outside their van to escort Sharp and his prisoner. In flawless English, they directed him to the car CIA had sent for them: a blue BMW M4.

The Dutch made little complaint about their country being used as a torture bus stop. They needed to keep the Americans happy, or the crucial CIA intelligence that helped keep Dutch citizens safe would dry up very quickly. The last thing the Dutch government wanted was the same problem the Belgians now had: a large, radicalised Muslim population and no intelligence network.

Novak simply walked where he was directed, with no clue as to how beautiful the Dutch sky was that night. He would see none of the shops in tax-free selling pornography the way Walmart sold Disney DVDs; or the array of African head-dresses on display in Departure Hall 3 where Kenya Airways and Emirates operated. Or the way its single-terminal struc-ture made it feel like the world's meeting point – possibly the centre of the world. Every conceivable nationality and race mingling under the one roof.

The M4 was a little Sharp touch. He knew Germany's autobahns lay ahead, and the best tool for those was one of the fastest coupes on the road: 450 horse power.

'Nice ride,' one of the KMar guards said.

Sharp said nothing as he helped Novak into the passenger seat. He didn't like the second guard. The one who was notably less enthusiastic than his partner.

Before Sharp got into his side he used what little Dutch he knew. '*Dank u wel.*'

The silent one got into his car and told his partner, 'Some-thing's not right about this.'

'What's wrong?' asked his partner.

'A CIA rendition with one CIA officer? I've seen these before and they bring four, five guys with them. Get MIVD.'

Sharp roared off towards the security gate, the M4's distinctive exhaust sound ringing out into the night.

'You can talk now,' Sharp said. 'It's just us.'

Novak squirmed. 'When can you take this hood off?'

'KMar's still behind us. I think one of them might be on to us.'

'Why would they be on to us?'

'Maybe they found it suspicious I'm here on my own with you. I was banking on them never having accompanied a rendition before.' Sharp revved the engine while waiting for the gate to open.

'What the hell are we in?' asked Novak.

'Something fast,' Sharp replied.

The plan was to take the E30 towards Germany through Hanover, then gun it straight cross-country on Autobahn 2 to Berlin. Which would get them there around seven in the morning. Reason enough for Sharp to have been precious about his sleep back on the plane.

That was the plan, at least.

It seemed fine when they reached the outskirts of Amsterdam and the KMar van peeled off before reaching the highway. Then Sharp informed Novak they had a problem.

'We've got a tail,' he said.

He'd noticed it back in Amersfoort, a black Transit van with two men in suits in the front. If it had been casual clothes, he would have felt okay. But something about the suits seemed off for that time of night.

He slowed right down, letting the van pass.

'MIVD,' he said.

The KMar guard had decided to use some initiative and made a call. MIVD were frothing at the mouth to catch CIA breaking protocol on their turf, and immediately sent a van out. They had one clear instruction: follow until they reach their destination. Which wouldn't work for Sharp. His whole plan was useless if the Dutch followed them into Germany. And if MIVD knew, there was a good chance word could reach NSA. Then their cover would really be blown.

'What's going on?' asked Novak, wondering why Sharp had gone so quiet.

'Hang on,' he said. taking the M4 from fifty to seventy in barely a few seconds.

'I would hang on if you'd take these cuffs off,' Novak said, clinging to the left edge of his seat with both hands. Unable to see, he couldn't anticipate the car's movement, and so bandied around in his seat from side to side.

The MIVD van was in pursuit.

Sharp told himself to remain calm and assess. Although MIVD had access to civilian police and roadblocks ahead were not out the question, there were no tolls ahead, traffic was light, and he was ultimately in a much faster vehicle.

The more wildly Sharp drove, the more anxious Novak became.

'Just take the hood off,' Novak pleaded.

Sharp gunned for a gap as a car in front pulled out to overtake a truck. All the driver saw was a flash of dark blue at his left wing, as Sharp veered slightly onto the grass verge to complete the overtake. The heavier ground was under Novak's side, and it was obvious they were not completely on the road anymore. Sharp grimaced. 'Hang on,' he said.

'You said that already!' Novak replied.

When the manoeuvre was over, Sharp exhaled heavily, turning into a laugh. 'You should be thankful you can't see this.'

With the MIVD van stuck behind a dawdling car that was taking forever to pass the truck, Sharp floored it and was soon up the road. By the time they reached Deventer near the German border he was satisfied they'd lost the tail. The only problem was MIVD would definitely have their plate.

On that front, Sharp knew they would have to just take their chances. He couldn't dump the car, and its speed might come in useful if they managed to safely extract Artur from Berlin.

He reached over and took off Novak's hood.

Novak gave his head a shake, enjoying the feeling of cool air on his skin again. Sharp motioned for him to turn around, and he unlocked the cuffs. 'I wouldn't take this as a typical rendition experience,' Sharp said.

Novak felt his reddened wrists. 'I'll be sure to point that out in my TripAdvisor review.'

Novak had never been to Germany by car before, and couldn't believe how simple it was to cross the border. There were more security procedures in place in most multi-storey car parks. As member states of the European Union had agreed, there would be no border controls – only at the border where the EU itself ended. There was just a blue sign by the side of the autobahn which read, "*Bundes-republik Deutschland*" inside a circle of E.U. stars. There wasn't so much as a stop sign, or a toll for the most cursory of ID checks.

Once you were in the E.U., you had access to all of it.

It was a myth that the German autobahn network didn't have speed limits. The *polizei* only cared if you were driving dangerously. For cars, there was simply an 'advisory' limit, but it wasn't legally enforceable. Sharp had spent enough time in Germany over the years to know this, which meant he could keep his foot on the floor for most of the night.

33

Stella walked tentatively towards the front gate of number 402, checking her position against the map on her phone. It matched up perfectly with the details Rebecca had left on the drive: a quiet residential street, filled with expensive, old Georgian houses. The cheapest of which would fetch mid seven-figures.

Before Stella reached the front gate she could hear a man's voice directing what sounded like small children.

When she reached the gate she saw a man in a suit with his tie pulled loose, heaving luggage into the boot of a red Lexus. Beside it, was a black Mercedes 4x4, registration 273D101.

A soft light from the hall spilled out onto the driveway, not bright enough for Stella to make out the man's face. His hair was dishevelled, his movements quick and nervy.

'Jonathan Gale,' Stella called out from behind the gate.

The man peered towards her. 'Who is it?' He was American.

He shoved a holdall into the boot of the car, while a young girl, no more than five, danced around the front steps, singing to herself. Gale recognised Stella as he approached the gate. He checked down either side of the street.

'I was wondering how long it would take you to find me,' he said.

Stella asked, 'That was you in the car yesterday?'

'My driver.'

'Thank you for that.'

Gale nodded, distracted. 'I was relieved to hear you got away but I'm really very busy.'

'Are you going on holiday? Strange time of night to take off.'

'Miss Mitchell. I don't know who you think you're dealing with here. I'm not risking my life or my family's life one more day.'

'You have diplomatic immunity,' Stella said. 'You've no reason to fear the police. Who are you so afraid of?'

'Who else would it be?' Gale looked at her in disbelief. 'Goldcastle, of course.'

Gale's daughter called out to him from the car. 'Daddy, I'm tired. When will we get to the hotel?'

'Go back inside, honey,' he called back. He waited until she was gone before continuing. 'They're the ones in the black Audi. Not in the car, at least. But they work for Goldcastle.'

'They're election strategists,' said Stella. 'Data miners. What are they doing mixed up in all this?'

Gale laughed desperately. 'They took Simon Ali from the backbenches to Downing Street in less than four years. You don't do that unless you have considerable power. Look around you, Stella. That's all this city is: money and power.'

Stella said, 'Goldcastle will do anything to get Abbie Bishop's laptop. Right?'

'Right.'

'So if you want to protect your family, tell me where it is.'

Gale was taken aback. 'Do you not get it? They're going to

kill you as soon as they know you have it. Due respect: they've killed far more important people than you or Tom Novak.'

'I'll take my chances,' she replied, unmoved by Gale's dire warning. Feeling like time was running out, she tried an old trick she'd been taught by her first editor: throw out two questions, one after the other. Chances are they'll give more away than if you asked one at a time. 'I know Abbie Bishop was stealing user data from GCHQ,' Stella said. 'Why was she stealing it? And what were you doing in Moreton House on Sunday night?'

Gale checked down the street again. There wasn't a car in sight.

'Abbie was hired by Goldcastle a long time ago,' he said. 'Long before those payments came through. No one could progress so quickly through GCHQ without their kind of...attention.'

'Why were they helping her so much?' asked Stella.

'Because she was the best agent they ever had. She was stealing personal data on U.K. citizens, so Goldcastle could shape the perfect candidate.'

'All this just to get someone elected?' asked Stella.

Gale answered, 'If you get a candidate elected, they'll do anything for you: shape policy, give tax breaks, open doors. You'll be in a sphere of influence for the next four years. Maybe longer.'

'How does her affair with Hawkes fit into all this?'

'She wasn't exactly sleeping with Nigel Hawkes for his sexual prowess. Goldcastle had her do it.'

'She was being paid to sleep with him?'

He mumbled to himself, 'Jesus... If they knew I was telling you all this.' He considered the phrasing. 'She was being paid to protect their investment.'

'Their investment?'

'Of course. Goldcastle were done with Simon Ali a long

time ago. They were going to back Nigel Hawkes in the General Election in six months.'

'Why would they do that?'

'Maybe there was something Goldcastle wanted that Ali wasn't willing to give them.'

'But backing Hawkes would mean...'

He nodded. 'Getting rid of Simon Ali. *Now* you're getting it.'

Stella asked, 'If Abbie was such a good agent for Goldcastle why would they want rid of her?'

Gale answered, 'I'm not sure we'll ever find out the answer to that.'

'Your car has been traced to Moreton House on Sunday night around the time Abbie died. There's other evidence of American involvement in this too.'

Gale rubbed his forehead. He'd had a pounding stress headache all day. 'I wasn't at Moreton House on Sunday night. I let someone use my car. An ally.'

'Who?'

'Goran Lipski.'

'That's your defence? You loaned your car to a disgraced GCHQ operative, who, so far, is the only person with forensic evidence that implicates him in Abbie's murder?'

'You think you've got it all figured out, don't you,' Gale said. 'Lipski wasn't what they said he was. GCHQ cultivated that profile over ten long years. Inventing stories about blackmail, and subterfuge.'

'Why would they do that?' Stella asked.

'He needed cover for what he was really involved in. Almost single-handedly he created a division of internal affairs for GCHQ. The first of its kind. If your country has a hero in this day and age, Goran Lipski would be it. His cover of being fired for corruption gave him cover to work with the dirtiest rogue agents in the field. Agents who were highly skilled, extremely motivated, and with secrets to hide. Lipski was as brave as they come. He couldn't even tell his own family the truth. He wasn't fired in disgrace: he never left GCHQ.'

'That's one hell of a secret to keep.'

Gale nodded. 'The only man who knew Lipski was still active was Trevor Billington-Smith. Otherwise, Lipski was a ghost.'

Stella asked, 'So how do Abbie and Malik get mixed up with Lipski?'

'Lipski figured out what Abbie was up to in GCHQ. He tracked her down, and she spilled her guts to him. She told him about a credible threat her agent in the field had discovered.'

'Malik,' said Stella.

'Exactly,' Gale replied. 'There was a threat against a U.S. target and Malik couldn't get anyone to listen. Lipski came to me to see if I could get the White House to delay Secretary Snow's visit. Without any explanation, CIA, NSA, everyone refused. Using Malik's intel, Lipski tracked down the bombing cell himself. On Sunday night, he told me the threat was imminent and he had to get Abbie Bishop out.'

Stella said, 'I don't understand. Why did he think *she* was in danger?'

'I never found out. But something happened earlier that night with Lipski and Abbie. Something that made him fear for her life, literally within the hour. I sent my car for him, which he took to Moreton House. By the time he got there she was already dead. A few hours later, Lipski was taken out before he could stop the bombers.' Gale backed away from the gate. 'I don't plan on ending up like Lipski and Bishop.'

Hearing Diane's voice in her head, Stella pushed for something clearer, more decisive. 'Are you saying that certain members of the British intelligence community actively aided and abetted the Downing Street bombing plot?' It was a broadsheet journalist's ploy: asking for the headline you want.

Gale said, backing away. 'This conversation is over. My advice to you? Don't walk away from this.' He paused. 'I think you should run.'

'If you don't speak out, who will?' Stella raised her voice as he got farther away. 'If you talk to me I can protect you.' She took one last shot. 'Think of your family, Mr Gale.'

'I am,' he replied, and kept walking.

His wife, having missed the exchange with Stella, passed him with yet more cases. Wherever the Gale family was going, it wasn't just a holiday.

Stella got off the Tube at Bayswater and ran the rest of the way to the hotel. When she reached the room, all of Dan's stuff was gone.

Rebecca's warning had at least prepared her for it, but it still felt like a blow.

She called Dan's mobile.

After two rings he answered without a word.

Stella didn't want to scream at him. She wanted him to see sense. 'Dan? Where are you?'

He didn't respond.

'I know about you and Patterson,' Stella said.

In the background she could hear the chirping and jingles of slot machines, and banal pop music. Someone next to him asked for a pint of lager.

'There's still time to do the right thing, Dan. Don't let them win.'

She waited a moment for him to reply.

'I'm sorry, Stel,' he said, then hung up.

She looked around the room: he had at least been kind enough to leave behind the files from Rebecca's memory stick – after making copies, then sending them to his Cloud system. She picked up her phone along with the room key and headed back out. She was damned if Dan Leckie was going to screw up her story.

If she was going to write about Abbie Bishop's death, she wanted to see where it happened for herself.

Stella got a taxi to Pimlico, dropping her at the start of Moreton Place. Having seen the police report she now wanted to check out PC Walker's story.

As soon as she turned onto Moreton Place it felt exactly as Walker had described. Given his vantage point when Abbie had fallen, Stella felt confident in Walker's story. The street gently curved to the left, giving Walker on the right-hand side a clear view of the balcony.

As she got closer, the depth of the balcony was what surprised her most. It was a good twenty feet, and confirmation that no one would feasibly jump through a French window, then run another few steps before jumping over the edge. It wasn't credible.

At the front door, a gold plate above the intercom said, 'MORETON HOUSE.'

On a whim, she tried the door. Locked.

She hit the buzzer for some of the other residents, getting no reply. Until the last one. What sounded like an Eastern European woman's voice.

'Yah?' she said, sounding put out.

Stella said, 'Hi, is there any chance you could buzz me in, I live in...' She then brushed her coat sleeve over the intercom, simulating a broken connection.

The intercom buzzed and the door unlocked.

As Stella climbed the stairs, a woman wearing white cleaner's overalls opened the door on the first landing.

'You buzz?' she asked.

Stella pointed upstairs. 'Sorry, I forgot my key.'

The cleaner nodded with disinterest.

There was no police crime scene tape across the front door of the safe house. In fact, there was nothing to suggest anything untoward had taken place there at all.

On the off-chance, Stella reached for the door handle. But before she could turn it, the door opened from the other side.

Without a word, Rebecca pulled her in by the arm.

Stella was cast into a vaguely recognisable scene from the police forensics photos taken on Sunday night, except the furniture had been straightened, and there was no blood on the living room carpet.

Rebecca chained and locked the door. 'I thought you'd come here,' she said, making her way to the living room. She had a laptop and two cups of tea set out on the table.

Rebecca held out her hand. 'Phone.'

Stella passed it to her. She had already removed the battery.

Rebecca pulled out the SIM card tray and carefully peeled off what looked like a contact lens attached to it. 'I needed to know where you were. So I put a tracker on it at the book-shop. Pretty easy on these old BlackBerrys.'

Stella remembered now how Rebecca had held onto her phone for an inordinate length of time.

Rebecca said, 'Smart move keeping the battery out. They're monitoring mobile activity around Moreton House. There's a lot of people looking for you.'

Stella moved towards the French window to get a better look at the balcony. 'You were right about Dan,' she said. 'He's been playing me this whole time.'

Rebecca said, 'Better you find out from me.'

'What are you doing here? I thought this would all be sealed off.'

'GCHQ still needs a safe house in London. They'll sell this place and move on elsewhere now its location has leaked to the press. For now, it saves me staying in a hotel.'

'I found Jonathan Gale,' said Stella. 'He's about to leave town.'

'I don't blame him.' Rebecca pulled up a tab on her laptop.

Stella took a seat next to her. After a few seconds of Rebecca typing, Stella remembered where she'd seen the unique screen set up before: the screenshots used in Novak's NSA story.

'Is that ECHELON?' Stella asked.

'Not exactly,' said Rebecca. 'ECHELON can only be accessed on-site. This is GCHQ internal records. It runs off the same design.' Rebecca pulled up the files on Goran Lipski. 'Every two years, every GCHQ officer is polygraphed. Out of a staff of thousands, the only one to fail in recent years was Goran Lipski. My boss, Alexander Mackintosh, had found fault with the findings, enough to raise an official complaint, accusing Lipski of, quote, "faking his lies". Trevor Billington-Smith might be the Director of GCHQ, but he's a political animal. Mackintosh is the brains. He figured out what Lipski was up to.'

'What was he up to?' asked Stella.

'Creating a one-man internal affairs department nobody knew existed. Except for Mackintosh. It was called Ghost Division.'

Stella said to herself, 'Jonathan Gale was right about Lipski.'

'Who?'

'It doesn't matter.'

Rebecca clicked quickly through some documents attached to Lipski's records. 'His death has already been classed as "Unsolved and Classified". Now he's gone, and Ghost Division has been shut down before it had barely begun.'

Stella said, 'I have a record of phone calls between Lipski

and the bombing cell, including on Sunday night, hours before Lipski was killed.'

Rebecca could see it now. 'He'd infiltrated the cell.'

'And on Sunday night, Lipski found out something about Abbie. Something that made him fear for her life. But he didn't get here in time.' Stella took out the police report from her bag. 'Which would explain the traces of her blood on his clothes.'

Rebecca spread the photos out on the table. 'He must have been the one who found her laptop.'

'So where is it now?' asked Stella.

Rebecca replied, 'Whoever killed Lipski must have got it already.'

Stella picked up a few of the photos and looked through them as she moved around the flat.

The place had been cleaned spotlessly: no trace of blood-stains on the cream carpet at the French window. Hollywood movies made jumping through windows look like punching through tracing paper. In reality, the force required to jump through any window, let alone a thick French window, was immense and would knock most people unconscious.

Stella read the file then looked out at the balcony. 'Abbie was five foot six, barely one hundred pounds. I don't buy that she managed to jump through this herself.'

Stella dropped the photos down on the coffee table. The one on top showed deep lacerations on Abbie's face, and also up the underside of her forearms – a defensive wound as she went through the window.

Stella said, 'We already know the autopsy report was faked. I can at least prove that much. The photo still helps.'

'What photo?' asked Rebecca.

Stella picked up a photo from the middle of the pile, showing the living room as the police found it on Sunday night. 'There was a bottle of wine on the table and a smashed glass. That's all.'

Rebecca snatched the photo from Stella's hand.

Wondering what had rattled her so much, Stella said, 'The bottle looks barely touched by the looks of it. Which matches what I know from the first autopsy report: she wasn't drunk.'

Rebecca stared at it.

Stella said, 'This isn't new information to you, is it?'

'I was told the police found two empty bottles of wine in the living room,' Rebecca replied.

Stella showed her the other photos of the rest of the flat. 'See for yourself. There was nothing else there. Were there any bottles in the kitchen bin?'

'Nothing.'

Stella couldn't understand what Rebecca's concern was.

Their attention was broken by a sudden beeping from Rebecca's computer.

She clicked to another open tab.

'Shit,' Rebecca said. She slammed her laptop shut and took it to the bedroom. 'Get your things.'

Stella stood up. 'What's going on?'

Rebecca explained on the move, dashing from room to room. 'The car that tried to drive you off Lambeth Bridge. I've been tracking it on the number plate recognition system. The car was just scanned a quarter of a mile away. Judging by the gap between camera scans it must be going about fifty miles an hour.'

Stella gathered up the crime scene photos and bundled them into her bag.

Rebecca stood at the open front door. 'Come on!'

The pair bolted downstairs, swinging themselves round the banister corners. Stella's heart felt like it was beating somewhere in her throat, her legs turning to jelly on the marble stairs.

The moment they got outside they looked at each other.

'What way?' asked Stella.

'It was coming from Piccadilly,' Rebecca said, setting off towards the far end of Moreton Place.

Stella ran to catch up. 'Can't we just hide down one of the basement staircases?'

Rebecca shouted back, 'We can't wait and hope. We need to move.'

Stella kept looking back, waiting for the appearance of a black Audi travelling at speed, but nothing came.

As they got towards the end of Moreton Place, she started to hear the sound of a powerful car somewhere ahead of them. Stella looked back again and saw a clear road.

'We should go back,' Stella panted, struggling to keep up.

'It's too late,' Rebecca replied. 'We'd never outrun a car on this length of street. We need to get out into the open. A busy road.'

They were about to turn the corner onto Belgrave Road, when out of nowhere a black 4x4 screeched to a halt side-on, blocking the women's path.

The driver shouted through the open passenger door, 'Get in!'

It was Jonathan Gale.

Back near the safe house end, a black Audi came screeching onto Moreton Place, the driver going at a terrifying speed.

The women piled quickly into the back seats. Stella tried to get the door shut but Gale had already taken off. The momentum of the acceleration was enough to close the door.

Gale pulled out in front of a bus that had to slam its brakes on, and swerve across the opposite lane to avoid a collision. Stella and Rebecca hadn't had time to get their seatbelts on, and ended up flung to one side of the backseats.

As they found open road, Gale said, 'What did I tell you.' His eyes were wide with terror, catching sight of the women in the rear-view mirror. 'Goldcastle.'

Stella watched the Audi quickly round the corner in pursuit, mounting the pavement to get past the bus.

Gale passed a black laptop case to the backseat. 'This is what you've been looking for. Take it and get out of here,' He struggled to cut a path through the night-time traffic of taxis and food-delivery cyclists. 'I'll hold them off.'

The Audi was making up a lot of ground, making insane overtakes by driving down the wrong side of the road.

Stella reached forward and took the laptop case, holding it close against her chest.

Rebecca could barely believe the one thing she'd been trying so hard to find was now right beside her. She told Stella, 'No matter what happens, don't let it go.'

Stella – too terrified to speak – nodded.

Up ahead, a car had broken down and was being serviced by an AA van, blocking the lane. All the traffic on that side had backed up, waiting for oncoming traffic to yield.

Gale floored it as cars attempted to pass the AA van, flashing their lights and tooting their horns at him.

'Get ready,' Gale shouted.

Then, barely fifty yards from the lane blockage, Gale pulled up the handbrake, locking up the rear wheels, then yanked hard right on the steering wheel, coming to a stop in the middle of the road. Gale's driver side faced the Audi, which skidded to a stop so quickly that the tyres smoked. The passenger shielded himself with his open door and pulled out a semiautomatic submachine gun. He took aim by leaning on top of his door. Both he and the driver wore woollen masks.

'Go!' Gale shouted at the women.

Stella threw her door open and ran towards the throng of traffic, keeping the laptop case close. Rebecca followed her out the same side, but tripped on the door edge.

If Stella thought she'd be safer in a crowd she was wrong.

The gunman hadn't been able to see if she was carrying anything, but he wasn't willing to take a chance. With Gale still in the driver seat, she was now his principal target. He didn't hesitate.

He opened fire on her, hitting a bus stop shelter as Stella hit the deck. What few pedestrians were around, ran away shrieking amidst the chaos.

Drivers abandoned their cars in the middle of the road, taking cover wherever they could.

By the time Rebecca had got to her feet, the gun was already firing. All she could do now was crouch by the foot of the door and hope.

The gunman turned his attention to Gale. 'Get out the car!' he shouted.

Gale got out slowly with his hands up.

The gunman approached swiftly, while the driver stayed in his seat with the engine still running.

He stood some ten feet away, gun held with professional poise. 'Where's the laptop?' he demanded. He was English.

'What laptop?' Gale said, his voice withdrawn and blank. He knew what was going to happen before it happened but it would at least mean the women could get away.

Stella ran out into the street holding the case up. 'I have it...'

The gunman looked right at her, then his real motivation became clear. He took a single step forward, then fired two shots into Gale's forehead.

Stella screamed, 'No!'

Retrieving the laptop wasn't his only order.

The gunman walked quickly and calmly to Gale's lifeless body, then fired a further two shots in his head, and two in his chest. He marched around the other side, seeing Rebecca sitting up against the back wheel. There was nowhere for her to run to.

The gunman pointed the gun at Rebecca's head. 'You know I won't ask twice,' he warned her.

Stella shouted, 'I have it.' She ran into the road, holding

the case out.

Rebecca shouted back, 'Run, Stella! Go!'

One look at Gale, and Stella knew she couldn't let the gunman do the same to Rebecca. She laid the case on the ground. 'Please,' Stella pleaded. 'Let her go.'

'Get up,' the gunman told Rebecca. 'Move.' He gestured with his gun towards Stella. When he was satisfied they were far enough away, he took the laptop out the case, turning it upside down so the hard drive entry was exposed. He lifted his foot up and stamped his heel several times into the hard drive unit. When he was through it was in pieces, including the magnetic platter where all the data was stored. Then he took out a small bottle of lighter fluid and sprayed it over the mangled circuit boards and plastic. He took out a lighter and flicked it on. When he dropped it on top of the case, Rebecca looked away.

In a second, the remains of the laptop were engulfed in flames.

In the distance, police sirens and blue lights came towards them.

The gunman ran back to the car, which took off in the opposite direction.

Rebecca tried to put out the fire, but it was too late. The platter was totally destroyed, Abbie's most vital secrets and the decryption code lost forever.

She stopped fighting the fire and fell to her knees.

Stella stared at the body of Jonathan Gale, sprawled in the middle of the street. She looked down at her trembling hands, then hid them in her pockets.

'I told him I had it,' Stella said. 'He looked right at me.'

'They were going to kill him anyway,' Rebecca replied. 'He knew too much.' Watching the police getting closer, she asked, 'What should we do? Maybe we should run.'

'No. I can't.' Stella sat against the front of Gale's car. 'I'm done running,' she said.

34

Nigel Hawkes was on his way back to Westminster after an emergency meeting at the U.S. embassy, and what was already a twenty-two-hour day. He asked Charlie Fletcher beside him in the backseat of his ministerial Jaguar, 'How the hell did Thatcher manage with only four hours sleep every night?'

Fletcher didn't answer. He was too busy browsing Twitter to see if Jonathan Gale's name had leaked yet. So far it hadn't, but it wouldn't be long. Then the British government would have a diplomatic nightmare on its hands.

Hawkes closed his eyes. His brief respite was broken by a text message. As soon as he read it, he called to his driver to stop the car.

The driver stopped on a double red line, prompting an orchestra of taxi horns behind.

Hawkes got out the car, already with his phone to his ear. When Fletcher made as if to follow him, Hawkes gestured for him to stay in the car.

Fletcher got out anyway, standing by the back door to keep watch.

Hawkes walked briskly down an alley. The conversation he was about to have wasn't for public consumption.

'What's going on?' Hawkes said. 'I was just summoned by the U.S. ambassador who tells me Jonathan Gale was shot in the street tonight. What the hell kind of operation are they running here?'

Alexander Mackintosh at the other end replied, 'It's out of our hands now, Nigel. We've done our piece. Let them do theirs.'

'Where are we with the laptop?' asked Hawkes.

'It's been destroyed,' said Mackintosh. 'Without it, the reporters won't be able to put the pieces together.'

'You haven't left anything sitting about on GCHQ systems?'

'Abbie Bishop had the only records on Goldcastle. We're in the clear.'

Hawkes said, 'There's still this Stella Mitchell problem. She's heard voicemails to me. From Abbie. It could make life difficult.'

'Has anyone else got them?'

'Only Dan Leckie, but Bill Patterson is taking care of him.'

'What do you want to do about Stella Mitchell?' asked Mackintosh. 'My team's standing by.'

Hawkes paused, thinking about what the front page of every British newspaper could look like by Sunday, all calling the end of his political career. 'Tell them to stand down.'

Mackintosh cautioned, 'Nigel, this could be our last chance to take her out in the open. The Americans have located Tom Novak: he'll be dead this time tomorrow. We can't afford any unfinished business.'

Hawkes said, 'Leave Stella Mitchell to me.'

Central London – Wednesday, 11.23pm

Stella had marched straight from giving her witness statement in the back of a police van on Belgrave Road to Lambeth, where she stopped at Dan Leckie's house. The rain was lashing down, but Stella was far beyond caring.

'Dan! Open up!' she shouted, whilst banging on his door. If he was in he wasn't answering.

She was about to start walking back towards the hotel when it occurred to her to just keep on walking to London Bridge. An hour's walk away.

She arrived outside *The Post*'s HQ at Streatham House, soaked to the bone. Angry, defeated, and looking for blood.

She marched past security. When they tried to stop her, she told them, 'I'm here to see Bill Patterson.'

The guard chased her to the lifts. 'Is he expecting you?'

Stella battered the "up" button until the doors opened. 'No. He's not expecting this.'

What few staff were still in the newsroom stopped their work and watched Stella beating a path straight to Patterson's door.

Patterson stood at his desk on his landline, tie undone. When he saw Stella approaching, he quickly ended the phone call. Whatever she was about to say to him, he didn't want the person on the other end hearing.

There was something wild about her appearance, her hair dripping wet, eyes piercing and white, even from a distance away.

Stella thundered through his door. 'Where the hell is Dan?' she bellowed.

Patterson was unruffled. He remained standing, going about his business: turning through copyedits of the Thursday morning edition. 'I thought he was with you.'

'I know you two have been plotting to steal my story.'

Patterson laughed. 'What story?'

'The affair Nigel Hawkes was having.'

'I've done you a favour, love. Trust me.'

Stella took out her phone and read from a message.

'"Keep her on the hook until she finds out who done in this Abbie bird." Sound familiar?'

He didn't even seem embarrassed at getting caught. 'What do you want? An apology? Look whose house you're in, Stella. Look who's been keeping you company the last three days. What did you expect? That we were all going to win awards for breaking a story about a bent politician who's been knobbing a bit of classified skirt? There's a reason this country hasn't got an equivalent of the Pulitzer Prize: no one gives a toss about the truth. Not me and not the punters. So yeah, I told Dan to turn you over.'

'He didn't keep me on the hook,' Stella said. 'He's taken off before anyone's found out who killed Abbie Bishop.'

'I've been in this long enough to know what you're thinking, though,' said Patterson.

'What's that?' asked Stella.

'You think Hawkes did it.'

Stella said, 'Abbie was sleeping with him because that's what she was sent in by MI6 to do: spy.'

Patterson finally sat down. 'Say it was him that did it. Would it really surprise you that a politician had a hand in a murder? There have been thousands of MPs over the years. You think none of them ever messed about with little kids? Or tried crack? Twenty-four Prime Ministers in the last hundred years, you think none of them ever cheated on their wives? In nineteen seventy-six, Jeremy Thorpe was on the verge of becoming Prime Minister when he ordered the murder of Norman Scott.'

Stella asked, 'Why are you covering for Nigel Hawkes?'

Patterson replied, 'Once all this Angela Curtis shit has died down, all the flags hanging out people's windows come off and we forget about Downing Street – when a snap election is called in six weeks Nigel Hawkes is going to be the next PM. You don't make enemies like that in my game.'

Stella laughed, the penny dropping. 'You were never going to use Dan's recordings, were you?'

Patterson said, 'Do you really think I'm dumb enough to use hacked voicemail recordings to out Hawkes as an adulterer? I won't let this place go the way of *The Herald*. There's a reason we survived that shitstorm: I don't take chances. I just needed Dan on a leash. And I'm not going to let Nigel Hawkes' name be dragged through the mud by hacks like Dan Leckie, or you.'

Stella could tell when she was on a hiding to nothing. 'Are you at least going to honour Dan's contract?'

'The recordings have all been destroyed,' Patterson said. 'That was part of the deal. He's not going to work here. He's not going to work *anywhere* after this. I've paid him a very generous amount for his services. Overly generous, in fact. I'm a fucking saint.'

Stella said with disgust, 'A one-off story like he was contracted wouldn't be far into four figures. That's barely a month's pay. There's no way he'd sell his story out for that.'

'True.' Patterson nodded. 'After I broke into his safe and found the recordings, I threatened to call his probation officer for violating his release terms for hacking. Unless he got me something juicy in return.'

'You blackmailed him,' said Stella.

Patterson shrugged. 'If that's what you call trying to protect someone, Stella, then sue me...'

Stella had no words left. Not tonight.

Patterson lit a cigarette as if it were post-coital, satisfied he'd won. 'For what it's worth,' he said. 'Dan never wanted to do it. He changed after he met you. Shame, really. We could have used him around here.' He grinned.

Once Stella got out the lift into the lobby, she took out her phone and prepared to call New York. She had to tell Diane the story was dead.

GTE Division, GCHQ – Thursday, 00.01am

After giving her statement, Rebecca hadn't felt like hanging around in London – despite Stella's offer to put her up for the night – and caught the last train back to Cheltenham. As always it was slow, two hours travelling up and around the Cotswolds.

The journey gave her time to think ahead of her night shift start at midnight. The events of the last six hours had drawn into question everything she had believed in: were her superiors really caught up in the biggest scandal to ever hit the British establishment?

The most painful thing about it was that none of her risks, none of her efforts mattered. Goldcastle's secrets had ended in a burnt heap on Belgrave Road beside Jonathan Gale's body. Abbie had taken her secrets to the grave with her. And as far as Rebecca saw it, the perpetrators were going to get away with it.

All that was left for Rebecca now was the past.

As Rebecca swiped her clearance card into the GCHQ entry gate, and was processed through the "Shower" security pod, she thought about how long she'd waited for such a moment.

The memory felt at once both far away and terribly vivid. It was only a few days after her father had died in the fire at Bennington Hospital. Thirteen-year-old Rebecca had crept halfway down the stairs of her childhood home late at night. Light from the kitchen stretched across the wide hallway. In the kitchen, two voices were conferring.

She crouched down on a stair, straining to hear.

The first voice she recognised easily enough: Sam Sulley, her father's closest and most trusted friend, who'd been looking after her in her father's absence.

She didn't recognise the other voice.

Rebecca went down the stairs as far as she could without being seen. She could only make out the other man's shadow on the linoleum floor.

The men were passing a bottle of whisky back and forth.

Sulley said, 'The only way to find out what happened to Stanley is getting into GCHQ.'

The other man replied, 'We don't have high enough clearance to see the report. Everything on Stanley is STRAP Three eyes only.'

To the man, it was a throwaway line. But that night, Rebecca went back up to her room, and as she lay in bed she felt a sense of determination brewing in her. A sense of purpose and happiness. All of which she knew she shouldn't have been feeling. It took some hunting around on the internet to find out what exactly STRAP Three meant. In the days that followed she felt a change taking place in her: she knew what she had to do with her life.

She would finally be able to find out the truth of how her father died.

As she rushed to her station, Rebecca's expression must have betrayed what she was really feeling – panic.

Matthew asked with concern, 'Are you alright, Rebecca?'

She couldn't remember the last time he had called her by her full name.

He moved towards her station then leaned down close to her. He was almost whispering. 'I'm not going to ask why you left that stapler on Alexander's keyboard the other day. But I am going to tell you to be careful.'

Rebecca tried to speak.

'Don't,' he said. 'Please. You don't have to tell me what you're into. I trust you. Just promise me you're being careful.'

She thought better than to deny his observation. 'I'm being careful,' she managed to say nonchalantly.

He said, 'I've lost enough colleagues this week.' He touched her on the shoulder then returned to his desk.

The classified systems were kept in a List X-maintained room. In GTE, this was off the main office floor, where no one could peek over shoulders at screens, or take photos of classified material.

List X maintenance meant the contractor that had built and installed the system – and the room itself – had passed the most stringent and all-encompassing security tests that British intelligence could devise. Everything from the air-temperature regulation vents, to the screws used to seal the computer units, had been checked and its sourcing approved.

There were no guards. Just three swipe-access doors down a long, brightly lit white corridor. The time between doors gave Rebecca plenty of time to think about how long she'd been trying to get there.

As Rebecca approached the third and final door, she glanced down at her hands. She was trembling.

She felt the clinical stare of a dozen cameras pointing at her, as she brought her shaking ID card up to the swipe slot. Beyond the window, the glass door of the List X room was tantalisingly close.

After swiping her ID, the light on the door turned green, and the lock released. She was through.

The air in the List X room felt different. To prolong the life of the computer terminals, the temperature was carefully regulated to be exactly the same at the floor as it was at the ceiling.

The computers had a multitier system that didn't require a different password or code for different types of clearance. An officer simply entered their name and employee number, then the system let them access whatever clearance areas they were approved for based on the BIGOT list.

Once Rebecca logged in, she was soon overwhelmed with the depth of material available to her. There were dozens of drop-down menus, each leading to thousands of files for GCHQ, MI6 and MI5.

By the fifties, MI5's old repository of hardcopy records had swelled to half a million files. Every single one had since been scanned, even the old "Y Boxes", containing the most highly sensitive files on defectors and spies – named as such for the yellow card slipped in the inside cover of the box.

As an ardent scholar of the Cambridge Spies who spied for Russia during the Cold War, Rebecca could have spent days lost in the files, reading personal memos written from the desks of such infamous figures as Kim Philby and Guy Burgess.

But for now, Rebecca's interest lay much closer to home.

She typed into the search bar: 'Stanley Fox.'

For a moment Rebecca hovered the cursor over the personnel file icon, almost scared of what she was about to discover.

After the cursory details on when Stanley joined GCHQ in 1979 – his formative years in cryptography and advanced mathematics – it appeared Stanley's work on encryption theory had led to him heading his own division within GCHQ.

By all accounts, Stanley had been a genius and spear-headed several major breakthroughs in cryptology, but without any major funding that reflected his success.

Curiously, in 2004, his division's operating budget had ballooned from a mere £137,000 to £4.2 million. His staff increased from three to forty. Whatever he was onto, he had the full belief of GCHQ top brass.

The budget topped out at £78 million in 2005. The strangest thing, though, was that this sudden injection of cash had coincided with an unexplained cull of Stanley's staff. At a time when the division's budget had peaked, Stanley was working entirely on his own.

Rebecca had never heard of one man being given an eight-figure operating budget. After some digging, she discovered that the cash wasn't being spent on staff, office space, or logistical resources. All £78 million was being spent on computing power.

Then, all operations halted the winter that Stanley had been hospitalised, following an acute mental breakdown. Taken to Bennington Hospital, a specialist in mental health, Stanley never returned to GCHQ. Just five months later the hospital burned to the ground, taking Stanley with it.

That was the end of it. The file pronounced Stanley Fox dead in the summer of 2006.

In a way, Rebecca was relieved there was nothing that toyed with what she knew about her dad. She was certainly surprised to learn how much his work had evidently been valued. It did, however, make her wonder what exactly he had been working on that was so valuable. What she couldn't understand was why any of it had been classified STRAP Three.

She was about to find out.

Scrolling down a few pages, the word was buried in a long paragraph, but it stood out immediately to Rebecca:

Goldcastle.

Operation Goldcastle, to be exact.

Rebecca was looking at the original mission file: the root document, stating an operation's start date and operating budget.

It had been authored thirteen years ago and carried the digital seal of the Advanced Cryptography division.

She had to look at the name at the bottom for several seconds before it really sank in. 'It can't be,' she mumbled.

The mission file had been signed off by Stanley Fox,

"Director of the Goldcastle Research Group". He'd been liaising directly with Alexander Mackintosh.

Another curious thing was a misspelled mention of Goldcastle – "Goldcaslte" – at the foot of a page. Rebecca clicked on it, and before she could make sense of what she was seeing, the page filled with a stream of folders, all related to Operation Goldcastle.

It took her a moment to work it out. If someone had chosen to hide all documentation related to a keyword – like Goldcastle – the user could disable all the hyperlinks, and make it look like the keyword didn't appear anywhere in the system.

What the person hadn't counted on was an innocent typo that had left one hyperlink still active. Leaving a back door to reactivate all the other dormant ones.

Someone had done their best to make it look like the files didn't exist.

Rebecca clicked to the most recent search result for "Goldcastle", the last of which appeared late on Sunday night. It was a 'ping request', which sent an electronic signal to a particular phone which activated its GPS receiver, giving the phone's location to within sixteen feet.

There were two ping requests.

The first was to a mobile at 11.35pm on Sunday. Giving a location at coordinates matching the Moreton Place safe house.

Rebecca took out her phone and searched for Abbie's number. Sure enough, it matched the number on the screen.

The second mobile had been pinged just after one a.m., giving a location next to Whitehall Gardens, beside the Thames.

Near to where Goran Lipski had been found.

But who had pinged the numbers?

The server logged the requester's ID each time. There was no way of hiding it. Someone at desktop number: 28399.

Rebecca's eyes narrowed. She was desktop 28402.

She pulled up the GTE floor plan, and scoured the desktop numbers near hers. The floor plan never mentioned names, as it was too cumbersome a task to update it each time personnel moved offices or departments. Instead, it listed the desks by job title.

28399 was listed as "Director of GTE Division."

Alexander Mackintosh.

The information prompted a memory from Sunday night. What had seemed at the time a throwaway line, but had been troubling Rebecca since Stella's observation about the wine bottles.

She quickly clicked out of the Goldcastle records and pulled up Abbie Bishop's autopsy report – the second 'official' one that showed two bottles of wine in her system.

Rebecca read the autopsy's issue time back to herself.

'This can't be happening,' she told herself.

From the glass door, standing in the dark, Mackintosh spoke, startling Rebecca.

'I remember the first time I saw a STRAP Three,' he said. 'I couldn't believe some of the things we were up to.'

Rebecca told herself there was no way Mackintosh could know what she had been looking at. The computer screens all faced the back wall, and the office's glass walls were frosted.

She tried to play things down, saying, 'You gave me a fright.'

He came in, letting the glass door close behind him. The soundproof seal suckered against the door frame. 'You shouldn't work in the dark like this, Rebecca. It's bad for your eyes.'

It was too late for her to log out.

When he saw what was on her screen, he exhaled. 'This is the trouble with working somewhere you can't delete anything,' he said.

'You never told me you knew my dad,' she said. She wasn't scared.

'He was a genius,' Mackintosh replied. 'That word gets thrown around a lot these days. Every time someone sends me a new recruit's application test they tell me they're a genius. They said that about you, too. Your dad was the real deal.'

'What does he have to do with all this? Goldcastle. Abbie. Lipski.'

He took a seat opposite her. 'Goldcastle tried to recruit him. He was the best cryptographer we ever had. And they had money to invest.'

'What did they want him for?' asked Rebecca.

Mackintosh stared into his hands. There was a part of him that was relieved to finally tell her. 'We kept telling him it was impossible. We all did. Then we tested it. We spent tens of millions of pounds testing it, trying to prove it didn't work. Up to two hundred and fifty-six-bit encryption. Out of thousands of tests, it came through one hundred per cent.' He looked up from his hands, meeting Rebecca's eyes. 'He coded a tool to break encryption... Even fifteen years ago everyone could see the possibilities. What it would mean.'

The revelation took Rebecca's breath away. 'No secrecy on the internet.' Her mind started racing at the different applications of such a tool. 'No anonymous instant messaging. The dark web would have a giant spotlight shining down on it. Nowhere for paedophiles to hide online. No illegal weapons or drugs on trading sites...'

Mackintosh added, 'It would cut terrorists off at the knees. No more messages that auto-delete after you've read them. We would see every word they sent, anywhere in the world. At least that was the plan. Until your father died. We lost everything in that fire. Him, and all his plans. That's why it's imperative to complete your father's work.'

'At what cost?' asked Rebecca. 'You want to keep the

country safe, but how many innocent people need to die for that to happen? Five? Fifty? A hundred?'

Mackintosh stood up, moving slowly across the room. 'Don't make the same mistake your father did, Rebecca. I beg of you. I tried and tried but he wouldn't listen.'

'Are you saying Goldcastle were involved in my dad's death?'

'I'm offering you a seat at the table with the people who really matter. And trust me, Angela Curtis is not one of them. She's not even going to be in Cabinet in three months' time, let alone Downing Street. I'm trying to protect you. You must believe me.'

'Like you protected Abbie?' she said. 'Two bottles, in case you're wondering. That's what your mistake was.

Mackintosh folded his arms. 'I'm sorry?'

There was a glimmer in his eyes of what she was getting at. It had been lying dormant in his mind since Sunday night, when, deep down, he knew he'd made a mistake.

She said, 'You told me the police found two empty wine bottles in Moreton House. But there are none in the crime scene photos, and forensics only found one half bottle of wine at the scene.'

'Come now, Rebecca,' he said. 'You can do better than that.'

Undeterred, she went on, 'If there was no evidence of two bottles at the scene, why would you claim that's what she'd had? Unless you were the person responsible for doctoring the first autopsy report.'

He smiled. 'I always knew you were the real deal too.'

Rebecca could see the pieces of the puzzle now. 'You pinged Abbie's location on Sunday night. You were directing the hit team, weren't you? Maybe you went along with them. I know she had been working for MI6. Was it Lloyd Willow's idea for Abbie to steal data from GCHQ systems? Or was that you?'

Mackintosh took a step back, turning away from her. 'This is ridiculous...'

Rebecca pressed on. 'Abbie told me in a message that you couldn't be trusted. She discovered that you had been helping a terror network infiltrate Downing Street, hadn't she?'

'Do I even need to be here, or shall I just let you carry on?'

'I've seen the press pass you had made for Mufaza.'

He turned to face her again. 'What?' His shock appeared genuine. 'You think I'm the one who made that?'

'It's on your computer, Alexander.'

'I don't know what you think you've found, Rebecca.' Mackintosh looked towards the door. 'Please,' he said. 'This can all be forgotten about. We can protect each other. You know what they're capable of. I can protect you, Rebecca!'

She stood up, the bit between her teeth now. 'MI6 is at the centre of all of this. They sent Abbie here. They put agents at Moreton House to secure the scene. The plan required someone powerful to lead it. Someone who could order a black ops team to take out any target they wished; who could relocate a Prime Ministerial press conference at short notice. He needed help for an operation like this, and he got it. From you, Trevor, and Nigel Hawkes. You all played your part. All to protect the real culprit: Sir Lloyd Willow.'

Mackintosh shook his head as two GCHQ internal security officers bustled in.

Rebecca backed away, raising her arms across her chest. 'What are you doing?' she snapped. She looked to Mackintosh. 'You can't do this!'

She fought, but her light frame gave the officers little trouble.

While one of them handcuffed Rebecca, the other said:

'Rebecca Fox, under the authority of section three of the Intelligence Services Act, nineteen ninety-four, I am arresting you on suspicion of espionage and disclosure of classified material without legal authority, as recognised in law under the Official Secrets Acts, which you are a signee. As of now, all powers, privileges and clearances are hereby suspended pending a full investigation.'

As the officers picked her up, Rebecca kicked her feet up against the edge of the desk, knocking her chair over as she tried to push back.

'As a senior GCHQ officer,' she called out, 'I demand you place Alexander Mackintosh under arrest for conspiracy to murder Abigail Bishop and Goran Lipski; and Sir Lloyd Willow for murder and treason...'

She kept struggling all the way outside to the corridor, where two more security officers carried her under the arms. Her feet barely touched the floor until she reached the holding cells in the basement, normally reserved for anyone arrested around or inside the perimeter fence.

Once her solitary cell was locked, Rebecca sat down on the padded bench trying to work out how to contact Angela Curtis with just one phone call.

35

Angela Curtis sat in her dressing gown with her feet up on the armchair with a pile of briefing papers in her lap. Only the glow of the television lit the room – not that she had been paying any attention to it. She had been nursing the same glass of wine for nearly an hour now, her thoughts wandering back to what Rebecca had told her earlier.

Roger Milton had demanded Curtis's schedule be cleared for what he called 'an early night'. Eleven p.m. was the best that could be managed.

When her private phone rang, Curtis had half a mind to leave it. She had tried that game as Home Secretary. It only ends with Specialist Protection knocking on your door until you answer.

She answered, 'No, I'm not asleep.'

Her night-shift secretary said, 'Prime Minister, I have Sonia Ali at the front door, along with Doug Robertson.'

'Christ.' Curtis sighed, rushing to her bedroom. 'Send them up.' She grabbed the first clothing to hand: that day's blouse tossed on the bed, along with her suit trousers.

Curtis let them in, giving Sonia Ali a hug as she went past. Doug Robertson kept his distance, carrying a briefcase.

He had the tanned face of someone who chased summertime around the globe throughout the year. He was a one-lawyer shop, representing a coterie of reclusive billionaires, foreign industrialists, as well as a number of ex-heads of state – one of whom had been Simon Ali.

Ali had happened to be one of the few people in the country who could afford Robertson's eye-watering retainer.

Showing them to the living room area, Curtis asked Sonia, 'Can I get you anything?'

'No, I'm fine,' she replied. Considering the circumstances, she seemed in pretty good shape. 'We won't be staying long. Do you know Doug?'

He nodded curtly. 'Prime Minister.'

Sonia couldn't help but glance through towards the bedroom. How odd it was to see a stranger's things all over the bed you had been sleeping in just a few nights ago.

Curtis hurried to switch off the TV, which was on something inane, then sat down beside Sonia.

'I didn't want to come here,' Sonia said. 'But Doug...'

Robertson sat in a chair on his own. He opened his briefcase and presented a blank white envelope to Curtis.

'What's this?' she asked.

Robertson explained, 'As Simon Ali's lawyer and executor of his last will and testament, it's my legal duty to furnish the succeeding Prime Minister with that envelope. The contents of which are unknown to me.'

'I don't understand,' said Curtis.

Robertson said, 'My client offered no guidance on the matter, other than an instruction that I witness your reading of the document.'

Curtis opened the envelope and started reading the letter inside.

Sonia sat in silence.

Halfway through, Curtis said, 'My god...'

When she was done, she exhaled. She looked at Sonia, who couldn't bear to make eye contact.

Curtis held the letter limply in her hand. 'Sonia—'

'It's about her, isn't it? Abigail Bishop,' she said, closing her eyes at the mere thought. 'I knew there was something wrong with him on Monday morning. He had this look. When you've been married as long as we have...' She trailed off.

Curtis held the letter out at Robertson. She said, 'If this ever got out...it would be nothing short of a disaster. For the government. For Simon's legacy...'

Robertson turned his hands up in acquiescence. 'It's not my place to advise, Prime Minister.' He'd already earned his £4000-an-hour fee.

Curtis took the letter to the bedroom – still in Sonia and Robertson's eye line – and took a lighter to it. Curtis dropped the paper into the fireplace, watching it burn until there was nothing left.

Premier Inn, Bayswater, London – Thursday, 1.00am

Stella returned to the hotel exhausted and distressed. A day like hers might have been painful yet somewhat tolerable for a war correspondent, but she wasn't used to covering dead bodies in city streets, and having guns pointed at her. To top it all off, she now had to face a video conference with Diane Schlesinger. She'd insisted on it after Stella had texted her about the evening's events.

In desperation, Stella went to her notes – while still wearing her jacket – rummaging wildly through the Gold-castle files from Rebecca, the Malik files from Novak, for something, *anything*, that could keep the story alive now.

The more frantic her search became, the more her frustration and anger grew. The ability of the conspirators to reach anyone, anytime, and anywhere, was too much to take for a journalist who had become used to success, and seeing truth succeed over corruption. She raised her arms, every cell in her body wanting nothing more than to swipe the entire desk clear, then walk out, thankful at still being alive. But she couldn't admit defeat.

She went to the bathroom with the intention of patching up her makeup to appear more presentable. She stared into the mirror, and instead of reapplying her makeup, washed off what little was left. There was nothing that was going to hide what she'd seen. In that moment, she didn't care what she looked like. All her pain was behind her eyes anyway. Nothing was going to cover that up.

'Don't you *dare* cry,' she ordered herself.

Five minutes later, as the Darkroom connection patched through to New York, Stella took some hotel stationery from the bedside table to make notes, then waited for the receiver screen.

Diane was at her desk, using her computer's webcam. 'Stella, how are you doing?' she asked, sounding tense.

Stella put a brave face on things. 'I'm alright. I got a bit of a fright earlier, but it's fine, though. I mean...I'm fine.'

Diane neglected to mention that, out of sight of the webcam, Henry Self was standing across the room, pacing nervously, arms folded.

'Where are you?' asked Diane.

Stella replied, 'I'm at a hotel in London. Somewhere safe.'

'What do we have so far?'

Stella broke eye contact. There was no getting around it. 'Well, let's see... I had been working with a journalist called Dan Leckie, who had phone recordings that proved Nigel Hawkes was having an affair with Abbie Bishop. Dan has now disappeared and I only have copies of some of the tamer, inconclusive recordings. The U.S. diplomat who had a laptop belonging to Abbie, which could have unlocked highly damaging intelligence documents, was shot tonight before he went on record with anything incriminating, and the laptop has since been destroyed, by what I can only assume is some British black ops team. The CIA agent with Novak isn't talking. Novak hasn't established contact with his source of the rendition video. And the only paper trail I have could land me in jail for violating the Official Secrets Act.' Stella moved slightly out of picture to open a minibar white wine. 'There might be a clue in Simon Ali's speech, but we don't have it and we have no way of getting it.'

It took Diane a moment to fully digest the direness of the situation. 'So, basically we're nowhere.' she said.

Stella took a drink, before replying, 'Basically. Have you heard from Tom?'

Diane said, 'Last we heard, he was with Walter Sharp in Albany and was attempting to fly to Europe to track down this kid, Artur Korecki. But we don't know where he is.' She glanced up at Henry, who was making a 'keep going' gesture. 'Stella,' she said, 'what do *you* think has been going on?'

Stella slowly drew her eyes back up from the empty miniature bottle in her hand to the screen. 'What I know for sure – what we can print – is that Abbie Bishop was having an affair with Nigel Hawkes that had been going on for several months. During that time, she was being paid five thousand dollars every month by a political consultancy firm called Goldcastle, to steal data from GCHQ. During that time, another MI6 agent on deep cover, called Goran Lipski, had infiltrated the cell that plotted the Downing Street bomb. When his superiors failed to act on his warnings, Lipski went to the Americans – specifically, Jonathan Gale at the U.S. embassy in London. Lipski was shot in the early hours of Monday morning and thrown into the Thames. Jonathan Gale was shot earlier tonight. We also know that Abdullah Mufaza gained access to Downing Street with a genuine press card issued to him by someone senior in GCHQ. Which gives us a solid connection between a rogue GCHQ operative and the Downing Street cell. That's what we have.'

Diane looked over the lid of her laptop at Henry, who shook his head.

She nodded thoughtfully, pushing her lips out. 'I think...' She wanted to be careful with her wording, being as charitable as she could. 'I think you need to come home, Stella. The story's over. We've got to get together a solid Downing Street piece now.'

While Henry looked down at his phone, Diane showed Stella a page of her notepad that had been sitting face-down on her desk. Diane had written "STAY ONLINE" on it. After winking, Diane said, 'Get back here as soon as you can, and we'll prep your Downing Street story.' She added, 'Stay safe, Stella.' Diane clicked her mouse, but only to minimize the Darkroom window rather than close it down completely.

All Stella saw at her end was a black screen, but she was still picking up audio.

Henry hadn't noticed Diane's trick. 'It's for the best,' he explained. 'There's something ugly going on over there, but she hasn't got it.'

Wanting Stella to hear something encouraging, Diane said, 'She's young. She's ambitious. She wants the big stories. That's why I brought her here.'

Henry said, 'But not at any cost. A couple of hours ago she was threatened by a gunman. I've got Martin Fitzhenry in the hospital, Tom Novak limping around god knows where, and we can't save a magazine with dead writers. You told me she was better than this, Diane.' He made for the door. 'She lost this one.'

Stella felt like she'd been punched in the gut.

The second Henry was out the door, Diane brought up the Darkroom screen again. 'Stella? Can you hear me?'

Still smarting from Self's assessment, Stella replied, 'I'm here.'

Diane said, 'Either way, we go to print on Friday, so I need whatever you can get by ten p.m. New York time on Thursday. You have – at most – twenty hours to close this thing. Now it's my behind on the line too. Don't think Henry won't flip when he finds out what we've done here. You need to find a way to bring this home. What are you going to do?'

Stella could sense her entire future hanging in the balance. 'Hawkes. Charlie Fletcher and I go way back. If I can get a sit down with Nigel Hawkes I can nail him.'

Diane didn't seem overly taken with the idea. 'If he doesn't fold, you won't be able to go back to him.'

'I can nail him,' Stella assured her.

Stella marched out the hotel, looking up and down Bayswater Road for a taxi. The street was deserted. Somewhere in the distance the shutters of a late-night kebab shop were slammed shut.

It was a crisp night.

Stella dialled a number on her phone.

The male voice at the other end sounded tired. 'Hello?'

'It's Stella, Charlie. I need to speak to the minister.'

Charlie replied, 'Are you drunk or stoned or something? It's the middle of the night. The only thing that'll get the Foreign Secretary out of bed at this hour is a North Korean missile.'

'Do you want a bet?' said Stella. She flicked to an audio file on her phone and pressed play.

Charlie held his breath while he listened to a recording of a voicemail left by Hawkes for Abbie Bishop.

'Not exactly future-Prime Minister material,' said Stella.

Charlie couldn't hide the stress in his voice. 'Where are

you now? I'll meet you. We can work something out about this.'

Stella said, 'I don't want to meet you. I want to meet Hawkes.' She flagged down a taxi. 'Tell him if he isn't waiting for me at Admiralty Arch, alone, in half an hour the recording you just heard goes up on our website.'

Grosvenor Crescent, London – Thursday, 1.12am

The Jaguar Sentinel XJ parked up on one of the most expensive streets in London. There were few other cars around, as residents used the secure underground parking facilities.

Against the wishes of her Royal and Specialist Protection detail, Angela Curtis had demanded minimal presence from them.

On the way up the front stairs to Nigel Hawkes' house, she was flanked by two discreetly armed RaSP officers, who had travelled in the Jaguar with her instead of in their usual convoy of armoured BMWs and Range Rovers. A third officer waited outside, guarding the front door.

Nigel's wife, Sheila, had the door open for Curtis before she reached it. Her husband was expecting her.

'Good evening, Angela,' Sheila answered. That she had failed to call her Prime Minister was no innocent slip up after years of barely friendly acquaintance. Her only relationship with Curtis was as her husband's political enemy.

Sheila closed the door and wrapped her cashmere cardigan a little tighter around herself. She asked the RaSP officers, 'Would you gentlemen like some tea or coffee?'

On her way into the drawing room, Curtis answered for them. 'They're fine.'

The two men stood in the hall, one facing the front door, one facing the kitchen at the back of the house.

Nigel was sitting on a leather chesterfield sofa. He had managed to throw on some casual weekend clothes after

Curtis' abrupt phone call approximately nine minutes earlier. He didn't get up when Curtis entered.

'The sort of welcome I've come to expect from the Hawkeses,' Curtis said, remaining standing in the centre of the room.

Nigel was too exhausted for anger or volume. 'I swore my allegiance to the crown, not your temporary office,' he said quietly.

Not rising to the remark, Curtis asked, 'Have you heard about this Jonathan Gale fellow?'

'It was in my evening security memo,' Hawkes replied.

'Do we have any leads?'

'You seem to have me confused with your Home Secretary.' Hawkes raised his hands then dropped them on his thighs. 'Is this what you got my wife and I out of our beds for, Angela?'

Curtis went to the bar and poured a whisky. 'I'm here about Simon Ali's speech.' She handed the whisky to Hawkes.

He gently swirled his glass. 'How bad is it?'

Curtis said, 'Worse than you could ever imagine.'

'How did you get it?'

'He left a copy with his lawyer to be given to the next PM. Doug Robertson delivered it to me earlier.'

Hawkes drained his glass, then held it out. 'Could I have another, please?'

Curtis turned away. 'Get it yourself.'

After pouring another measure, Hawkes leaned on the bar, his back to Curtis. He said, 'If you came here to tell Sheila, you're wasting your time. I already told her. Or are you going public with it?'

'Public with what?'

'About the affair.' Hawkes walked to his snooker table and rolled the black ball to the far end. 'It wasn't serious. Abbie Bishop and I.'

'How long had it been going on?' asked Curtis.

'Six months.'

'That's how long she'd been getting paid by Goldcastle. The very consultancy firm you hired four weeks ago to run your election campaign. My source in GCHQ has shown me exactly what Goldcastle has been up to: hacking referendums and elections using illegally acquired online data on U.K. citizens. Do you think Goldcastle have enough to clinch the election for you?'

'Come on, Angela,' Nigel groaned. 'There are no cameras in here. Who are you trying to impress? I didn't get into this job to privatise the NHS, do nothing about carbon emissions, and let bankers get away with daylight bloody robbery. But we let those things happen because it keeps us in jobs. Those people who finance our campaigns: they're the ones in charge. Every day we say things we don't mean because we know it will play well. That's what we do. We win elections, then we find ways to stay in power. You're like one of those people in a pub, carping about millionaires hiding savings in offshore tax havens. Give that same person a million pounds and a creative accountant, I guarantee they'd do the exact same thing. Because that's what people do: they protect their own interests.'

'That's not what I'm doing,' said Curtis. 'I want to see this country prosper. And politicians like you be held to account.'

Hawkes laughed. 'A party political broadcast from Angela Curtis...'

Curtis asked, 'Do you admit you have no compunction about Goldcastle's methods and hoodwinking the public?'

'If a bit of imaginative news and targeted advertising is enough to swing an election or a referendum, then what does that say about the electorate? Do they deserve my respect? I suppose you'll go public with the Abbie story in a few days. Try to sew up the election early for yourself. Trust me, Bannatyne will eat you up in the debates...'

'Look at me, Nigel,' she said.

He turned around.

Curtis moved towards him. 'I wanted to look into your eyes when I asked you.'

Hawkes braced himself.

She asked, 'Did you have the Simon Ali press conference moved from the Foreign and Commonwealth Office building?' Curtis watched him carefully, gauging his reaction.

'Why would I do a thing like that?'

Curtis said, 'Roger Milton's been looking into it for me. The Foreign Office had new scanners installed last week. Scanners that would have flagged the ceramic balls in Mufaza's suicide vest. Whoever moved the press conference wanted Mufaza to get in.'

After a pause, Hawkes said, 'I don't know anything about that.'

Curtis snapped, 'We've got a mole in GCHQ handing out press cards to terrorists, credible threats being covered up, and I'm telling you whoever moved that press conference is involved.'

Hawkes' phone started ringing, breaking the icy silence.

He answered, 'Not now, Charlie. I'm–' He rubbed his temple. 'Tell her I'll be there in half an hour.'

After he hung up, Curtis said, 'You're in demand tonight.'

Hawkes patted down his pockets, checking for his wallet and keys. 'I have to go out for a while,' he said, making for the hall.

Curtis stopped him before the door, placing her hand on his chest. 'It was terrorism, Nigel. Terrorism that was *allowed* to happen.'

He didn't say a word.

She took her hand away and allowed him to leave.

Curtis looked up and saw Sheila sitting on the stairs.

'Could you step outside, please?' Sheila asked the RaSP officers. Once they were gone her gaze shifted to Curtis, who came to the bottom of the stairs. 'I don't know what you think Nigel has done.'

'Where was he on Sunday night?' asked Curtis.

Sheila replied, 'He was here. With me.'

'His ministerial diary says that he was taking calls until eight o'clock.'

'Nigel's a busy man, Angela. I respect his privacy.'

'Of course.' Curtis turned to leave.

'I know that you know about her,' Sheila said suddenly. 'That Abbie woman. It wasn't his fault. She tricked him. If anyone's to blame for all of this it's her.'

Curtis said, 'Oh, I think there's a bit more blame to go around than that.'

The Mall, London – Thursday 1.32am

Stella sent a text to Diane: '*On way to meet Hawkes.*'

Diane replied, '*Don't show him the pitch if you're not sure he'll swing at it. It could be dangerous.*'

Stella muttered, 'Bloody baseball analogies...' before pocketing her phone.

She got out the taxi at the top of the Mall at Admiralty Arch. When she saw no one else there, she checked the time on her phone. He had five minutes.

The Mall was deserted all the way down to Buckingham Palace half a mile away. The only movement was the swaying of the Union Jacks jutting out from the trees over the road.

Then Stella saw a man with mid-length swept-back grey hair come out of Horse Guard's Row, where his driver had dropped him off. He had his overcoat collar turned up against the breeze.

He had left his security behind. He couldn't risk bringing them along. Every journey, no matter how insignificant, was logged by the Met's Protection Command.

Stella could tell from his gait that it was Hawkes. The air of superiority, his face pointing slightly upwards.

'We're off the record,' he said, looking around shiftily. 'Can we take this somewhere a little less visible, Miss Mitchell?'

'Follow me,' Stella replied, taking him towards the bottom of the staircase at The Duke of York column, away from the main road.

'Did you know,' Hawkes said, 'when the Duke died, the entire army gave up a day's wages to pay for this column.' He gazed up admiringly at it. 'Try suggesting such a thing now.'

'Maybe if we had leaders that were deserving of it,' Stella countered.

Hawkes pinched up his trousers as he took a seat on the bottom stair. 'If you're here to blackmail me, Miss Mitchell, tell me now. It's late. And I'm tired.'

Stella stood in front of him. 'I'm interested in why Abbie Bishop was murdered.'

'So am I.'

'Did you know what she was doing for MI6?'

'We never talked about that. We always left work at the front door whenever we saw each other.'

'How did it start?'

Hawkes couldn't maintain eye contact. He looked off towards St James's Park in the background. 'We met at the U.S. embassy about nine months ago. My wife Sheila and I had been growing apart for a while. Suddenly here was this beautiful young woman who looked at me like I was... I hadn't felt like that in decades.' He trailed off with a wistful smile. 'I know I sound like some besotted, stupid old man.'

'You could say that,' Stella said.

'Yes, well... I knew it was only a matter of time before someone found out. We were very careful. Plus, I have a few extra resources I can pull on: cars, drivers, non-network phones. With my diary as full as it is, it wasn't difficult to explain away some lost hours to my wife. Six months later I realised I was in love with Abbie.'

Stella asked, 'Did Abbie ever mention concerns about her safety?'

'No, never.'

She flicked through her notes. 'Your public diary shows that you were taking various diplomatic phone calls at your office until eight p.m. on Sunday night. Where were you the rest of the night?'

Hawkes snorted at the implication. 'You really do have a low opinion of me, don't you. I was at home. With my wife.'

Stella took a beat. 'When did you find out Abbie had died?'

'Monday morning was chaos. It was about midday that I saw her name in a security briefing.'

'How upset do you think Goldcastle will be about it?' Stella decided it was time to ramp things up a bit. 'My documents show she was stealing from GCHQ. Was she doing it for you?'

'Good heavens, whatever for?'

'GCHQ have been collecting data on millions of U.K. citizens from social media sites and internet searches. That data could give Goldcastle insights into the electorate that could swing an election.'

Hawkes snorted. 'That's paranoid conspiracy stuff.'

'That data could be very useful if you were looking to challenge Simon Ali in the General Election.'

'A Foreign Secretary challenge his own Prime Minister? The Party would never stand for it. Simon Ali had never been more popular in the polls. Everyone knew he was going to walk the next General Election.'

Stella could feel him getting more comfortable the longer the conversation went on. She decided to raise the stakes. didn't want to let him go yet. 'I know that Simon Ali's press conference was moved at the last minute. What sort of person would be authorised to move that without the PM's permission?'

Hawkes blinked quickly. 'From a security perspective? I suppose it's possible someone from Specialist Operations.'

'What about Sir Lloyd Willow?' asked Stella.

He mulled it over. 'It would be somewhat irregular, but not impossible.'

Stella knew the question would turn their conversation nuclear, but she had to go for it. The clock was ticking. 'What about someone in the Foreign Office?'

Hawkes laughed in disgust. 'I didn't move the press conference, Miss Mitchell.'

'What was Simon Ali going to say in his speech? What was he going to confess to?'

'I haven't the *slightest* idea,' Hawkes said, getting to his feet. He fired off a text to his driver who had been circling the Mall. 'You can print whatever you like about me, Miss Mitchell. I don't care what recordings you've got. You think you have me over a barrel because I don't want an affair story coming out before I run for PM? You got your recordings from Dan Leckie – yes, I know all about that. Do you really think an editor of the calibre of Diane Schlesinger is going to let you use those? It's my understanding those recordings have now gone astray, which leaves me rather in a state of deniability.' Hawkes started to walk away.

Stella called after him, 'Bill Patterson will hold those recordings over you for the rest of your career.'

Hawkes turned back. 'I took this meeting as a courtesy, because Charlie Fletcher told me you were someone who should be taken seriously. This is the first time Charlie's been wrong about anything. This meeting never happened.' He wandered back towards the Mall, where his car promptly arrived for him.

Stella shook her head as he drove off. She'd taken a

chance to force him into some kind of admission. She'd tried to bluff him, and Hawkes had called it.

There was now only one person left who might still be able to save the story.

Dan's block was on one of the shadier parts of Lambeth Road, forever feeling like someone could jump you at any moment – especially after midnight, under cover of low-hanging trees and a lack of street lights.

Stella knew it was a long shot, but it was the last chance she had before calling Diane to tell her the story was definitely over.

She knocked hard on the front door, thinking she might have to wake Dan from what would surely be a deep, intoxicated sleep.

After calling his name a few times, she tried the door handle.

It didn't turn. It didn't have to. The door was off the latch and tipped open at the slightest touch.

Stella entered the living room stealthily, then flicked the light on. Everything was as she remembered it. There was no sign of forced entry or burglary. Dan had simply left the latch off the door.

There was a piece of paper lying out on the coffee table, surrounded by empty cans of lager that had been used as ashtrays. The paper had been folded over. The front of it said "STEL"

Stella could see her breath as she opened the letter.

"*Dear Stel. I'm sorry again about running off. I always liked you and we had a good run back in the day. I needn't have bothered screwing you over with the recordings. Patterson's refused to pay me and now he won't put a word in at any other papers like he promised. Basically it's over for me. This was my last shot and I buggered it up. I've left the web address and password to my dropbox account on the other side of this. It's got all the MP3s of the Hawkes voicemails in it. Including the ones Patterson was keeping from you last time. Light the bastards up, Stel."*

She dialled Dan's mobile immediately. It went to voicemail.

'Dan,' she said, 'it's Stella. I'm at your place and got your note. I'm worried about you. Will you call me back as soon as you get this? I'll find you another job, I swear I will. I'll come find you wherever you are.' She hung up.

She sent a text to Rebecca: '*I need a trace on a mobile. EMERGENCY*'

36

Artur had barely slept since he got to Berlin. It was nothing more than his eyes closing over, followed almost immediately by a sense of panic at his precarious position. Then he was wide awake again.

He had bedded down under a bridge in the Government Quarter of Wilhelmstrasse, where a small community of Middle Eastern refugees had gathered. Sleeping on flattened cardboard boxes, his jacket for a blanket, Artur found himself beside a Syrian father and son, the boy all of five years old.

From their camp, it looked like they'd been there a while. The boy played happily a few feet away from his father, who sat cross-legged on the pavement, staring into space, wondering how he was supposed to build a life for his son from a filthy blanket on the street in a strange country. He only knew the German for 'hungry', 'sorry' and 'thank you'.

He had never felt cold like December in Berlin.

The father had handed over his life savings to traffickers back in Hungary. He and his son had nearly asphyxiated whilst stowed away in a truck bound for Calais. They ended up in the notorious 'Jungle' migrant encampment, which was as dangerous as the war zone they had just left.

When Artur looked at the pair, he felt like a fool for acting so hard done by the past week.

Before he left the camp that morning, he gave the boy a can of Coke he'd been saving for his breakfast, then said '*Auf wiedersehen*' and ruffled the boy's hair. The boy hurried over to his dad with the Coke, amazed by his present.

As Artur made his way back to Pariser Platz for the second day, he wondered how long he might keep up his routine. Days? Weeks? What if Novak never came? Where to then?

He straightened his clothes as best he could, but he, too, looked homeless.

Pariser Platz was quieter than usual because of a freezing wind blowing across the square. The decorations on the enormous Christmas tree in the centre jingled and chinked in the wind. At the main entrance, a group of Spanish and Italian tourists were braving the cold to photograph the Brandenburg Gate.

Artur pulled up his denim jacket collar and took the same spot as the day before: on a bench on the west side of the square. For the next hour, he would look hopefully and expectantly at each male, who, from a distance, looked even vaguely like Tom Novak.

Sharp parked up on Lennéstrasse on the edge of the Tiergarten park for an hour. When it was time, he and Novak set off on foot towards Pariser Platz, taking a slight detour down Behrenstrasse – passing the haunting Memorial to the Murdered Jews of Europe, which looked like a parking lot full of tombs.

Before they reached the Brandenburg Gate side of the square, Sharp stopped walking. He told Novak, 'You're going to have to do this alone.'

'What do you mean?' asked Novak.

'If Artur has a tail, the cleanest way to get to you or him is a long-range shot. The square's too open for a shooter to risk a hit close up. I'll stay on the edges where I can spot any sniper positions.'

'What are you going to do,' asked Novak, 'stare at them intently? You're unarmed.'

Sharp reached down to his ankle and revealed a Glock 26 9mm attached to a holster. It was designed for concealed carry. 'The advantage of not getting searched at airport security. It's no rifle, but at longer range I could certainly *deter* a sniper.'

Novak opened up Sharp's jacket and said – only half-jokingly – 'I guess it's too optimistic that you might have a bullet-proof vest in there for me?'

Artur sat with his hands in his jacket pockets, legs stretched out, his body stiff with cold. Nearby, a tourist walked past eating a hot dog, the smell wafting towards Artur. It took him a moment to remember when he had last eaten. He had been so hungry the night before that he resorted to looking through a bin, but after finding some scraps couldn't bring himself to eat any of it.

Then, in the distance, a figure emerged from the far end of the square. His walk hesitant, cagey.

Artur couldn't believe he'd actually come.

Novak recognised Artur from his videos, except he was more drawn, pale and with dark rings around his eyes.

Before Artur could rise from the bench, Novak gestured for Artur to remain sitting.

Sharp had held position in front of the DZ Bank building, set a little back from the main square, giving the clearest view of

the surrounding area. Sniper conditions were far from perfect
with the wind up and gusty, but visibility was extremely clear
for a long-range shot. With steady cloud coverage there would
be no sudden shifts in light.

Artur's chosen meeting place was the definition of
shooting fish in a barrel. Sharp had always thought of old-
fashioned intuition as experience mixed with skill. And his
intuition told him that the situation didn't feel right.

He walked around the perimeter of the square, head
down in a free map he'd picked up from the Hotel Adlon,
which overlooked the entirety of *Pariser*.

Novak sat down beside Artur and said, 'Don't make any big
gestures. Relax. Talk quietly. Are you alright?'

All Artur wanted to do was throw his arms around Novak,
and embrace him like a brother. He spoke in English as best
he could, 'They tried to kill me.'

Novak said, 'I have someone helping me here. That guy
walking in front of the Allianz building in the black jacket and
cap. Don't be alarmed if he comes over. He's CIA but he's
with me. You can trust him.'

Artur started to smile. 'I can't believe you actually came.'

Remembering Sharp's instructions, Novak said, 'In a few
seconds I'm going to get up, slowly. You get up as well and
walk beside me. Two friends, just walking. We're going to walk
towards the east side of the square, okay?'

'Okay.' Artur's voice cracked a little, overcome with relief.

Novak stood first, then Artur followed. Dizzy from exhaustion and hunger, Artur stepped to one side to regain his
balance, leaning into Novak.

At the same moment, a cry of 'Shooter!' from Sharp's
direction was followed almost immediately by a rifle shot. The
shot hit the iron bench and would have been a direct hit on
Artur had he not moved.

The tourists near the Christmas tree scattered in all directions, a mass exodus only increasing the sense of panic. A woman nearby screamed, '*Terroristisch!*' as she ran towards the fountain to escape.

Novak covered Artur's head and pulled him behind the bench for what little cover it provided. More shots rang out, ricocheting off the bench once more.

Novak and Artur were helpless. There was too much open ground to get to the Christmas tree.

Hunkered down in front of the Allianz building, Sharp could tell from the angle of the shots that the shooter was somewhere in the Hotel Adlon, around the second or third floor. It didn't take him long to spy the rifle sticking out of an open window on the third floor.

Sharp aimed his Glock at the window, then shouted at Novak, 'Go!', giving them cover as he fired.

Other than Novak and Artur, the square had emptied.

'We've got to go,' Novak yelled, still covering Artur as best he could.

'I can't,' Artur replied back, hunched over.

Novak hauled him to his feet as Sharp delivered more covering fire, blasting out the shooter's hotel room window. The rifle shots stopped just long enough for the pair to get out from behind the bench. Keeping as low as possible, Novak guided Artur across the full width of the square. Novak's heart was beating so hard and so fast it felt like one constant, intense throb.

Novak made a beeline for the U.S. Embassy, as two armed *Bundespolizei* officers on patrol took up firing positions. All they could see was Sharp with a weapon pulled.

The moment Sharp saw them, he took cover behind the Christmas tree and attempted to flash his CIA badge. He shouted '*Ich bin* CIA!' But before he could extend his badge, one of the panicked *Bundespolizei* – thinking they had a terrorist incident on their hands – was about to shoot. Luckily for Sharp, the man's partner stopped him in time.

Sharp held up three fingers, then pointed to the third-floor window of the Adlon. With the police focussed on the shooter now, Sharp set off after Novak and Artur.

They were still in the shooter's range, and as the police turned their guns on the blasted-out window, a shot caught the back of Artur's leg. He collapsed in a heap. The sudden tug of Artur's weight to one side also felled Novak.

He struggled to his feet, dragging Artur with him.

'*Schnell bewegen!*' the police shouted at the pair — *move quickly*.

Novak struggled with Artur, who was like a dead weight around Novak's waist. There was still a good hundred yards to the embassy entrance.

We're not going to make it, Novak thought.

Then, Artur's body suddenly lightened and he was back on his feet.

'I got you,' said Sharp, taking up Artur under his other arm.

As they neared the embassy gate, Sharp called out, 'I'm Officer Walter Sharp, CIA!' He managed to hold out his badge with his free hand. 'These men are CIA-protected witnesses.'

The embassy patrolman opened the wrought iron gate, and hustled them across the forecourt. 'Stay down!' he shouted, as more shots rained down at Novak and Artur's feet.

When they reached the marble lobby, Artur sat on the ground, starting to get his breath back. His eyes were wide with shock. He couldn't hear anything.

Then Sharp, still on his feet, turned around.

Novak saw the blood dripping from Sharp's mouth, then Sharp started to fall. Novak caught him, which slid Sharp's jacket to one side. Revealing a gushing gunshot wound below his right shoulder.

Sharp's eyes closed.

'Oh, Jesus...' said Novak, his hands filling with blood. 'We need an ambulance! We need a doctor!'

37

THE FOURTH FLOOR, GCHQ - THURSDAY, 9.10AM

Mackintosh had built up a head of steam dashing up two flights from GTE to the Director's Suite. He bounded past Trevor's secretary, and shoved the door open with both hands.

'Have you lost your mind?' Mackintosh shouted.

Trevor gestured to his secretary, standing helplessly at the open door, that it was alright. Once the door was closed, Trevor quietly seethed. 'The only thing lost around here, Alex, is your self-control.'

Mackintosh caught his breath. 'They've let her go.'

'I know, and there was nothing I could do about it.'

'Why didn't you call Nigel?'

'Normally, I would have,' said Trevor. 'But it seems Rebecca Fox has friends in high places. Higher than the Home Office.' He handed Mackintosh a piece of paper across his desk. 'Phone records from the holding cells. Fox didn't call a lawyer. She didn't call a union rep. She called a secure Hannibal phone located somewhere within Downing Street.'

Mackintosh exhaled in frustration. 'Curtis.'

'Contact must have been made at some point,' said Trevor. 'Likely with Roger Milton during Rebecca's recent excursion to London. Curtis hasn't strayed beyond Whitehall in the last forty-eight hours.'

'We can't let her back in here.'

'It's the PM's call, Alex. Fox has been signed off for the next week as a courtesy.'

'A *courtesy*?' Mackintosh exclaimed.

Trevor retorted, 'It was your mistake. She had full authorisation for STRAP Three clearance, approved by Angela Curtis personally. Curtis has the right to grant emergency clearance to GCHQ officers. I'm sticking to the letter of the law on this one.'

Mackintosh said, 'The law says it needs to be in writing. The officer can't just make a phone call.'

Trevor held up another piece of paper, showing Curtis's signature at the bottom. 'Filed with the Foreign Office an hour ago.'

'Whose side are you on?' Mackintosh asked.

Trevor replied, 'Maybe if I had some guarantees about the Honours list in May. I'm the only GCHQ Director in fifty years who hasn't been knighted.'

'This is about your *knighthood*?'

'I believe a little reward for my efforts is not unreasonable.'

'Unreasonable?' barked Mackintosh. 'Trevor, how the hell would it look if the Director of GCHQ was given a knighthood after the press pass debacle, and all the other GCHQ failures that have caused the attack?'

Trevor stared back in incomprehension. 'I did everything that was asked of me.'

'You did,' Mackintosh acknowledged, 'But you're going to have to wait.'

Trevor's hands were trembling with rage as he collected his briefing papers for his meeting. On his way past he told Mackintosh, 'It's unwise to make an enemy of me, Alex. The things I know? Could bring down the entire house of cards.'

The News Office, London Bridge – Thursday, 11.12am

Within forty-five minutes of Stella calling Diane the night before, telling her she was in possession of all of Hawkes' and Bishop's voicemails, Diane had set her up in a windowless office in the shared News Office building overlooking London Bridge. Diane had worked with several other reporters there – now senior editors themselves.

Stella was just glad to have proper office equipment, rather than sitting at a small desk, with a hotel Wi-Fi service that wasn't even secure enough for an eBay transaction, let alone exchanging documents on national security.

Not one for taking chances, Stella had put black tape over the thin sliver of glass on the office door, that otherwise would have looked out onto the newsroom floor of a national broadsheet.

In the last two days, Stella had slept for four hours, and she was starting to flag. She felt like she was travelling half a yard behind her body.

An intern back in New York was typing up transcripts of all the voicemail recordings, then pinging them back to Stella's IronCloud. Now she had the voicemails on record, she started the frame of a story connecting Abbie Bishop and Nigel Hawkes, and subsequently Abbie and Goran Lipski – all serving as an opening into the Downing Street attack. She had Jonathan Gale and the anonymous attackers in the black Audi. And somewhere around the edges, looming over every-thing, was Goldcastle.

She was fifteen hundred words in, when her laptop screen flicked to a full-screen notification:

"Darkroom – INCOMING CALL: Diane Schlesinger"

Stella hit Accept.

Diane was sitting at the desk in her bedroom with her reading glasses on. It was barely seven in the morning, New York time, but she'd been up since five.

'How's it going, Stella?' Diane asked.

Before she could reply, someone knocked on the office door.

'Not now,' Stella called out. 'Sorry,' she said to Diane. 'I was saying, I need another two thousand words. To really nail it.'

Diane thought about it. 'Fine. Do it.'

Stella asked, 'Have you even been to bed?'

'I was asleep for a little while, then I had to take a phone call.'

There was more knocking on the door, louder this time.

Stella shouted, 'Piss off!'

Then a notification appeared at the top of the screen: "INCOMING CALL: Tom Novak."

In a panic, Stella announced, 'It's Novak! Sorry, Diane, can you hang on?'

With a grin, Diane told her, 'Take it, take it...'

Stella clicked "Accept call". 'Novak!' she beamed. 'Where are...' She squinted at the screen. He was on his phone. Standing in front of an office door with black tape over the window. 'Are you...?'

'Outside?' said Novak, knocking again. 'Yeah. You wanna let me in? I've got an entire newsroom staring at me right now.'

Stella scrambled to the door. When she opened it, she covered her mouth in relief.

He was wearing an oversize navy t-shirt that had "VIR-GINIA" written across it in collegiate writing. He put his arms out a little as if she was to inspect him. 'Not much of a wardrobe to choose from on CIA charter flights.'

Stella threw her arms around him so hard it knocked him back a step.

'Are you okay?' she asked.

Novak replied, 'Am *I* okay? What about you? Diane told me what happened.'

Stella let go of him. 'I'm fine,' she nodded. 'A little banged up, but alright. Where the hell have you been?'

'I was renditioned by CIA.'

Stella closed the door. 'Very funny.'

Novak took out a wad of paper from his backpack. 'Luckily, I've got notes.' On his way to Stella's desk, he waved hello to Diane. 'Hey, boss.'

Diane said, 'Now that I have the two of you in the same room for once I better make this quick. Stella, I brought Tom up to speed with where you are. Tom, what have you got?'

Novak laid out his notes, standing at Stella's desk. 'I got Artur Korecki on the record on the plane from Berlin. Berlin police took down the shooter, who's been identified as Leonard Schulle. A gun for hire. And a pretty successful one until this morning. My CIA guy, Sharp, took a bullet, but we had a doctor on the flight over. He's going to be fine. He's only on background – no name or rank to be used.'

Diane said wistfully, 'I'd love to have those tapes of Malik from Camp Zero.'

'They're long gone, I'm afraid,' replied Novak. 'But we at least have video of CIA renditioning an MI6 agent. Malik made a phone call to Abbie Bishop in Camp Zero, trying to warn her about a threat against her. And Malik has a proven link to Abbie Bishop, thanks to Stella's end. Stella?'

Stella took up her notes. 'Abbie Bishop was Malik's handler. We're a little closer to proving links between Goldcastle and the data Bishop stole. I have a source in British intelligence who can link some of their payments to Bishop with the company.'

Diane was scribbling notes in shorthand as they spoke.

Novak said, 'It's worth noting as well that Robert Snow was going to oppose the new Freedom and Privacy Act. That could have made him some powerful enemies in the U.S. government.'

'And on Downing Street,' Stella said, 'the press pass that Mufaza used to access it was made by someone at GCHQ.'

Novak turned to her. 'Are you serious?'

Stella showed him the printout from Rebecca.

Diane continued scribbling for a few more seconds. 'Right...a few things. If we're going to come out and call someone in GCHQ a terrorist conspirator, we'd better shore up our story here. One: if Goldcastle were paying Abbie Bishop why would they want her dead? Two: what were Goldcastle doing with the data and who knew about its theft? Three: who moved that press conference? And four: we need something – *anything* – to link that black Audi to British intelligence. That's the ball game. Stella has one source on an eyewitness at Moreton Place who's been identified as MI6. But I'd like something on paper.' Diane stood up, pacing in front of the laptop. 'I'm going to ask you a question Henry's going to ask me in a couple of hours: How confident are you in this story?'

Novak and Stella shared a look with each other, knowing full well the gravity of what they were saying.

Novak was leaning forward on his knees, his face etched with tension. 'It's good.'

'Stella?' Diane said.

Stella answered, 'It's good.'

Diane said, 'Remember a few years ago, Dan Rather's *Sixty Minutes* story questioning George W Bush's military record? It ended with his producer being fired, and Rather took early retirement. And you know what? It wasn't that they were wrong. They just couldn't prove enough of it was *right*.'

Stella and Novak nodded.

Diane checked her watch. 'There's ten hours before we go to print here. Now's not the time to run scared. This is a *big* story. You've been waiting your whole lives for this. Are you ready to get to work?'

They both replied, 'Yeah.'

'And remember: keep all source names off any drives. Use initials only. If this Freedom and Privacy Act goes through, we might end up having to turn over all our servers.' Diane said, 'That's it. Let's finish this thing.' She logged out.

As soon as she was gone Novak exhaled, tilting his head to the ceiling. 'What now?'

Stella turned back a dozen pages in her notes, the ones she wrote up after her meeting with Hawkes. Being off the record didn't have to mean that a meeting never happened. She just couldn't directly use anything he had said in her final copy.

'I met Hawkes last night,' Stella said.

'And?'

'He's too experienced to give anything away. His wife is his alibi.'

Novak rubbed his newly shorn hair, the relentless pace of the week starting to take its toll. 'What have we got that's a constant through George Abassi, Abbie Bishop, the Downing Street attack, the black ops team who went after you, Rebecca, and Jonathan Gale?'

Stella suggested, 'MI6? Lloyd Willow could have moved that press conference.'

'It's possible,' Novak agreed. 'As Foreign Secretary, Hawkes is the minister responsible for MI6.'

Stella added, 'And the press conference was moved from the Foreign Office itself.' She rummaged through her notes. 'I was working on something before you got here. Voicemail messages between Abbie and Hawkes.'

Novak looked at the transcripts with concern. 'Did you get these from Dan?'

'Yeah, he left them for me.'

'Left them? Where is he?'

'I don't know.' Stella kept looking through the transcripts. 'He took off. And there's no signal on his mobile. Wherever he is, he doesn't want to be found.'

Novak cleared his throat. 'I think we, uh...need to talk about the bigger problem here.'

'Like what?'

'First, we have to prove Bishop and Hawkes were having an affair. How are we doing that?'

'The voicemails.'

'We're not actually using them, are we?'

Stella paused her search. 'Why not?'

'Because they were recorded illegally by a convicted phone hacker? Didn't Diane ask where you got them?'

Stella sighed in frustration and moved back from the desk. 'They're second-hand, Novak. The *facts* are still in those voice-mails. We're not using them as a source, we're using them to confirm what we already know.'

Novak started walking circles. 'What do we know for sure? What source do we have on the record, that will put their name to something?'

Stella couldn't see any other way around it. 'There are still ways for us to use the tapes. They're still–'

Novak put his hands to his head. 'The tapes are *illegal*, Stella!' he shouted.

Stella shouted back, 'Oh, great. The mighty Tom Novak is going to lecture me on journalistic ethics when it comes to sources!'

Neither had the energy for anything further.

They were now at opposite ends of the room.

Novak had calmed himself enough to return to his normal speaking volume. 'I screwed up, Stella. I know, I screwed up massively on the biggest story of my life. And once all this stuff comes out about my NSA source, I'll be out of a job, and very likely in jail. By the time I get out, I could be in my late forties. Do you know many forty-year-old journalists who lied about sources who make it back to the top?' He stepped cautiously towards her. 'I don't want to see you make the same mistakes I did. Believe me, I know how badly you want it. But you don't want it like this.'

Stella stood against the desk, reliving the night before. 'They shot him like it was nothing, Novak,' she said. 'Jonathan Gale was about to run away with his family. Now a little girl and a wife have lost a father and a husband. Because of me. Because of this story. I can't walk away. Not after the things I've seen. We have to get these guys. I don't care what it takes.'

Novak held his temples, trying to think of a way out. 'What if we could take something existing in the recordings, and work around them instead.'

'What do you mean?'

'Like a name, or a phone number, something that leads to something or someone else. Then we get *them* on the record.'

Stella handed him a transcript page. 'This is what I was going to show you. There was one voicemail that stood out.'

The transcript showed:

"*[voicemail left for NH]: several <beeps> then END OF CALL.*"

Stella clicked to the original MP3 recording she'd downloaded earlier from Dan's dropbox. She put in one of her earphones and held the other out to Novak.

He came back to the desk and listened with her.

There were more than several beeps. Eleven to be exact.

'That sounds like a phone number being dialled,' Novak said.

Stella asked, 'Why would she start dialling in the middle of a voicemail?'

'Hang on,' Novak said. 'Hawkes and Bishop must have been using burners. Exclusive use for calling the other. Someone in Hawkes' position wouldn't take a chance on something like that.'

'There's eleven beeps,' Stella said. 'That's got to be a U.K. mobile. And there's no one else recorded on here other than Abbie Bishop or Hawkes.'

'We know the first two digits are going to be 0 and 7.'

Novak flicked to the keypad on his phone and hit the zero then seven. 'Phone keypad frequencies are standardised. My number seven sounds the same as yours or anyone else's.'

Stella tried it on her phone too. 'The tone's the same for one, four and seven. And for two, five and eight. And for three, six and nine.'

Novak shook his head. 'You're hearing the primary frequency – the louder one is the same – but there's a quieter secondary frequency in the background. You'd need to be an experienced musician to make it out, but it's there.' Novak turned Stella's laptop to face him and quickly navigated to a website called Find DTMF Tones. 'I used this before on the NSA papers. You wouldn't believe the tools that developers put online for free.' He converted the MP3 recording to a WAV file, then uploaded it to the website. After one click, the website reported back on the phone number dialled.

Stella wasn't slow in realising its value. 'I could get Rebecca Fox to trace this number.'

Novak's eyes widened. 'What other source do we have on Hawkes and Bishop?'

Stella shook her head, taking long blinks as she rejected possibilities. 'An affair that went on this long, someone had to know.' She snapped her fingers. 'Hawkes said he needed phones, cars, and logistics to keep it a secret. For that, you need a trusted aide.' Stella scooped up her things and shovelled them into her bag.

'Where are you going?' asked Novak.

'I need to find Charlie Fletcher.'

38

Walter Sharp and Artur Korecki had been resting on some couches pulled into Diane's office. The blinds were closed, and none of the *Republic* staff had been told who the strange men were who were taking up so much of Diane's day.

For Sharp, dizzying jetlag was the least of his worries. He had been bandaged around his shoulder and his arm was in a sling.

Artur, meanwhile, couldn't do enough for Sharp. Fetching him glasses of water to take his painkillers, helping him take his boots off, fluffing a cushion for him while Diane and Mark Chang interviewed him. While Sharp gave his version of events from Camp Zero, Artur set up a chair outside the room, taking on the role of Sharp's personal bodyguard.

When Sharp was done, he said to Diane, 'That's it. That's everything.'

Diane looked worriedly at his statements. She said, 'Officer Sharp. You do realise that your statements place you in the interrogation room alone with George Abassi. Although your name won't appear anywhere in this story, I wanted to make you aware of the possibility you could be identified from some of these details.'

'I understand, ma'am,' Sharp replied.

Diane said, 'Mark?'

Chang tapped his pen on his pad. 'We need a second source on Abassi,' he said. 'Stella has GCHQ files detailing Abassi's work, and Tom has a CIA transfer request for taking him to Camp Zero.'

Diane could see the problem. 'We need a second source that definitively says Abassi was at Camp Zero on Sunday night.' She looked to the ceiling, searching for a curse. 'Nan...*tucket.*'

While Mark and Diane struggled to think of a solution, Sharp said, 'I might be able to help with that.'

Two hours later, a call came from reception to Diane's office.

As Sharp left Diane's office, Artur sprang to attention.

'Relax, Artur,' Sharp told him.

At reception, a young man with a Middle Eastern complexion was waiting with a padded envelope in his hand. He was wearing a baseball cap unusually low down his forehead.

The man was insistent with the receptionist. 'I don't want Diane Schlesinger. I want Walter Sharp.'

'Sir,' the receptionist said, going back through her notes, 'there is no one here by that name.'

Sharp said from the edge of the newsroom. 'Fahran.'

The man's eye lit up. He said quietly to Sharp, '*Khaleel.*'

One of the many Arabic words for friend.

'Are you alright?' Fahran asked.

'It's nothing,' replied Sharp. He took the envelope. '*Shukraan,*' he said – *Thank you.*

At the height of the War on Terror, CIA had set Fahran up in an apartment in Queens. An apartment that he now called home. Along with his wife and three children. Fahran was risking his immigration status to hand Sharp the envelope.

Sharp peeked inside, admiring the analogue tapes – the

ones Fahran had taken before General McNally's crew had ransacked the Camp Zero command.

Sharp said, 'When you think of the money we've spent safeguarding our most vital digital documents. You know what the Russians still use to this day?' Sharp closed the envelope with a smile. 'Typewriters.'

Fahran said, 'You cannot hack what is not online.' He put out his hand.

Sharp shook it. 'Thank you.'

When Sharp returned to Diane's office, she and Mark Chang were still in animated discussions about what to do with the Abassi side of the story.

Sharp dropped the envelope onto Diane's desk, and said on the way out the door, 'Double-sourced.'

39

Rebecca had no intention of sticking around for a return to work in a week's time. As far as she was concerned her GCHQ career was over. She'd glimpsed inside the world of classified material that had been shut off to her for so long. Now all she wanted was to start again, even if she had no idea where that would be, and what it would look like.

She unpinned all her research on her father and Bennington Hospital from the living room wall, putting the contents into a plastic zip wallet. With that, and a small holdall of clothes, she didn't look back as she closed the door behind her.

She left the keys on the kitchen worktop. The flat was let through a GCHQ employee programme, and she was damned if she was going back to the Doughnut to drop off keys to Human Resources.

While she made her way towards the town centre, her phone began to ring. Out of habit she took out her regular mobile, then realised that wasn't the one ringing. It was the Hannibal phone Roger Milton had given her.

She did a quick survey of the street – empty in all directions – before answering.

'Thank you for getting me out,' Rebecca said.

'We're going to have to be more careful,' Curtis answered. 'They know I'm helping you now.'

'I'm out. I'm done. If I keep going like this I'm going to get locked up for a very long time. Last night was long enough.'

'I can't let you do that, Rebecca.'

'What do you mean?'

'I need you inside GCHQ. For a few hours.'

'You're the Prime Minister. What do you need me for?'

Curtis lowered her voice, as if someone had come into close proximity. 'Do you trust me, Rebecca?'

'Well...yes.'

'I need you to remember that while I pass you on to someone else.'

Rebecca didn't understand what was happening.

The next voice she heard was Trevor Billington-Smith's.

'Rebecca,' he said.

She stopped dead in her tracks.

'I want to apologise for what happened last night. I didn't know anything about that. I need you to trust me as you've trusted Angela. It doesn't just concern Goldcastle and Abbie.' Trevor paused. 'It concerns your father, Rebecca.'

'My father?' she said.

'I need you to go back to GTE and await my instructions.'

40

FOREIGN AND COMMONWEALTH OFFICE, WHITEHALL –
THURSDAY, 6.30PM

Charlie Fletcher came steaming out the King Charles Street entrance of the Foreign and Commonwealth building, looking urgently from left to right. He spotted Stella across the road, standing under a streetlight which illuminated a cloud of descending mist.

He'd decided to come down without his suit jacket to make it clear he didn't plan on hanging around long.

'Stella, this is madness,' he said, leading her to a secluded archway. 'You can't lord these messages over me every time you want something. You asked for the minister, I gave you the bloody minister, alright?'

'I don't want the minister,' Stella said. 'I want you.'

'Your shit's on Nigel, not me.'

'Is it? What about Bill Patterson? I have it on good authority you two set Dan Leckie up.'

Charlie backed up a step. 'Don't talk rubbish.'

Stella stayed up in his face. 'Did the pair of you really think no one would ever ask how someone like Dan got Nigel Hawkes' phone in the first place?'

'What. Do. You. Want?'

'My magazine's going to publish that it was you who sold out the minister.'

The panic filled Charlie's eyes like a submarine taking on water. 'Hang on–'

'One question, yes or no: was Nigel Hawkes having an affair with MI6 agent Abbie Bishop?'

Charlie spoke to the sky, 'I cannot believe this. I cannot believe you're actually doing this...'

Stella took out a notebook, turning to a fresh page. She added, 'And we're on the record.'

Charlie laughed and started walking away.

'Yes or no, or we're printing your name with "refused to comment".'

He stopped walking.

'Yes or no,' said Stella, 'then you become an anonymous source close to the minister.'

He still had his back to her. 'And my name disappears?' he asked.

'Your name's going to disappear from the corridors of Whitehall altogether if you let Hawkes pull you down with him. He's finished after this, Charlie. You know he is.'

Charlie turned around. 'An anonymous source close to the department.'

'Okay,' Stella agreed.

He came closer. Then he took a long breath. 'Yes,' he said. 'Hawkes was having an affair with Bishop.'

'Did you cover it up for him?'

'Yes.'

'From the rest of the cabinet?'

'Yes.'

'From Simon Ali?'

'It was my job. Hawkes was going to carry on whether I was his aide or not. The corridor outside my office is like an open audition call for Machiavellis in Ted Baker suits. All of them willing to do whatever I'm not.'

Stella didn't let up. 'I'm tracing a mobile that may have been used to contact Abbie Bishop. Did you ever source a phone for Hawkes? A burner?'

'I never did anything like that.' Seeing how unconvinced she was, he added, 'Stella, I don't *know* about any phone. I never even *met* Abbie Bishop. I would just move his schedule around so they could hook up.'

'Where?' she asked.

'Moreton House, mostly. Never anywhere that kept records or had cameras, like hotels or anything. I tried to warn him. He wouldn't listen to me.'

Now that Stella had him on the ropes, she asked, 'What's Hawkes' connection to Goldcastle?'

'Jesus...' Charlie put a hand to his forehead and closed his eyes. 'I warned Nigel that that was never going to stay a secret for as long as everyone wanted.'

Using the one nugget she had on Goldcastle, she said, 'I know that Abbie Bishop was being paid five thousand dollars every month by them.'

Desperate to get away before someone saw him, Charlie said, 'Look, I swear. All I know is that Hawkes was shagging her, and I tried to stop it. I thought that Goldcastle might have been paying her to sleep with him, you know, to put him in a vulnerable position. But I never found out. That's it, I swear!'

Stella now had printable proof about Hawkes' affair. Charlie looked too terrified to be lying.

'Okay,' Stella said, putting her notebook away.

Before he left, Charlie said, 'These people are animals, Stella. Watch yourself.'

41

Rebecca felt eyes piercing her from all sides as she walked through GTE. Word had spread of her arrest the previous night, but no one really knew why she'd been released.

When she reached her station, Mackintosh – who had been alerted by security to her presence – shut his office blinds as she went past.

Rebecca was relieved to see Matthew's desk unattended.

When she logged in to her computer, an OTR message appeared on her screen. '*Rebecca, this is Trevor. Open up ECHELON. Then pull up phone number 07700900243.*'

Rebecca did so, bringing up the metadata for the entire user history: every call, every text, every voicemail, when and where they occurred and who to.

In GCHQ tests, metadata alone had proven to be more accurate than message content in locating or identifying a user. By itself, metadata didn't give too much away. But once cross-referenced with other numbers of interest it became easy to place two targets having a secret meeting together, or to form patterns of behaviour that indicate occupation, lifestyle and habit.

The first thing Rebecca noticed was how regularly the

phone was switched off. Every Wednesday between half eleven and quarter to twelve in the morning, and didn't come on again until a little after half past. Never earlier.

Mobile phone masts in the area had picked up a lot of activity on the phone in the Westminster area. It got Rebecca thinking about something that happened every Wednesday, midday until half-past. Something that any person involved would turn their phone off for: Prime Minister's Questions.

Trevor messaged: '*Done? Now bring up Sunday night's entries.*'

Rebecca could feel a surge of anticipation as she scrolled through the endless stream of data. When she reached the most recent data, she noticed a circled, red R next to the call log.

Someone operating ECHELON had activated the phone's microphone for live recording during a set time. The operator ID was Trevor Billington-Smith's.

Trevor: 'Download all recorded calls from 23.00 – 00.30 Sunday night.'

Rebecca: 'What does this have to do with my dad?'

Trevor: 'Patience.'

Rebecca downloaded the calls to her personal drive.

Rebecca: 'Done.'

Trevor: 'Make backups and send them to Stella Mitchell and Tom Novak at The Republic.'

Rebecca: 'That's classified intelligence. I can't do that.'

Trevor: 'Why not? You've done it already. I already sent them a cache of files on Goldcastle. Everything they still need to make their story.'

Rebecca got a lump in her throat. But it also meant Trevor knew she'd stolen files and hadn't done anything about it.

Rebecca: Why can't you do this yourself?

Trevor: 'Goldcastle are cleaning up shop. I'm in Westminster until later tonight and can't access the files where I am. If this waits until I get back the files will be gone. This is our last chance.'

Rebecca: 'Whose phone is it?'

There was a long pause.

Rebecca: 'Hello?'

A pop-up informed her that Trevor had logged out.

Why would he log out before he told me what to look for? she thought.

She had a bad feeling about staying visible at Trevor's end any longer. She logged out, and sent all the ECHELON recordings for the number on Sunday night to Novak's *Republic* IronCloud.

Greenhills Road, Cheltenham – Thursday, 8.15pm

Trevor Billington-Smith was in his five-bedroom Edwardian villa on his own, typing messages to Rebecca in his study.

It had been a few minutes since he had first heard what he thought was the familiar creak of the front door. But he knew he'd locked it from the inside, so he had paid it little mind.

Then he heard a creak on the old oak staircase leading to the study.

'Hello?' he called out.

The creaks grew louder, then a shadow stretched under the bottom of the door.

Trevor reached for the panic alarm attached to the under-side of his desk – a traditional banker's desk with a leather top.

A young man spoke from the other side of the door. 'I wouldn't bother if I were you. I cut the connection to that outside.'

Trevor moved his Anglepoise lamp to see towards the door.

The door slowly opened.

'You're no James Bond, that's for sure.' He held his keys up. 'I let myself in.'

Trevor sighed in relief, reaching towards his heart. 'Matthew! You nearly gave me a heart attack. What are you doing sneaking in here?'

He walked towards his father, holding something Trevor couldn't make out.

'Why did you cut the panic alarm?' Trevor asked.

'I tried to warn Becky,' Matthew explained. 'I told her to be careful. I gave her every chance to walk away.'

Trevor's heart started pounding as he realised that Matthew was holding a length of thick rope.

Trevor whimpered, 'Matthew. Son. What are you doing?'

Matthew shook his head. 'I hate that you've put me in this position. You've risked everything we've built.'

Trevor pushed his chair back until it met the wall. Then he stood up.

Matthew lunged for his father, catching him by the arm and twisting him around.

Matthew closed his eyes as he wrapped the rope around his father's neck and pulled. 'I'm sorry,' he managed to say. 'I'd rather it was me who did this, instead of Goldcastle's people.'

Through flashes of childhood memories – hundreds of snapshots flitting through his head like a strobe light – he grunted at the strength required to stop his father wriggling free. As he pulled the rope as tight as it would go, Matthew groaned, 'God forgive me.'

42

WESTMINSTER, LONDON – THURSDAY, 6.53PM

Parliament Street was almost at a standstill, the pavements crammed with people looking for their first view of the reopened Downing Street. Stella, on her tiptoes, could see nothing but a solid mass all the way down to Westminster underground station, so she doubled-back through Derby Gate, the small lane bisecting Parliament Street and Victoria Embankment next to the river.

She was momentarily distracted by a notification on her phone:

"IronCloud has received a new file ready for download for *stella.mitchell@therepublic.com*. Enter your key to decrypt file."

On an evening like this, it was extremely welcome news. Still on a high after her meet with Charlie, her mind raced with the possibilities of what was in her IronCloud.

In that brief moment of looking down at her phone, she didn't notice the black Range Rover pulling into the lane behind her. By the time she clocked the four men in suits marching towards her, it was too late. One of the abductors slid a hood over Stella's head, and covered her mouth with his hand. The other three bundled her into the back of the car.

Some men smoking outside the pub on the corner of the

main road took a few steps towards the melee, but seemed unsure of what they had really seen in the gloom.

The last man into the Range Rover flashed his badge at the men on the corner.

'Metropolitan Police Specialist Operations,' he shouted. 'Back away.'

The driver lit up a blue flashing light on the dash and one in the back window, then raced out into the middle of Parliament Street, siren blaring.

The Range Rover was on the road barely a minute before pulling into the Ministry of Defence.

The guard at the MOD security gate had been briefed ahead of time and was expecting them. He had the barrier lifted so when SO1 approached it didn't even have to slow down.

Stella knew she hadn't travelled far. At a guess she thought she was at New Scotland Yard – a stone's throw away from the MOD – as the only other possibility would have been MI6, which would have been at least another minute or two away.

They descended a ramp into an empty underground car park, the tyres squealing on the waxy tarmac.

When the car stopped, Stella felt a gust of wind as the door opened. It was already below freezing outside.

They had stopped at what looked like a set of decrepit services lifts. Stella didn't fight as she was pulled from the car. She knew it would be pointless.

One of the men called a lift which opened immediately, revealing a dazzlingly modern interior – brushed silver walls on one side, glass panels on the other, and a 4K-resolution touch-screen.

Two of the men stayed with the car, while the other two led Stella into the lift. The more senior officer of the two placed his hand on the screen, which scanned his fingerprints.

The men said nothing the whole way down. When they reached the only floor available – the equivalent of five storeys below ground – the glass panels on the left side opened with a clean swoosh, revealing a long corridor.

The senior officer put a guiding hand on Stella's lower back, pushing her out.

The corridor was lit by rows of LED lights down both sides, going past all kinds of offices, briefing rooms, a decontamination suite, a crisis control room with full media suite, a store room (filled with canned goods, blankets and bottled water), and several bunk suites.

At the end was a glass cubicle. Through it and to the right, stood a soldier in a uniform no civilian would recognise: the Royal Army Pindar Corps. A unit set up solely to guard a facility very few people knew existed.

At the cubicle, the SO1 officer placed his hand on another screen by the cubicle – the same kind as in the lift. When the doors opened he led Stella inside. When they came out the other side, the RAP officer opened the door he'd been guarding for the past three hours. Inside was a conference room, with a video wall that ran almost thirty feet wide and ten feet high. It had the ability to break down a national emergency to every essential facet. Today, it was all black. On standby.

The SO1 officer let go of Stella and removed her hood. The room wasn't brightly lit, but it still took a moment for her eyes to adjust.

The SO1 officer left the room without a word.

Stella didn't know whether to expect a gun to be pointing at her. When she realised she was in a safer place than she first thought, the relief washed over her. Stella said, 'You scared the shit out of me.'

Angela Curtis sat the end of the conference table, eating a salad with a crescent of briefing papers spread out in front of her.

'Forgive the dramatic precautions,' Curtis said, still chewing. 'You'll understand when you see what I have to give you.'

Stella looked around the room. 'I heard rumours about this place a few years ago.'

'Secrecy is still one of the things we do well.' Curtis sounded effortlessly powerful. 'You can't imagine the things they tell you when you get this job. Unrepeatable, of course.'

'I'm not eager to test that,' Stella assured her.

Curtis took a drink of tea. 'They called this place Pindar after the Greek poet. When Alexander the Great raided the city of Thebes in the fifth century BC, out of thousands of houses razed to the ground, Pindar's was the only one still standing.'

Stella said, 'So when the world burns in a blaze of nuclear explosions, or whatever apocalyptic war games you train for down here, Britain, like Pindar's house, will still be standing.'

'Britain must march on, Miss Mitchell.'

Stella smiled at the soundbite answer. 'Except, Prime Minister, Pindar's house wasn't spared because he had access to a few million pounds of military and technological hardware. It was out of respect. For Pindar's reputation. His legacy. Alexander knew that if word reached the other territories that Pindar's house had been desecrated, the backlash against him would be so great, so *monumental*, he'd regret the day he ever set sail for Thebes. Do you really think that's how the rest of the world sees Britain? Twenty, maybe even fifteen years ago perhaps. But now?'

Curtis said, 'There's still greatness in this country. I wouldn't be here if I didn't believe that.'

Stella countered, 'There's not a single issue the rest of the world looks to us on. The only thing America needs us for is unpopular wars and chat show hosts. Is this,' she gestured at the surroundings, 'the only thing our country builds now? Is this our great endeavour? Expensive places to hide?'

Curtis smiled in a restrained way and reached for a document in front of her. It had been badly crumpled. From when she'd cast it aside – with faultless sleight of hand in her bedroom – as Doug Robertson and Sonia Ali sat in the next room. She'd only burned the envelope that had contained the document. 'You have to understand I only choose to give this to you because I trust your integrity. And most importantly, so do the public.'

'You're leaking me something?'

Curtis held out the paper. 'If you want it.'

The headed paper threw Stella immediately: "From the desk of the Right Honourable Simon Ali MP".

After a few lines, the words seemed familiar. It wasn't until the end of the second paragraph that she realised what it was she was holding: the complete version of Simon Ali's speech.

'How do I know this is genuine?' Stella asked, still staring at it.

Curtis replied, 'It came from Simon's lawyer.'

'Right, but...' Stella exhaled. 'Do you believe what Simon Ali says in this? Is it true?'

Curtis said, 'I'm afraid to say I'm in absolutely no doubt.'

Stella kept reading. 'This also says that he was going to come out against the new Freedom and Privacy Act.'

'Robert Snow would have, too,' Curtis added.

Stella said, 'You do realise the impact releasing this document will have on your government?'

'Realise?' said Curtis. 'I'm banking on it. I'll go on the record. You can quote me as a source close to Simon Ali. That can confirm the veracity of the document.' Curtis waited for answer. 'Well?'

Stella plucked her notepad out of her jacket pocket. 'Once this comes out, it's going to clear the path for you come the General Election.'

Curtis tried to feign ignorance. 'I have an idea how it might be interpreted, yes.' Noticing her tea had gone cold, she topped it up with more hot water. 'Just as I have an idea how one of your competitors might interpret it if I invite them down here instead.'

'You're threatening me with what will happen if I don't run this?'

'I'm just a fan of clarity, that's all,' Curtis answered.

'It's so easy for you, isn't it?' Stella said. 'This. The plotting, the machinations. Don't make out like you're doing me a selfless favour giving this to me.'

Curtis said, 'I can't make changes to this country without power. Without power I can't lead.'

'Once I print this, there's no going back, Prime Minister.'

Curtis stared Stella down, daring her. 'Look into my eyes and tell me I'm not ready.'

Stella was in no doubt.

Curtis held up three fingers. 'You have three minutes to make notes.'

The News Office, London Bridge – Thursday, 7.34pm

Novak had been deep in the zone for most of the day: his notes laid out in front of him, the structure he wanted clear in his mind. He had the three things essential to every reporter: purpose, coffee, and a deadline.

The intensity of the experience – being back on the home straight on a major story – reminded him of the days of the NSA papers. When no one really knew who he was, and he was just some guy writing at his desk. He'd find himself on a crowded street or the subway, with no idea the maelstrom his life would become over the subsequent months.

A lot of the time, the public couldn't even tell you what publication a major story originated from, let alone which journalist wrote it. But everyone knew who Tom Novak was.

Reliving his past glories, a single pop-up on Novak's laptop was about to change everything:

"IronCloud has received a new file ready for download for *tom.novak@therepublic.com*. Enter your key to decrypt file."

Thinking it was the transcript of Sharp's interview, Novak decrypted the file, eager to get to work plugging the best quotes into the story. He was perplexed to find an audio file, rather than a transcript. Thinking that Diane had sent over the raw audio of the interview instead, Novak put in his earphones with a grumble. An audio transcript would take twice as long to get through.

But as Novak skimmed the first twenty minutes and got only the same rustling noises, he fired off a quick email to Diane, asking her if she had checked the microphone before recording.

Before Diane could reply, Novak heard voices on the recording.

Muffled conversation.

Too faint to make out. Seeing as someone had taken the not inconsiderable time to send it via IronCloud rather than basic email, Novak opened an audio equalizer program. With a few basic adjustments to certain frequencies, the conversation became much clearer.

'Oh my god,' he said in amazement. 'We've got it...'

43

Stella returned to her and Novak's temp office a little shaky in the knees. The state of the room had deteriorated significantly since she'd last been there. Novak had strewn notes all over the floor, trying to form a timeline of events. His desk had several polystyrene cups from the coffee machine down the corridor. It looked like he'd been in there for days.

As soon as he saw Stella come in, he finished up the call.

'Okay, I gotta go.' He tossed the phone aside. 'What's wrong?' he said, his eyes feverish and wild.

Stella collapsed into a chair in exhaustion and handed Novak a piece of paper. 'Simon Ali's speech.'

'What?' he said. It took several seconds for it to sink in. 'Where did you get this?'

'Angela Curtis.'

'I don't understand.'

Stella took a long drink from a bottle of water on the desk. 'I was just lifted off the street by SO1 and taken to her. She said that Simon Ali's personal lawyer was sent that on Monday morning.'

Novak didn't have to read much to get a sense of its

importance. 'This is unbelievable. The President's own
Defense Secretary coming out against the Freedom and
Privacy Act.'

'George Abassi was right,' Stella added. 'He told Sharp
the threat against the U.S. target was from the President. This
gives us motive.'

Novak paced back and forth, over-caffeinated. 'What if
the President angle is off?' He paused. 'What if it was Goldcastle? What if they ordered a hit on Snow and Ali for endan-
gering hundreds of millions of dollars in private contracts
when the Bill passed.' Novak scribbled down "Ali" "Snow"
and "Freedom & Privacy" then circled them. 'That's what I
think we should start with.'

Stella closed her eyes, trying to get their ducks in a row.
'Hang on. How did Goldcastle know what Simon Ali was
going to say? They would only order the hit if they knew that.'

Novak cued up one of the files from his IronCloud,
pointing to the source phone number that came with the
recording Rebecca had sent. 'Recognise this?'

Stella read back the number on the screen. 'The number
from Abbie's voicemail. The dial tone.'

'This is an outgoing phone call from that number that
took place on Sunday night at eleven twenty.'

Novak hit play.

Male One: 'We need to talk.'

Male Two: 'I can't right now. I need to finish this speech.'

Stella said quickly, 'That's Simon Ali.'

*Male One: 'We have a problem with Bishop. She's gone off the
reservation.'*

Simon Ali: 'What does that mean?'

Male One: 'She wants out. She says she's done.'

Simon Ali: 'Then talk her round.'

Male One: 'I've tried. She won't listen.'

Simon Ali: 'Why? Goldcastle are paying her like the rest of us.'

Male One: 'It's complicated.'

Simon Ali: 'Have you spoken to anyone at Goldcastle?'

Male One: 'I met with Jarrod earlier on.'

Simon Ali: 'How mad was he?'

Male One: 'He was fucking...black with rage, Simon. I've never seen him like that.'

A long pause.

Male One: 'We need to bring her in.'

Simon Ali: 'Bring her in?'

Male One: 'If we bring her in we could still save this.'

Simon Ali: 'Do it.'

Novak clicked out, then into a different recording. 'An hour later, the number receives another call.'

Simon Ali (shouting): 'You fucking killed her! What the hell did you have to do that for? You said you were just going to bring her in.'

Male Two: 'Simon, calm down. Calm down. There was nothing we could do. It's done now. It's over.'

Simon Ali: 'You did this, didn't you. You told them to take her out. I can't do this anymore...'

Male Two: 'Stop blubbering, you bloody fool. Keep it together, man.'

Simon Ali: 'I don't care anymore. I'm done.'

Male Two: 'What do you mean you're done. You can't be done!'

Simon Ali: 'We can't carry on like this. We're sanctioning murder. For what?'

Male Two: 'You know as well as I do it's more complicated than that.'

Simon Ali: 'If I went public. What could Goldcastle do about it?'

A pause.

Male Two: 'Simon. I shouldn't have to tell you how bad an idea that would be. You know they would never let that happen.'

Simon Ali: 'Watch me.'

End of call.

Stella couldn't sit down any longer. 'My god, Novak. That's a Prime Minister. On record.'

Novak moved the mouse to another file. 'There's one last

call you need to hear.' He handed her a pair of headphones. 'You'll need these, though.'

Stella put them on.

He clicked play.

Halfway through the call, Stella put her hand to her mouth. She didn't want to listen to the rest, but she knew she had to. At least once the whole way through. When it was done, she slid the headphones off, traumatised.

'It's definitely him, isn't it?' Novak asked.

Stella nodded gravely. 'Yeah. It's him.'

'We still have a question of why Goldcastle wanted Abbie killed,' said Novak.

'She wanted out,' said Stella. 'The first call says so.'

'Then *why* did she want out?' Novak asked. 'We know she never touched any of the money Goldcastle gave her.'

Stella said, "This is all well and good, Novak, but how can we use it? It's stolen.'

'No, it's not,' he replied, handing over a printout of the legal framework that came attached with the recordings. 'It was authorised by GCHQ. According to the government and anti-terror legislation, that is a legal wiretap on a phone call. And it was leaked to us by an anonymous source. It's as legal to use as a printed email.'

Novak ruffled his hair. As badly as he needed sleep, he knew he wouldn't be getting any for at least another twelve hours. 'We gotta take this to Diane,' he said.

'Okay.'

'You've worked tough stories before. I know you've been in tough editorials before. Believe me when I tell you, nothing can prepare you for how brutal this editorial is going to be. They'll need to send this to a red team.'

Stella groaned. 'The red team on my phone hacking story made me doubt my own name.'

Novak said, 'If we get this wrong legally – and I mean even a little bit – GCHQ and the British government will end up owning *The Republic*. One of the most respected figures in the British establishment will have got away with murder, and every single person involved in one of the biggest conspiracies in political history will get away scot-free.'

Being ironically rosy, Stella said, 'Alright. So, nothing much at stake, then.'

44

Sometimes stories emerged that, if true, could have profound consequences for those involved. Sometimes public disgrace, financial penalties, or – in the case of Goldcastle – criminal charges. Ruining someone's life with a story was easily and quickly done. Putting it back together was not so easy. Corrections were never as prominent as the stories that necessitated them. And sometimes legal cases, even after winning, could be expensive enough to bankrupt a publication. Which was why red teams existed.

At *The Republic*, a red team was a group of journalists, editors, or respected figures in the magazine who had no prior knowledge of a story. They hadn't been briefed and hadn't sat in on editorials. With their fresh eyes, it was easier to appraise the veracity of sources, or see where a journalist might have been tricked or blindsided.

Diane believed that sometimes you can want a story too badly. That's when you can overlook something obvious.

Mark Chang had brought in three other senior staff writers, from the finance, culture, and politics desks. Diane also brought in Vincent Bruckner from Bruckner Jackson Prowse, as well as Henry Self, who had only absorbed what few details of the story Diane had passed on in their late-night rundowns.

They gathered around the conference room table in front of a camera linked to a Darkroom feed sent back to London, where Tom and Stella answered question after question. For nearly two hours they'd gone back and forth over every detail of the story: the sources, the recordings, the chronology, the links between the various strands.

'The plane used for Abassi's rendition,' Bruckner said. 'What do we know about that?'

Novak raised his pen to show he'd field it. 'The FAA has a Gulfstream registered under the tail number N511GA. It came off the line eight months ago, and was sold to a CIA contractor three weeks after. The paperwork is in your folders under tab four B.'

Bruckner asked everyone, 'How's the room with Walter Sharp?'

'Something feels a little off with him,' said one of the staffers.

'What's off about him?' Novak fired back, a little too defensively.

Out of shot, Stella tapped him on the foot with her own.

What Novak resented was the senior staffers using their red team status to throw their weight around, trying to impress Diane. Not to mention scoring some points against Novak. Journalism wasn't like the book industry where many were glad to see another's success. Books weren't a zero-sum game. But there were only so many news stories going around, from finite sources. For every story that broke, there was an editor across town yelling at a reporter, demanding why *they* hadn't brought it in. Much of the public might have loved Novak, but there was a simmering resentment among some of *The Republic* staff at the disparity between how much coverage Novak received, and how much work he seemed to put in. For some on the red team, it was the first time in months they had seen Novak anywhere other than on TV.

Novak corrected himself, 'Sharp's worked his whole life to keep the bad guys out. The bad guys are now living in his house and he wants them out. He knows what they did to Abassi and he wants someone somewhere to pay.'

The staffer winced. 'Vengeance is not a good angle for a source. This is what I'm saying: if he so much as confirms a black op even exists, then he gets sent down to Leavenworth.'

Bruckner pressed him. 'What's your concern?'

'Motive,' replied the staffer. 'If he's out for revenge he's more likely to embellish.'

'Thank you for that *important* lesson,' Novak said sarcastically. 'I have, after all, only been a reporter for fifteen years.'

Diane fired him a warning glance. 'Tom.'

Another staffer spoke up. 'While we're on motive, I want to raise an issue I have with Arthur Korecki. I–'

Novak interrupted, 'That's not his name. *Artur* Korecki. There's no H.' He tossed his notes aside then rubbed his eyes. 'Look, I get that you're enjoying being in a room with Diane and Henry for longer than your usual five-minute pitch meetings on a Wednesday morning, but if you're going to do this seriously can we at least get the names of the players right?'

The staffer continued, 'Korecki's not reliable. There are clips of his videos on conspiracy websites. It's Alex Jones-type stuff. Even the name TruthArmy...is he one of these nine eleven inside-job guys?'

Novak replied calmly, 'He has never said, nor claimed, that nine eleven was an inside job. He has never made any public statements or made any videos on that subject. Can you, *please*, talk to me about the material you actually *have* that's unreliable?'

The staffer went on, 'What about these payments made from Goldcastle Group to Abbie Bishop every month?'

Stella turned to the relevant page in her folder. 'This is in tab five A. We traced the payments to an address in Liecht-enstein.'

The picture in the folder showed a crumbling two-storey building, surrounded by rubble and already demolished properties.

Stella said, 'As you can see, the address is for a shell company. Liechtenstein's a tax haven. Sixty-two square miles, population of thirty-seven thousand, yet it holds around seven billion dollars in its banks. There's also no border control between it and Switzerland. You get guys literally driving cases of cash back and forth. A company registers with an address like this one, and it can wash vast sums of cash through it at very little expense.'

A staffer from the finance desk asked, 'How is it linked to Goldcastle?'

Stella replied, 'About seventeen accounts down the line, but we have a solid link to a Goldcastle subsidiary in the U.S.'

'So you're saying that Abbie Bishop was employed by MI6, then sent in to steal data from GCHQ on behalf of Goldcastle?'

Novak said, 'Yeah.'

'Do you know why Goldcastle were having her steal the data?' the staffer asked.

Reluctantly, Novak replied, 'We're getting to that,' while he wrote something down on a notepad, out of sight of the webcam.

The staffer said, 'As you're so convinced that Bishop was murdered as part of some conspiracy, why would Goldcastle – or anyone else – want her dead?'

Novak showed Stella the notepad discreetly. It said "Ass hat" on it with an arrow directed at the screen.

'We don't know,' Novak said.

The staffer flashed his eyebrows up in surprise as he made a note. He mumbled just loud enough for the mic to pick it up. 'Definitely rusty.'

'*Excuse* me?' Novak said.

The staffer threw down his pen and shook his head. 'You haven't got it.'

'I agree,' another said. 'It's a no for me.'

Diane put her hand up. 'Hang on. We're not taking a vote just yet.'

Bruckner sat with his forefinger placed over his lips. It was impossible to tell if he was impressed or bewildered at what he was listening to.

Wanting to break the tension, Henry clapped his hands. 'Why don't we take a break,' he said.

Both ends of the Darkroom call went mute during the break, but the camera feed kept going.

Novak did a full-body stretch in his chair. When he relaxed, he said, 'Sorry. I let that get away from me a bit. But two hours... Honestly, there's only so much grandstanding I can take.'

Stella laughed. 'Seriously? Tom Novak complaining about someone else grandstanding?'

'Yeah, laugh it up, Mary Poppins. It's your byline too.' Novak groaned loudly. 'What are we going to do?'

Stella was perfectly calm, judiciously scrolling through her phone. 'The story's good, Novak. We need to trust that.' She showed him the screen from a news website.

The breaking news headline: "*Director of GCHQ Trevor Billington-Smith found dead at home.*"

Novak said, 'Goldcastle are wrapping up loose ends.'

When they returned from the break, Diane led things off. 'Let's start over,' she said. 'Because there are some things we haven't got to yet. I want to hear it from the top. Stella, you go.'

Stella found her place in her notes, but at this stage, she could have done it all from memory. 'On Sunday night, Abigail Bishop was killed at Moreton House in Pimlico, a GCHQ safe house. There was a go signal from the man at GCHQ who located Bishop by her mobile, which had received a ping request. Location confirmed, a hit team arrived at Moreton House. Abbie Bishop ends up dead. Her autopsy, as detailed in tab one C, clearly shows she was not intoxicated as claimed by MI5's doctors. We also have a police source and a corroborating source in British intelligence, that state key witnesses on the ground were in fact MI6 agents who gave police false statements and gave false identities. Why? She found out about a plot to assassinate Simon Ali and Robert Snow, and threatened to expose the people behind the conspiracy. I had this confirmed just a few hours ago through a senior source in GCHQ.'

'Sorry, guys,' Diane said, making quick notes. 'What is the confirmation?'

Stella answered. 'Seeing as he's now dead, I can name him: Trevor Billington-Smith. Former Director of GCHQ. They just found his body at his home. He had sent me memos from Abbie Bishop, highlighting her security concerns. You should have the memos at your end now.'

As they came through, Diane skim-read the first. 'Heavens to Betsy.' She turned her laptop screen to Bruckner.

Stella continued, 'Though she was being paid by Gold-castle to steal GCHQ data, learning of the plot against Snow was the last straw for Bishop. She wanted out. But Goldcastle needed her. When they failed to persuade her to stay in the fold, they convinced senior political figures to deal with it. That's where our phone recordings come in. Tom?'

Novak cued up the recordings, playing the first one of Ali giving the go-ahead to bring in Abbie Bishop. He explained, 'Bishop had been having an affair with Nigel Hawkes: another aspect of her deal with Goldcastle, which was to keep an eye on their investment.'

'Investment?' asked a red team staffer.

'Trevor Billington-Smith passed us emails between Goldcastle CEO Jarrod Warner and senior figures in GCHQ and MI6, discussing Warner's anger that Ali and Snow might be coming out against the Freedom and Privacy Act. Warner talks openly about what the process might be for replacing Ali as Prime Minister.'

Novak hit play on the first two phone calls.

When they were done, the room was silent. No one moved. No one wrote anything.

Novak then played the third.

Male One: 'Lloyd. It's me. Sorry, I know it's late. We have a problem.'

Male Two: 'Let me guess: Simon Ali.'

Male One: 'He's not listening to reason on this Abbie Bishop thing. He's talking about going to the press.'

Male Two: 'Jesus. We have to do something.'

Male One: 'What can we do? We have between now and the next time someone points a camera and microphone in his direction.'

A pause.

Male Two: 'There might be something...There's a memo going around. From an MI6 agent in the field out in Nimruz. A terror cell in Birmingham. I've been contacted by GCHQ's internal affairs man, Lipski. He's talked to them apparently. He says they're going to move tomorrow.'

Male One: 'What are you saying?'

Male Two: 'I'm saying it might already be too late to stop them. If they were to get through...'

Male One: 'You're out of your mind, Lloyd. We can't let that happen!'

Male Two: 'Nigel, listen to me. Lipski says they have guns stockpiled. It's going to be a Paris-style attack. They'll hit Snow, hit Ali, then SO1 will take them out from the roof. It'll be over in seconds.'

Male One: 'I can't believe you're actually talking about this.'

Male Two: 'Then tell me what the alternative is! Do you understand how many lives we could save with Goldcastle's technology? How many other terror attacks could be averted as a result?'

Male One: 'You're talking about state-sanctioned assassination of a sitting Prime Minister.'

Male Two: 'No, that's what you're talking about. I'm talking about securing vital intelligence technology that's going to keep our country safe for the next fifty years! My analysts assure me that given the armed detail on duty at Downing Street, the cell will be lucky to put down even five people. Also, I don't think you're considering what this will mean for your own future. Goldcastle want a leader they can really invest the next decade in. Think what you could achieve in ten years, Nigel. You know what they can do. If Goldcastle believe in you, Nigel, the General Election won't be a vote. It will be a coronation.'

A long pause.

Male Two: 'Nigel?'

Male One: 'Okay. Let's take him.'

When the recording stopped, everyone was in their own little worlds of disbelief.

Bruckner was the first to manage to speak. 'They mentioned a gun attack. Why the disparity with what actually happened?'

Novak said, 'There was a cache of guns found at the terror cell's base in Birmingham, possibly for use in a follow-up attack.'

'What about the press pass?' Diane asked. 'The evidence shows conclusively that the press pass for Mufaza was made weeks ago by Alexander Mackintosh in GCHQ.'

'I agree,' Stella said. 'What Lloyd Willow says in the call doesn't stack up. Tom and I think Willow and Goldcastle were testing Hawkes to see if he was really worth them all going to the wall for. The Americans had already decided to take out Robert Snow. They just wanted to see if Hawkes could be trusted with the biggest secret of all. But Lloyd Willow did what Goldcastle wanted him to do: get rid of Snow and Ali. His mind was made up long before he convinced Hawkes to order the hit.'

A staffer, exasperated with the scale of the conspiracy, complained, 'What on earth were Goldcastle doing that was so valuable to everyone? They've got politicians killing rivals? For what?'

Stella fielded it. 'The documents our senior GCHQ source sent show the data Abbie Bishop stole for Goldcastle was to test a new decryption program. It would render all online encryption useless. Everything online, or via a phone signal, would be wide open for GCHQ and NSA to see. The software was valued by GCHQ analysts as being in the region of four billion pounds.'

Henry exhaled. 'Not a bad pay day.'

Stella emphasised, 'That's just for a ten-year contract, by the way. So yeah, I'd call that motive for protecting an investment. Ali wouldn't support it, so they found a man who would: Nigel Hawkes.'

Diane said, 'Tom, maybe you can take us through the American angle on this now.'

He cleared his throat. 'On Sunday night, Abdul al-Malik, an MI6 agent working undercover in Nimruz, Afghanistan, was renditioned to a CIA black site in Poland called Camp Zero in a small town called Szymany. He warned that his handler in London, Abbie Bishop was in danger. Malik knew what she was going to do, and knew Goldcastle and the British would do whatever they could to silence her. He told my CIA source that he had evidence of a credible threat against a U.S. target – which we now know to be Robert Snow – and that Malik's own life was in danger. He said the men pursuing him would do anything to ensure the threat was successful. The man he named as being behind the threat was the President of the United States.'

'What do we have on this guy, Malik?' Bruckner asked, shuffling between tabs in the dossier.

Novak answered, 'We have the Korecki tape of Malik coming off the plane; the paperwork on the aircraft being CIA property; our CIA source is on background confirming Malik's testimony; we have the prisoner transfer request, and multiple documents from MI6 confirming Malik's operations; and Diane has the tapes from Malik's interrogation in Camp Zero.'

Bruckner said, 'And what do we have on Downing Street?'

Stella said, 'We have the press pass created at GCHQ; multiple memos from a senior GCHQ source confirming the conspiracy; files from Operation Tempest, as well as Malik and Lipski's warnings of a credible threat; the original autopsy report showing that Bishop was not intoxicated; testimony from the first policeman on the scene at Moreton House, PC Leon Walker. And we have this.' Stella held up a piece of paper.

Bruckner leaned towards the screen. 'What is that?'

'It's a direct transcript of Simon Ali's speech,' Stella answered. 'From a source close to Simon Ali. The speech confirms his opposition to the Freedom and Privacy act, and assumes responsibility for the death of Abbie Bishop, as well as confirming that he would stand down at the next election.'

When someone asked, 'Can that be verified?' Diane answered, 'I can vouch for the veracity of the source. It's unimpeachable.'

Stella looked at Novak, and put down her pen. 'That's it,' she said. 'That's everything.'

No one seemed to know who should talk next. Given the circumstances, a few seconds felt like the length of a Wagner opera.

Diane broke the silence. 'Vincent. Where's legal with this?'

Even for a man as experienced in media law as Bruckner, he seemed taken aback. 'First of all – and I want to be absolutely clear on this – Stella or Tom need to take all of this to London police. The audio and the copy of the speech. They're under no obligation to reveal how they got it. Their sources are protected.' He leaned his head to one side. 'One could argue persuasively that you needed time to corroborate these sources. Something in the region of twenty-four hours from now would not be unreasonable.'

'Conveniently enough time to prepare for publication,' Henry said, withholding a smile. 'I want to go round the room. Diane?'

'The story is *good*,' Diane said. 'It's *really* good.'

'Mark?' Henry asked.

Chang had been unusually quiet. Mostly out of respect for what Stella and Tom had managed to put together in just four days. He answered, 'Diane says it's good, I don't need to know anything else. I'm in.'

Once all hands were counted, Tom and Stella felt like they'd heard the bell ring at the end of a twelve-round slugfest.

Their story had survived the red team.

Henry asked, 'How long till we publish?'

Diane said, 'We can hold the printers a few more hours. Online we can go until tomorrow morning, London time. We'll need to take this to Downing Street soon. Give them a chance to comment. Even if we run "Downing Street declined to comment". We'll need to ask MI6, GCHQ, NSA, CIA and anyone else too. But they won't acknowledge Goldcastle.'

'The British government will not have that luxury,' Stella added.

Bruckner raised his pen in the air. 'I do see one potential problem with regards to the source you're using on this phone recording. The GCHQ officer, she's still employed there, am I right?'

'Correct,' said Stella.

Bruckner made a quick expression of pain. 'They're going

to charge her under the Official Secrets Act. The nineteen eighty-nine amendment removed any public interest defence. I assume she was aware of this when she disclosed these documents?'

'She knew what she was into,' Diane said as an aside.

'We still need to protect her,' added Novak.

'That's very noble of you, Tom,' Bruckner said, 'but she cannot disclose information relating to security or intelligence. *This*,' he motioned to the vast amount of paperwork in front of him, 'is not a grey area.'

Having reported on a number of stories dealing with the Official Secrets Acts in the past, Stella herself was not inexperienced with the law.

'But the disclosure itself must be deemed damaging,' she said.

Bruckner retorted, 'You're accusing the British Foreign Secretary and chief of MI6 of conspiracy to murder.'

Stella said, 'The damage has to be proven to be against the state. Our story is only damaging against a handful of individuals because they've committed, or been party to, a crime.'

Bruckner nodded, thinking it over. He looked at Henry and Diane. 'It could work.'

'Also,' Stella added, 'there is a precedent there with Katharine Gun.'

'Who's Katharine Gun?' asked Henry.

Stella answered, 'She was a translator at GCHQ who leaked an email from the NSA asking for help in spying on countries crucial to the United Nations Security Council vote on declaring war on Iraq. Gun admitted the leak and was about to go to trial. At the last minute the Attorney General dropped the case. Some say because Gun's defence team was going to demand the disclosure of whether the Attorney General believed the war would be legal.'

Bruckner said, 'This isn't about a war and it isn't the UN.'

'No,' said Stella, 'but Gun's legal team was also going to hinge their argument on the defence of necessity.'

Bruckner began to smile. 'Leaking the email was an attempt to stop an imminent loss of life... That's clever.'

Stella said, 'This didn't stop after Monday morning. Jonathan Gale was shot in cold blood just last night. Novak, Officer Sharp and Artur Korecki are all lucky to be alive after Berlin. How do we know there aren't more lives still at risk?'

'What do you think, Vince?' asked Henry.

Diane interjected, 'I think we have the legal view, Henry. We're not lawyers. We're *journalists*. We're not here to get convictions. We're here to tell people what happened.' She jabbed her finger on top of her notes. 'This *happened*.'

Henry straightened his notes up. 'That's good enough for me. Let's get this up.'

As the others cleared out the room, Diane was the last one left.

She told Tom and Stella, 'We need to get ready now. Every newspaper, every commentator, every blogger and vlogger and anyone with an axe to grind is going to come after us. They're going to question your integrity. Your reporting. It's going to get ugly. But no matter what happens, I'm going to have your backs.' Diane lifted the hefty pages of notes. She smiled, then – her voice filled with pride – said quietly, 'It's a *fucking* good story. Let's finish it.'

45

Stella had arranged to meet Sid Vickering at the Golden Café, just a few hundred yards from his house.

Golden Lane Estate had been built in the fifties, almost from scratch, after enduring some of the heaviest bombing of the Second World War. The council estate and tower blocks that now sprawled across the area appeared stuck in a time warp, immune to the vast gentrification that had taken place in nearby Shoreditch and Bethnal Green.

Stella waited with a cup of tea in a polystyrene cup, her hands joined around it for warmth. Her breath was visible in the cold interior.

Sid wandered in, wearing a grey cotton tracksuit without a t-shirt under the hoodie, exposing a tuft of chest hair. He'd fallen asleep on the sofa in front of the American horse racing the night before.

'Stella,' he said, plonking himself down. 'Chief Inspector says you've to give me something. D'you want to know what I said?'

Stella passed a memory stick to him. 'Was it tawdry and completely lacking in wit?'

He smiled, then waved his hand 'no' at the waitress who was gesturing if he wanted something.

'He said you had some news about Dan,' Stella said.

'They found him this morning on the shore of Loch Lomond. They found an empty bottle of Mirtazapine with him. His prescription. No suspicious circumstances.'

Stella stared at the table. Until Sid confirmed it, she'd still been holding out for better news.

'You said you found a note at his house?' he asked.

'Yeah. I left it there.'

Sid held out the memory stick. 'What's all this about?'

'Fulfilling our legal obligations.' Stella got up, leaving a pound coin on the table. 'Go to *The Republic* dot com in about an hour, you can read all about it.'

Stella returned to News Office expecting to find Novak in good spirits, plugging in any White House comments to his sections. Whatever they had to say didn't affect the story. She was surprised to find him in his chair, pushed back from the desk, sitting low in the seat, lost in thought.

'Everything, okay?' Stella asked.

'Sure,' he replied, forcing a smile. 'The White House has no official comment to make at this time.'

'That's...fine, right? We knew they wouldn't bite.'

'The story's good. There's one problem, though.'

'What?' Stella sat down, still wearing her coat.

Novak said, 'A few minutes after they replied, my lawyer called. He got a call from the State Department. As of about twenty minutes ago, they've decided to widen the scope of their investigation into my NSA leak. It now wants to include our Goldcastle story as part of the NSA hearings.'

Stella scoffed. 'They're just trying to muscle us off.'

'I know,' Novak said calmly. 'Included in that, though, is their intention to subpoena you.'

'I don't understand.'

'They're going to investigate whether you've ever broken any national security laws in the United States.'

'Fine. Let them.'

'Stella—'

'No, seriously. They're trying to get to you through me. I'm not letting them do that!'

Novak huffed. 'One question, Stella: Have you ever witnessed Mr Novak, or have you yourself, ever revealed United States classified intelligence? And the answer you're going to have to give – unless you want to commit perjury – is yes. Because that's exactly what we had to use to prove George Abassi was in CIA custody at Camp Zero. The CIA prisoner transfer request given to us by Officer Sharp. And if we don't name Sharp – which I know you would never do – both of us will end up in jail. That's the ball game.'

Stella's eyes scoured the floor, trying to think of a solution. 'What are we going to do? We can't drop the story, Novak.'

'I know.' He turned his hands up. He couldn't see any other way. 'You have to take my name off the story.'

Stella stared at him, not knowing whether to laugh or not. 'You're actually serious.'

He said, 'Without my name on the story they can't link me to you, in a journalistic sense, according to my lawyer. It would kill their question.'

'I'm not letting you take your name off the story, Novak!'

He let the moment pass, then said, 'Sometimes I'll be watching a movie. You know when they put up old TV clips to establish what period the movie's in, what the political climate was like?'

Stella said, 'Sure.'

Novak went on, 'More often than not they use Walter Cronkite or Dan Rather. They never used clips of my dad. You know why? He never did anything important enough. He wasn't a reporter, he was an anchor. When Russia invaded

Afghanistan, Dan Rather crossed the border disguised as an Afghan peasant. Cronkite told the world that John F. Kennedy was dead. Seymour Novak never broke a story in his life. I remember one night he came home buzzing. I could tell something great had happened. I assumed he'd got hold of a great story, something important. I asked him what happened. You know what he said to me? The station's new ratings were so good that their ad buy was up eleven per cent. I was sixteen. That was when I knew my dad wasn't a news man like Murrow or Matthews. He was a TV presenter. From that point on, all I wanted to do was to break stories. To bring the truth out from under a rock and tell people, here's this thing that you didn't know before, and now you do. That's what I want. I want to be *that* guy. Because I want to do something more substantial than have a tweet go viral. Because I can't get excited about increasing a TV station's ad buy. And this story is more important than whether my name is on it or not.'

Stella joined her hands together as if in prayer, leaning forward in her chair, imploring him. 'Tom, you have to seriously consider what you've gone through to get us this far. No one will ever know you were involved.'

'*I'll* know,' Novak said. 'So will you guys. Diane, Mark, Henry. Anyone that truly matters.' He got up, and on his way past laid his hand on Stella's shoulder. 'It's going to be a huge story, Stella. It's all yours.'

After explaining the situation, Stella hoped Diane would understand her concerns. Instead, Diane argued that the State Department could drag their investigation on Novak out for months, and that Stella could be out of operation for the best part of the next year. Right at a time when the magazine needed her to be following up on Goldcastle. It wasn't exactly a story that didn't have legs.

In the end, Diane had told Stella that as much as it pained her, she couldn't let the story go out with Novak's name now. The litigation fees alone would condemn the magazine to closure.

With Novak's name removed from the byline, Diane was about to finish up the Darkroom call and send the final copy-edits to the printer, when Stella stopped her.

'Hang on,' she said. 'Is this okay for everyone?' She scrolled to the sidebar of the report credits and typed, "Additional reporting by Dan Leckie."

Diane could see the change at her end. Diane deferred to Novak. 'Tom?'

Novak said, 'Yeah.'

His half of the story went out under "Republic staff writer."

46

Angela Curtis was the last of the ministers to make her way to the front bench of the Commons chamber. The benches on both sides were filled to capacity. It was standing-room only.

It had been a beautiful piece of political orchestration on Roger Milton's part: he'd been briefing all morning that *The Republic* were going to publish details of Nigel Hawkes' affair with Abigail Bishop. A story that Diane Schlesinger was all too happy to confirm when asked by rival media. She had just neglected to tell them that that was but a fraction of the story.

Curtis was surrounded by her Cabinet ministers, yet she looked isolated as they talked amongst themselves, leaving her consulting her notes.

Ed Bannatyne, sitting beside Curtis, whispered to her, 'It was good of you to come down, Angela.'

Distracted, Curtis replied, 'I'm sorry?'

'Good of you to come down. To show your support for Nigel. That's who the Urgent Question will be for, won't it? There are all sorts of rumours flying around.'

'I expect so.'

Hawkes looked unruffled, close allies nearby, some patting him on the shoulder, telling him he'd weather whatever storm was coming, and that *The Republic* was just looking for lurid gossip.

Urgent Questions were an opportunity for members of Parliament to direct questions to a particular minister – usually done straight after regular Question Time sessions. It was up to the Speaker of the House's discretion whether the question was indeed urgent enough and in the public's interest.

The Speaker took his glasses off and announced, 'An urgent question from Angela Curtis.'

It was highly irregular for even a minister to request an Urgent Question, let alone the Prime Minister. Hawkes sat back a little in relief, comforted that Curtis was at least going to go after someone on the opposition benches first.

The chamber went quiet as Curtis rose, wondering not only what she was going to ask, but who the question was for.

She took hold of the sides of the Despatch Box. 'Thank you, Mr Speaker. My Urgent Question, is to ask the Foreign Secretary to explain to the House...'

So much noise erupted from all sides of the House, Curtis had to break off. There was clamouring all around her.

The Speaker called repeatedly for order, but the chamber simply wouldn't listen to him.

Curtis carried on anyway. 'To *explain*, what exactly was the nature of his intervention with intelligence relating to the Downing Street bombing cell?'

The noise turned to a dismayed confusion. No one had any idea about this.

She held up a stack of paper. 'These are transcripts of phone calls made by the Right Honourable gentleman on Sunday night, where he discusses with a senior MI6 official, about a known credible threat from a terror cell and how they might collude to let them gain access to Downing Street. Can the Right Honourable gentleman confirm that he is responsible for allowing the worst terror attack in British history to take place, and knowingly allow the murder of Simon Ali?'

The Speaker had never heard noise like it in all his years. No one ever had.

Curtis sat back down again, the calmest person in the chamber.

Nigel Hawkes didn't know what to do with himself. He half-rose, then seemed to change his mind.

As if to encourage him, the Speaker chimed in. 'The Right Honourable gentleman will stand to answer the question. There are no rules governing a minister asking an Urgent Question of his or her own party.'

Hawkes stood up, his normal resolve shot to hell.

Everyone waited for him to make his way to the microphone. Instead, he buttoned his jacket, and pushed his way through the throng of standing MPs to reach the exit.

Hawkes' allies rose from their seats to catch the Speaker's eye. So many rose that the Speaker had little option but to call time. He couldn't pretend he'd seen none of them.

'Will the Prime Minister give way for a question?' the Speaker shouted, struggling to be heard.

'No, I will not give way,' Curtis shouted back, prompting a fresh barrage of waved papers and cries of 'Give way!'

Though she wasn't being picked up by the Despatch Box microphone, the microphones hanging from the ceiling did. She called back more forcefully, 'I will *not* give way! I will *not*! The minister must *answer* the questions.'

Once Hawkes made it to the Central Lobby, he dialled Charlie Fletcher on his mobile. Fletcher – who had watched the whole debacle at his desk in the Foreign and Commonwealth Office – answered, just as Hawkes saw Metropolitan police officers approaching.

Hawkes said, 'It's over, Charlie.' Then he hung up.

News Office Building, London – Friday, 12.21pm

Both Novak and Stella had imagined what they would do when the story broke. In the end it happened over a few tepid beers in their cramped News Office room. They pulled up *therepublic.com/uk* on Stella's laptop.

At the top left corner of the report were the social media and email links. Underneath was a share counter. Within a minute of the story going live the shares began.

Each time they refreshed the page, the shares jumped up.

Reading through the article, just Tom and Stella in the room, it was hard to imagine the impact the story was having worldwide.

After only half an hour, the story had been shared more than one hundred and seventy-five thousand times.

By late afternoon, Twitter's top five worldwide trends were:

#Goldcastle

Nigel Hawkes

Abbie Bishop

#TheRepublic

Angela Curtis

For the website, Kurt had helped redesign the front page, so its entirety was taken up by what Diane had christened The Goldcastle Papers.

The strap underneath said:

"British Foreign Secretary and MI6 Chief implicated in Downing Street terror attack".

One of the main inset pictures showed a snip from a mobile phone video, of Abdul al-Malik standing at the top of a plane stairway. His hood removed. His face finally revealed to the world.

The caption underneath: "MI6 agent George Abassi."

GTE Division, GCHQ – Friday 3.01pm

Word had spread of Alexander's arrest earlier that afternoon. He hadn't made it past the main entrance before being taken in. It turned out he wasn't such a tough nut to crack. After ninety minutes he'd given up the identities of the driver and passengers of the black Audi.

An hour later, at seven different addresses across the capital, the police were kicking in the doors of people who in almost every technical sense didn't exist.

Aiding the search was newly reinstated PC Leon Walker, who had been instrumental in confirming the identities of all seven members of the MI6 black ops team.

With no one at the helm of GTE or the directorship, the entire building felt rudderless. Compounded, too, by the arrest of Sir Lloyd Willow in the previous minutes.

It wasn't the way Rebecca had wanted to leave the place that had given so much to her. Now it had taken from her. Trevor, Alexander and Abbie were all gone, and Matthew was missing.

Now, leaving was all that was left.

She was about to switch off her computer, when a message came from an unknown user through her OTR:

User: 'Aren't you forgetting something?'

Rebecca scanned the office, looking for anyone watching her.

Another message came through:

User: 'What about Abbie's encrypted files?'

Rebecca sat back down and dragged her keyboard nearer.

Rebecca.Fox: 'The decryption code is gone.'

User: 'So you'd agree if I could open it, that would impress you?'

Rebecca had only one response to such a statement:

Rebecca.Fox: 'Troll.'

She would have shut down her computer if it wasn't for the attachment that came with the next message: a folder containing some kind of file.

User: '*Open the Goldcastle file inside, then decrypt.*'

Rebecca looked around her once more. She opened the program, then clicked on the Goldcastle file inside.

A final message came through.

User: '*Answers don't come to you, Rebecca. You have to find them.*'

Then the messenger logged out.

Rebecca stared incomprehensibly at the screen. It had been a long time since she'd seen or heard that phrase.

She decrypted the attachment, revealing the original classified file on the fire at Bennington Hospital.

It was headed: '***NOFORN, STRAP 3 EYES ONLY.***'

It detailed a covert operation, instigated by Goldcastle, and led by MI6, to raid Bennington Hospital with a view to stealing Stanley Fox's research on breaking encryption. Whether the ensuing fire, and death of Stanley, was part of the mission was unclear from the report. The result was that Goldcastle ended up with Stanley's complete research records. Research that could inform their own efforts to recreate his system of breaking encryption.

Rebecca rushed back to OTR, pulling up everything she could about the last contact. As was the nature of OTR, there was no trace. In desperation she wrote:

Rebecca.Fox: '*Are you there? Please write back.*'

But she knew that wasn't going to happen.

She waited for nearly half an hour. Then logged out.

Once she had packed up everything from her station, Rebecca made her way to the swing doors marking the GTE exit.

When she looked out, all she saw was empty desks. Now on her own again, it felt like she was walking once more with ghosts.

EPILOGUE

Sharp held his arms out when he saw Novak walk in. The pair embraced at the booth, slapping each other's backs in the way men uncomfortable with sentiment are prone to do.

Artur, wolfing into a multi-storey, oozing burger, quickly wiped his mouth and gave Novak a hug. Wally sat opposite, already looking a little emotional at meeting Novak for the first time.

He stood up with his hand out. 'Thank you,' Wally said to Novak.

All four sat beaming through their lunch, sharing fries and wedges and talking about the future.

Novak said, 'Artur, I saw your video's gone viral, man.' He pulled up the YouTube page showing the video stats on his phone.

The video entitled, "CIA abduction of MI6 agent George Abassi", had collected over a million views in under twenty-four hours. After re-uploading his previous videos overnight, Artur's subscribers had rocketed from three hundred and sixteen to ninety thousand.

Novak said, 'I got both your I-589s through from Citizenship. You all set?'

'Man, I can't wait to be American,' Wally exclaimed.

Artur wasn't quite as enthusiastic. 'Do you think they will let my mother come?' he asked.

Novak looked at Sharp.

'Let's wait and see, son,' Sharp said. 'The most important thing is your mother knows you're safe here.'

'And how are you doing, Officer Sharp?' Novak asked.

Sharp nodded. 'I'm good. My lawyer thinks the State Department's going to drop the case against me pretty soon. Seems like they've had enough of their dirty laundry aired in public recently. They're giving me till the end of the month to let the wound heal up good.'

'What's CIA saying?'

'They're basically home free,' said Sharp. 'The Brits are taking all the flak for this one. How about you? When's your next hearing?'

'A few days.' Novak shrugged. 'They could spin it out for weeks.'

'How does your lawyer figure your chances?'

'I could be going down. Probably eighteen months, minimum security.'

Artur tapped Wally on the arm, pointing out a cute girl standing on the pavement, looking at her phone. The pair squabbled over who was going to go out, then they got up together. After some small-talk with the pair, the girl typed something into her phone, looking sceptical. A moment after her internet search came back, she exclaimed to Artur, 'No way! You started TruthArmy?'

'Me *and* him,' Artur corrected her. 'We're a team.'

Novak, grinning, said to Sharp, 'They're gonna be alright here.'

Quiet came over the table, as the two men realised it was the first time they'd been alone since they got back.

'There's something I've been wondering since Berlin,' said Sharp.

'What's that?' asked Novak.

'You could have just left Artur there. You didn't need him for the story. You already had his video.'

Novak threw out his bottom lip and gave a very Brooklyn, nonchalant shrug.

'You couldn't leave him out there, could you. High and dry.'

Novak shrugged again.

Sharp said, 'That's all you gotta say, huh.'

Novak thought for a moment, then said, '*Semper fi.*' He held out a fist.

Sharp bumped knuckles with him. '*Semper fi*, brother.'

GCHQ, Cheltenham – Six weeks later

Angela Curtis stood at the lectern set up in the basement under GTE Division. Only a dozen or so people had been invited to the talk, and, except for two, no one really knew what it was about.

Curtis said, 'I expect you're probably wondering why I've asked you all to come here on a Monday evening, and to lie whenever anyone asked what you're doing.'

To her right, stood Roger Milton and Rebecca Fox.

'I know GCHQ's had a rough ride lately,' Curtis went on. 'You've all heard the public outcry. We can be supportive and reassure each other that it was just a few bad apples, and when it comes down to it we're all honest, committed patriots.' She glanced down at her notes, remembering the beat Roger Milton told her she needed. 'But we also have to be honest with each other. More honest than we can afford to be in public about such things. For months – possibly years – GCHQ had an intelligence leak. About as major as one can imagine. That's why I'm making it one of my first priorities to equip GCHQ with the sort of investigative powers it's so desperately needed. Of course, this isn't the kind of initiative that I can talk about on the election trail. But I want to assure all of you here, I won't rest until GCHQ is given every resource to continue keeping this country safe. When it came to creating the role I'm about to announce, there really was only one candidate. I've got to know Rebecca Fox very well recently. She has proven not only her talent and dedication, but also her commitment to the ideals of GCHQ: to protect this great country. So, it is with great pleasure I introduce GCHQ's first Director of Internal Affairs Division, Rebecca Fox.'

Everyone applauded as Rebecca shook Curtis's hand.

Once she'd managed to carry off her fairly workmanlike speech – sorely lacking in adjectives – Rebecca stole a moment with Angela Curtis.

Rebecca said, 'I saw the polls this morning, Prime Minister. You must be pretty happy.'

Curtis replied, 'This is the bit where I play dumb and say something about there being a long way to go, and it's never over until the last vote's counted…'

Rebecca said, 'Of course.'

Curtis looked around, checking no one was within earshot. She turned her back slightly to the rest of the room. 'It'll be nice to be able to call each other without using a Hannibal phone.'

'I don't know,' Rebecca said, looking around the basement. The new office was still under construction, with metal beams and ventilation shafts exposed where the ceiling tiles had been taken away. 'I think talking to you in future will likely mean something bad has happened again.'

'I suppose so,' Curtis said. 'I'm told the CPS has strong cases against Hawkes, Alexander, and Matthew thanks to you.'

'It's mostly thanks to Abbie,' Rebecca said.

'It's not mostly thanks to Abbie that Goldcastle has gone into administration. Jarrod Warner's looking at twenty years.

The next summit I have with the American President isn't going to be too cosy.'

'How's Alexander holding up?'

'He's doing okay. He and his lawyer assure me he knew nothing about the Downing Street attack or about Abbie. He said he was ordered by Nigel Hawkes to cover it up after the fact. He wanted to extend to you his regret over what happened. As well as his thanks.'

'Thanks?'

Curtis said, 'If it wasn't for you, he'd be facing a conspiracy to murder and commit acts of terrorism. And Matthew would have got away with it.'

'I still think it was him who killed Trevor.'

'I spoke to John Pringle at the Met about that. They can't make the case. Anyway, with the conspiracy and terror charges, he'll be going away for long enough. John says they can at least demonstrate it was him who hacked the UKPCA and sent the press pass to Alexander's computer.'

'Everything leaves a trace,' Rebecca said to herself.

Curtis asked, 'Did you get Roger's memo on your title?'

'I did.'

'You don't like it?'

'I know Ghost Division was Goran Lipski's idea. It's a bit Tom Clancy, don't you think?'

Curtis laughed. 'You think GCHQIA is catchier, do you?' She offered her hand. 'Congratulations, Director Fox.' She leaned in a little closer. 'I wouldn't be in this position without you. You still have that phone, right?'

Rebecca said, 'Always on me.'

As Curtis drifted off to take a call Roger Milton had been fielding, one of Rebecca's new team members approached tentatively.

'Sorry, boss,' he said. 'I didn't want to interrupt.' He handed Rebecca an A4 envelope. 'That's everything I could find on the OTR contact.'

Rebecca took out the analysis.

'It's weird,' the analyst said. 'They didn't fully encrypt their IP. I mean, what's the point in using OTR if you don't want to hide?'

Something in the analysis notes seemed to strike a chord with Rebecca.

She handed the analyst her glass. 'Looks like we've got our first case.'

E. Barrett Prettyman Federal Courthouse, Washington, D.C. – The next day

Novak sat alone on the front steps of the courthouse, its vast windows capturing the full power of the morning sun. From there, he looked out across Constitution Avenue, watching a thin haze unfurling around the Capitol Building's iconic dome.

Novak had on his winter coat and a pair of Persol sunglasses, managing to remain – for now – incognito. There were still few people around: he was over an hour early for his hearing. For Washington D.C., with the President at Camp David alongside his new Defense Secretary Bill Rand, Novak was the main show in town.

Stella rounded the corner, wearing her brown mac and a thick scarf wrapped around her neck, carrying two coffees. She, too, wore sunglasses – slightly oversize – her hair tied back.

'This might be my last decent cup of coffee for quite some time,' said Novak from a distance. He took his sunglasses off. 'I hope it's good.'

'What are friends for,' Stella said. As she handed him his cup, she stifled laughter, turning away slightly with her hand to her mouth.

Novak looked at the cup top, then gave her a withering look. 'What's that?'

She'd had the barista write the customer name as "Jeremy Webb".

'That's funny to me,' she replied. She sat down beside him, taking her sunglasses off. 'Cold today, isn't it.'

His mind on the proceedings that awaited him, Novak said, 'I guess.'

'Must be close to zero out here.'

'Thirty.'

'I'm sorry?'

'It's Fahrenheit over here. Zero is thirty.'

'Oh, yeah.' She paused. 'Must be close to thirty.'

'Uh huh.'

She paused again, longer this time.

Just when Novak thought she'd move onto something else, Stella added, 'Did you know the coldest ever day in Washington was minus fifteen? Which is about...what's that in Fahrenheit–'

Novak snapped, 'What are you, Weather Woman, or something...'

'Don't do it,' she replied quickly.

Novak knew what she was talking about. 'Stella...'

She said, 'You're telling me I can't make one last attempt at convincing you?'

'You absolutely can,' Novak replied. 'But my lawyer, Diane, and Henry have already tried, and failed.'

'I believe my argument will be more substantive.'

'*More* substantive. Than a lawyer, your boss and your boss's boss?'

'Yeah.'

'And will this substantive argument involve simply repeating your existing arguments to me, but with some additional adverbs and a more desperate tone?'

'No.' She reconsidered. 'Maybe. Possibly.'

Novak said, 'Then no, you can't convince me.'

'It's a bad idea,' said Stella, 'and it gets you nowhere. Also, did I mention it's a bad idea?'

'It's not a bad idea. I'm not who people think I am.'

'Are you an accomplished journalist, who writes for one of the last great Fourth Estate establishments, who broke a massive story that started an entire debate over online privacy and NSA overreach, and who is about to make the biggest mistake of his life in owning up to something completely irrelevant to the facts of a story, and that will potentially send him to prison for the better part of a year?'

Novak thought about it. 'I guess.'

Stella said, 'Then you're *exactly* what people think you are. I left out that you're also one of the most brilliant writers I've ever worked with. Someone I'm proud to say I work with. Yeah, you messed up. But you also forget that you did some amazing reporting after the NSA papers leaked. On a purely selfish level, I don't want to lose you. Because it feels like we're only just beginning.'

Novak said, 'If I say nothing, it's a lie of omission. I don't want to live with that. And I'm not handing over my laptop.'

Stella groaned. 'God, man... Do you think this is an Arthur Miller play or something? You're not ratting out "the guys from back home", you moron. No one is going to remember your ideals in eighteen months. You give up your laptop, which they won't be able to decrypt anyway, and that's that. You go home, Novak.'

'What happens the next time I have a source?' asked Novak. 'How safe would anyone feel handing me potentially damaging material after they've watched me roll over for the government on this? If you were a source with a story, why would you come to me with *anything* after this?'

Stella couldn't think of an answer.

Novak lowered his voice, eager for her to understand. 'This isn't one of those times you can say whatever is necessary to get away with it, then tell yourself it was alright because your fingers were crossed behind your back.'

'Did you tell Diane?' asked Stella.

'Last night,' he replied.

'How did it go?'

'How do you think? I was given a once-in-a-lifetime source, and I bungled it. I gave the White House the one opening they needed: I lied. I lied about how I got the intel. And even though the intel was real, the source was real, and we spoke repeatedly, what the headline is going to be later on is: "Tom Novak Lied". This is the only way to spare the magazine. To spare you and Diane.' Novak checked his watch. 'I should go in. The press will be all over here soon.'

Stella stood up with him. 'You know I would have happily sat next to you in there.'

'I know, Stella. It worked.'

'What worked?'

'Diane,' he said. 'I know she brought you in to pull me out of my slump. I was barely batting one hundred and I—'

Stella waved her hand. 'Tom, please. Don't with the baseball metaphors. I can't even...'

'What I'm saying is: it worked. You brought me back.' He linked his arm with hers. 'Come on. You ever seen a guy get up in front of about three hundred people and detonate his reputation?'

'Can't say I have.'

'Then you're going to love this.'

As they walked in, she hugged his arm a little tighter. 'Really is cold today.'

Novak had been in his seat beside Kevin Wellington from Bruckner Jackson Prowse well in advance of the beginning of the hearing.

'Tom Novak, early?' said Kevin in mock-amazement.

'Is that your pep-talk this time?' Novak asked. 'I was looking forward to a little speech about American justice today.' He smiled as he noticed the tag still on the bottom of the sleeve of Kevin's new suit. It amused Novak, the idea of him buying a new suit for the occasion. Like he was going to his high school prom.

'You don't need any pep talks today, Mr Novak,' Kevin replied.

'Oh yeah? Why's that?'

'You're not an asshole anymore.'

Novak grinned. 'Let's not get *too* carried away.'

The clerk of the court stepped forward and called out, 'All rise. The Honourable Chief Judge Randolph Wickers presiding.'

Novak stood with Kevin as the judge read out the charges:

'Mr Novak, you've been charged under the Espionage Act, obstruction of justice, and possession of classified materials.' Then Judge Wickers asked the question that had so consumed Novak for the past month. 'Mr Novak, how do you plead?'

Novak said, 'Not guilty, your Honour.' Then added, 'I'm not a rat.'

Judge Wickers did a double-take at Novak, as many in the public gallery – filled to capacity – laughed among themselves.

Wickers said, 'Mr Novak, do you see a tightrope walker going across the ceiling?'

Novak said quizzically, 'Your Honour?'

'Or a man in a top hat introducing trapeze artists?'

'No, your Honour.'

'Do you know why that is?'

'This isn't a circus?'

'That's correct. Which means, don't treat my courtroom like one. That's the *one* warning you get. Mr Wellington, throw a muzzle on your client before I charge him with contempt.'

Kevin spoke up. 'Actually, your Honour, my client would like to make an amendment to a previous statement.'

'Previous statement?' said Wickers, baffled. 'We haven't *started*, counsel.'

'Your Honour, my client wishes to file a defence of recantation. From his Congressional hearing dated December eighth.'

'A recantation of what?'

'Of how he came into possession of classified material.'

Wickers said, 'Counsel, does your client understand that in doing this, he's admitting an unlisted charge of perjury? Which he may yet be charged with due to this admission?'

Wellington pursed his lips, restraining his frustration. 'Unfortunately, he does, your Honour.'

Wickers said, barely hiding a grin, 'You must have wished you stayed in bed today, Counsel. What's your defence, Mr Novak?'

Novak did up the single button on his jacket as he rose. 'Your Honour, my testimony on December eighth didn't accurately portray how I came into possession of classified NSA materials. There was no prior establishing of a relationship with a source online, as I claimed. The truth is, I found the memory stick after a White House press conference.'

The gallery started murmuring, enough for Wickers to reach for his gavel.

'Settle down,' he said, maintaining control of the chamber.

Novak went on, 'As I was under oath at the time, I wish to invoke the defence of recantation, which allows a witness to amend a previously unreliable statement.'

Wickers added, 'Without the inconvenience of being charged with perjury. If I decide to see it that way.'

'Something like that,' Novak said.

Wickers took a moment, then held out his hand. 'Mr Wellington, if you'd like to pass me a copy of your client's amended statement...'

While Wellington approached the bench, a lone English voice spoke up from the gallery.

'Excuse me...your Honour, excuse me...'

Murmurs sparked up around the court.

The man called out, 'Judge Wickers, may it please the court: I am Mr Novak's source.'

There were gasps from the gallery. Everyone turned towards the lone voice at the back of the court.

Wickers banged his gavel repeatedly, calling for order. 'What's your name, sir? Stand up, please.'

The man, who looked around sixty, got to his feet. He was wearing a blue corduroy suit, and was holding a Trilby hat in his hands.

'Mr Novak,' the man said, 'I'd like to apologise for putting that virus on your phone and laptop. I was trying to protect you. To keep Artur Korecki's video from them...'

'Do not address the defendant, sir,' Wickers called to him. 'You're in contempt of my court. What's your name?'

The name would mean nothing to those in the public gallery, or the attendant media. But for Tom Novak and Stella Mitchell, the name meant plenty.

The man turned his hat anxiously in his hands. 'My name is Stanley Fox. I think you'll want to hear what I have to say.'

THE END

* * *

Novak and Mitchell return in *Capitol Spy*

Buy it for Kindle or in paperback on Amazon here.

Extract on next page...

EXTRACT FROM CAPITOL SPY

Andrei Rublov had been awake for nearly two days straight, but sleep was the last thing on the thirty-year-old Russian's mind. He had more than enough caffeine gunning through his system to keep him sharp, and he was still feasting on an adrenaline rush after meeting his anonymous source the previous night.

The files the source had supplied him with were comprehensive to say the least. But it was one file in particular – just three pieces of paper slipped into a cream manila folder – that Andrei knew would change everything.

It would unquestionably be the biggest story of his career, and have serious consequences for some very powerful people.

Now he had to get out of D.C. as soon as possible.

It didn't take him long to pile his things into a backpack: only small daily essentials like his toothbrush and dirty laundry needed to be packed. In the two weeks he'd been in the rented apartment, he hadn't allowed himself to get too comfortable. He had been in the journalism game long enough to keep a go bag ready on such a story.

As he took the bag to the window he did a quick scan of

the studio apartment, checking he wasn't leaving anything relating to the story behind.

If his source's file proved right, the apartment would surely be turned over soon enough.

Now he had to stay alive for long enough to get on a plane. He hadn't decided yet on Ronald Reagan or Dulles. Wherever had a flight leaving for a non-extradition-treaty country in the next hour.

Going home to Moscow wouldn't be an option for quite some time. Maybe ever again.

Andrei didn't even want to risk getting cornered in the stairwell, so he went out the bedroom window of the flat-roofed two-storey, ducking and weaving his way down the metal fire escape with panic-filled footsteps.

Now he was out in the open, a sense of dread seeped through his stomach. He felt the unmistakable paranoia of being watched. A feeling he had grown used to in Moscow.

In the darkness he couldn't see far. A grab team could have been parked around the corner for all he knew. There would be a time for euphoria about the size of his story, and that would be once he was safely on an airport runway.

There wasn't much going on in the Garfield Heights district of the nation's capital. Somewhere in the distance a solitary dog barked, followed by the sound of a trash can being kicked over.

It was too late for the dealers, and too early for everyone else, leaving the dark, pre-dawn streets deserted.

As Andrei's breathing quickened, the thick bursts of fog from his mouth came out faster. It was barely thirty Fahrenheit out, but there wasn't enough space in his head to contemplate the cold.

He pointed the key at the Chevy Impala rental he'd been driving – looking all around, expecting someone to appear from the shadows at any moment. The sound of its perky assertive beep as it unlocked seemed to ring out around the surrounding buildings. Much louder than Andrei wanted.

He set off so quickly the back wheels spun on the cold tarmac. He fumbled with his phone as he raced through the endless, identical blocks, managing to get connected to the car via Bluetooth. He tapped "Ronald Reagan Airport" into his Sat Nav.

Ronald Reagan was the closer of the two D.C. airports: Andrei didn't want to be on the road a minute longer than he had to.

He merged swiftly onto Suitland Parkway that took him to I-295, then the Anacostia Freeway.

There were quicker ways to get through Capitol Hill, but this kept him on major roads which were better lit and more liable to have other drivers on them.

The proximity to other cars provided little sense of security though as he caught sight of a black van slowly but steadily progressing up the slow lane, sitting some four cars back.

Andrei crooked the rear-view mirror to get a better angle on it. As the road gently curved right, he could see a tall silhouette in the driver's seat, no passengers.

Andrei pressed the call button on his phone, then said aloud in Russian, 'Call Natalya.'

It was nearly two p.m. in Moscow, which Andrei hoped would make it likely she would answer. After a few rings it went to voicemail.

His voice cracked with a mix of triumph and fear. 'Talya! It's Andrei.' He took a beat, long enough for a calming breath. 'I've got confirmation. I know who it is. And they're right here in Washington. I met my source last night and they know everything. They gave me a dossier...' He shook his head. 'I think I'm being followed. They could be after you too. Listen to me, Talya: you've got to get out of Moscow right now.' He glanced in the rear-view mirror, noticing the black van creeping forward, overtaking. Now just two cars back. 'If anything happens to me...You know what to do.'

He hung up, then put his foot to the floor, using all the power his 3.6-litre V6 engine had to offer, taking him up to seventy miles per hour. The van was soon far back and seemingly uninterested in following.

Andrei exhaled. Panic over.

In a bid to stay on roads with some kind of CCTV coverage he took a left off Anacostia onto East Capitol Street, taking him over the Anacostia River. In no time he was on Pennsylvania Avenue.

Wanting to zoom in on the Sat Nav map, Andrei pinched his fingers across the phone screen. 'Weird,' he said to himself, as the screen went black, then seemed to reload.

The directions told him he was only ten minutes away from Ronald Reagan National Airport. He checked his rear-view mirror again. It was still clear.

For a newcomer to Washington, it was easy not to realise you were on a road leading to the epicentre of American political power. The east side of Pennsylvania Avenue coming through Dupont Park was so unassuming, it was like driving through some little Midwest town, with its modest storefronts and tidy hedgerows.

Then something magical started to happen around the intersection of 13th and 11th Street: in the distance the illuminated white dome of the Capitol Building slowly emerged. The sight of it made Andrei's heart swell, as the scale of what he was about to go public with truly hit home.

The stakes didn't get any higher.

What didn't help was the sudden reappearance of the black van. It was being driven more aggressively now, swinging right out of Potomac Avenue, and following much closer. Its lights were on a purposely hostile full beam, which also made it impossible for Andrei to make out the face of the driver.

Andrei flicked his rear-view mirror aside, but the Impala's interior was flooded with the van's headlights.

Andrei cursed to himself, 'Shit.' He knew he was in it now.

He wasn't going to take any chances, and keyed '911' into his phone screen. All he had to do was hit the green call sign if he got rammed.

The black van was all over his back bumper, but made no move to take him off the road. It was just following malevolently close.

Andrei knew he had to lose the tail somehow or else he'd be followed into the airport and his destination spotted: he'd be starting all over again at the other end. The sort of people that were after him had assets all over the globe. He needed a clean break or he was as good as dead.

He used every inch of the road to make the tight left turn onto Constitution Avenue, touching forty-five as he clipped the apex.

As the road straightened - heading west past the Smithsonian Museums and other grand white buildings that lined the road – Andrei's speed crept up.

Fifty...

Fifty-five...

Sixty...

His knuckles were white on the steering wheel. The buildings to his left a blur in his peripheral vision. He only had eyes for the black van.

Arlington County Emergency Communications Centre – same time

Marcy Edwards was on hour seven of her night shift. Apart from restroom breaks, she hadn't left the 911-police group pen. Dinner had been a large bag of tortilla chips and guacamole.

Such were the demands on emergency call workers in

Virginia: the combination of stress and emotional anxiety had left the state with a crippling shortage of operators like Marcy. Even if starting salaries of $35k a year managed to entice qualified applicants, hardly any of them hung around longer than a few months. Having to listen to calls from crying children asking for help because "mommy's been asleep for four days," or talking someone through a call while someone's house was robbed.

Operators couldn't afford a 'bad call', or be off their game even once. Lives depended on it.

Marcy's call line lit up. She answered, 'Nine one one, what's your emergency?'

She heard the sound of a car engine before a voice.

'My name is Andrei Rublov,' the caller said, voice raised. He sounded scared. 'I'm a reporter for Russia Now. I'm in a silver Chevy Impala going west on...Constitution Avenue. I cannot control my car.'

Marcy asked routinely, 'Are you under the influence of alcohol or drugs, sir?'

'No! The car is not under my control.' Frustrated at his inability to explain, he tried again. 'The car is...'

In the background the engine could be heard getting louder.

Marcy said, 'Andrei? Are you there?'

'It's the Arlington bridge,' Andrei cried. 'I'm going to go off it...'

Marcy shot a look out the window. Her building was just half a mile from the bridge. 'Andrei, listen to me. No matter how bad you might be feeling, take your foot off the gas and slowly pull over to the side of the-'

'I can't! Aren't you listening to me? I'm not suicidal but my car is going to go off the bridge...'

Marcy raised her voice. 'Andrei, there's no reason for you to go off the bridge. Just listen to me-'

Two of Marcy's colleagues, off-call, turned to see what was going on, thinking she had a jumper.

Andrei's heart sank. He knew what was going to happen. It was inevitable. 'Are you recording this?'

'Yes, I am.'

'I need to say something...' The thought of what he was about to say put a lump in his throat. '...for posterity.'

Marcy, trained in keeping despondent callers in a positive frame of mind, said, 'You're not going to die, Andrei, just keep talking to me, stay with me.'

Nearly drowned out by the engine, he said, 'There's a mole in Congress.'

'I'm sorry?'

'There's a mole!' he yelled. 'There's a Russian spy in Congress. Senator-'

The line went dead.

Marcy pressed her earphone in harder. 'Andrei? Andrei talk to me...' Seeing the line was definitely dead, she hit a speed dial on her keypad. 'D.C. dispatch, this is ECC. I need a vehicle response to Arlington Memorial Bridge. I need a visual on a silver Chevy Impala.'

Arlington Memorial Bridge

The black van pulled up just short of the bronze statues of men on horseback – the Arts of War - marking the start of the Arlington Memorial Bridge.

Traffic came to a standstill in a matter of moments.

Drivers on the bridge hurried out their cars and ran towards the gaping hole in the concrete balcony. Down in the river, a silver Impala sank below the surface.

Seconds later at ECC, an operator beside Marcy Edwards took a 911 call.

'Oh my gosh...' the female caller said, struggling to keep

her composure. 'He just went off the side of the bridge. He was going so fast...'

There was a conversation in the background of someone having to be dissuaded from jumping in after the car. 'It's already under water. You'd freeze in there before you even reached him...'

Back at the Arts of War, the black van calmly set off again across the bridge.

The man in the driver's seat sent a text message: "Done. Who's next?"

* * *

To continue the story, buy *Capitol Spy* for Kindle or in paperback on Amazon here

ACKNOWLEDGMENTS

This book is dedicated with love to ELD.

Thank you:

To DW, who read an early draft and made some invaluable suggestions.

To Chris Ryan, for crucial advice on how the Downing Street attack could happen. Chris is a really generous guy, and told me a host of fascinating snippets. If you get the chance, shake his hand. I guarantee you won't forget it for a while.

The list of what is fact and what is not in *Official Secrets* would be much too long. Suffice to say: this is a work of fiction, but you would not believe how much of it is factual.

Official Secrets required a huge amount of research. The following were invaluable, and I highly recommend reading for pleasure as well as insight:

Hack Attack by Nick Davies (the book to read on the U.K. phone hacking scandal)

Blackwater and *Dirty Wars* by Jeremy Scahill (both essential reading on what the war on terror has really meant on the ground)

Intercept by Gordon Corera (history of GCHQ)

The History Thieves by Ian Cobain (history of British classified intelligence)

No Place to Hide by Glenn Greenwald (fascinating book on the Snowden leaks, the major inspiration for Novak's NSA Papers story)

The Snowden Files by Luke Harding

Legacy of Ashes - A History of the CIA by Tim Weiner

Within Arm's Length by Dan Emmett (Secret Service agent's memoir)

The New Spymasters by Stephen Grey

See No Evil by Robert Baer (CIA agent's memoir; blistering stuff)

The Perfect Kill by Robert Baer (how assassins work)

McMafia by Misha Glenny

The Killing School by Brandon Webb (what it's like going through the U.S. Army Sniper school)

Data and Goliath by Bruce Schneier

10 Downing Street by Anthony Seldon (out of print picture-book history)

Everybody Lies by Seth Stephens-Davidowtiz

The Penguin Book of Journalism ed. Stephen Glover

The Universal Journalist 5th Ed. by David Randall

The History of MI5 by Christopher Andrew

There were many, many more books that helped me along the way, but the ones above are some of my favourites. If you liked Official Secrets I think you'd get a kick out of them.

A brief word on American/British English usage throughout:

As many of you will know, I live in Scotland, so I use British English as my standard. However, there are occasions when it is necessary to use American English spellings. For example, when referring to the U.S. Secretary of Defense, or the U.K.'s Ministry of Defence, I use the relevant native spellings as they refer to official titles of that country. I try my best to be consistent with this considering it is a transatlantic series.

There are a lot of sacrifices required in order to write a book. It might be a gloriously sunny day and all you want is to get on your bike and ride out into the countryside. You also often need to stay up long into the night with work first thing the next morning. Or you have too much to do to finish that damn chapter, so you can't spend the weekend with your family.

To all the people in my life who are willing to make these sacrifices with me, thank you.

Finally, to anyone reading this: thank you for buying this book. It took a lot of long hours and hard work to complete, but every new reader that discovers it makes it all worth it. I hope you'll come back and join Novak and Mitchell in Book 2: *Capitol Spy* and Book 3: *Traitor Games*

Printed in Great Britain
by Amazon

64381138R00270